UNLOCKING BLACKBEARD'S SKELETONS

Hope you enjoy this adventure!

Robin Reams

Unlocking Blackbeard's Skeletons

Robin Reams

Copyright © 2019 Robin E. Reams

All rights reserved. No part of this book may be used, reproduced or transmitted in any form or by any means, electronic or mechanical, including photograph, recording, or any information storage or retrieval system, without the express written permission of the author, except where permitted by law.

ISBN 978-1-59715-199-3

First Printing

Dedicated to my co-authors:
God and my Savior, Jesus Christ.
Also, in loving memory of my sister.
Holly Reams
1993–2009
I couldn't have written this without constant
help from Heaven. I love you so much!

❂ ❂ ❂

Jesus said, "For where your treasure is,
there your heart will be also."
LUKE 12:34

❂ ❂ ❂

But the LORD said to Samuel, "Do not look at his
appearance or at his physical stature, because I have refused
him. For the LORD does not see as man sees; for man looks
at the outward appearance, but the LORD looks at the heart."
1 SAMUEL 16:7

CONTENTS

Acknowledgments viii
Author's Note ix

Chapter One ~ Bearded Rogues 1
Chapter Two ~ Mid-Knight Message 14
Chapter Three ~ Tunnel Land 29
Chapter Four ~ Pie and Pirates 42
Chapter Five ~ Locket of Truth 55
Chapter Six ~ Not-So-Tough Cookie 66
Chapter Seven ~ Violent Seas 77
Chapter Eight ~ Father in Disguise 88
Chapter Nine ~ Bloodstained Cobblestones 103
Chapter Ten ~ Crafty Hands 119
Chapter Eleven ~ Death's Head 132
Chapter Twelve ~ Secrets in Ink 145
Chapter Thirteen ~ Old Slough Predicament 158
Chapter Fourteen ~ White Feathers 169
Chapter Fifteen ~ Thrashers' Prey 180
Chapter Sixteen ~ Cold Hearts 195
Chapter Seventeen ~ Pirate Banyan 208
Chapter Eighteen ~ Captains' Parley 219

Chapter Nineteen ~ Scuttlebutt 235

Chapter Twenty ~ Smoking Gun 248

Chapter Twenty-One ~ Farewell, Adventure 263

Chapter Twenty-Two ~ Spinning Lies 276

Chapter Twenty-Three ~ Painful Verdict 292

Chapter Twenty-Four ~ The Hunt 308

Chapter Twenty-Five ~ High Tide 324

Chapter Twenty-Six ~ Flickering Candlelight 337

Chapter Twenty-Seven ~ Circling Buzzards 353

Chapter Twenty-Eight ~ Hangman's Noose 369

Chapter Twenty-Nine ~ Lonesome Sound 385

Chapter Thirty ~ Christmas Treasure 398

Get the Scoop ~ Blackbeard the Pirate 415

ACKNOWLEDGMENTS

Thank you, God, for Your unfailing love and constant guidance. The ability to write stories is a gift that I am honored to have. To my family, friends, and readers, I extend my heartfelt thanks for your support and prayers. I am also grateful to Edwina Woodbury and Chapel Hill Press, Inc. Of course, to my sister, Holly, who enjoyed history as much as I do and has left me with so many memories, including the hours spent researching family history. Our shared interest in Blackbeard and visiting historical sites during our childhood ignited my imagination while working on this book. Thanks, Mom and Dad, for helping me continue to pursue my love of writing.

AUTHOR'S NOTE

The adventure you are about to embark on is historical fiction. As much as possible I used real facts and events as a foundation for this story, but my own imagination created this book. It takes a lot of hard work to gather the necessary information to make historical fiction realistic. I have studied books on piracy, navigation, sailing ships, colonial living, native plants and animals, Indians, wars of the period, governments, layouts of towns, and religious beliefs. Additionally, I spent many hours researching colonial documents, attending pirate reenactments, visiting museums, walking historical sites, and talking to historians. Although the main character is my creation, many of the supporting characters are based on real people I discovered by digging into the available records. I took artistic liberties with their personalities and features since they are fictional characters in my story. For the most part, the places mentioned in this book are real locations, and I tried to describe them as close to what they were in 1718. Many of the dates used are from the colonial records tracking the real Blackbeard's whereabouts during the last days of his life. Historical researchers learn new things about the past every day, so it will be interesting to see what they uncover in the future.

IT'S TIME TO SET SAIL—
THE ADVENTURE AWAITS ...

CHAPTER ONE

☠

BEARDED ROGUES

July 2, 1718 ~ Wednesday

Clopping horse hooves blended with the restless thumping of Lizzie Beard's heart as the wagon traveled over the old wooden bridge crossing the greenish-blue waters of Bath Town Creek. Her eyes searched boats anchored in the broad creek and tied to the handful of wharfs lining Bath's waterfront, looking for tangible evidence proving the rumors true. During the last days of June, a group of sea-roving men visited Bath, causing quite a stir. The reason for their visit was unknown except for the late-night meeting at Governor Charles Eden's two-story home on Bay Street. The strangers left two days later, promising the arrival of their comrades within two weeks. As far as Lizzie knew, the information was accurate; however, one intriguing detail made the story sound more like gossip than truth. The new arrivals were supposedly associated with pirates.

Chances of such a controversial rumor being true seemed unlikely, though Port Bath stayed busy with merchants selling and trading goods. Merchant ships sailed from southern ports beyond Charles Town to northern colonies up the Delaware Bay, making Bath a potential target for those who captured ships and stole their contents, an act of piracy—or, as some called it, treason.

Despite the rumors, Lizzie's aunt decided they would go into town for supplies they needed, trusting God to protect them from danger. Going to town was a treat Lizzie and her four cousins enjoyed, especially when it meant taking a break from schoolwork.

Feeling the light summer breeze against her face, Lizzie peered eagerly at the ships dotting the broad creek as it meandered into the Pamtico River. Two ships were within view: one unloading crates and barrels of merchandise at the dock and another headed for the ever-changing Ocracoke Inlet, the only access to the Atlantic Ocean. Something else caught her eye, a third ship anchored off the point not far from a private dock owned by Tobias Knight, the secretary and tax collector for the colony. Unlike the others, this ship was smaller, only having one main mast instead of two. Lizzie's mind began to whirl as she considered why the ship's crew chose to anchor near Secretary Knight's landing. Could it be possible the unusual ship had any connection to the promise of new strangers?

A high-pitched shriek drew Lizzie's attention away from the ship to her youngest cousin seated beside her in the wagon. The six-year-old's hazel-brown eyes beamed with excitement as her hand frantically patted Lizzie's arm.

"What is it, Hannah?" Lizzie questioned the little girl, who was clearly finding it difficult to stay still as the wagon rolled into town.

"Look out there," she said, pointing at the ship that had intrigued Lizzie. "Do you see the ship near Mr. Knight's place?"

Captured by her outburst, ten-year-old Rebecca and eleven-year-old Alice leaned over to see what their little sister was pointing to.

"Why would a merchant ship want to anchor out there? Wouldn't it be easier to anchor it closer to the dock?" Rebecca wondered aloud.

"Don't be silly!" declared Alice. "They're visiting Mr. Knight."

"It's a pirate ship," snickered their fourteen-year-old brother, apparently listening from the front of the wagon.

"Trent Lee!" Aunt Grace scolded her oldest child from her seat beside him. "You know better than to speak of such nonsense!"

"Yes, ma'am," Trent mumbled, flashing his signature grin as their horse Honeybee set her hooves on the dusty Beaufort Street.

Immediately taking a right at the bricklaying shed of Thomas Roper, they continued down Bay Street bordering the waterfront. Honeybee pulled the wagon through town, passing several homes and the Blue Heron Inn operated by Thomas Unday. By the time they neared the town landing, Lizzie could see a merchant ship tied to the wharf surrounded by numerous privately owned boats. The entire town was abuzz as tradesmen went about unloading the shipments.

Trent paused in front of Dr. Patrick Maule's home at the intersection of Bay Street and Craven Street before pulling into the lot of Harding's General Store on the opposite corner. The store's owner, Thomas Harding, was standing across the street at his shipyard, where he chitchatted with a man wearing a white wig. Knowing that Governor Eden was one of the only men in town who wore a wig, Lizzie wondered why he was visiting the shipbuilder's lumberyard in the middle of a workday. She had no time to ponder as Trent tied off the reins to their chestnut-colored mare.

The dark-haired boy hopped down from the wagon to assist his mother. Meanwhile, Lizzie helped her three cousins get down and quickly clutched Hannah's hand. The six-year-old had a fascination with the corral of multicolored horses next door at the horse mill where the cornmeal and flour was ground.

Trent held open the freshly painted white door so that they could enter the store managed by Giles Shute and his wife, Charity. Lizzie led Hannah up the steps, following Alice and Rebecca as they joined their mother on the porch. Inside were shelves stacked with tools, cloth, and goods such as flour and cornmeal, all surrounding a wooden counter at the back. On the end of the counter sat six glass jars filled with a variety of colorful candy. Each flavor was a delight to the taste buds, a child's dream come true. The room smelled of the mouthwatering sweetness, as if the walls themselves were peppermint sticks.

Lizzie breathed deeply, savoring the sweetness as she allowed her sixteen-year-old senses to slip back into her childhood, a time cut short by terrible circumstances. Life began to down spiral seven years prior in 1711 after months of heated battles that pitted neighbors against each other. Later this period was known as Cary's Rebellion, a religious conflict started by the former governor Thomas Cary. As it turned out, the war was only the beginning.

Opposing sides destroyed many of the planted crops. The crops that did survive the war quickly deteriorated in an unusually severe summer drought. As the summer wore on, the colonists faced another tragedy: yellow fever, a rampant mosquito-carrying disease that claimed many lives.

In July, Lizzie's grandfather James Beard went south to the major Carolina port of Charles Town on a business trip. Two weeks later, a letter arrived addressed to her papa, Edward Beard, letting him know that his father had become ill with the fever and died on the twenty-first. The letter also held information of an oral will James managed to make, leaving his business and plantation on Bath Town Creek to both his son and second wife, Elizabeth. He had already given his daughter, Susannah, the land he owned on the Neuse River as a wedding gift when she married John Martin Franck in early June.

After receiving the news, Edward made plans with his wife, Martha, before heading down to Charles Town to take care of his father's burial and unfinished tar shipments. At the time, John Martin Franck was on a business trip to New Bern, but thankfully Martha's sister, Grace, and husband, Jared Lee, lived on the banks of the Neuse River neighboring Susannah and Edward's farms. With Jared's help, they were able to continue the complicated process of getting the tar and pitch from the pine trees.

As if James Beard's sudden death wasn't hard enough, Lizzie's momma and aunt received news of their own mother contracting yellow fever. Traveling with their children, Martha and Grace went to Bath to be with her. Susannah went with them to visit her grieving stepmother, Elizabeth, who lived next to the Worsley family.

Martha and Grace were able to spend time with their mother while Susannah kept their five children on the Beard plantation. Sadly, the fever claimed the life of their beloved mother, Mary Worsley. Shortly after Mary's burial in September 1711, Martha also fell ill. Weeks later, the Worsley family would have another burial plot, this time belonging to Lizzie's mother. Both losses left the family's faith shaken as they struggled to understand God's plan.

The combination of war, drought, and the yellow fever epidemic created a perfect storm for the abused Tuscarora Indians. They launched their attack on the colonists, making their deadly move at dawn on September 22, 1711. People sought safety in Bath, bringing horrible stories with them. Having just buried Lizzie's mother, Aunt Grace decided to stay in Bath with her newborn baby, nine-year-old niece, and three children—ages seven, five, and three.

By October, Aunt Susannah received a letter from her husband, John Martin Franck. Although he was at New Bern during the first attacks, he was able to use his role in New Bern's society to receive news more quickly. Uncle Martin's grim letter reported what they feared most. Not only were their homes on the Neuse River burned down, but Uncle Jared was dead, murdered by the Tuscarora Indians as he and the workers defended the Beard family's tar business.

Sighing, Lizzie shifted her attention back to the present as she heard Mrs. Charity Shute talking to Aunt Grace.

"Hello, Grace, how are you today?" inquired Mrs. Shute, who stood at the counter wearing a pale blue dress and a radiant smile.

"Very well. How's your family?" Aunt Grace responded.

"Good. Mother is keeping my three youngest ones today. Philip is helping his father in the storage room," she explained, referring to their oldest child, who was nineteen. "What can I get you?"

"Unfortunately, we're out of our own stock of flour and cornmeal. I need five sacks of flour, four sacks of cornmeal, a sack of sugar, and some material," Aunt Grace said.

"Of course, we always have a supply of freshly ground cornmeal and flour, but we're out of sugar. Giles ordered a shipment over three weeks ago. Everyone has been asking for it. Let me go see if any sugar came in this morning while you look at the cloth. We just got some new patterns," Mrs. Shute replied, leaving to find her husband.

Aunt Grace went to the table to look at the bolts of cloth. Trent browsed the hunting knives while the girls searched glass jars of candy, pointing to their favorites in a clamor of giggles. Standing with her cousins at the candy counter, Lizzie glanced at her aunt. She noticed a look of longing on her face as she gently ran her fingertips across the edge of a fancy feathered hat perched on a shelf.

Always putting others first, the hat was something Aunt Grace would never buy for herself. The last seven years had been difficult for her. Lizzie admired her tremendous courage and felt blessed to have her as a substitute mother figure. Just the emotions would have defeated most women, but not Aunt Grace. She was a Worsley, tough and determined to press forward.

With the help of her father, Thomas Worsley Sr., and two younger brothers, Aunt Grace managed to keep up the 375-acre plantation next to her father's place. James Beard owned the plantation prior to his death and willed it to Lizzie's father, Edward, and James' widow, Elizabeth. Upon his return to Bath in the spring of 1712, Edward approached his stepmother with the details of his father's oral will. To his surprise, Elizabeth was engaged to be married to her next-door neighbor, Captain William Masten, a Dutch-born man she had grown close to after James' death. Since she was a young widow without children, it was customary for her to remarry quickly. Once she married William and moved to his 400-acre plantation, she signed over her dower rights as James' widow, allowing Edward to have his father's land.

Since their homes on the Neuse River burned during the Indian attacks, Edward offered the Bath Creek plantation to his sister-in-law, Grace. She and Edward sold their land on the Neuse River to his sister, Susannah Franck, and husband, Martin, whose 640 acres bordered Edward's land.

Grace and Edward had a lot in common after losing their spouses, but there was a great deal of difference in how they handled the next few years. While Grace turned to her faith in God and support of her family, Edward distanced himself. He returned to Bath after making his father's last tar shipment to find his wife gone, the colony devastated from the Tuscarora Indians, and the leaders in desperate need of his assistance. Having a seaworthy ship, Edward was able to help the colony by using his father's ship, the *James*, to bring in supplies.

Finally, in 1715 the Tuscarora Indians agreed to a peace treaty, and the war-ravaged area started to rebuild, though the process was slow. Busy with time-consuming duties, Edward spent more time at sea as he turned his attention to trading goods. The benefits provided their family with much-needed hard currency, but personally he began to fall apart. Obviously, the death of Lizzie's mother affected him deeply. What started as an honorable sacrifice for his friends turned into a way for him to escape his pain. For the last two years he had been absent in Lizzie's life, a burden she kept to herself.

Mrs. Shute appeared from the back of the store and reached for the sacks of flour stacked on a shelf behind the counter. Seeing her return, Aunt Grace picked up several bolts of cloth and carried them to where Mrs. Shute was gathering their order.

"You're in luck, Grace. The sugar came in. Giles is bringing it," Mrs. Shute proclaimed. "These colors will make nice dresses."

"I think so, too. I'll need four yards of each and three yards of blue for Trent's new shirt," Aunt Grace stated. Glancing at the girls she continued, "And add a stick a candy for each of the children."

Surprised by her aunt's special treat, Lizzie thanked her as she joined her cousins in deciding which flavor to choose. When all five of them had made their selections, they waited for Mrs. Shute to finish cutting the new material. Just as she was folding the fabric, Mr. Shute came in wearing a white apron tied around his waist and a big grin.

"Good day, Grace. Here's the sugar. I'm glad you came in today. I was just trying to figure out how to get the large crate I received this morning over to your place. Also, there is a letter here addressed to your brother-in-law, Edward. I know you haven't heard from him, so you must sign for it along with the crate. You'll have to pay for the letter, but the crate has been prepaid," the storekeeper declared.

Shock overwhelmed Lizzie's mind as she heard her father's name. She wondered what was in the crate and who sent the letter.

Aunt Grace raised her eyebrows as she pulled coins from her brown cloth handbag. "Where did they come from?"

"The addresses on the crate indicate it came from Charles Town and went to Mrs. J. M. Franck of New Bern. It appears Susannah repackaged the crate and addressed it to you. Edward's letter came from Philadelphia. Does he know someone in Pennsylvania?"

"I'm sure he does from his travels with the tar business. Trent can help you load the crate," Aunt Grace replied.

"I pulled a muscle in my back last week, but Philip and my new hired hand will load it for you. His arrival from New Bern couldn't have come at a better time."

The shopkeeper gathered the flour, cornmeal, and sugar while his wife found some brown paper to wrap up the fabric and candy sticks. With a turkey feather and blackberry-based ink, Mr. Shute figured the total on a scrap piece of parchment paper. Finishing the tally, Mr. Shute pulled out a leather-bound ledger from the cubbyhole beneath the wooden counter. Flipping through its alphabetically sorted pages, he searched for the Lee surname containing their past purchases and current credit total. He dipped the feathered quill into the small inkwell, careful not to waste any as he wrote down the new items. Like other families, Aunt Grace charged items to their account, paying the amount owed by the end of the month.

"Could you please sign here for the crate and letter?" Mr. Shute requested as he slid a piece of parchment paper to Aunt Grace and handed her the feathered quill.

"Look! Look! Look!"

Turning, Lizzie spotted six-year-old Hannah standing on her toes near the front window pointing at something outside. In her excitement, she knocked over the window display, sending items crashing to the floor. Horrified, Aunt Grace rushed over to make sure she was okay while apologizing to Mr. and Mrs. Shute. Thankfully, nothing broke, even though Aunt Grace insisted Hannah say she was sorry.

Curious to see what had captured her attention, Lizzie peered out the window, forgetting to help her aunt clean up as her eyes fixated on the scene outside. In the center of the dusty street walked a group of men wearing unusual clothes and guns. Shocked by their weapons and the shaggy hair on most of their faces, Lizzie couldn't help but stare wide-eyed as the noisy men passed by on their way to the Salty Sailor Tavern, the rougher of the two alehouses. As Lizzie watched, she felt drawn to the strangers by an unknown force. One man captivated her more than the others. He was a tall man dressed in black and appearing to be about Aunt Grace's age. His shoulder-length, curly black hair stuck out from a three-cornered hat while miniature braids of facial hair hung from his cheeks.

"Is that hair on their chins?" Hannah wanted to know.

"Who are they, and why do they have guns?" Alice asked.

"The hair on their faces is a beard," Mr. Shute explained as he came over. "They anchored their ship near Knight's plantation yesterday. Some people have called them scallywags or bearded rogues. There is even a rumor going around they might be pirates."

"Giles!" Mrs. Shute blurted out, clearly as shocked as Aunt Grace was by her husband's remark.

"So, the rumors are true, then? They are pirates?" Trent questioned, his voice full of excitement and curiosity.

"Maybe. If they are, it makes sense for them to carry guns, and a fearsome beard certainly stands out in a crowd of properly shaven men. They walk around like everything's normal. I heard they met with Governor Eden like the other men who came. King George I of England offered a royal pardon to pirates who promise to refrain from further piracy by swearing their allegiance to his Crown. The pardon must come from a governor," Mr. Shute proclaimed.

"That's enough, Giles. The children will have nightmares," Mrs. Shute told him as she handed Aunt Grace the letter, packaged material, and wrapped candy. "Hope you have a good day, Grace."

"Thank you, Charity. Hope you do, too."

"Pull the wagon to the back, Trent. The boys can get these sacks of flour and cornmeal," Mr. Shute instructed as he went through the doorway leading into the back room.

Waving to Mrs. Shute, Lizzie followed her aunt and cousins outside. As her brown eyes adjusted to the sunshine, she found herself gazing down the dusty street at the Salty Sailor Tavern. Something inside her childishly hoped to catch another glimpse of the so-called pirates. She imagined the lively group of men seated at a corner table sipping brandy and recalling past adventures on the high seas.

By the time the girls walked around the shaded porch, Mr. Shute was already directing Trent on how close to bring the wagon. His auburn-haired son, Philip, and a new hired hand stood nearby wearing old work clothes and black tricorn hats. Philip had two younger brothers named Samuel and Joseph and a little sister, Penelope.

As Trent stepped down from the wagon, Philip spoke up. "Hey, Trent. What have you been up to? Caught any fish lately?"

"Haven't had a chance to go," he muttered, giving his mother a disappointed look.

"Well, don't feel too bad. It's been a while since I last went," Philip revealed, teasing Hannah by flicking one of her brown, braided pigtails. "Good afternoon, Miss Lee."

"Good afternoon, Philip," Aunt Grace answered.

"Grace, I want you to meet our new helper," Mr. Shute said, motioning toward the young man standing beside his son.

"It's a pleasure to meet you," Aunt Grace greeted the young man. "My name is Grace Lee, and this is my family."

Hastily snatching off his hat, the young man raked his fingers through his short, light brown hair attempting to tame the sweaty mess. "Nice to meet you, too, ma'am. Do you know Jared Lee?"

Clearly stunned by his question, Aunt Grace hesitated. "Jared was my husband. How do you know him?"

"My father used to work for Mr. Lee prior to the Indian War. I'm Jake Griffin, the oldest of Jacob and Sadie Griffin's children."

Aunt Grace smiled. "Oh, my goodness. You were our neighbors when we lived on the Neuse River."

Memories flooded Lizzie's mind as she remembered playing with Jake as a child. She had thought he was about a year older than her.

"Philip, please take Jake into the back room and retrieve the crate with Miss Lee's name on it," Mr. Shute suggested.

Motioning for Jake to follow him, nineteen-year-old Philip led the way inside, quickly returning with the wooden crate between them. Whatever the crate held was heavy, as the two boys struggled to carry it across the porch toward the waiting wagon.

"There you go, Grace. Do you need help getting it into your home?" Mr. Shute questioned as Philip and Jake helped Trent load the sacks of flour, cornmeal, and sugar.

"We can manage. Thank you for all your help."

"You're welcome, we look—" Mr. Shute started as he suddenly stopped mid-sentence to stare at something beyond them.

Turning to look, Lizzie's eyes widened as she discovered the source of Mr. Shute's attention. Walking up the back steps of the loading dock was a shaggy-looking man wearing striped britches and a blue shirt. The man carried an iron rod in his left hand and a piece of parchment paper in the other. Fearful of what the stranger would do, Lizzie was shocked when the man addressed Aunt Grace.

"Sorry to interrupt, ma'am," the man stated in an unusual dialect that caused Lizzie to wonder if he was a sailor. Speaking to Mr. Shute he continued, "Sir, do ye own this store?"

"No, Thomas Harding does. I oversee it though."

"Good, I'll just leave this list with ye. I'll be back in about an hour to fetch our supplies," he declared.

Bewildered, Lizzie watched the stranger cross the street to the Salty Sailor Tavern. Further down Craven Street, the blacksmith, Collingswood Ward, stood outside his forge surveying the scene.

"Do you think he was a pirate? I don't remember him being in the group we saw going over to the alehouse," Trent mumbled.

"It's possible. By his appearance and dialect, he was certainly a sailor. I didn't see him earlier when the boys and I were at the dock getting our shipment from the merchants," Mr. Shute responded.

"What's on the list?" Trent wanted to know.

Unfolding the wrinkled parchment paper, Mr. Shute shrugged. "Smoked ham, dry beans, flour, cornmeal, candles, and, well, basic sailor needs. I see supply lists like this all the time. Perhaps Collingswood knows something. I saw him walking over here from the forge. He must have gotten the iron rod from the blacksmith."

"It doesn't matter, Trent. We must be going. All of you still have some school studies to complete," Aunt Grace urged. Looking at Jake she added, "Would you join us Saturday evening for supper? Trent can pick you up around five o'clock."

Jake looked surprised by her offer. "That is mighty kind of you, Miss Lee, but I don't want to burden your family."

"Having you over for supper is no burden. I look forward to catching up and sharing old memories," Aunt Grace insisted.

"Okay, Miss Lee, I'll come," Jake agreed. "But there is no need for Trent to pick me up. I have a horse."

"After you cross the bridge, take the road to the left. Our plantation is the second on the waterfront. We really must be going. Have a nice day," Aunt Grace replied as she went down the back stairs.

"See you soon," Mr. Shute called after them.

Taking the bundle of fabric, Trent placed it under the seat while his mother climbed up. At the same time, Lizzie helped Alice, Rebecca, and Hannah maneuver around the crate and supplies. Settling down beside Hannah, she glanced at the store catching a glimpse of Jake as he paused to look at them before entering the storeroom. Lizzie listened to Trent whistle for Honeybee to start trotting homeward as the steady sounds of clanging metal echoed from the blacksmith's forge down the street.

Multitudes of thoughts spun in Lizzie's mind, ranging from Jake's appearance in Bath Town to the crate Aunt Susannah sent and the mysterious letter addressed to her papa. Despite her excitement to discover what surprises the crate and letter held, she couldn't stop thinking about the bearded rogues. Why were they here in Port Bath? Only time would tell.

CHAPTER TWO

☠

MID-KNIGHT MESSAGE

July 5, 1718 ~ Saturday

Warm sand burned Lizzie's bare feet as she walked through the garden picking ripe red tomatoes. Coming to the end of the row, she pushed back her straw hat to wipe sweat from her forehead. The day was hot and humid, the type of day when she would be daydreaming about going for a refreshing swim after a hard day's work. Today, however, her thoughts were elsewhere as she fantasized about the contents of her papa's letter.

Even though it had been two years since they had contact with him, Aunt Grace refused to open the letter, saying they should wait to give it to his sister. Feeling the letter must be important, Lizzie disagreed and urged her to open it, knowing Aunt Susannah wasn't planning to come to Bath anytime soon. In her note to Lizzie, Aunt Susannah said she would see her at Christmas, mentioning how excited Edward, Mary, and Elizabeth were. Lizzie was looking forward to spending time with her three young cousins.

It turned out the crate held a giant spinning wheel belonging to James Beard's sister-in-law, Susannah Murrey Beard. Great-Aunt Susannah lived with her husband, William Beard, in Charles Town. With both parents deceased, their three sons decided to send the spinning wheel to their cousin, Susannah Beard Franck, who shared their mother's name. Since Lizzie's father had been close to Great-

Uncle William as a boy, Aunt Susannah wanted her to have the spinning wheel to keep as a Beard family heirloom. This excited Lizzie, who was thrilled to have her own spinning wheel. The giant wooden wheel spun sheep wool into thread.

Still obsessing over the letter, Lizzie had just started down the next row when she heard their dog barking. Snapping out of her trance, she spotted a light brown horse with a cream-colored tail and mane trotting up the path with Jake Griffin on its saddle. Walking over to the old pecan tree near the house, she set her basket down and clapped her hands together.

"Come here, Killer," Lizzie called, getting the little brown and white dog's attention.

Killer ran to Lizzie, allowing her to scratch behind the dog's perky ears, giving Jake a chance to dismount his horse. He took the reins and led his horse to where Lizzie stood in the shade.

"Hello," Jake proclaimed, removing his three-cornered hat. "Mr. Worsley asked me to come early to nail down loose tin on a barn."

"Uncle Thomas told us you were coming. He's talking with Aunt Grace and getting everything ready. You can put your horse in the pasture with Honeybee and Butterscotch," Lizzie offered.

"Thanks. I'm sure Buckwheat would like some water. It's so hot today," he mumbled, shifting his eyes as if he was uncomfortable.

Lizzie felt Jake's awkward behavior had something to do with her. "I'll show you where the water trough is."

Passing the garden between the house and barn, Lizzie led the way to the fenced-in pasture. As they walked by, Alice, Rebecca, and Hannah shouted across the barnyard from where they were picking vegetables. Their yells triggered Betsy, the white-faced brown cow, to welcome Jake with a loud moo. Smiling, Jake waved in return.

"Those girls have grown up," he commented to Lizzie. "Time has flown by. I never thought I would meet anyone I knew in Bath. I'm grateful Mr. Worsley hired me. It's been great working for Mr.

Shute, but there wasn't much for me to do until the next shipment comes in. When his back heals, I doubt he'll need me. The truth is, I need work and somewhere to stay. I don't think I can bear another night in the loft above the blacksmith's forge, not in this heat with that fire always burning. Anyway, I was going across the street to see if the cooper needed an assistant in his barrel-making shop when Mr. Worsley came in asking Mr. Shute if he knew anyone seeking work."

"We could use some help. Grandfather's servants tend the crops, but the repairs fall behind. The servants can't handle all the work. Uncle John typically works alongside the servants, but Grandfather wants him to take on more responsibilities since he's twenty-three and doesn't have a family yet. Unfortunately, Uncle John can't get the hang of it in time for our busy season. We've been harvesting the first of the tobacco, so Uncle Thomas had to cut back on his attorney duties. He wasn't interested in running the plantations. His passion is the law," Lizzie explained.

Now at the fence, she lifted the rope looped around the post and pushed open the heavy wooden gate, holding it open for Jake. Once inside, he led his horse to the water trough and removed the saddle. He placed the saddle on the fence before joining Lizzie. Walking to the barn, Lizzie wrestled with the question haunting her.

"Jake, have you seen those bearded men in town?"

"The pirates?"

Lizzie hesitated. "Yes, them."

"Two came into the store this morning for tobacco."

"Do you really think they're pirates?"

"I would say yes, although pirates aren't much different than ordinary seamen. So far, the only commotion they caused occurred last night. They must have gotten drunk at the alehouse. I heard them from the loft above the forge singing sea chanties around midnight. No one was happy about it this morning, but like Mr. Shute said, there is no law against singing," Jake reported as they rounded the corner of the barn where the wagon stood under the shelter.

Fourteen-year-old Trent had the wooden ladder propped against the barn as he waited for his uncle's instructions. Beside the ladder laid a pile of silver sheets of tin, a bucket of nails, and a hammer. Aunt Grace held onto her straw hat as she examined the roof with her brother.

The tall, short-haired Thomas Worsley talked with his frowning older sister, explaining the repairs needed for the tattered roof. Being two years older than his brother John, it was he who shared his father's name, Thomas, and the obligations of running the family business. Since he was rearing a family himself, it was even more important to help carry on the Worsley family heritage. The farm had to sustain not only his family and Grace's but also their father and three younger siblings: John, Mary, and Charlotte.

"Afternoon, sir. What would you like me to do first?" Jake wanted to know, inspecting the tin by raising his hand to shield his eyes from the bright sunlight.

Uncle Thomas gave a cheerful greeting accompanied by a handshake. "The roof has been nailed down, but it needs to be replaced. I have the materials you'll need. Do you think you can do it?"

"I should be able to," Jake answered.

"Please be careful. Is there anything we can do to help, Thomas? If not, we'll get back to the garden," Aunt Grace asked.

"No, I think we can handle it. Trent can help, though."

Leaving them to mend the roof, Aunt Grace led the way to the garden where the girls were taking the baskets of ripe vegetables to the house. Picking up her handwoven basket at the pecan tree, Lizzie carried it to the back porch, pushing thoughts of pirates aside.

"Girls, please go upstairs and get the pillows. Lizzie, take two of these baskets to the root cellar. While you're there, bring back some potatoes for supper and the new goose feathers. Two sacks should be enough to refill the pillows," Aunt Grace instructed.

Lizzie headed to the side of the house where the root cellar went beneath it. Lifting the double wooden doors, she hoisted her tan skirt to keep from tripping on the stairs going underground. The darkness forced Lizzie to feel her way along the brick wall until her bare feet left the last step and touched the damp soil. She wished she thought to bring a lantern, but there was no point in turning back even though she despised the eerie darkness. Using her hands to feel the air, her fingertips brushed the burlap sacks of goose feathers propped against the wall at the base of the stairs. Fumbling past them, she found the wooden crate of freshly dug potatoes, located an empty pail, and filled it. Grabbing the burlap sacks on her way up with the potatoes, she returned to the sunshine, pausing to close the doors behind her.

Back on the porch, Alice cut the thread holding the pillow together so that Rebecca and Hannah could pull out the old feathers. Aunt Grace sat in her rocking chair with a wooden bowl in her lap, snapping the ends off green beans. Tossing the burlap sacks to her cousins, Lizzie sat in the rocker next to her aunt. She placed the pail of potatoes beside her and grabbed a bowl of beans. As she began to break off the ends, she naturally picked up a familiar rhythm.

Soon, the air was full of laughter as the children recalled the spring day when they collected the goose feathers. Every year when it was time for the geese to shed their feathers, they would capture them. Rebecca and Hannah chased each goose to where Trent waited with a hooked pole. After hooking the bird's leg, he flipped the goose over so the girls could hold it down. Next, Alice slipped a sock over its head to protect them from its beak. Aunt Grace and Lizzie plucked the feathers, removed the sock, and let the squawking goose loose.

In no time, the girls finished pulling out the old feathers and began stuffing the pillows with new ones, giggling as loose white feathers drifted in the air, landing on their heads. Once they filled the pillows, Lizzie took a break from snapping beans to help stitch up the end of each pillow. Taking a needle and thread, she sewed a nearly perfect row across the cloth, sealing the feathers inside. Sewing was something every girl learned to do at an early age. Girls as young as Hannah practiced their stitches daily on a small piece of cloth stretched over a wooden circle called a sampler. They began with simple stitches and eventually moved on to fancy embroidery. Turning sixteen in May, Lizzie had advanced to embroidery, which she practiced whenever Aunt Grace didn't need her help with the seemingly endless job of sewing on buttons, hemming skirts, or patching holes.

Double-knotting the thread, Lizzie finished the last pillow, tossing it to Hannah as Alice and Rebecca completed their pillows. She spotted Uncle Thomas walking toward them, wiping sweat from his brow as he came to a stop at the bottom of the stairs.

"Grace, I'm headed out. Jake told me you invited him for supper when you were in town. It's going to take him a few days to replace the tin. I told him to rest tomorrow since it's Sunday and resume his duties Monday morning. I also gave him permission to sleep in the shed behind the smokehouse. He might as well stay here while he's working. Once he's done with the barn, I'll get him to replace some fencing and paint the porch. Giles won't need him until next week when the ships come in. I invited Jake to join us in worship, but he didn't say much. Perhaps you can mention it. He can at least eat dinner with us at Father's," he announced.

"Alright, I'll see what I can do. We'll see you tomorrow."

"We may be a bit late. You know how it is trying to get the family ready to go somewhere," he replied, referring to his wife, three-year-old son, and seventeen-month-old boy. "Sunday dinner should be interesting. Charlotte is cooking by herself. She needs to get used to it, because when Mary and Thomas Bustin tie the knot she'll be doing all the cooking for Father and John."

Aunt Grace smiled. "It won't be long. Tell Sarah and the children we said hello."

"I will. Good-bye, girls."

Waving to their uncle, Lizzie and her cousins watched him mount his black horse. As he left the yard, Aunt Grace finished snapping the beans and got up to check the pork roast she was cooking. The girls followed her with the pillows while Lizzie lingered on the back porch sweeping the mess with the straw broom her aunt left near the back door. Cleaning up the old feathers, she placed them in the washtub the girls had been using and combined the bowls of green beans to make it easier to carry inside. Opening the back door, Rebecca and Hannah nearly knocked her down.

"Thanks for sweeping up the feathers," Rebecca declared.

"Yes, thanks, Lizzie. Momma told us to take the washtub to the barn," Hannah added.

Both girls bounced off the porch carrying the washtub between them. Heading into the kitchen, Lizzie placed the green beans on the counter and turned to her aunt, who was standing near the fireplace peering into a three-legged iron cauldron on the hearth.

"What can I do, Aunt Grace?" she asked, tying on an apron.

"Please peel the potatoes. Alice is combining the eggs with yesterday's and pouring the milk left over from making butter this morning into a pitcher. There's enough of Betsy's milk for supper."

Washing her hands, Lizzie grabbed a knife to peel the skin off the potatoes. She sliced them into smaller chunks to speed up the cooking time, placing the cut potatoes in a pot. Meanwhile, Aunt Grace put the green beans in another pot, adding water and pork fatback seasoning before hanging the pots on iron hooks suspended over the fire by a rod. Moving on to the ears of corn, Lizzie shucked the outer layer of green husks, revealing the cream-colored kernels inside. Laying the seven ears of corn in a fourth pot, she filled it with water and placed it on the hearth close to the burning wood. Aunt Grace prepared the cornbread by mixing cornmeal with water and patting it out so that it could fry in the cast-iron pan.

"There isn't anything else to do right now. You might as well go wash off," Aunt Grace suggested.

"We shouldn't take long," Lizzie said as Rebecca and Hannah skipped into the kitchen and went through the doorway.

Hanging her apron on one of the wooden pegs nailed to the wall, Lizzie followed her cousins into the room where they ate their meals. The four of them walked down the hallway and climbed the stairs to the second level. There were four rooms upstairs, two smaller ones at the top of the stairs and two larger ones toward the front of the house with windows overlooking the waterfront. Hannah, Rebecca, and Alice shared one of the larger rooms across from their mother's.

Reminding her cousins to wash behind their ears, Lizzie left them to their scrubbing, entering the room next to theirs and across the hall from Trent's. Closing the door, she poured water into a bowl from a pitcher and started washing her face with lavender-scented lye soap. Soon she was clean, which was an accomplishment considering how dirty her feet were. Opening the tall wooden wardrobe in the corner, she chose a petticoat, a light pink dress, and a pair of stockings. With her outfit complete, she unbraided her hair and brushed through it before tying a pink ribbon around her ponytail and finishing with her black, high-buttoned shoes.

Going next door, Lizzie found the girls clean and dressed in their white petticoats. Alice was at the wardrobe picking out a dark green dress before passing Rebecca a light purple dress and Hannah a yellow one with embroidered white daisies. Having helped them fix their hair ribbons, Lizzie led the way to the kitchen where Aunt Grace was moving cornbread from the frying pan to a basket lined with cloth.

"Go change, Aunt Grace. We can finish," Lizzie offered.

Turning around, Aunt Grace gave her a nod. "Everything is ready. Hannah, go tell Trent and Jake to wash up for supper while your sisters set the table. Let's use Mother's fine china."

Hanging up her apron, Aunt Grace left the girls as she went upstairs. Lizzie stirred the potatoes, checked the corncobs, and tasted the green beans to be sure they had enough seasoning. Alice and Rebecca got out the china, a family heirloom only used for special occasions. The two girls set the table with forks and cloth napkins. Finally, Hannah placed a vase of white daisies and yellow black-eyed Susans on the table. Aunt Grace returned wearing a dark blue dress, though she kept her straight, dark brown hair up in a bun. She handed Hannah the basket of cornbread as Trent and Jake came in.

As the boys went into the next room, Lizzie removed the pots from the fireplace while Aunt Grace spooned food into bowls for the girls to carry to the oak table. Alice and Rebecca joined Trent on the wooden bench as Lizzie took her usual spot on the other side of the table with Hannah between her and Aunt Grace. Jake sat in a straight-backed chair at the end of the table.

"Let's hold hands and bless the food," Aunt Grace said, reaching for Hannah and Rebecca's hands.

Taking Hannah's right hand, Lizzie realized she had to hold Jake's hand instead of Trent's. Feeling uncomfortable, she stretched out her hand. By the look on Jake's face, she could tell Aunt Grace caught him off guard. Glancing at Trent, Jake took his hand before reaching out to grab Lizzie's. Closing their eyes, Aunt Grace asked God to bless the food and thanked Him for their blessings.

Aunt Grace passed the potatoes to Rebecca. "Thank you, Jake, for helping with the barn. We're blessed you came when you did."

"I appreciate the work, ma'am. Mr. Shute doesn't need me every day. Mr. Worsley said I can sleep in your shed. It beats the heat of the blacksmith forge. My food and lodge can come out of my pay."

"The Lord always takes care of us. We're going to the Divine Service in the morning to worship God. We go to my father's house to eat afterwards. You're welcome to come," Aunt Grace hinted.

Jake shrugged. "I don't know. I'll think about it."

"What plans do you have in Bath?" Aunt Grace asked.

Jake took a bite of pork roast before answering. "I wasn't planning to stay long, just through the summer. I arrived here a week ago and got the job with Mr. Shute, which pays for food and supplies. By the way, Miss Lee, this food is delicious. I haven't eaten like this in years."

Aunt Grace smiled. "I'm glad you're enjoying it."

"Where were you planning to go?" Trent questioned.

"I heard there is work up north in Philadelphia, Pennsylvania, on merchant ships," Jake explained, sampling the corn on the cob.

"Aren't you a bit young to be going to Pennsylvania to join the crew of a merchant ship?" Aunt Grace inquired.

"Not really. I turned seventeen in January. I've been an apprentice on merchant ships since I was fourteen. My apprenticeship ended this year. After three years, I learned a lot about ships."

"Where has time gone? You were only a child when we last saw you, and now you're a young man," Aunt Grace sighed.

"I didn't recognize any of you the other day. As I moved forward after the tragedy, I tried to forget those years of my life."

Assuming Jake was referring to the Indian attacks of 1711, Lizzie became tense. She knew her aunt wanted to know more about the attack, even if it meant hearing the awful details Jake no doubt witnessed firsthand as a survivor. The details of Uncle Jared's death remained a mystery due to the lack of information when similar attacks were simultaneously occurring all over the colony.

"I know your parents are proud," Aunt Grace acknowledged.

The expression on Jake's face changed, revealing a wounded soul. He told them his parents and three younger sisters died in the first Indian attack on the fateful September morning. Although he didn't say how he escaped death, Jake did say he ran to the nearby Neuse River plantation where Jared Lee rounded up a group of men. Back at the Griffin homestead, there was nothing they could do but bury his family. Jake lived with Uncle Jared for a few days before the plantation came under attack. The men stayed to fight so that their wives and children could escape by boats up the river to New Bern, the closest safe-haven fort. Jake went with them to safety, never to see Jared Lee again. For the next three years, he lived with an older couple until he turned fourteen and applied for an apprenticeship with a merchant.

After Jake finished his story, the conversation focused on less depressing topics, making the evening more cheerful. Soon their plates were empty, and at Aunt Grace's insisting Jake agreed to take Trent up on a challenge to play a game of chess. Quickly washing the dishes, the girls joined them in the parlor while Aunt Grace sat in her rocking chair with her latest sewing project. Pulling up chairs, the girls slid over to the small oak table Trent and Jake were sitting at to see the game. Knowing chess could be far from a quick game, Lizzie found herself amused with Hannah's impatience as she whispered questions in her ear.

Jake called checkmate as their dog Killer started barking wildly. Placing her sewing project in the basket beside her rocker, Aunt Grace got up about the time there was a knock on the front door. As she opened it, Lizzie saw that the visitor was Uncle Thomas. Alarmed by his return, she realized a young Indian boy was with him. The youngster, no older than Hannah, had tanned skin and eyes nearly as dark as his shoulder-length black hair. His name was Scripo, an orphan of the Tuscarora Indian War and one of Tobias Knight's servants.

"Thomas? What brings you here at this hour?" Aunt Grace asked, letting the two of them in. "And why is Scripo with you?"

"Sorry to bother you, ma'am, but Master Knight told me to deliver his letter tonight," young Scripo piped up.

"The lad came to my place a half an hour ago. He gave me this. It was addressed to both of us," Uncle Thomas declared, holding out a piece of folded parchment paper.

Taking the letter, which had a red wax seal bearing Tobias Knight's symbol, Aunt Grace began to read. Letters of importance had seals of red wax to ensure they remained private. A letter sealed with black wax brought news of the death of a loved one. Wondering what the letter said, Lizzie watched her aunt's facial expression, knowing the contents were serious.

Finishing, she looked up at her younger brother. "Looks like we need to go meet with him. Let me grab my shawl."

"Okay," Uncle Thomas replied. "Ride back to Mr. Knight, Scripo, and let him know we will be there shortly."

Nodding, the young Indian boy took off as Uncle Thomas turned to Jake. "Can you stay here in the house until we return?"

"Sure," Jake agreed.

Thanking him, Uncle Thomas opened the door for Aunt Grace, who was back from her room wearing a white shawl.

"We shouldn't be long. Girls, mind Lizzie and don't stay up past bedtime," she instructed, heading out the door.

When the house had grown still, Rebecca tapped Jake on the arm. "You know, Lizzie is really good at chess, too."

"I bet she can beat you," Hannah giggled.

The last thing Lizzie wanted to do was play chess. She was anxious to know the reason Mr. Tobias Knight needed to meet with her aunt and uncle so suddenly. Uncle Thomas' request for Jake to stay only added to the mystery. Was it dangerous for them to be home alone?

"Well, Jake? Want to take on Lizzie?" Trent teased, getting up.

"Why not? Let's see how good you are," Jake joked.

Sitting in Trent's vacant chair, Lizzie watched Jake set up the new game as Trent swapped seats, allowing Hannah to sit on his lap for a better view. When Jake was ready, he motioned for her to go first. Choosing a pawn from the front line, Lizzie slid it forward two spaces. Jake made a similar move with his pawn and for the next couple of turns they inched their way into the opposing territory. Finally, Lizzie spotted an opportunity to slide a bishop diagonally five spaces, grabbing Jake's attention by taking out his rook.

"Smart move," he mumbled, studying his side of the board.

The game continued for some time, each making carefully calculated moves until at last Lizzie saw an opening for a checkmate. She slid her queen into position and looked at Jake with a smile.

"Checkmate," she declared triumphantly.

Jake looked stunned. "What? How did you—never mind."

"We told you Lizzie was good," Rebecca laughed.

"You weren't kidding. Someone taught you well, Lizzie."

"Yes, they did. You were quite a challenge, though," she admitted as she turned to her cousins. "It's time for bed, girls."

"But Momma isn't home yet," Hannah pointed out.

"They've had plenty of time to go and come back," Alice added.

"The meeting just took longer than they expected. She said to go to bed if she didn't get back in time," Lizzie reassured them.

"Lizzie's right. Go on," Trent urged his sisters as they groaned.

Saying goodnight to their brother and Jake, the girls went upstairs to their bedchambers. Lizzie followed to help them get ready for bed. Once the girls were in their white nightgowns and mob sleeping caps, they knelt beside the rope bed Rebecca and Hannah shared. As they said their bedtime prayers, Lizzie bowed her own head, listening to their heartfelt requests to God. When they finished, Lizzie tucked her two youngest cousins under a quilt their mother made before moving to the single bed Alice slept in. Wishing them sweet dreams, Lizzie returned to the parlor where she joined the conversation between Trent and Jake. They discussed numerous topics, but the most interesting was Jake's description of the places he had seen while serving on merchant ships. An hour passed when Trent, now yawning, announced he was heading to bed, saying goodnight as he turned in.

Glancing at the front door, Lizzie's mind drifted to Aunt Grace and Uncle Thomas. She tried to stop worrying, but realized it was nearing midnight.

"They're okay," Jake muttered, grabbing her attention.

"Guess you're right. I have to trust God will bring them safely home," she replied, silently sending up a prayer. Looking back at Jake, she realized he had an odd look on his face. "What's wrong?"

"Nothing."

"Something's bothering you."

"I just haven't been relying on God lately," he confessed.

"What do you mean? Everyone is supposed to rely on God."

Jake shook his head. "You have reasons why you believe certain things, and I have my reasons. Anyway, let's talk about the letter. Why do you think Tobias Knight wanted to meet with them?"

"I have no idea. It must be important, though."

"How well do you know the Indian boy? It could be a false letter of some kind. Can he be trusted?"

"Of course he can be trusted. During the Indian war there were a lot of raids. Scripo was an abandoned baby, an innocent victim of the war. Mr. Knight and his wife, Katherine, took him in and raised him. Even though he is now a house slave they treat him well, almost like family. Scripo has always been nice. Besides, the letter had a red wax seal and the Knight symbol."

"Alright, alright, it was only a theory."

"You don't trust Indians, do you?"

"Not since those murderers killed my folks."

"I understand your anger, but not all Indians are bad. The tribes who didn't participate in the raids dealt with attacks, too. Scripo's family could've belonged to one of those tribes," Lizzie continued as Killer started barking again.

Lizzie exchanged a look with Jake, who rose from his seat. The latch on the front door jiggled and in walked Aunt Grace.

"Thank God you're safe. I was worried," Lizzie proclaimed.

"It took longer than I anticipated," Aunt Grace admitted.

"Why was the dog barking at you?" Jake asked.

"We must have scared her when we came into the yard. Hopefully she'll calm down and won't wake everyone up."

"What did Mr. Knight want to talk about?" Lizzie inquired with curiosity, noticing her aunt's face was pale.

"It's late. We can talk about it later. Would you please find a quilt for Jake?" Aunt Grace requested, changing the subject.

"I'll be okay, Miss Lee," Jake assured her.

"Nonsense. I won't take no for an answer."

Exiting the parlor, Lizzie passed the table on her way down the hall. Reaching underneath the staircase, she lifted the heavy lid of the oak chest that stored quilts, wash towels, and other fabrics. Choosing a patchwork quilt made from scraps of clothing, she returned to the parlor, apologizing for not having a pillow. Although Jake insisted he didn't need one, Aunt Grace, true to her thoughtful nature, assured him he would have a pillow by Monday night.

Saying goodnight to Jake, Lizzie waited for Aunt Grace, who saw him to the door. Going upstairs, they wished each other sweet dreams. Lizzie entered her bedchambers while Aunt Grace went to hers. As she dressed in her white nightgown and mob sleeping cap, Lizzie couldn't help but wonder about the conversation between her aunt, uncle, and Mr. Knight. Whatever happened shook Aunt Grace's spirit, causing the color to drain from her face. Climbing beneath her quilt, Lizzie stared at the wooden boards of the ceiling thinking about the way her aunt dismissed her question. *What was going on?* Her own spirit would not rest until she knew what the letter said.

CHAPTER THREE

☠

TUNNEL LAND

July 12, 1718 ~ Saturday

Seven days had passed since the private meeting between Aunt Grace, Uncle Thomas, and the secretary of Bath, Tobias Knight. Despite Lizzie's questions, her aunt always changed the subject or said there were chores to do. This led Lizzie to the conclusion Aunt Grace had no intention of telling her what happened in Tobias Knight's study. For whatever reasons, Aunt Grace's lips were staying sealed. If Lizzie wanted to know, she would have to piece together the mystery.

All morning, the girls had been helping Aunt Grace wash the quilts and bed linen with lavender-scented lye soap. They hung them up to dry on the long clotheslines strung from poles in the backyard. Finishing the bedsheets, Aunt Grace sent the girls inside to bring out their clothes. Meanwhile, Aunt Grace dried her hands on her apron and went to the barn to see how close Jake and Trent were to completing the new barn roof.

In no time, the girls returned carrying armloads of clothes, dropping them next to where Lizzie waited. As they went back inside for the second load, Lizzie began to sort the clothes in piles, the colored clothes beside Aunt Grace's washtub and the white clothes beside hers. Sitting in her chair, she picked up one of her aunt's aprons and started to put it in the soapy water, pausing as she felt something in the pocket. Pulling out the object, she realized it was a piece of paper. Carefully unfolding it, she spotted a familiar red wax seal on the back of the paper where the ends met.

Excitement raced through Lizzie's mind as she gazed across the yard at her aunt who was talking to Trent as he held the ladder for Jake. She couldn't believe her luck. All week she had tried to figure out what the letter said and here she was holding it in her hands. Suddenly, a wave of guilt filled her heart. Perhaps she should return the letter to the apron and pretend she never saw it, or maybe she needed to give it to Aunt Grace. Then again, it could be God's way of letting her know trouble was ahead. Deciding God wanted her to know, Lizzie made sure no one was looking and opened the letter.

Dear Mr. Thomas Worsley and Miss Grace Lee,
I have important news regarding your brother-in-law. I cannot disclose the news in this letter. Thus, I am asking you to come talk with me tonight if possible.
Sincerely, Tobias Knight

Breathless, Lizzie considered the news Mr. Knight referred to in his letter. Clearly, her papa was in trouble, but why were Aunt Grace and Uncle Thomas keeping it secret? The back door to the kitchen slammed shut, reminding Lizzie the girls were back. Quickly folding the letter, she slid it into the pocket of her own apron as her cousins dropped their last load of clothes.

"What can we help do now?" Alice asked.

"You can help scrub these clothes until your momma gets back," Lizzie suggested as she submerged the apron in the soapy water.

Eleven-year-old Alice picked up one of Hannah's work dresses and put it in the other washtub. Working alongside her, Lizzie held the wooden washboard as she scrubbed the apron up and down on the ribbed tin. Once clean, they twisted the soapy water out of the clothes and handed them to Rebecca and Hannah, who rinsed them in a third washtub of plain water. When Aunt Grace returned, Alice went to help her little sisters hang the clothes on the line.

Eventually they finished washing and the girls went inside to make a picnic dinner to eat under the pecan trees. Lizzie sliced tomatoes while Aunt Grace fried bacon and Alice peeled off pieces of lettuce. Rebecca made the sandwiches as Hannah found an old quilt for them to sit on. After everything was ready, they brought the sandwiches outside, calling for Trent and Jake to join them in the shade. The boys sat down as Hannah asked the blessing.

"God is great. God is good. Let us thank Him for our food. By His hands, we are fed. Give us, Lord, our daily bread. Amen. Dig in!"

Picking up a sandwich, Lizzie recalled how Grandfather Worsley taught them this prayer when they were little. It had been Grandfather Beard who added the "dig in" part, a tradition Lizzie had started with her cousins.

"Do you like these sandwiches, Jake?" Hannah questioned.

"I sure do. Can you guess what my favorite part is?"

Hannah shook her head. "No, what?"

"Tomatoes are so juicy it runs down your hands."

The six-year-old giggled as tomato juice dripped from Jake's chin. Lizzie knew the little girl had enjoyed Jake's company over the past week. In fact, the whole family had kind of adopted him.

Finishing their meal, Aunt Grace announced her plans to go berry picking while Trent and Jake went fishing. Taking the quilt inside, the girls tied on their bonnets. Armed with baskets, they set out for the woods bordering their property to the south. Over the years, the plantation next door had sold numerous times. At one point, it belonged to Lizzie's step-grandmother, Elizabeth Beard Masten, and her husband, Captain William Masten, before they moved to the other side of Romney Marsh three years prior. The most recent owner, Governor Charles Eden, also lived there for a short time, but sold it in April to John Lillington, a real estate appraiser who planned to sell the property.

Gazing at the rock-filled black soil, Lizzie walked behind her aunt and cousins as they skirted the cornfield. Passing head-high rows of slender green stalks, they arrived at the woods where the thickets of blackberries were. Spreading out, the girls began to pick the ripe, deep purple berries off the thorny bushes, leaving the red berries to mature. Lizzie worked alongside Hannah, picking berries beyond the little girl's reach. Moving along the row, she remembered Grandmother Worsley taking her, Trent, and Alice berry picking when they were little and how she rewarded their efforts with a blackberry pie. Thinking about her made Lizzie's heart fill with sadness. Oh, how she missed her loved ones in heaven.

The sound of squeaking caused Lizzie to turn around. To her surprise, she spotted a carriage headed toward them. As it drew closer, she recognized the man at the reins. It was Grandfather Worsley.

"Hello!" he exclaimed.

"Father, what are you doing here?" Aunt Grace answered.

Pulling on the reins to stop his brown-colored mare, the lanky man climbed down to give them a hug.

"I'm heading to Tunnel Land. Thomas has something he wants me to look at. I caught Trent and the new lad, Jake, down by the dock. He said they were going fishing, and I could find you here gathering berries. I know you're busy, but I wanted to see if you would go with me."

From his unusual demeanor, Lizzie knew this wasn't an ordinary invitation. Governor Eden's former plantation had acquired the nickname "Tunnel Land" due to the legend of a tunnel leading from the wharf to the cellar of the mansion. Personally, Lizzie had never seen a tunnel or heard of anyone finding its entrance, yet the legend remained. Although it wasn't odd for Uncle Thomas to be at Tunnel Land, it was strange for him to ask Grandfather to come.

Lizzie assumed her uncle was appraising the mansion and cluster of outbuildings for John Lillington.

"Alright," Aunt Grace agreed. Turning to Lizzie she added, "Keep picking berries until I get back. Listen to Lizzie while I'm gone, girls."

Leaving her basket, Aunt Grace climbed into the carriage behind Grandfather Worsley. Waving to them, Lizzie couldn't stop wondering what was going on and if it had anything to do with the letter. Mulling over the situation, she became convinced she needed to find out the details. She quickly devised a plan to keep her cousins busy.

"Alice, I need to go check on something."

The eleven-year-old nodded. "Okay."

Seeing the curiosity in her brown eyes, Lizzie didn't linger. Walking around the end of the bushes, she waited until she was out of sight before picking up her pace. As she came to the edge of the field, she held up her dress so that she could run, making her way to the waterfront. Coming to an overgrown path parallel to Bath Creek, she crossed the property line and zigzagged through the woods until she came to a field of tobacco already topped out with the signature white blossoms. Staying hidden among the tall, yellow-green stalks of tobacco, Lizzie came to the edge of the field and, having nowhere else to hide, peeped through the long, pointed leaves at the vacant house.

To her amazement, the place was swarming with men, and at least one woman now that she had spotted Aunt Grace and Grandfather. Uncle Thomas stood on the porch with a feathered quill in one hand and parchment paper in the other, giving out orders. Some of the men were neighbors, but many were strangers dressed in shabby clothes.

Watching the plantation owners and strangers form a semicircle around the stairs, Lizzie caught a glimpse of what they were looking at. Fifty or more Africans stood shoulder to shoulder facing the

Bath County planters. Stunned by the sheer number of dark-skinned men, Lizzie couldn't help but wonder where they came from. She knew many plantation owners had anywhere from two to five slaves to help tend their crops. Even her grandfather had three African men who worked alongside his white and Indian servants. These African men were different, though. Judging by their muscular bodies and youthful faces, she knew they were the best quality of slaves the colony had seen in years, possibly since Port Bath's founding in 1703.

For some time now, plantation owners had to travel either north to Virginia or south to Charles Town to purchase slaves for their farms. Unfortunately, those colonies always got the best slaves, which forced the Bath County planters to take the feeblest men. The fact that these able-bodied Africans were here during such a crucial time would be huge for the colony.

Wishing she could hear what Uncle Thomas was saying, Lizzie clasped her hand over her mouth as her eyes fell upon a familiar face. Feeling as though the humid July heat would choke her, she drew in a shaky breath. The man approaching her uncle was tall and wore a long black beard tied up in miniature braids. He was the same man they had seen in town, the man whom everyone thought was a pirate.

Apparently, she was the only one alarmed by the bearded man's presence. The more Lizzie watched the crowd, she began to get the feeling the man had brought the massive number of slaves into the colony. Could this be a business deal? Was the pirate story just a disguise to keep Governor Eden and the townspeople from knowing about this mysterious shipment? Why keep it secret?

Lizzie's mind spun with scenarios, yet none of them made sense. Clearly her family was in on this deal, but why? Watching Uncle Thomas sort the Africans into groups, Lizzie realized he was separating them by the families living along Bath Town Creek. Wondering why he was overseeing this event, she suddenly recalled the letter tucked in the pocket of her apron. Fumbling to retrieve it, she pulled out the letter and reread it, hoping to make a connection between the late-night visit her aunt and uncle made to Knight's plantation and the puzzling encounter at Tunnel Land.

Glancing at the crowd, Lizzie searched the faces expecting to see Secretary Knight. To her surprise, he wasn't there. Surely, he knew about this meeting next door to his home. Regardless of his position in the government, Mr. Knight had been living in the colony for years and had many friends, including the Worsley family. He had to know about it, and perhaps even planned it out with Uncle Thomas. The question was, what did this have to do with her papa?

Confused, Lizzie retraced her steps through the tobacco field. Coming to the overgrown path, she marched past seedling trees, briar patches, and the thick undergrowth of wildflowers as she crossed the property line leaving Tunnel Land's secrets behind. Following the woods, she made it to the blackberry bushes, where she could hear her cousins. Not wanting to scare them, she announced her return.

"What took you so long?" Rebecca asked.

"Sorry," Lizzie replied, ignoring her question.

Thankfully, the girls said nothing more as they excitedly showed her their full baskets of juicy blackberries. Relieved she wouldn't have to explain, Lizzie picked up her own basket and finished helping pick the last of the ripe berries. About twenty minutes later the carriage came into view, bringing with it the images Lizzie had seen and the questions she yearned to ask but dared not. By the time her grandfather and aunt came to a stop, she could barely absorb what they were saying as her cousins showed off the baskets full of hard work.

"My goodness! You girls certainly gathered lots of berries. They'll make a great pie," Grandfather proclaimed proudly.

"I think your hard work deserves one," Aunt Grace added.

"Can we fix a pie tonight, Momma?" Hannah begged.

"Alright. Climb on, your grandfather's taking us home."

Cheering in happiness, they clambered up on the carriage. Although cramped, the three girls managed to fit on the wooden bench behind their grandfather and Aunt Grace with six-year-old Hannah seated on her mother's lap. Holding the baskets of blackberries, the carriage lurched as Grandfather urged his brown-colored mare homeward. Coming to the main yard, he let them off at the back door, said his good-byes, and headed north to his adjoining property. Lizzie watched him go as her cousins took the baskets inside the house before joining Lizzie and their mother at the clotheslines.

"Lizzie, why don't you and Alice take down the quilts?" Aunt Grace suggested as she removed sheets from the second line.

Pulling a quilt off the line, Lizzie helped Alice while Rebecca folded dresses and Hannah matched stockings. After the quilts were folded, Alice started on Trent's shirts and knee britches, giving Lizzie the awkward duty of folding Jake's clean clothes and bed linen.

"Momma!" Hannah exclaimed, tugging at her mother's arm as she pointed at the waterfront. "Here come Trent and Jake."

Turning, Lizzie spotted the boys down by the dock. Grandfather Beard had constructed the crudely built wharf years ago to get the crops of corn, sweet potatoes, tobacco, and cotton out of the fields to sell. Seeing Trent and Jake walking to the house, Lizzie noticed they were carrying a string of fish along with their cane poles.

"Look what we caught!" Trent yelled, holding up his fish.

"Fish for supper sounds good," Aunt Grace called back.

Trent grinned. "Come on, Jake. Let's clean these croakers."

Taking their fishing poles to the barn, the boys went to scrape the scales off the fish while the girls finished the laundry. When everything was neatly folded, they picked up a load of clothes to take inside following Aunt Grace and her armload of bed linen. Realizing she had to return Jake's clothes and sheets, Lizzie asked Alice to carry her clothes upstairs so that she could take Jake's to the shed. Rounding the corner of the barn, Lizzie made her way to the smokehouse where they kept salted meats hanging from the rafters. Behind it was the tool shed, a small wooden-planked shack big enough to hold rakes, shovels, hoes, and equipment used to tend the garden and fields.

As she pushed open the creaking door, Lizzie paused to allow her brown eyes to adjust to the dimly lit room. By the sunlight streaming in from between the planked walls, she could make out a pallet in the corner. Walking over to it, she spotted the quilt and pillow Jake borrowed and a lantern perched on an overturned bucket. She placed his belongings beside the quilt, feeling guilty he had to stay in such a dirty place while they lived in the luxury of their two-story home.

Sighing, she reached for the door handle as it swung open, causing her to jump. Startled, she held up her hand to shield her eyes from the blinding sunshine.

"What are you doing?" came Jake's unmistakable voice.

"I-I was returning your washed clothes," Lizzie stuttered, her cheeks flushing as she saw the curious look on Jake's face.

"Oh. I didn't expect anyone to do my laundry. Food and board were the only things in our agreement."

Trent's voice interrupted the cloud of awkwardness, causing Lizzie to exhale in relief. Stepping into the sunshine, she followed Jake around the barn expecting to see Trent waiting. What she didn't anticipate seeing was two visitors riding astride horses. Recognizing the stepbrothers, she suddenly felt another rush of awkwardness.

Although they were known as the Gale boys, the oldest brother, Thomas Harvey Jr., was a stepson of the former chief justice Christopher Gale. The younger brother, Miles Gale, was the oldest of Mr. Gale's children, which included two girls ages fourteen and twelve.

"Looks like you had good luck fishing, Trent," Miles said.

"Yes, we caught a bucket full," Trent answered, holding up the fish he was carrying to the house. "Jake showed me a few different techniques he learned."

"Jake?"

"Sorry, I should've introduced you. Miles Gale and Thomas Harvey, this is Jake Griffin, a friend of our family."

"We already met," Jake stated in a surprisingly flat tone.

"Yes," Miles replied arrogantly. "I believe you were working with Philip when I bought supplies."

"What brings you here?" Trent asked as his mother came up.

"Hello," Aunt Grace greeted their visitors.

"Good afternoon, Miss Lee," Miles responded.

"We wanted to invite you to a party we're hosting at our house next Saturday. Guests will arrive around four o'clock. I hope you will attend, Miss Lee," twenty-three-year-old Thomas declared.

"Thanks for the invitation. I don't think we'll be attending."

Making eye contact with Lizzie, Miles quickly spoke up. "Mother has been planning this party for weeks, Miss Lee. Since Father left on his business trip to England it's all she's talked about. Mother would feel terrible if you didn't come. Please reconsider."

Listening to his plea, Lizzie knew his request had little to do with his mother's feelings. Whether he would admit it publicly or not, his main intentions were to have Lizzie attend the party. Unfortunately, Aunt Grace gave in.

"Alright, we'll come."

"Wonderful!" Miles exclaimed happily, grinning at Lizzie.

"We'll see you next Saturday, then. Good day, Miss Lee," Thomas proclaimed as he dipped the brim of his three-cornered hat and turned his horse around to leave.

Tilting his own hat down to show respect, Miles added, "Looking forward to seeing you next Saturday, Lizzie."

Nudging his horse with his boots, Miles joined his stepbrother. Lizzie stood beside Jake feeling uncomfortable. The interest Miles had shown and hints he had been dropping over the last few months were obviously leading up to something. Lizzie tried to avoid him—not because he was a bad person, but because she wasn't ready to pursue a relationship with anyone. She hoped and prayed he didn't get up the nerve to ask Aunt Grace's permission to court her.

"Come along, girls, I need you to take these quilts inside so I can start supper," Aunt Grace instructed as she handed each of them a patchwork quilt. "Trent, after you take the fish to the kitchen, could you and Jake bring in some more firewood?"

"Yes, ma'am," he piped up, taking in the fish while Jake headed to the woodpile behind the barn.

Receiving her own quilt from Aunt Grace, Lizzie trooped up the stairs of the back porch behind her three cousins. Leaving Aunt Grace in the kitchen to begin supper, the four girls proceeded up the flight of steps leading to their bedchambers.

Alice led her sisters to their room, where Lizzie could hear them talking about Miles and his interest in her. Trying to ignore them, she entered her room and walked to her bed. Bending down, she checked the goose-feather mattress, making sure it was still on the ropes crisscrossed underneath it and tied to the wooden rails. She put on her bedsheets and arranged the quilt her mother made from her outgrown clothes. Going downstairs, she came into the kitchen just in time to help Aunt Grace.

"Lizzie, please start frying the fish. I have already battered them and got the lard heated," her aunt suggested as she cut the cabbage.

Tying on an apron, Lizzie carefully placed several battered fish in the frying pan. Meanwhile, Aunt Grace got Alice, Rebecca, and Hannah to help with the cornbread hoecakes and cabbage so she could start the blackberry pie. In no time, their supper was ready. After saying the blessing, Aunt Grace passed the plate of fish as Trent started the conversation.

"Is that pie?"

"Yes," Aunt Grace confirmed.

"Hope you like blackberry pie, Jake," Hannah proclaimed.

Jake smiled. "I do. My mother called it briarberry pie."

"Because of the briars?"

"Exactly. Do you like the croaker fish we caught? Can you guess how it got its name?" Jake questioned the little girl.

"It croaks like a frog," she responded as everyone laughed.

Once everyone quieted down, Trent changed the subject by asking his mother why she didn't want to go to Mrs. Gale's party. Although she claimed she had plans for next Saturday, Lizzie knew part of the reason had to do with Sarah Gale, a sophisticated woman around whom Aunt Grace felt awkward. Over the years, the Gale family had held an important role in the politics of Bath. According to rumors, Christopher Gale had even been at odds with Governor Charles Eden on occasion. Lizzie also knew her aunt's change of heart had to do with the potential relationship between her and Miles. Aunt Grace had in no way suggested she should pursue a relationship with him, but Uncle Thomas had insinuated there was no reason she shouldn't give the sixteen-year-old a chance. Most of the girls her age had been courting, and some were even engaged to be married. Even Miles' sister, Elizabeth, had recently announced her engagement and plans for a wedding in February after her fifteenth birthday.

"Is Jake invited?" Trent wanted to know.

"Sorry, Jake, I didn't think to ask. I'm sure Sarah would welcome you. I'll get Thomas to speak with her," Aunt Grace stated.

"There's no need to go to the trouble, Miss Lee. Sounds like it's going to be a fancy party. I would feel uncomfortable," Jake said.

"Please come, Jake," Hannah begged.

"Jake has made his decision," Aunt Grace reminded her.

Upset, Hannah picked at her food as the table fell into an unpleasant silence. Eventually Trent spoke, though Lizzie wished he hadn't.

"I was surprised to see both Thomas and Miles."

"Why? You know Miles came to see Lizzie. He's smitten," Rebecca replied as her sisters giggled.

Lizzie felt her cheeks grow warm with embarrassment. She wished it was possible to sink into the floor where she could hide.

"He is *not* smitten," Lizzie shot back defensively.

"Look who's standing up for her sweetheart," Alice teased.

"This is ridiculous. Miles Gale is *not* my sweetheart."

"It sounds like it," Hannah pointed out.

"Aunt Grace, please tell them to stop," Lizzie pleaded.

"Alright, girls, leave Lizzie alone. Her private relationships are not topics to discuss over supper," Aunt Grace declared.

Lizzie debated reminding her aunt she didn't have private relationships but chose not to stir it up again. While the rest of the family ate their pie with conversation, she nibbled on hers in silence.

Lost in thought, her mind drifted to Jake's comment about briarberry pie. The only other person she knew who called them briarberries was her papa. She felt ashamed to have forgotten it was his favorite pie. Changing her focus, she mentally revisited the scene she witnessed at Tunnel Land. Somehow there was a connection between the man everyone called a pirate and the mystery of her father. She just had to figure it out.

CHAPTER FOUR

PIE AND PIRATES

July 15, 1718 ~ Tuesday

The dog days of summer were in full swing, making life miserable and crops dry. It had rained just enough to refresh the vegetables Sunday afternoon on the family's way home from dinner at Grandfather's house. Unfortunately, the heat made it difficult to stay indoors even at night. Luckily, they could feel a breeze off the water as they sat on the front porch in the evenings.

Lizzie enjoyed watching the sun set beyond the trees and seeing the stars appear in the night sky. After hours of math and English studies, it was nice to relax. Tonight, there was an added excitement since they were going to catch fireflies. Waiting on the steps with jars, the girls watched for the first glow to light up the darkness.

"There's one!" Hannah shouted as she jumped up from the bottom step with Killer wagging her tail behind.

Joining Hannah in the grass, Rebecca, Alice, and Lizzie left the stairs in search of the tiny bugs. It didn't take long for Lizzie to spot a firefly as it landed on her outreached hand flashing its soft glow. Cupping her hand, she released the bug into her jar and continued her search by the barn. Soon, a dozen fireflies were crawling around in her jar. Deciding she had enough, Lizzie started to retrace her steps to the front porch. Something near the corral caught her eye. Pausing, she realized the dark shadow was a human.

Fear swept over Lizzie as she stood frozen. The shadowed figure eased along the fence in the direction of the dock, slipping into the night without the slightest clue of identity. Stunned by what she saw, Lizzie hastily made her way around to the front of the house where Aunt Grace sat in her rocking chair. Beside her, Trent whittled by the light of the candle inside the lantern.

"You filled your jar fast," Aunt Grace proclaimed when she saw the jar of fireflies Lizzie held in her shaking hand.

"Yes, ma'am," Lizzie replied absentmindedly.

"Are you alright?"

"I'm fine. I just thought—"

Before she could finish, Killer started barking as she ran down the path. Lizzie could see a horse and rider trotting toward the house.

"Jake's home!" Rebecca announced excitedly as she and Hannah ran to meet him and Buckwheat.

Watching her cousins, Lizzie sat on the steps with her jar of fireflies, listening to the chirping crickets and croaking frogs in the woods. She tried to remember all she could about the shadowy figure, but she wasn't even sure it was a human. Holding the jar up to the light glowing from the lantern, she could see the little bugs crawling all over the jar trying to escape.

"What did you want to tell me?" Aunt Grace asked her.

Looking up at her aunt, Lizzie debated whether she should mention the shadowy figure or if she had seen anything at all. There was no sense in scaring everyone if she couldn't be certain what she saw.

"I caught extra fireflies for Hannah," she mumbled.

Aunt Grace laughed. "She does seem to chase them more."

"Jake, we're catching fireflies," Hannah said as she proudly held up her jar for him to see.

"Wow! You caught a lot, Hannah."

"I'll get your supper ready, Jake," Aunt Grace called.

"Okay, Miss Lee. Let me take Buckwheat to the barn."

Jake trotted Buckwheat to the barn while Aunt Grace went inside. In no time, he returned carrying something in his right hand.

Hannah greeted him with a big hug. "How was your day?"

"Pretty good. Philip and I worked through dinner so I'm starving. Two ships came in this morning. We had a mess getting the crates and barrels from the town dock to the store. It took all afternoon to help Mr. Shute reorganize the storeroom. Philip said he didn't think he would be able to get out of bed tomorrow," Jake commented. "By the way, Trent, Mr. Shute gave me a copy of the *Boston News-Letter*."

Trent put down his wood carving. "Why?"

"He thought you might want to read the article about pirates," Jake explained, holding up the newspaper.

Trent jumped up to follow Jake to the kitchen. The girls took their jars of fireflies inside to learn more about the pirates. Sitting around the table, they waited to hear the news as Aunt Grace joined them. While Jake ate his meal, Trent read the article aloud.

The *Boston News-Letter* was usually two weeks old because of the time it took to print in Massachusetts and ship to Bath. From what the article said, four pirate ships had blockaded the major southern port of Charles Town in the third week of May. The leader was the notorious pirate captain known as Blackbeard. He captured several ships in the harbor and held the people onboard hostage until the government of Charles Town met his demands. After holding the port under siege for nearly a week, Blackbeard received his requested chest of medicine. He then released his prisoners, who included a town councilman and his four-year-old. Shortly after the incident, one of the four pirate ships wrecked near the inlet at Fish Town. The ship had been one of the vessels reportedly captained by Blackbeard as his flagship *Queen Anne's Revenge*, though it appeared the pirate had escaped on a smaller ship called the *Adventure*. There was a warning to all colonies to keep watch for Blackbeard and his crew of pirates.

"Do you think those men we saw in town are the same pirates?" Alice asked when Trent finished reading the article.

"There's a lot of hearsay going around. Most of it involves the idea of those men being Blackbeard's crew," Jake revealed.

Lizzie noticed her aunt had become tense. Although she doubted the man they saw in town was the pirate captain Blackbeard, it was curious to note the man did have a black beard. The name would indeed be a perfect disguise. If it was Blackbeard, then what was he doing at Tunnel Land with Uncle Thomas and the other group of planters? Surely, it was just a coincidence.

"Why did they wreck one of the ships?" Rebecca inquired.

"They claim it was an accident, but I've been around ships long enough to know there is more to the story. Captains know about changing tides so they were either drunk or had a purpose for getting rid of it. Perhaps Blackbeard needed a less recognizable ship. Everyone has heard of *Queen Anne's Revenge*," Jake informed them.

"I've never heard of it," Trent mentioned.

"You haven't been traveling the waters. *Queen Anne's Revenge* has been up and down the coast causing trouble. Over the last two years, Blackbeard made a big name for himself," Jake continued.

"How many pirates are there?" Hannah questioned.

"Hundreds, maybe even thousands, but Blackbeard is only one of the many captains. Mr. Shute thinks the pirates are leaving soon. While Philip and I unloaded merchandise, several of them came in for supplies. We stacked enough barrels of food and freshwater on the loading dock to last a month. Mr. Shute said they purchased other necessary items, paying with gold coins. They also got barrels from the Salty Sailor Tavern," Jake responded, finishing his supper.

"That's enough about pirates," Aunt Grace announced, taking Jake's plate. "Why don't you go play chess?"

Recognizing that her aunt wanted the pirate conversation to end, Lizzie ushered the girls into the parlor. Trent and Jake joined them, sitting at the small oak table to play chess. Taking a seat in a rocking chair, Lizzie picked up her sewing project while Alice and Rebecca practiced their stitches on their samplers. Hannah pulled a chair up to the oak table to watch the chess game.

By the time Aunt Grace came into the room, Lizzie was deep in thought considering all the information in the *Boston News-Letter*. If Blackbeard was the same man they saw in town, then what was his purpose for coming to Bath? Obviously, he was somehow involved in bringing the Africans to the colony, but why was Uncle Thomas entangled in it? Lizzie remembered the letter Tobias Knight sent and the mention of her papa. Perhaps there was a connection between her father and the scandalous pirate. What if Blackbeard captured her papa's merchant ship and was holding him captive?

Fear engulfed Lizzie at the thought of her papa's potential captivity. Not paying attention, she pierced her index finger with the sewing needle. Placing her finger to her lips to stop the trickle of blood, she glanced at the chess table where Jake was getting up. She wished she could ask him what he thought about her speculations.

"Giving up already?" Trent teased him.

"For tonight I am, we'll have to finish tomorrow night. I'm too tired to keep up an intense game like this."

"It's time for us to go to bed, too. Come along, girls," Aunt Grace insisted as she put away the dress she had been hemming.

Rebecca and Alice put their samplers into the basket beside their mother's rocking chair while Hannah gave Jake a hug. After saying goodnight, the girls went down the hall with Trent.

"My goodness, I forgot to give you a slice of pie, Jake," Aunt Grace said as she passed the kitchen.

"I can cut him a slice while you tuck the girls in bed," Lizzie offered, realizing this gave her an opportunity to question Jake.

Aunt Grace nodded. "Thank you, dear. Goodnight, Jake."

"Goodnight, Miss Lee," Jake responded.

Walking to the cupboard, Lizzie retrieved a plate and went to the counter where her aunt had left a partially eaten blackberry pie. Uncovering the pie, she cut Jake a medium-sized piece.

"Do you think the pirates will leave soon?" she questioned as she handed him a fork.

"Yes, if it really is Blackbeard, I'm sure the news of their mischief down in Charles Town written in the *Boston News-Letter* messed up their plans to hide out here in Bath," he pointed out.

"If they are, is it possible they still have hostages?"

"The *Boston News-Letter* stated those held captive were released after the demands were met," Jake reminded her.

"What are the chances they kept some hostages? Couldn't they find out if the hostages were business owners?" she persisted.

"It's possible. Why are you interested in the hostages?"

Lizzie suddenly felt uneasy. The last thing she wanted to do was tell Jake the truth. He didn't need to know what she saw at Tunnel Land or the mention of her papa in Tobias Knight's letter. Regrettably, she had no choice but to give him an explanation. The hard part was trying to explain while he ate her papa's favorite dessert.

"My papa has been at sea for several years. He used to run Grandfather Beard's tar business before the Indian War. Since then, he has been on merchant ships. We haven't heard from him in a while so I just wondered if maybe his ship had been captured," Lizzie declared.

"Pirates capture ships all the time. It would be hard to find out. Some pirates just steal the contents of the merchant ships while others torture those onboard, sometimes even killing their victims. Occasionally, pirates dump victims on deserted islands. Maybe your father is one of the lucky ones and a passing ship will pick him up."

"Maybe so."

"I better get to sleep," Jake said, finishing the last bite. "Trent will have me up early to go fishing. He's got a secret hole to show me and already has the boat in the water. Thanks for the pie. Goodnight."

"Goodnight."

Covering the pie and heading upstairs, she paused to wish her aunt sweet dreams as Aunt Grace entered her bedchambers. Once in her room, Lizzie closed the door and picked up her old rag doll sitting on top of her oak chest. Holding the doll to her heart, she sat at her desk thinking about her papa. Glancing at a small box on her desk, she decided to reread the mysterious letter Tobias Knight wrote. She reached for the wooden box, a treasure trove of trinkets ranging from her mother's hairpin to an Indian arrowhead she found while walking through the fields. Sifting through her box of knickknacks, she found the embroidered handkerchief once belonging to her mother, the hiding place she had been keeping the letter. Taking out the note, Lizzie read the words. A mix of emotions overwhelmed her.

"What should I do, God?" she whispered.

Smoothing the doll's dress, Lizzie's mind went back to the last Christmas she shared with both her parents. Grasping her mother's hairpin, she felt a sense of urging come over her. She couldn't shake the feeling that her beloved papa was on the pirate ship. Tears welled up in Lizzie's eyes as she tried to decide what to do. She considered talking to Aunt Grace but doubted her aunt would be completely open with her. Her questions about the existence of new African slaves yielded nothing. Even Trent couldn't get a straight answer. They were supposed to believe it was normal for so many men to appear out of nowhere. Lizzie knew where the slaves came from, but she couldn't tell her aunt she had been spying. Could it be possible her family paid for the Africans? Would they pay a pirate? Was there a chance they were secretly paying a ransom for her papa's safe return?

Blinking back tears streaming down her cheeks, Lizzie glanced into her box of treasures, her blurry eyes falling on a golden necklace she hadn't worn in months. Picking it up, she wiped her eyes so that she could read the inscription: *LB*. Two tiny letters were the only thing special about the oval-shaped locket, but to her it wasn't just her initials. Her papa had given her the necklace seven years before for her ninth birthday in May 1711, four months prior to her momma's death. His words that day were meant for a little girl who missed her papa during his weeks at sea, but tonight those words rung true in the consciousness of her memory.

Lizzie, my darling, no matter where I am in this world, when you wear this necklace my heart will be close to yours.

Putting on the necklace, Lizzie let the oval-shaped locket hang over her heart, knowing what she had to do. No matter how dangerous the mission was, she would never be satisfied until she knew her papa was not on the ship anchored near the Knight plantation. Weighing the situation, she concluded her only chance to find out if her father was on the ship was to go. After all, Jake said the men purchased enough food to last a month. They were clearly planning to leave soon. Making up her mind, she decided to spy on the ship tonight. Hopefully, she could then determine how to board the ship in search of her papa.

Trying not to wake everyone, she took off her shoes, slowly opened her door, and tiptoed out of the room. Grabbing the handrail mounted to the wall, she crept down each step, holding her breath in hopes of calming her pounding heart. When she reached the back door, she quietly opened it and stepped onto the back porch. She put on her shoes while telling herself there was no need to be afraid. This time, she wouldn't allow her eyes to fool her with shadowy things.

By now, the nearly full moon was well in the sky as she headed for the dock. She remembered Jake's comment about Trent leaving the boat docked for their fishing trip, a stroke of luck since it would make her efforts much easier. Crossing the yard, Lizzie heard a growl coming from the barn. As the animal came out into the moonlight, she realized it was Killer. Unfortunately, once the little dog recognized her, she ran to Lizzie's side wanting her ears scratched.

"Go back to sleep, Killer," Lizzie mumbled.

At first, Lizzie thought she had successfully coaxed Killer into keeping her secret; however, as she walked to the dock, she could hear the little dog whimpering. Coming to the dock, she untied the rope holding the small fishing boat to one of the poles and climbed aboard, pausing as she felt something tug at the hem of her dress. Turning, she spotted Killer holding the dress firmly in her jaws.

"Let go, girl!" Lizzie urged as the little dog ripped a piece of the cloth and dropped it beyond her reach.

Frustrated, Lizzie told Killer to sit and stay while she got situated on the board positioned across the center of the boat. Picking up a wooden oar, she began her journey in the darkness, slowly pushing the boat through the water one stroke at a time.

Having no idea what to do when she made it to the ship, Lizzie decided to row down the creek toward the Knight plantation. Using all her strength, she pushed the small boat through the water past the end of their property and across the waterfront of the vacant Tunnel Land. Soon, the Knight plantation was in view. The two-story white-planked house had a wide front porch to welcome visitors who came to speak with the secretary of the colony, Tobias Knight.

To Lizzie's surprise, a glow illuminated the windows of the downstairs parlor, indicating Secretary Knight was entertaining guests. It was strange considering how late it was. Based on the moon, Lizzie figured it was about midnight. Two lanterns lit up the dock, revealing a twenty-five-foot periauger tied to the post.

Approaching, Lizzie saw the huge ship she had seen anchored in the channel for the past two weeks. Noticing the men aboard the ship had rowed their periauger to the dock to visit Mr. Knight, she viewed this as an opportunity to search the ship for her papa without the dangerous men onboard. Quickening her pace, she rowed out to where the majestic ship glowed in the light of its lanterns.

Once at the ship, Lizzie spotted a rope ladder extending into the water. Loosely tying the small boat to the ladder, she began to climb, ignoring the anxiousness fluttering in her stomach. Reaching the top, she took a deep breath and sent up a prayer before tentatively peeping over the railing. From the dim light of the nearest lantern, she could make out at least two, maybe three men at the front of the ship. Judging by the laughter, they appeared to be playing some sort of game.

Looking over her shoulder at the glowing house, Lizzie took a shaky breath and swung her left foot over the railing. She eased across the back of the ship, pausing to peep inside a room off the main deck. Seeing nothing through the crack in the door except a desk of strewn papers, she opened the second door, which yielded stairs leading down into the ship. Guessing her father might be below deck if he was a captive, Lizzie chose to take the stairs. With every step, she grew more nervous, praying no one would see her.

At the bottom of the stairs, a flickering light from the next room danced across the wall, causing goose bumps to rise on Lizzie's arms. She considered going back to the fishing boat, but thoughts of her father changed her mind. Nervously biting her lip, she pressed her shoulder against the wall and eased to the edge of the door frame, bravely peeping around the corner. Her brown eyes scanned the room, realizing with great relief there was no one there.

The right side of the room had a brick cook pit and on the left wall a long oak table. Crossing the room, she cautiously entered the adjacent cabin, which was full of hammocks hanging from the ceiling in rows. The room smelled musty from the stuffy sea air, making it difficult to breathe without coughing. Not wasting time, Lizzie walked past the rows of hammocks to the door on the other end of the room. Pressing down the thumb latch, she peered inside the pitch-dark room, deciding it was a perfect place for a prisoner.

Needing more light, Lizzie went back to the kitchen and returned with one of the lanterns. Holding up the lantern, she descended the stairs, going even deeper inside the ship. This new room turned out to be a storage area with barrels and crates of goods piled against the walls. Spotting a heavily latched door, Lizzie walked toward it, placing the lantern on the floor so that she could unlock the iron latch. From the light of the lantern, she saw chains made of black iron on the walls, clearly a sign the room was meant for hostages.

Before she had a chance to examine it, someone grabbed her and covered her mouth. Struggling in her attacker's grasp, she tried to free herself by kicking and shoving as her heart pounded.

"Stop fighting. It's me, Jake."

Shocked, Lizzie felt a sense of relief flood over her as Jake released his grip around her shoulders and let go of her mouth.

"You scared me to death!" she hissed, catching her breath.

"Have you lost your mind?" Jake exploded. "What are you doing here? Do you realize how dangerous this is?"

"Yes, but while I watched you eat that pie tonight, I thought Papa was being held prisoner on this ship. I just had to find out."

"What are you talking about?"

Sighing, Lizzie filled him in on her suspicions, beginning with Mr. Knight's letter. She told him what happened at Tunnel Land and how Uncle Thomas stood next to the bearded man without fear. Finally, she recalled the newspaper and her need to see if her papa was on the ship before the crew left the colony.

A noise echoed from the deck above as voices filled the musty air. Jake grabbed the lantern and motioned for her to follow. Crawling on their knees, they hid behind barrels and prepared to blow out the candle. Knowing they had no way of relighting the lantern, Lizzie prayed the men wouldn't come in. Eventually, the voices ceased.

"Stay here and keep hidden," Jake instructed, passing her the lantern. "I'm going to see if we can get on the deck without being spotted. We must hurry before the periauger returns."

Jake snuck around the barrels and went up the stairs leading to the room of hammocks. Lizzie watched, hoping he would be successful. Before long, he came back wearing a look of disbelief on his face.

"Did you find a way out?" she inquired in a hopeful voice.

"Possibly, but it's going to be tough. Two men were in the galley getting brandy. They were talking about putting barrels in the cargo hold in the front of the ship. I followed them to the deck. The men are loading the last of the cargo into the periauger at Knight's place."

"They're stealing from Mr. Knight?" Lizzie blurted out.

"If they are, the Indian boy and five others are helping."

"You mean Scripo?"

"Yes, him. Can you swim? Our boats are gone."

"Gone?" Lizzie breathed, hardly able to comprehend what he was saying. "But how? I tied mine to the ladder."

"And the canoe I used was tied to your boat. Apparently, you didn't double knot your rope."

"I—I'm so sorry...," Lizzie stuttered, fighting back tears.

"I guess it doesn't matter if you can swim or not. It's our only chance at escaping. I'll do what I can to help you."

Following his lead, Lizzie stayed close as they crossed the sleeping quarters and entered the kitchen, or galley as Jake had called it. Leaving the lantern on the table, they eased up the second flight of stairs. Nearing the top deck, Jake held out his arm to keep Lizzie behind him. With her back against the wall, she waited in the darkness. Voices drifted in the air, sending chills down her spine. She could hear someone giving orders to go down into the galley.

Frightened, Lizzie didn't wait for Jake to tell her to retreat. With her heart beating rapidly, she descended the stairs. She continued down into the storage room, pausing for Jake who had gone back for the lantern. As soon as he got inside, she slammed the door.

"What are you doing? Don't slam the door!" he protested as he handed her the lantern and furiously jiggled the door latch.

"I was too scared to think they might hear us," she panted.

"This is worse. The door is locked," he said, sinking to his knees with his head against the door.

"What? How are we going to get out of here?"

"We'll just have to wait for someone to open the door."

Sitting on the steps, Lizzie tried to remain calm, but she couldn't stop feeling guilty. Thankfully, Jake found a few spare lanterns that would come in handy, at least until the candles burned out.

"Jake, how did you know where to find me?"

"I heard Killer whining and found her with a piece of cloth. She took off running to the dock where the boat was missing. I remembered the talk we had, so I decided to take the canoe up the creek."

"I convinced myself Papa was on this ship. It was a big mistake. I'm glad you came after me, I don't know what I would do if I was trapped in here alone," she whispered.

"Hold on a moment," Jake mumbled, raising his hand.

"What is it?"

"The ship is moving, possibly out into the Pamtico Sound. With the door locked we're stuck," Jake answered gravely.

Lizzie felt miserable. Jake was upset and had a right to be. Her foolishness had them trapped on this ship. What would her family say when they found them missing? Feeling sick with fear, Lizzie held back tears and sent up a prayer begging God to help them and to forgive her for putting not only her own life but Jake's in danger.

CHAPTER FIVE

☠

LOCKET OF TRUTH

July 17, 1718 ~ Thursday

Hunger gnawed at Lizzie's stomach, making her light-headed. It had been thirty-seven hours since she and Jake last ate supper. To their disappointment, the iron-banded wooden barrels in the storage room contained liquor, not food. This dilemma, combined with the dwindling candle in the only remaining lantern, had hurried Jake's attempts to break out of their prison. By using the blade of his knife, Jake had tried to pry open the door. Despite his efforts, he hadn't succeeded, which made their situation seem hopeless. Jake was pretty sure they had passed through the inlet at Ocracoke Island, their last opportunity to jump ship and swim ashore.

Leaning her head against the wall, Lizzie thought about being stuck with Jake in what she concluded was a pirate ship. Listening to him share his life experiences, she realized serving aboard merchant ships as a young man had been a fight for survival. With scant meals and backbreaking work, it was amazing how Jake managed to make it on his own. His experience comforted Lizzie, who knew that her survival depended upon his knowledge of ships and the skills he learned.

Tired and restless, Lizzie drifted into an uneasy sleep trying not to think about the rats. At some point, she heard Jake's voice.

"Lizzie! Someone is unlocking the door. Get behind the barrels."

Grabbing the lantern, Lizzie scrambled to her hiding place. Meanwhile, Jake got behind the door, signaling with a nod for her to blow out the candle. Trying to calm her nerves, Lizzie blew out the flame, sending them into darkness. The door swung open, allowing light to stream in. Peering between barrels, she could see a broad-shouldered man descend the stairs as Jake lunged on top of him. The two tussled on the floor until another man jerked Jake off his comrade.

"Settle down, lad. Why are ye here?" the second pirate inquired.

"I'm not talking to you," Jake spat, wiping blood from his nose.

The first pirate got up rubbing his jaw from where Jake punched him. He took Jake's knife from the protective sheath tied around his waist and put it to Jake's throat as the other pirate held his hands behind his back.

"Let me have the squirt, Owen. I'll cut him up in pieces with his own knife and throw him to the sharks."

"As much as I'd like to see ye do it, John, Captain won't like us roughing up the lad until he questions him. He must have a reason for sneaking aboard. We'll return for the barrel of rum."

The pirate named John grumbled as he took Jake's arm and escorted him to the stairs. Marching up the steps, he paused to glance across the room. Lizzie held her breath, hoping he wouldn't spot her. Apparently satisfied, he led Jake up the remaining steps with Owen following behind. Thinking she was safe, Lizzie leaned forward. To her horror, she heard the locket hanging from her necklace clang against the iron band wrapped around the nearest barrel. Realizing what happened, she held it as Owen returned to examine the room.

"Did ye hear something?" he asked John.

"The noise came from over there," John acknowledged, pointing in Lizzie's direction.

Horrified, Lizzie crouched as close to the floor as she could, knowing there was nowhere to go. She prayed they wouldn't discover her.

"It's probably a rat. They're everywhere," Jake hastily commented.

"I don't need ye telling me about the rats. I know what they sound like and that was not what I heard," Owen snarled.

Although she couldn't see what was happening, Lizzie's ears picked up the sound of wood sliding across the floor.

"Look what we have here! Seems like it wasn't a rat after all," exclaimed Owen's voice as Lizzie felt his hand grab her arm.

"Let go of me!" she hollered, struggling to free herself as the pirate lifted her off the floor and pushed her against the wall.

Using every bit of her strength, Lizzie kicked the pirate's legs hoping he would release her. She temporarily succeeded; however, he quickly recaptured her, this time holding his arm around her throat.

"Ye are quite a feisty lassie, just the type of gal I like," Owen chuckled as he brushed his hand through her hair.

"She's right handsome to look at, but who says ye get her?" John hinted, suddenly more interested in Lizzie than Jake.

"Alright, we can share her," Owen said. "Look what she's got around her neck. Give it to me, lass."

"Never!" Lizzie shouted.

"Take it off or I will yank it off ye."

Shaking in fear, Lizzie regretfully fumbled with the latch of her beloved necklace. Handing it to her captor, she wistfully watched the pirate hold up her locket with a look of triumph on his face.

"It must mean a lot to ye," Owen proclaimed.

"Leave her alone," Jake snapped.

"There isn't anything ye can do to get ye girl back, lad. She's ours now," John declared with a snicker.

"Take us to the captain," Jake demanded.

"Nay, I think we'll leave this pretty little thing locked up. Captain doesn't need to know about her," Owen countered.

"I'll tell your captain about her and how you conspired against him to keep her for yourselves. I think he will be very interested in what I have to say," Jake shot back.

"Fine, we'll take both of ye to see Captain."

"What?" John exploded. "Why are ye listening to him?"

"Because he got me thinking," Owen informed him. "Since we found her first, Captain can make sure no one takes her from us."

John nodded in agreement as he shoved Jake up the stairs. "Good idea. Come on, let's go see Captain."

Owen grabbed Lizzie's forearm and led her up the stairs. She tried to calm her pounding heart, but it was useless as her fear mounted. Walking through the room of hammocks, the pirates led them to the kitchen and up the stairway to the deck. Having been in the storage room, the bright sunshine blinded Lizzie, so she had to squint to see.

The deck swarmed with pirates carrying out their tasks. Several of the nearest ones stopped working when they saw her and Jake.

"Where did they come from?" one of them questioned.

"The storage hold. Tell Captain we have visitors," Owen told him as he and John took them to a small room off the deck.

Once inside, the pirates forced them to sit in two straight-backed chairs facing the desk in the center of the room. Glancing around, Lizzie concluded it was where the captain stayed. There was even a map laid on the desk with some sort of metal measuring device.

A sudden slamming of a door made Lizzie jump. The noise accompanied an angry voice. Though she dared not turn to see who it belonged to, she already knew it was the captain.

"I was informed strangers are onboard and one is a young lady."

"John and I found them in the hold when we went to fetch a rum barrel," Owen explained.

"Do ye really expect me to believe such nonsense?"

"It's true, Captain, honest," John confirmed nervously.

"Honest? Ha! I doubt either of ye have been honest in years. Someone brought these two onboard, and I want to know who."

"Ye should ask them why they were there," Owen suggested.

For a moment, there was silence followed by creaking floorboards as the captain came around the desk and sat across from Lizzie and Jake. His tall stature and braided black beard were giveaways to his identity; he was the same man she saw in town and at Tunnel Land.

Lizzie couldn't help but stare at the captain, both captivated by his appearance and fearful of what would happen to them. His demeanor changed when he made eye contact with her.

"What are ye doing on my ship?"

"We made a mistake, sir. I promise we won't say a word to anyone of your whereabouts. Just let us go," Jake requested.

"Ye are crazy. We're going to finish smashing ye face, break those legs, and throw what's left to the sharks!" John reminded him as he grabbed Jake's arm.

"Except for the girl, she's worth keeping," Owen added.

"Let him go. The bloody nose is enough until they give us some information. Have ye forgotten the oath ye swore? It clearly states no woman shall be on this ship," their captain pointed out.

"The articles say we aren't allowed to *bring* a woman aboard. Since we *found* her, the rules change," Owen replied.

"We just want to get back to Bath," Jake urged.

"Are ye spies? Surely, Eden didn't plan to double-cross us," John demanded as his captain held up his hand for him to stop.

"Get our company something to eat. I'm sure they're hungry."

"Are ye going to feed them?" John snorted.

"Aye, is there a problem?"

"I guess not. Come on, Owen."

"Wait! I want my necklace back," Lizzie insisted.

"What necklace is she talking about?"

Grumbling, Owen thrust the locket into his captain's hand before following John outside. As the door shut, the captain examined the necklace by dangling it in front of him.

"Sorry about ye nose, lad. It doesn't look broken. What are ye names?" When neither spoke, he persisted. "Well, let's start over. I'm Captain Edward Teach, but my friends and enemies call me Blackbeard. Now, I need to know ye names."

"I'm not sure it's wise to tell you, sir," Jake answered.

Blackbeard was clearly surprised by his statement. "I see. Perhaps the young lady can shed more light. Where did ye get this necklace?"

Lizzie shifted uncomfortably in her chair, not wanting to tell the notorious pirate captain how special the necklace was to her.

"It was a gift," she finally said.

Blackbeard glanced at the locket, running his fingers over the engraved letters before looking at Jake. "Tell me, lad. What reason did ye have for coming aboard this ship, and why did ye bring her?"

"He didn't—" Lizzie began as Jake nudged her with his elbow.

"*We* didn't plan to get stuck on a ship," Jake interrupted.

"How do I know ye aren't spies, then? Why else would ye be on my ship? Ye claim it's a mistake, but ye story is suspicious. What were ye looking for? Did someone send ye?" Blackbeard inquired.

"You have it all wrong, sir," Jake started.

"Do I? Well, lad, ye need to explain it because I'm getting the idea ye are lying. Ye came aboard for something, now tell me the truth."

Jake didn't respond, which made the captain angry. A sickening feeling settled in Lizzie's stomach as she wondered what Blackbeard would do to them. She instinctively began to pray.

"Very well. Since ye won't defend ye actions then I'll arrange to leave ye on a deserted island," Blackbeard announced.

"Thank you, sir."

"Ye won't be thanking me when ye can't find freshwater, lad. Anyway, the girl stays onboard," Blackbeard continued.

"Can't you release both of us on an island?" Jake protested.

Blackbeard shook his head. "Nay, she must stay here."

"That's not fair."

"Pirates aren't usually fair, lad. To tell ye the truth, the only thing stopping me from allowing my men to do as they please with ye and the girl is this necklace," Blackbeard revealed.

"You can keep the necklace," Jake offered.

"Jake!" Lizzie gasped, staring at him in shock.

Realizing her mistake, Lizzie looked at her hands to avoid the nasty glare Jake was giving her for revealing his identity.

"Now we're getting somewhere. What is ye name, lass?"

Frozen in fear, Lizzie didn't say a word.

"Sworn to silence, are we? I can see this necklace means a lot to ye," Blackbeard concluded as he held out the necklace for her to take.

Hesitating, Lizzie slowly stretched out her hand to take her necklace from the pirate's palm. As her fingers clutched the golden chain, the pirate captain grabbed hold of her hand and leaned forward so that his long, black beard brushed against her skin. This action caused Jake to come up out of his seat.

"Sit down, lad, or ye will be sorry," Blackbeard threatened as Jake eased back in his chair. "Is the engraving on this necklace ye initials?"

"Don't answer," Jake declared.

"I wasn't talking to ye, Jake," Blackbeard stated. "They are ye initials, aren't they, lass? I know by the look in ye eyes. It takes years to learn how to hide one's feelings which the eyes reveal."

Letting go of her hand, Blackbeard stood and walked over to Lizzie. Terrified, she sat motionless in her seat, clinging to the locket. The pirate captain squatted in front of her and placed his rough, calloused hand under her chin, forcing her to look up at him. She stared into his bearded, suntanned face as tears of fear gathered in her eyes.

"My, how pretty ye are," he muttered.

Just then, the door to the captain's cabin opened, causing Blackbeard to stand up. Feeling relieved, Lizzie tried to relax as Owen and John brought in cups of water and two plates of food.

"Have ye gotten anything out of them?" John asked.

"Nothing yet, but perhaps food will change their minds."

"Captain, I informed the quartermaster of the situation. He'll declare a vote when ye finish interrogating them," Owen reported.

"Let me finish then," Blackbeard responded as both men exited the room, leaving Lizzie and Jake alone with the captain. Sitting in his chair, Blackbeard looked at them from across the table. "Go ahead and eat. Ye must be starving."

Remaining still, Lizzie sat in her chair, gazing at what looked like pinto beans on a bent plate. Beside her, Jake did the same.

"It wasn't a suggestion," Blackbeard growled.

Glancing at Jake, Lizzie bowed her head in silent prayer, asking God to bless the food and protect them. When she finished, she picked up the spoon and began to eat.

"Don't eat fast, you'll get sick," Jake warned.

Blackbeard watched them eat with his elbows on the table and chin propped against his fists. Lizzie didn't dare look up at him, though she sensed him staring at her with his piercing eyes.

"Thanks for the meal, sir. Is there any way we can forget this happened? I'll remain a captive if you'll let her go," Jake pleaded.

"Ye drive a hard bargain, Jake, but I can't."

"Please, sir, I'll do anything. Just release her," Jake begged.

"It's commendable to sacrifice ye life for hers; however, my decision is in her best interest," Blackbeard stated as he stood and walked to the small window overlooking the ocean. "Seven years ago, I acquired a necklace with a locket. I had it engraved with the letters L and B, my daughter's initials."

"What?" Jake exclaimed as Lizzie stared at the pirate.

Blackbeard returned to the table. "That's right. She's my daughter. Ye look too much like ye mother to deny."

A wave of emotion flooded over Lizzie as she listened to the pirate's words. She couldn't believe what she was hearing. Was this fearsome pirate captain really her father, or was he lying to catch them off guard? Lizzie's mind spun, trying to recall the letter Mr. Knight wrote to Aunt Grace and Uncle Thomas. Didn't Mr. Knight say there was important news regarding their brother-in-law? What if he wasn't talking about her papa's capture? Maybe the midnight meeting was about his arrival in Bath Town, not as a sea captain but as the feared pirate Blackbeard. Gathering her courage, Lizzie challenged his claim.

"How do we know you aren't tricking us?"

"Smart girl, Grace has taught ye well. Everything I've said is true, Lizzie. Ye are my daughter," Blackbeard acknowledged.

Hearing her name made tears stream down her cheeks. There was no doubt he was her father. He even mentioned Aunt Grace, which added to her confidence of his identity.

"I don't believe this," Jake mumbled. "Lizzie boarded this ship to find her father and the whole time you were a pirate."

"How do ye know one another?" Blackbeard questioned.

"I came to Bath a few weeks ago. Miss Lee offered me a place to stay, and Mr. Worsley gave me a job. My parents were Jacob and Sadie Griffin," Jake answered.

"Sorry about the death of ye family, lad. Jacob was a good man. Thomas told me ye were a hard worker," Blackbeard proclaimed.

"Thanks," Jake muttered. "I don't mean to pressure you, but surely you can drop us off on an island somewhere?"

Blackbeard hesitated. "We have a bad situation. It isn't safe to put Lizzie off on an island. Too many men sail these waters. The only choice is for ye to stay aboard. Our plans are to go to Pennsylvania before going south. Perhaps I can convince the men to return to Ocracoke on our way to Bermuda. Until then, we need a cover story. Do ye have any experience on ships, Jake?"

"Yes, sir, I've been an apprentice since I was fourteen."

"Ye experience may prove useful. I can keep ye onboard by forcing ye to serve as a pirate. Unfortunately, Lizzie's fate is more complex. Many of the men were respected members of Bath's society. They may not recognize ye, but over time they'll figure it out. I'll have to pull them aside privately. We can't let the remaining crew know ye are my daughter. As for the men who lived in Bath, I must ask ye to never speak of it. If their identities leak to the others it could cause a split in the crew that could be dangerous," Blackbeard explained.

The door to the captain's quarters opened. Standing up, Blackbeard motioned for the new arrival to join them.

"I have something important to discuss with ye, Thomas."

Shutting the door, the dark-haired pirate walked toward the table while Blackbeard sat back down.

"What's on ye mind, Captain? Owen and John told me about the stowaways. Everyone is waiting for ye to begin the meeting."

"Thomas, we have a problem. Three weeks ago, William Howard told me he wanted to leave the crew and return home to his father after we got things straight with Eden. When he left, I knew I had a critical decision to make. Selecting a new quartermaster and suggesting to a crew of pirates they should vote him in is no easy task, but neither is filling those shoes."

"Ye can trust me," Thomas interrupted. "We're friends."

"I know," Blackbeard sighed as he stroked his beard and glanced at Lizzie. "Do ye remember my daughter, Lizzie?"

Thomas' jaw dropped. "Are ye serious?"

"I'm afraid so, my friend," Blackbeard responded gravely.

"She's so grown up. How will ye protect her from pirates aboard other ships or better yet our own crew?" Thomas inquired.

"I can't without help. The only thing I can do is declare her off limits and have her stay with me. Jake is the son of an old friend. He has three years of experience on ships. My plan is to force him into service until we leave Pennsylvania and head south. Maybe we can convince the crew to stop at Ocracoke Island," Blackbeard replied.

"Until then, what are ye planning to do with her? She can't stay locked in here for the next month," Thomas pointed out.

"Aye, but she'll be safe with either ye or Jake."

"Ye know if she spends time with the lad the others will get jealous. Maybe she can help Cookie with the cooking and washing. Cookie's one of us," Thomas suggested.

"Good idea. Keeping this secret in our inner circle of Bath County pirates is wise. Come on, let's get this over with," Blackbeard sighed as he got up. Looking at Lizzie and Jake he added, "Stay here."

Lizzie watched her father and his quartermaster leave with concerned looks on their faces. Realizing how delicate their situation was, she considered the risk her father was taking. In her mind, she replayed the last few hours, which seemed unreal. Here they were on a pirate ship with the legendary Captain Blackbeard, who also happened to be her father.

Her mind went back to the day she first saw him walking the streets of Bath. No wonder she felt captivated by him. Stories and newspaper articles about the violent Blackbeard came flooding into her mind. Had her papa changed into the evil man the stories portrayed? Was she the daughter of a killer? What caused him to become a pirate in the first place?

Clutching her necklace, she felt tears trickle down her cheeks. For the next few weeks, she would hopefully get what she wanted more than anything: the opportunity to seek the answers of her past and spend time with the mysterious man she called Papa.

CHAPTER SIX

☠

NOT-SO-TOUGH COOKIE

July 24, 1718 ~ Thursday

Life on a pirate ship was certainly interesting. At first, the steady rocking of the waves caused her to be nauseated, but after seven days at sea Lizzie was much better. For the previous two days, she had spent her time doing odd jobs with her new friend, Joseph Curtice. The pirate, known as Cookie, was surprisingly kind and often shared one of his longwinded stories. Thankfully, her father's plan had so far gone smoothly for both her and Jake, who spent his days on the deck working alongside the rest of the crew. This arrangement had a downside, though, because it restricted her time with Jake. She hoped to see him today when she and Cookie mopped the main deck.

Dipping the wood-handled mop into the wooden bucket of seawater, Lizzie scrubbed the floor of the sleeping quarters. Not only was it difficult to clean the floor, but the unscented lye soap didn't put a dent in the awful musty smell of sweaty clothes engulfing the room. She wondered how the pirates could sleep in this terribly ventilated place and was thankful she slept in the captain's cabin.

Focusing her mind, Lizzie thought about her papa's description of the meeting with the crew. The men didn't have much to say about his decision to keep her and Jake onboard, at least not while he was present. According to Cookie, there was a heated discussion in progress when he went downstairs after meeting them. Cookie didn't mention what they said, only that Blackbeard should watch his back.

His comment frightened Lizzie, who wasn't sure what to expect. She was quickly learning that her papa had enemies. This wasn't surprising if the reports of his brutal nature were true. It was still hard to believe that she was the daughter of Blackbeard.

Hearing Cookie's unique sailor dialect calling her, Lizzie recalled the first time she heard it back in Bath. As fate would have it, Cookie had been the man they saw on Mr. Shute's loading dock, and just as Trent suspected, he was a pirate. Entering the other room with her mop and bucket, she spotted the pirate waiting in his striped britches and faded blue shirt. Interestingly, his initial tough-guy nature had dwindled to reveal a kindhearted soul she had grown to cherish.

"Miss Lizzie, I believe we're ready to go up on deck. Have ye finished swabbing the sleeping quarters?" Cookie asked.

"Yes, sir," Lizzie responded.

"Ye don't have to call me 'sir.' Everyone calls me 'Cookie.' Let's go scrub the bugs and seagull droppings off the deck. Don't forget the hat I gave ye," he said as he started up the stairs with his mop and bucket.

Grabbing the tricorn hat off the kitchen table, Lizzie placed it on her head and ran to catch up. As she struggled to carry her cleaning supplies, she pondered where Cookie got the hat. He gave it to her with no explanation except for the statement that he had a trunk of spares.

"I need to stop at the captain's cabin. I'm sure there is another name for it, but we call it the necessary or outhouse," Lizzie mumbled as she followed him into the bright, late-afternoon sunlight.

Cookie chuckled. "Of course, ye can go to the head. There's no sense in letting ye pipes burst."

Giggling at his odd way of saying things, Lizzie entered her father's quarters. Walking to the tiny room in the corner, she reached into the wooden bucket by the door and picked up a corncob to wipe with before closing the door behind her. A stream of light beamed through the small bluish-green tinted window. Bending to pull up her dress, Lizzie's hand brushed something near her shoe. Panicking, she dropped her dress and ran out. Turning around, she spotted a rat the size of a squirrel with ugly, dark gray fur and a long naked tail. Without thinking, Lizzie screamed as the rodent hissed, revealing its sharp fangs.

Hearing her scream, Cookie rushed in. "What's wrong?"

"It—it's a rat!"

"Calm down. They tend to stay in the head. I'll take care of it."

Leaving the captain's cabin, Cookie returned carrying a mop. Jabbing the rat with the rag mop, he shooed it out of the head and chased it onto the main deck. Once he was gone, Lizzie reentered the tiny room to finish her business before joining him outside. To her surprise, he was carrying a one-eyed, solid black cat in his arms.

"You have a cat?" Lizzie inquired, watching him rub the cat's fur and massage its ears. "What happened to its eye?"

"I'm not sure. She was injured when I got her. She's a fine mouser and has never been afraid of rats. Rodents eat away at our food supply and can even gnaw wood. Tuffy is an honorary member of our crew," he explained, placing the cat on the deck.

The cat took off while Cookie picked up his mop and bucket. Trailing behind him as he headed for the front of the ship, Lizzie soaked in the scene of pirates. Several paused from their work to look at her. She considered how many recognized her as a fellow Bath native. Looking for Jake, she caught someone staring. Startled, she felt uncomfortable as the pirate's cold gaze seemed fixated on her.

As Cookie put down his bucket, he must have seen the fear in her eyes. "Are ye all right? Ye look like ye have seen a ghost."

"He's watching," she whispered, nodding in the pirate's direction.

Turning to see who she referred to, Cookie's demeanor changed. "Don't let Israel scare ye, lass. Ye are safe with me."

Still uneasy, Lizzie stole a look at the pirate. Luckily, he was no longer standing near the giant wheel in the center of the deck. Dipping her mop into the bucket, she tried to get his gaze out of her mind by asking Cookie how the steering worked. He explained the wheel steered the ship by pulling a rope through a pulley attached to the rudder on the bottom of the ship. By turning the wheel, the long ropes pulled the rudder to one side, changing the ship's course.

As they scrubbed the deck, Cookie continued to talk about sailing. He told her the front of the ship was the bow and the rear was called the stern. It was obvious he had been at sea most of his life even before he joined a pirate fleet. Eventually, the subject turned to her father.

"I've noticed something different about Captain. He's like his old self. Six weeks ago, we were an army of four hundred men and four ships. Blackbeard has been distant ever since the incident at Fish Town involving our flagship, *Queen Anne's Revenge*. Ye have changed him. It looks like he's fond of Jake, too," Cookie observed.

Glancing over her shoulder, Lizzie searched the faces working the sails. She spotted her father dressed in his black attire and three-cornered hat. Jake was with him wearing spare clothes Thomas gave him.

"Cookie, can I go see my fa—, well, Captain?" Lizzie requested, catching herself although he knew their relationship.

"Go ahead. Ye can help me finish later," Cookie agreed.

Lizzie crossed the deck as a light breeze blew stray strands of her curly, dark brown hair into her face. Breathing in the salty sea air, she walked to where her father and Jake were talking about the sails.

"Hello," Lizzie greeted her father as he turned around.

"Lizzie? What are ye doing out here?"

"Cookie and I are mopping. Do you have a moment to talk? I wanted to discuss something with you," Lizzie hinted.

"I'm busy. We can talk later," Blackbeard suggested. Looking at Jake he added, "Keep up the good work, lad. I want ye to help check the barrels for leaks. Edward Salter will show ye what to do. He's a cooper by trade, my main man when it comes to barrels."

Without another word, the pirate captain walked to the front of the boat, leaving Lizzie with Jake. Frustrated, Lizzie let out a deep breath as she watched Jake sit down on an empty crate.

"Why does he ignore me?" she mumbled.

"He said he was busy," Jake pointed out.

"That's always his excuse. If he really wanted to talk, he would spend time with me in the evenings instead of playing cards or checkers. The truth is he doesn't want to answer my questions."

"Maybe he's uncomfortable talking to you. From what I gather, your questions won't have simple answers," Jake responded.

Pondering his words, Lizzie realized she hadn't considered what things her papa didn't want her to know about his current life. Gazing at the worn sail in Jake's lap, she watched him stitch a neat row across the cream-colored material with the largest sewing needle she had ever seen.

"I didn't know you could sew."

Jake smiled. "Don't tell Trent."

"You're pretty good. Why are you using such a big needle?"

"Sailcloth is made from stiff material called hemp. It's easier to sew with a longer needle, and silver needles won't rust. Hemp is a stringy fiber of an herb plant. Ropes are also made from hemp," he explained as the barrel maker, Edward Salter, walked up.

Taking off his tricorn hat, the dark-haired cooper wiped the sweat from his brow with a tattered sleeve. "Ready to check the barrels?"

"Yes, sir," Jake answered, putting the sail aside and turning to Lizzie. "I'll see you later."

Walking to the front of the ship, Lizzie resumed her duties. An hour later, she and Cookie had the deck clean. Squeezing the seawater out of her mop, she handed him her bucket to dump overboard.

"Let's get started on supper, Miss Lizzie. Take the mops and buckets to the galley. I'll be there shortly," Cookie told her.

Without an explanation, he headed down a ladder into the hold. Lizzie made her way to the back of the ship, descended the stairs, and put up the cleaning supplies. Cookie came in carrying two headless chickens.

"Where did the chickens come from?" Lizzie blurted out.

"Pirates eat chicken like the colonists. Most of us came from respected families. When we sailed on ye father's flagship, *Queen Anne's Revenge*, we captured some merchant ships stocked with cows and hogs. We ate ham, pork chops, roast beef, and steaks. There were times food was scarce, but it's normal when ye are feeding hundreds of men. At one time, there were seven hundred pirates in our fleet."

"Seven hundred pirates? I can't imagine. It's even harder to envision having live cows and hogs on a ship like a farm," Lizzie declared, watching him put the reddish-brown hens on the table.

"There are twenty-four people with ye and Jake, so two chickens will do. Go boil some water while I fetch the flour. I used the last this morning," he commented.

Lizzie set to work knowing Cookie would soon be back. Struggling to pick up the heavy pot, she hung the cauldron on the iron hook over the charcoals of the brick cook pit. Taking a jar, she opened the freshwater barrel sitting nearby. After dumping several jars of water into the cauldron, she replaced the barrel lid and lit a fire underneath the cauldron like Cookie taught her.

The water had just begun to boil when Cookie returned with the sacks of flour. Grabbing a headless chicken, Lizzie pulled out the reddish-brown feathers. She was glad Cookie had already beheaded the chickens outside. Just thinking about it brought back memories of Aunt Grace killing the chickens, a process that started with twisting the neck and chopping off its head with a sharp ax.

Once the hens were clean, Cookie dipped them in the steaming water. Lizzie plucked out the remaining feathers. Cutting off the feet, Cookie got out the insides, giving Lizzie the gizzards, hearts, and livers for his so-called famous chicken pastry. Seasoning the naked chickens, Cookie put them in a fresh pot of boiling water. While the hens cooked, Lizzie washed off the table as Cookie got the flour. Helping him mix and roll out the dough, she cut it in strips so that he could add them to the pot. The leftover dough made biscuits.

By the time the food was ready, Jake and Edward came up from the bottom of the ship. Lizzie wondered how Jake's new job went but decided not to ask him in front of the cooper.

"Cookie, is supper ready?" Edward asked.

"It's close."

"Good, bring up the food when it's done. Blackbeard plans to eat under the stars," Edward informed him.

"Alright. Go ahead and take the rum," Cookie responded.

Edward asked Jake to help him carry the rum barrel. Since the chicken pastry was ready, Cookie took it off the fire while Lizzie moved the biscuits to a bowl. As Cookie toted the food to the main deck, she stayed behind to gather the pewter spoons, cups, and bowls into a basket. She filled a container with water for her and Jake to drink before taking the basket upstairs.

Lizzie felt a cool breeze through her hair as she stepped out on the deck. Her eyes fixated on the bright rays of light as the sunset slowly dowsed the sky with color. Resting her basket on Cookie's makeshift table, consisting of a board stretched over two barrels, Lizzie stood next to him to help serve the men.

A line of pirates formed as they picked up a bowl and waited for their meal. Doing her job, Lizzie gave each a biscuit, listening to the conversations of the pirates. Eventually, the quartermaster, Thomas, came into view, followed by Jake and finally Captain Blackbeard. Once the men had food, Cookie fixed bowls for Lizzie and him and pulled out stools from beneath the table. Sitting down, Lizzie prayed over her food. Looking up, she realized Cookie was smiling at her.

"Listening to ye talk to the Maker every day, I'm beginning to consider talking to Him again myself. Perhaps ye can put in a good word for me the next time ye talk," he commented.

"God would be happy to hear from you."

"I've got skeletons in my cellar He wouldn't like."

"Skeletons?" Lizzie exclaimed in shock.

"I don't mean real skeletons, I mean figuratively. Ye know, things ye done wrong in the past. I guess ye call them sins."

"I'm glad you don't have real skeletons around here," Lizzie joked. "Just because you're a pirate doesn't mean you can't change. God will forgive you."

"Ye make it sound so simple, lass," Cookie mumbled.

Before Lizzie could reply, three crew members came for more pastry. Meanwhile, some of the others began to play music with a mouth harp and a flute. To Lizzie's amazement, a few men sang as others tapped spoons to the music. Watching Cookie and another pirate light candles, she recalled the first time she set foot on the ship over a week ago. The glow of candlelit lanterns had illuminated the *Adventure* that night. Now it didn't seem as mysterious.

"Don't light any more, Husky. Remember the bylaws—plus it saves the candles," Cookie advised.

"I know, all lanterns and candles out by eight. Ye shouldn't have cooked so late. It's probably about nine o'clock," Husky complained as he joined the group of singing pirates.

Taking her empty bowl to the table, Lizzie looked at Cookie, who had tidied up the dirty bowls. "Is Husky his real name?"

Cookie chuckled. "Nay, it's John Husk. He's the strongest man we've got. Look at his shoulders. He could carry a hog. Let's get closer to hear the music. My hearing isn't what it used to be."

"What's the name of this song?"

"It's called 'Henry Martin.' Legend has it, the song was about a man named Henry and his brothers."

Lizzie could see the men starting to get wild as they drank heavily from the rum barrel. Even her father had his pewter cup full of rum as he joined the singing. Seeing Jake alone, she told Cookie she was going to go sit with him.

"Hey, Jake, do you mind if I join you?" she inquired.

"Sure," he replied, making room for her on the crate.

As she sat down, the pirates began chanting the song, which told the story of Henry Martin and his two older brothers who lived in Scotland. They cast lots for who should go to help maintain their family by turning robber on the salt sea. Henry hadn't been gone long when he spied a ship. He cried out to the ship and discovered it was a rich merchant bound for London Town. For two or three hours, the ships fired their cannons until Henry gave the death shot sending them to the bottom. News arrived in England that the rich vessel sank and all the merry men drowned.

"Have you heard music like this?" Lizzie wanted to know.

"Yes, it's a sailing song. Crews sing to pass time and stay in one accord while hoisting sails. The ships I've been on had someone who brought instruments like the flute or Jew's harp. I overheard that Blackbeard forced a trumpet player into service a few months ago. He was on the French slaver called *La Concorde* when Blackbeard's company captured her. He renamed the ship *Queen Anne's Revenge*. The man who plays the long trumpet is over there," he declared, pointing to one of the five black men playing music with spoons.

"It's interesting how the African men are treated almost like everyone else," she said, wondering what trumpets sounded like.

"I noticed the same thing. Lately, I've worked with a pirate about my age named JJ. He says the Africans have more opportunities as pirates than as sailors or farm workers. They work more than average pirates, but they have a pretty good life. When Blackbeard splits loot among the crew, he gives them a share, too. The captain, quartermaster, sailing master, boatswain, and gunner get extra for their skills."

"Speaking of duties, how did your new job go?"

Jake shrugged. "Okay, I guess. From now on, it'll be a daily job unless the wind picks up. I'll have to check for signs of rat droppings and make sure the barrels aren't leaking."

Listening to the unique music, Lizzie gazed at the stars. It was amazing how different the sky looked with no trees to obscure it. Jake noticed her staring up at the sky.

"I remember my first glimpse of the starry sky on the open water. It's something I will never forget."

"I don't think I'll ever forget this either. The sky is different out here, like the stars are brighter somehow," Lizzie observed.

"The first ship I apprenticed with had a wise old sailor who became a friend. I didn't realize he was teaching me how to read stars."

"When I was little, Grandfather Beard told me about following the North Star. Then there's the star in the Bible that guided the wise men to baby Jesus in the manger. Is that what you mean?"

"Captains use the stars to navigate by. Stars reposition slightly as the seasons change, so captains normally carry a map with major stars on them. They can tell which way is north or south in the middle of the ocean. They also study the sun's angle, the drifting clouds, or seagulls," Jake explained.

"What do seagulls and clouds have to do with navigation?"

"Clouds are always moving, and seagulls don't fly far from land. To see any bird tells a captain land is near," he told her.

"There's so much to learn. It's different from life at home. Speaking of home, I wonder what everyone is doing. I miss them."

Jake laughed. "I miss them, too, even Hannah's questions."

Lizzie giggled at the thought of Hannah constantly asking everyone questions. She hadn't considered the effect the little girl's inquisitive mind had on Jake.

"Guess you missed the party. Wasn't it Saturday night?"

"I forgot about the party Mrs. Gale was hosting. You're right. It was supposed to be last Saturday night," Lizzie replied.

"Do you think your aunt and cousins went?"

Lizzie shook her head. "I doubt it. Under the circumstances, Aunt Grace probably changed her mind. My absence would have caused a lot of unnecessary attention."

"So, what's the deal with you and the Gale boy?"

"There is nothing between me and Miles Gale."

"But Trent said—" he began as she interrupted him.

"Trent lacks understanding. I'm not going to pursue a relationship with Miles just because he shows interest in me."

"Sorry I ruffled your feathers. One could get the idea you have feelings for this fellow," Jake pointed out.

"Well, I don't."

"Alright, I won't bring it up again. I don't know what the fuss is about. He was so arrogant at the store, I told Philip someone needs to put him in his place. No one deserves to be talked down to."

The two of them fell into an awkward silence only disturbed by the pirates' boisterous singing. Although part of her wanted to find out what Miles said, Lizzie decided not to ask Jake. Not only did she have situations at home to deal with, but now she had problems here. She just couldn't shake the feeling her father was hiding something from her.

CHAPTER SEVEN

☠

VIOLENT SEAS

July 31, 1718 ~ Thursday

Trying to stand in the blustery wind, Lizzie grabbed her dress hanging on the clothesline she assembled earlier this morning. Although the clothes were still damp, Cookie instructed her to remove them before the wind blew them overboard. She dreaded taking down the underwear, a job Cookie usually took care of. Looking up at the dark clouds, she felt certain it would be a stormy afternoon.

A gust of wind ripped one of the shirts from the line. Lunging forward, Lizzie tried to catch it midair, but the red material slipped through her fingers. Hoping the shirt would catch on something, she was surprised to see Jake holding the runaway shirt in his hands.

"Today's a bad day to hang clothes," he said, handing her the shirt.

"Tell me about it. Thanks for catching the shirt. The last thing I need is a pirate upset over lost clothing," she responded.

"It belongs to Israel Hands. I've been warned about him."

"Maybe he's the one Cookie said Papa needed to watch out for." Jake's eyes widened. "Shhh! He's Blackbeard, remember?"

"I'm sorry," she whispered, looking to see who was nearby. "I keep forgetting to call him 'Captain.'"

"Well, don't forget it again," he urged. Cocking his head to one side he added, "Is that your dress?"

Reaching to take it off the line she replied, "Yes, it's mine."

"How did you get the outfit you have on?" Jake asked.

"Cookie has a trunk of spare clothes. He gave me a shirt and two pair of britches. I cut out the inside seam of the britches and sewed them together. It gives me something else to wear."

"You're almost as talented at sewing as I am," Jake joked. "There's a bad storm coming. Why isn't Cookie helping you?"

"He saw the dark clouds and told me to get the clothes in while he went back to the galley to put out the fire. We fixed a pot of soup this morning and had just relit the cook pit to warm it up."

"Fires are dangerous on a stormy day. Guess we'll have to eat cold soup and hardtack. I'll help you get the clothes down," Jake proclaimed as he began to remove the clothes from the line.

"You do the underwear. That's Cookie's job. What's hardtack?"

"It's a hard piece of bread with no taste. When the weather is bad or the food rations are low, the cook brings out hardtack. On my last voyage, we ate hardtack for two months with grog."

"Grog?" she inquired in confusion. "I've never heard of it."

"Grog is watered-down rum. It goes further and keeps the sailors from getting drunk. Freshwater turns sour on long voyages, so they drink beer, rum, or brandy," he informed her.

"I hope our freshwater doesn't get bad. I don't think I can drink any of those things. What are the differences in them?"

"Rum comes from sugar. Beer is from grains such as barley, and brandy from fruits. Wine is similar because it comes from grapes."

Putting the last of the clothes in the basket, Lizzie gazed at the black clouds. "Do you think it's going to get rough?"

"It looks bad, but Blackbeard is on top of things."

He pointed at the mast where Blackbeard was staring into the rigging. Tilting her head, Lizzie saw a pirate hanging from the wooden beam holding up the mainsail. He clung to the beam while looking into a spyglass at the southern horizon where the storm was brewing.

"Blackbeard sent Nathaniel Jackson up the ratlines to see how much lightning is accompanying the storm. Lightning is a good indicator to how bad the storm will be," Jake told her.

"Ratlines?"

"See the ropes resembling a spider web? Those are ratlines. They give you a foothold and make it easier to climb. With the ship swaying, you can easily fall to your death. I'm sure he's also looking for waterspouts. Ocean bound storms can stir them up. Hurricanes are the main worry. They come from the south out of the warmer waters of the Caribbean anywhere from mid-June through October."

"I pray we won't go through one of those. A few years ago, there was a bad storm. Aunt Grace took us down to the cellar. Mr. Shute told us a hurricane grazed Ocracoke Island," Lizzie recalled.

"Thankfully I never experienced a hurricane at sea. Maybe this storm won't be one either. Come on, I have to check the barrels."

Carrying the basket, Lizzie followed Jake down to the kitchen. Cookie was acting like a wild man. Confused, she looked at Jake.

"Cookie's putting things away. When the wind and waves rock the ship, anything not secured will fall. Someone might get hurt."

Lizzie placed the laundry basket in the corner while Jake went to the bottom of the ship. Noticing Cookie stacking the cooking supplies in a wooden chest, she gathered the pewter plates from the table.

"Thank ye. Sorry I left ye with the clothes. I saw Jake come in. Did he say what Captain's orders were?" Cookie inquired.

"The only thing Jake was told to do was check the barrels."

"Aye, the barrels need checking, the cannons need securing to the floor, the mainsails lowered, and the smaller sails tied off. There's a lot to do," Cookie sighed, shaking his head.

Working together, they put everything away except the bowls for the half-warmed soup still in the cauldron. Scooping some out, Lizzie blessed her dinner and quietly ate. Meanwhile, Cookie went to tell the crew dinner was waiting. Spooning soup into her mouth, Lizzie heard footsteps coming up from the hold. Looking up, she saw Jake was back, wearing a frustrated expression on his face. Wondering what was wrong, she quickly swallowed and got up to serve him.

"Cookie said to eat before the storm. You can eat with me," she insisted, grabbing the long ladle that dipped down into the soup.

"Okay," Jake agreed, pulling up a chair.

Bringing him the soup and a cup of water, Lizzie returned to her seat and went back to eating. "Was everything alright down there?"

"The barrels were fine, but I spotted rats," Jake grumbled.

"Cookie will have to take Tuffy down there."

"The one-eyed monster?" he suggested sarcastically.

Without thinking, she instinctively slapped his arm. "Don't be cruel. Tuffy may be disabled, but she can still do her job."

"Why did you hit me?" he complained, rubbing his arm.

Lizzie shook her head. "I didn't hurt you."

"Getting into a fight is probably how she got disabled. We could shoot the rats, but I guess it's safer to let the monster—uh, cat—kill them," he commented, quickly changing words as Lizzie eyed him.

Suddenly someone's voice echoed outside. Before Lizzie knew what was happening, Jake jumped up and climbed the stairs, taking two steps at a time. Wanting to see what was going on, she followed him. Stopping on the top step, she stood on her tiptoes to peer over Jake's shoulder. By now, it was drizzling rain on the crew who had gathered in front of her father.

"Here, ye! Here, ye!" Blackbeard shouted. "The storm should be over us within the hour. Cookie has soup, so take turns eating. Continue to secure loose objects both on deck and down below. Look alive! Our lives depend on ye brains!"

"Aye, aye, Captain!" chanted the crew as everyone broke off in different directions to complete their tasks.

Turning, Blackbeard spotted Jake and Lizzie in the doorway out of the rain. As he walked up, Lizzie noticed the concern on his face.

"Jake, did ye do as I asked?" the pirate captain questioned.

"Yes, sir, the barrels are fine. We have a few rats, but I'll take care of it after the storm passes," Jake answered.

"Good. Report to Garret," Blackbeard ordered, referring to the boatswain who oversaw the sails and rigging. "He's taking down the mainsail. Storm winds tangle the sails and can snap the mast in half. Take ye boots off. Going barefoot prevents slipping on a wet deck."

"Okay," Jake responded, bending to remove his boots.

Blackbeard set his gaze on Lizzie. "It'll be dangerous out here, Lizzie. Ye need to stay below deck. Do ye understand?"

"I understand, Papa," she muttered, knowing no one could hear her. "Be careful. I'm praying for you. I love you."

By the look on his face, Lizzie could tell her words startled him. Although he didn't say anything, a smile flickered across his grizzly black beard, a sign he loved her, too. Watching her father's tall figure walk away, she silently asked God to protect them.

"Here, take my boots and stay off this deck. I mean it," Jake said forcefully, holding up his boots.

"You don't have to repeat the warning."

"Yes, I do. You were crazy enough to board a pirate ship in the middle of the night. Like Blackbeard said, use your brain."

Rolling her eyes, Lizzie took the boots as Jake trotted barefoot over to the pirates working on the sails. Just as she was preparing to go downstairs, Cookie came up with Owen and Stephen.

"Get two bowls of soup, Miss Lizzie," Cookie instructed.

Entering the kitchen, Lizzie took Jake's boots to the corner where she put the laundry basket. Filling the bowls, she served the men although she felt uncomfortable around Owen, the pirate who grabbed her in the storage room two weeks before. Placing the bowls in front of them, Owen glanced up at her while Stephen talked about the storm. He winked at her, which gave her the chills. Thankfully, Cookie came to pour them a cup of beer, saying it would keep them energized.

As they were leaving, two African men sat down. Lizzie ladled out cold soup, which Cookie gladly complemented with his so-called remedy for each sailor's lack of momentum. Soon, Blackbeard and Thomas Miller were coming down the steps.

"Looks like it's going to be a nasty storm," Cookie declared, pouring two more cups of his remedy.

Sitting down, Blackbeard rejected the drink. "Don't pour me any beer, Cookie. I've got to stay focused."

"Come on, it'll give ye a boost," Cookie urged.

"Nay, it will cloud my mind. It's fine for the crew, but I must stay sharp," Blackbeard insisted.

"Same for me, Cookie, but thanks anyway," Thomas added.

"Alright, here's some plain old water," Cookie proclaimed, placing cups of water on the table as Lizzie brought the soup.

The two men choked down the food in such a hurry that Cookie didn't even sit down with his own soup before they were leaving.

"Let me know if ye need me," Cookie called after them as he shook his head and looked at Lizzie. "Ever since I slipped during a storm last fall, those two haven't let me help on deck. They think I'm either clumsy or too old. I am the oldest, but they aren't far behind. If they didn't need a cook, they'd leave me on an island."

"They wouldn't leave you," she comforted him. "Besides, I'm glad you're here to keep me company."

Cookie smiled. "While it rains, how about a story?"

Outside the wind roared as it whipped through the small sails. The sound made Lizzie shiver, but the booming thunder bothered her the most. Sitting with Cookie, she listened to his story from the old days about a storm they rode out when he joined her father's crew. As the *Adventure* rocked through the waves, she imagined the man her father once was. According to Cookie, their first voyage together involved a sunken treasure ship off the Florida coast two years earlier.

Thunder echoed through the quarters, making both Cookie and Lizzie jump. Holding onto the table to keep from sliding to the floor, she tried not to get seasick as the *Adventure* floated over the waves. Cookie restarted his story as a member of the crew barged into the kitchen. Heading for the doorway dividing the galley from the sleeping quarters, the blonde-haired man disappeared into the next room.

"That's Philip Morton, our gunner. In battle, he loads the cannons. During storms, he ties down the eight cannons and secures the port holes so water can't come in," Cookie explained.

"Cookie, come help me!" Philip called from down below.

Jumping up, Cookie went to help. Moments later Tuffy came in, pausing to stretch as she pranced into the room. Lizzie noticed her claws were gripping the wooden floorboards to keep upright. Coming over to Lizzie, the one-eyed black cat nudged her leg, begging for a rub. Picking her up, Lizzie massaged behind the cat's ears, avoiding her sharp claws. Evidently satisfied, Tuffy squirmed, wanting to get down. Placing her on the floor, the cat hurried to the sand-filled box Cookie made for her to do her business.

A shout from the deck made Lizzie look up. Wondering if she should get Cookie and Philip, she decided to go see who was hollering. Holding onto the walls, she made her way upstairs and opened the door. Seeing anything was difficult due to the furiously blowing wind and hard, driving rain; however, her eyes focused on an object in the center of the deck. Squinting, she realized the object was Jake.

Lizzie rushed onto the deck to help Jake up. To her relief, he sat up just as she was crossing the deck. Unfortunately, between the wind and rain she lost her balance and fell onto her back. Gazing up at the black sky, she rolled onto her stomach and tried to get up.

Each attempt failed because her shoes couldn't gain traction. Now she understood why her father told Jake to go barefoot.

"Lizzie, what are you doing?" Jake yelled from close by.

"I thought you were hurt. Don't worry. I'm heading back inside as soon as I can get up," she promised loudly, taking off her shoes.

She had just managed to stand up with the assistance of the railing when Jake shrieked. "Look out!"

Turning, Lizzie saw a sail had broken loose from the cleat holding it to the ship. Caught by the wind, the sail caused the massive wooden beam to swing across the deck. Before she knew what was happening, her shoes slipped from her hand as she found herself tangled in the flapping sail. Struggling to get loose, she flipped over the railing, free-falling until her body hit the choppy waters of the Atlantic Ocean.

Going underwater, she tried to get her head above the waves. Gasping for air, the current forced her down into the turbulent water again. The salty water stung her eyes and wind-chapped lips as she thrashed in the sea. Lizzie begged God for help as her limbs grew tired from her efforts to keep from drowning. Then a strange thing happened. Like an answered prayer, her new pieced-together skirt rose around her, holding her up out of the ocean.

"Lizzie! Lizzie!" shouted a voice behind her.

Startled to hear her name, Lizzie felt a sense of peace come over her. Wondering if the voice belonged to an angel, she suddenly understood this may be the end. Thoughts of her mother rushed into her mind. The idea of seeing her again made her unbelievably happy until she thought about her papa. Faced with conflicting emotions, Lizzie realized she wasn't ready to leave this world.

"Lizzie! Are you all right?"

Floating over waves, Lizzie lifted her head to see where the voice came from. At first, she saw nothing except water, but then she spotted the *Adventure*. Gathering her strength, she attempted to swim in its direction. She briefly pondered if anyone saw her fall and how they could rescue her in the inclement weather.

"Lizzie! Lizzie! Hold on!"

Relieved, Lizzie recognized Jake swimming toward her.

"Thank God!" she exclaimed, grabbing his outstretched hand.

"Are you okay?" he panted. "Looks like the rigging cut your forehead. You scared me when you didn't answer."

"My head hurts."

"Well, let's see if we can get to the ship. It's going to be hard."

Nodding, Lizzie tried to follow Jake. Periodically, they would stop to rest, but for the most part the swimming was continuous. Completely worn out, she felt as though her limbs would fall off.

"Jake, I have to stop again," Lizzie gasped. "I can't keep going."

Jake sighed. "Alright."

Resting, Lizzie glanced in the direction from which they had just come. Between the wind and rain, it was amazing they got this far. Looking at Jake, she saw something flash in the water. Thinking she was seeing things, she pushed soggy hair out of her eyes.

"What's that?" she questioned, pointing at the gray objects.

Jake's voice was eerily relaxed. "Stay calm. They're sharks."

"Sharks!" she screamed.

Terrified, she threw her arms around Jake's neck, holding on for dear life. She didn't know a lot about sharks, but she did remember they could bite off an arm or leg.

"I said to stay calm," Jake mumbled through a mouthful of her soggy brown hair.

"There's another one!" she squealed, clinging to him tighter.

Jake wrapped one of his arms around her waist. "Lizzie, let go of my throat. I can't breathe. Your forehead is bleeding. Some sharks can smell blood. Stop kicking. Hopefully they'll leave."

Relaxing a bit, Lizzie tried to calm her pounding heart as four sharks circled them. Resting her chin on Jake's shoulder, she gazed up at the *Adventure*'s hull towering overhead. She was about to ask what he planned to do when a rope landed beside them with a splash.

"Jake, are ye alright?" yelled Blackbeard's voice.

"Lizzie's hurt, but we have a bigger problem. There are sharks swimming nearby," Jake called back as he reached for the rope.

"Wrap the rope around ye. We'll pull ye up."

Jake put the loop over their heads, tightened the knot, and tugged on it to let the pirates know they were ready. Commotion sounded from the *Adventure* as the men pulled up the rope. Feeling the tug, Lizzie held tightly to Jake while keeping an eye on the sharks. When they surfaced, she and Jake were hanging slightly above the water.

By now, the rope was straining under their combined weight as the pirates pulled them up a few inches at a time. Halfway up, Lizzie sensed the rope loosening seconds before they abruptly plummeted. As they tumbled back into the ocean Lizzie swallowed mouthfuls of seawater. When the pirates hoisted them out of the water for the second time, Lizzie choked and gulped for air. Finding it difficult to breathe, she felt as though she were going to faint.

Eventually, the pirates pulled them over the railing. Barely coherent, Lizzie could hear someone vaguely talking as her body touched the saturated deck. The next thing she knew, someone was hitting her back as they sat her up. Coughing and gagging on seawater, she heard her papa's voice commanding the crew to go back to their positions. Someone spoke to her, but she was too weak to respond. She slowly slipped into unconsciousness.

Lizzie had no idea how long she remained in that unconscious state, but her ordeal had drained her. When she finally regained awareness of her surroundings, the initial thing she noticed was a familiar voice.

"There's something bothering me," muttered Jake's voice.

"Go ahead," came Blackbeard's quiet answer.

"Lizzie has questions you don't want to address and maybe shouldn't, but she has the right to ask them. You owe her that much."

"Ye are pretty straightforward. I'll consider ye request."

Footsteps echoed through the room, making them stop talking. From the distinct dialect, Lizzie knew it was Cookie.

"Has she woken up yet?" he asked.

"Nay. I can't keep waiting. Thomas needs me," her papa replied.

"Can I have some water?" Lizzie questioned, feeling groggy.

"Ye are awake," Blackbeard stated from his seat beside her.

He pushed a strand of her dark brown hair away from her eyes as he helped her sit up on her bed. Confused about what happened, Lizzie suddenly realized she was no longer wet.

"Ye gave us quite a scare," Cookie said, handing her a cup.

Sipping some of the water, she felt a sharp pain above her right eye and reached up to touch her sore head.

"Ye had a bad cut but it didn't need stitches. Captain changed ye clothes. They're drying," Cookie told her.

"Get some rest. I need to get back to the crew. They're trying to save the sails. Thomas said there's damage to the mast, too. Cookie will be nearby. I'll check on ye later," Blackbeard declared. Looking at Jake he added, "Ye look tired. Go rest in ye hammock awhile."

Her papa exited the room with Jake. As Cookie sat on the stool, he asked if he could share a story. Nodding, Lizzie closed her eyes and listened to his sea-roving tale, silently praising God for saving both her and Jake's life.

CHAPTER EIGHT

FATHER IN DISGUISE

August 3, 1718 ~ Sunday

Curiosity intrigued Lizzie as she watched her papa from the doorway of her sleeping quarters. Blackbeard sat at his oak desk with a large parchment paper spread out. The artifact was tattered at the edges, suggesting the document's importance. She noticed several objects on the table, one of which her father picked up. Watching him stand the brass object up and move it across the paper, she concluded it was a measuring device.

Pausing, Blackbeard grabbed a feathered quill and dipped it into the inkwell before writing something on a piece of paper. Studying the document, he wrote something else while stroking his wiry, black beard with his free hand. Apparently sensing she was watching, the pirate captain suddenly glanced up at Lizzie.

"Good morning. I didn't see ye standing there. Bring one of those chairs over here."

Lizzie picked up a straight-backed chair and sat down beside him. Her eyes glimpsed the document stretched out on the oak desk. The artifact was a detailed map of the coast of Carolina, Virginia, and the northern colonies of Delaware and Pennsylvania.

"What's this for?" she questioned, pointing to the brass object.

"It's a divider, a tool used to determine the longitude or distance east to west on a plat. I estimate how long it'll take to reach our destination," he explained, handing her the object with two sharp points.

"So, you can predict when we'll arrive in Pennsylvania?"

"Aye. I'd say we're seven to ten days out, depending on how many ships are heading into the Delaware Bay. The area is busy this time of year. If we hadn't taken the oath it would be a fine opportunity to—" Blackbeard began, stopping abruptly.

"A fine opportunity for what?"

"The oath—uh, never mind," he replied. "Dividers are a helpful tool in a sea artist's box."

"I've never heard of a sea artist's box. What is it?"

"Every captain has a box of items like a divider, a compass, and a spyglass. Mine came from ye grandfather. He taught me about navigation. Out here in the ocean it takes both skills and knowledge to survive. I was voted in for my knowledge."

"You were voted in?"

"Captains and quartermasters are voted in. I was an ordinary crew member, but it didn't take long for me to learn the Caribbean waters from my mentor, Benjamin Hornigold. While serving on his ship the *Benjamin*, I earned the right to captain my own ship. Although my crew is committed to me, they can vote me out. It's different than King George's appointed governments in the colonies."

Lizzie could tell by the way her papa spoke about King George I that he wasn't pleased with the way the king handled things. This fact interested her but wasn't surprising. Even levelheaded Aunt Grace didn't have much taste for the German king.

From what Lizzie understood, the current king of Great Britain and Ireland took the throne after Queen Anne's death in 1714 instead of her half-brother, James, from the House of Stuart. The politics of the situation was difficult to grasp. Lizzie figured the basic theory was the belief of some loyal colonists that James, a Scot, should've been king instead of George, who was German and knew little English. By neglecting James' rightful place on the throne, the

350-year-long reign of the Scottish lineage broke. Not only was King George I unfair to the Scots, but the political and religious battles trickled down from Great Britain to the colonies in the New World.

Knowing her father named his flagship *Queen Anne's Revenge*, Lizzie wondered if it had anything to do with his dislike of King George. She was about to ask when someone entered the cabin.

"Captain, the damaged mast is ready to hoist back in place."

"I'll be out there shortly, Joseph," Blackbeard responded as the pirate headed out the door. Looking at Lizzie he added, "I need to see what's going on. Are ye staying here?"

"I thought about writing a letter to Aunt Grace. I'm sure she's worried. Maybe you can mail it in Pennsylvania. Do you have extra paper I can use?" she asked as he rolled up the map.

"There's paper and sealing wax in the top desk drawer," he confirmed, grabbing his tricorn hat. "The pounce is in the shaker beside the inkwell. Don't write about me or the crew and just put ye initials. Details are dangerous. Ye never know who might read it."

"Okay, I'll try to write in code words. What's pounce?"

Her papa looked surprised. "Ye haven't heard of pounce? It's ground-up powder from cuttlefish bones, a sea creature like an octopus. Sprinkle it on the ink to make it dry. I've got to go."

Watching her papa leave, Lizzie opened the top drawer and pulled out parchment paper. She picked up the turkey feather quill, dipped the nib of it in the silver inkwell, and began the letter.

Dear AG,

We are fine. I am not sure when we will return. Try not to worry. You probably know why I chose to come. There may not be another chance to write. I miss you and love you so much.

Love always, LB

Rereading the letter, Lizzie struggled with emotions. She hoped Aunt Grace could decipher what she was trying to say. Picking up the small shaker, she shook the pounce over the dark, walnut-based ink.

Waiting for the ink to dry, she searched the drawer for the sealing wax. Rummaging through the stack of papers, Lizzie paused to open a small silver box. Upon opening it, the strong smell of tobacco filled her nostrils, making her quickly close what she now knew was a snuffbox. She finally found a red stick of wax, the typical color used for letters. Lizzie was about to look for the signet that sealed the wax to the paper when her eyes caught something. The parchment paper on the bottom of the stack had Jake's name on it. Interested, Lizzie realized the wording was the same.

Articles and Bylaws for the Adventure

I. Crew members must obey the captain in battle but can vote to overrule him during peace time if majority rules.

II. Crew members vote on important decisions and get an equal share of food, liquors, and provisions.

III. Captains will call crew members by list to board prize ships. In addition to their share of the prize, each can claim a shift of clothes. But if any takes more jewels or money than is allotted punishment is by marooning.

IV. No one can play card games or dice for money.

V. All lanterns and candles out at eight o'clock. But crew can remain on the open deck after such time to drink.

VI. All pistols and cutlasses must be clean for battle.

VII. No boys or women allowed. Those guilty of disguising or sneaking a woman onboard will face death.

VIII. Penalty for desertion in battle is death or marooning.

IX. No fighting on the ship. Quarrels should end onshore with sword and pistol.

X. Talk of leaving crew is not tolerable until each man has earned an agreed amount of plunder. If a crew

> member gets crippled in battle crew will compensate his injury.
>
> XI. The captain and quartermaster get two shares of a prize; a share and a half go to the boatswain, sailing master, and gunner; one and a quarter for the rest.
>
> XII. Musicians must rest on the Sabbath Day.

At the bottom of each page was a different crew member's name. Some, such as her father; his quartermaster, Thomas; and Jake had signatures beside their printed names; however, most of the papers only had a marking resembling the letter x. Going back to the first page, she noticed it was a list of names.

Official Roster for the Crew of the Adventure

Edward "Blackbeard" Teach - Captain
Thomas Miller - Quartermaster
Israel Hands - Sailing Master   Philip Morton - Gunner
Garret Gibbons - Boatswain   Edward Salter - Cooper
Joseph "Cookie" Curtice - Cook
Joseph Brooks ~ Joseph "JJ" Brooks Jr. ~ John Carnes
Stephen Daniel ~ John Giles ~ John "Husky" Husk
Nathaniel Jackson ~ John Martin ~ John Philips
Owen Roberts ~ James Blake ~ Thomas Gates
Richard Greensail ~ Richard Stiles ~ James White
Jake Griffin

Lizzie panicked when she heard the door to the cabin open. She fumbled with the papers and wrestled them back into the drawer.

"Hey, Lizzie."

Hearing Jake's voice, Lizzie relaxed. "What are you up to?"

"Blackbeard wanted his compass and backstaff."

"A what?"

Jake laughed. "A backstaff. It's used to judge the latitude by the sun's shadow. It's important when figuring which way to go. Many seamen consider it a black art like witchcraft. What are you doing?"

"I'm writing Aunt Grace. Papa said to be careful what I wrote."

"He's right. I'm sure they'll be glad to hear from you."

"Yes, we missed both Hannah's and Alice's birthdays. Too bad you didn't get to see the detailed map Papa was looking at."

"Sounds like a rare Spanish plat. Their maps are better than the English. Blackbeard must have taken it from a captured prize. Edward Moseley is the surveyor general for maps of the Carolina coast."

"Really? Colonel Moseley used to live on Bay Street in Bath. He now lives in the Chowan Precinct but still owns lots in town, including the blacksmith forge. He rents to Mr. Collingswood Ward." Glancing at the pile of papers partially stuffed in the drawer, Lizzie decided to get Jake's opinion. "I found papers in this drawer. Maybe you can help me understand what they are."

"Don't tell me you've been snooping."

"Snooping? Papa told me the paper and sealing wax were in the drawer, so I figured the signet was, too. I got curious when I spotted your name on one of the documents," Lizzie stated.

Coming over, Jake put one hand on the desk so he could look over her shoulder. "It's the crew roster. Captains keep records of everyone on the ship. During my apprenticeship, the captain had a roster so he knew how much to pay depending on how long we were onboard. JJ says pirates do the same. The quartermaster keeps the communal plunder, which is the stolen treasure. When the pirates split up, they get their share of the loot."

"What about these papers? They're the same except for the names at the bottom. You signed the last one," she pointed out.

"Those are the ship's articles. Everyone signs a copy of the articles swearing they'll abide by the rules. The men who can't spell their names mark the page with an x. JJ said there was a man last year who failed to keep his word so Blackbeard left him on a deserted island."

"So, if these are pirate rules, then why did you sign them?"

"Blackbeard said it would be a good idea in case the men wanted to see my signature. I took the oath with my hand on a Bible."

"The Bible? I can't believe they have one onboard!"

"Me either," Jake agreed. "It's on his shelf. If I remember correctly there's a part about not stealing. My mother made us memorize ten things and not stealing was one of them."

"You're talking about the Ten Commandments. They're in the first part of the Bible, in Exodus," Lizzie recalled.

"I've got to go. Blackbeard's probably wanting to know where I am," Jake said, grabbing the backstaff and compass from the shelf.

As Lizzie put the papers back, she wondered what was in the bottom drawer. Reminding herself she needed the signet, she opened it and peered inside. The first thing to capture her attention was a black, leather-bound book. Picking it up, she realized it was a pocketbook diary. Thumbing through it, she discovered a folded paper tucked behind the last page. It bore the signature of Governor Charles Eden.

"Look at this. It has Governor Eden's signature."

Jake joined her at the desk. "What have you drug out now?"

"I found this in Papa's pocketbook diary."

"I doubt Blackbeard wants people looking at his private journal."

"Would you just look at this?"

He took the paper she handed him. "I think it's one of those pardons Mr. Shute talked about. You know, the pardons King George I issued to pirates who swear their allegiance to his throne in exchange for a pardon from their previous crimes."

"This has 'Captain Edward Teach alias Blackbeard' written at the top. Why do these papers use that name?" she questioned.

Jake shrugged as he started out the door. "I've heard some of the crew call him Teach. Blackbeard's waiting on me. Stop snooping."

Rolling her eyes, she held up the signet. "I wasn't snooping."

Watching Jake leave, Lizzie placed the pardon in her papa's journal. Sliding the pocketbook in the drawer, she heated the wax stick with the candle's flame in the lantern. As it began to melt, she pressed the red wax onto the folded letter. Holding the brass signet against the red wax, she slowly pulled the rest of the wax stick away. After it dried, she lifted the signet revealing the imprinted letter B.

Placing the signet and wax in the drawer, she took her letter to the room where she stayed with her papa. Going to her makeshift bed, she pulled out an old snuffbox Cookie gave her from its hiding spot beneath her bed. Unwrapping the blue handkerchief, she placed the letter under the snuffbox. Lizzie opened the box, grateful she removed the smell. Peering inside, she touched her locket, remembering the last time she wore it—the day she found out her papa was Blackbeard. Sliding it under her bed, she grabbed the tricorn hat Cookie gave her and located the Bible Jake told her about.

With a single braid of dark brown hair hanging from beneath the hat, Lizzie went into the sunshine carrying the Bible. Allowing her eyes to adjust to the light, she spotted her papa supervising the men as they repaired the cracked mast. The pirates were nailing a wrought-iron hoop around the base of the mast where the storm damaged it.

Making her way to where the ladder stood against the cabin, Lizzie sat on a wooden stool in the corner. She opened the Bible and read the first Scripture she came to in the book of Psalms. An hour passed before she noticed Cookie walking over with a tired look on his face.

"You look exhausted. Would you like some water?"

"Nay, I'm fine. Thomas insisted I take a break from helping John Giles patch sails. The hole was big enough to put a periauger through. Garret Gibbons is normally in charge of the sails, but he's busy with all the rigging work," Cookie answered as he sat down on the deck.

"Looks like you're close to finishing."

"We still have to fix the eyebolts on the portside where the rigging broke loose. Then we'll tie off the sail," he informed her.

"Where's portside?"

"It's the left side of the ship. Starboard is the right. That storm wounded this ol' girl. She needs a careening. We haven't done it since we captured her in April. It requires supplies and beaching her."

"How do you careen a ship?"

"Careening means scraping the creatures off the bottom. Next, ye need to replace damaged planks, caulk the seams, and paint it. There's a lot of work involved, but like I said we need supplies," he continued. Pointing to the Bible he added, "What are ye reading?"

"Since it's Sunday, I decided to read the Bible. Jake told me there was one onboard. He also explained the pirate articles. There's something I don't comprehend, though. You work on the Sabbath, but you can't make music. Working on God's day of rest is a sin."

"Living at sea has daily tasks. We can't stop working, but we can rest from making music. It's our way of recognizing the Sabbath."

Gazing at the deck, Lizzie noticed her papa walking up with the backstaff. It resembled a bow and arrow, having two metal pieces with a connecting wooden arch. As the tall, bearded captain approached, Cookie scooted over.

"Ye don't have to move, Cookie. I'm just going up the ladder to get higher," Blackbeard stated as he climbed the rungs.

Watching him climb on top of the captain's cabin, Lizzie stared in amazement as he steadied himself and held up the backstaff. With his back to the sun, the pirate captain positioned the object while sliding a wooden piece across the arch.

Cookie explained how a backstaff read the ship's latitude, the distance north or south. By holding it up to the horizon, you measure the distance of the sun's shadow to where the sky and water meet. A compass confirmed which way was north with a metal pointer. It was new to average sailors, even though English navigator John Davis invented it a hundred years earlier. Before the backstaff, sailors used an astrolabe, which was hard because you had to stare into the sun.

Blackbeard's voice echoed across the deck, causing the crew to stop working. "Listen up! Land is in the horizon, a clear sign we're nearing Delaware Bay. For the next hour, we're going to stop working on the repairs and start disguising the ship. Unless we resemble a merchant ship we won't slip past the authorities. If all goes well, we'll get a chance to go ashore when we arrive in Pennsylvania."

As the men fulfilled their duties, Cookie stood up. "Come on, we need to get the potatoes ready for our soup."

"Cookie, do ye need Lizzie?" Blackbeard called.

"I can manage, Captain. Go ahead, Miss Lizzie."

With Cookie holding the ladder, Lizzie climbed to the cabin roof. She took her papa's hand as she tottered across the arched roof like a child learning to walk. Coming to the edge of the two-foot-tall railing, she gazed at the ocean below, spotting several gray dolphins as they jumped out of the gorgeous greenish-blue water.

"Look at the pod of dolphins!" she exclaimed. "Sometimes a couple come up in Bath Creek. I love watching them play."

Admiring the pod of ten dolphins, Lizzie couldn't stop giggling as the gray animals raced the *Adventure*. Watching these six- to eight-foot-long creatures moving through the water, she thought about how creative God was to make such amazing animals.

"I thought ye might enjoy gazing through the bring-them-near. The Capes of Delaware are those rocky cliffs on either side of the bay," Blackbeard said, handing Lizzie his spyglass.

Holding the spyglass up to her eye, Lizzie peered through the long tube at the mass of land in the northern horizon. Even from this distance, she could make out the rocky cliffs of the bay.

"I see why you call it a bring-them-near."

Blackbeard chuckled. "The nickname suits it well."

"Feels like it's covered with paper," she observed, handing it back.

"Aye, the tube came from vellum, a paper-thin piece of calfskin. Maps are sometimes made from calfskin, too."

Watching her papa close the spyglass by sliding the three interlocking pieces into each other, Lizzie debated whether she should speak with him about his past. Recalling Jake's warning about not pushing him for answers, she decided to tread lightly.

"I'm excited to see Pennsylvania. In July we received a letter from there addressed to you. Aunt Grace wouldn't open it, but she did open the crate Aunt Susannah sent. It's interesting how we saw you in town the same day. We even met Cookie," she began.

"When ye came aboard Cookie told me about seeing ye at the store. I met with ye uncle while I was in town. Thomas gave me the letter, but he didn't mention a crate."

"Did he meet with you at the Salty Sailor Tavern, or are you referring to the gathering at Tunnel Land?"

His eyes widened. "How do ye know about the gathering?"

Going back to the night Scripo brought Mr. Knight's letter, Lizzie explained how she concluded her papa was on the pirate ship. She told him about finding the letter in Aunt Grace's apron and how she watched the meeting at Tunnel Land from among the tobacco leaves.

Silence came over Blackbeard as he stared into the horizon. He sat down on the rooftop, allowing his long legs to dangle over his cabin door. Joining him, Lizzie tucked her dress under her to keep the wind from blowing it up. Glancing at her papa, she noticed how pale his skin was. Finally, he drew in a deep breath.

"I assume Grace doesn't know any of this."

"No, sir. I had to explain my actions to Jake when he found me on this ship. I know I should've talked to Aunt Grace, but I couldn't get her to tell me about Mr. Knight's letter. She didn't even give a reason for all those Africans suddenly appearing."

"We arrived in Bath with a hundred men. Sixty of them were African slaves. Since half the crew were returning to the colony, we dispersed the Africans among our families. My portion went to ye grandfather to help with the farmwork," he proclaimed.

"Why didn't you come see me? You were so close."

"Ye grandfather wouldn't allow it. I can't blame him. He knew I wasn't staying and thought it would only hurt ye. Since I couldn't see ye in person, I watched ye from the shadows one evening."

"That was you? I saw a shadowy figure while we were catching fireflies. It was the same night Jake showed us the *Boston News-Letter* with an article about you. Later, I snuck out and came aboard."

"I didn't know ye saw me. Anyway, ye said Susannah sent a crate to Grace. What was it?"

"Aunt Susannah received a giant spinning wheel from your cousins in Charles Town after your aunt died. She wrote me, explaining how special your aunt was and said she wanted me to have it."

"My aunt was a good woman. She tried to keep us in the Presbyterian faith. Father would've never made it without her and Uncle William. We lived with them for a while after Mother died. I was about eight, but Susannah was only a few weeks old."

"I wish I could have known them. Did Grandfather Beard and Great-Uncle William grow up in Charles Town, too?"

"Nay, they grew up in Bristol, England. As a young lad, I enjoyed listening to stories of the old days when they were boys making mischief. My favorite stories were about my grandfather. He came to England from Scotland with nothing but the shirt on his back. It was hard times, especially for a man of Scottish descent."

"Wow, I didn't know we were Scottish. What about you and Aunt Susannah? Do you remember England?"

"I was born on the island of Barbados in the Caribbean. We moved to Charles Town the year before Susannah was born. My childhood memories are of Charles Town. I traveled with Father on his merchant ship as his apprentice. He taught me about sailing and gave me my love for the sea. One of our trading routes was to Port Bath. The first time I saw ye mother was at the general store. After several trips to Port Bath, we fell in love. We later married and bought land on the Neuse River with Grace and Jared. When ye was four, Father bought land beside us on the Neuse River so we could live near each other. About the same time, he married my stepmother, Elizabeth Moore, in Bath Town. They were going to live in town where the horse mill is now but decided to resale the lot and live where ye are living with Grace."

"So, was the Pennsylvania letter from a friend of yours?"

"It was a warning. The governor isn't recognizing pardons," he mumbled, suddenly acting like he was going to leave.

Not wanting the conversation to end, Lizzie changed subjects. She could tell by the anxiousness on her papa's face he was beginning to distance himself from her. It was now or never.

"I would love to know more about Grandfather Beard's family. Aunt Susannah doesn't like to talk about him. It makes her sad. I miss him, but I miss Momma more," she revealed, fighting tears.

Another awkward silence filled the emptiness, causing her heart to ache. Lizzie wanted to embrace her papa like she did when she was little, feeling his strength radiate through her. This man sitting beside her wasn't the same as she remembered. He was somehow different.

"Ye dark brown hair and soft smile remind me of her."

"I spent many nights thinking about her," she whispered. "I think about you as well. I've missed you, Papa. When you didn't come home, I wondered what I did to keep you away."

Her father looked at her. "I can't believe ye thought my leaving had something to do with ye."

"What was I supposed to think?" she inquired, wiping the tears from her eyes. "I haven't seen you in over two years."

"I'm sorry ye felt that way, Lizzie. My life has been a mess, and since I became a pirate it was best to stay away."

"Why did you choose this life instead of me?"

"Ye don't understand."

"Then help me understand."

Shaking his head, Blackbeard let out a sigh. "We received a letter from John Morgan telling us Father died. It was my duty as his son to go to Charles Town and arrange his burial. He had been on a business trip. John showed me papers regarding Father's tar business and the debts he owed. To clear the debts, I had to take his shipment to the Caribbean. This happened in July, so when I left, everything was well at home. When I returned in the spring, the colony was a disaster after the Indian War and Martha was dead."

His voice cracked with emotion at the mention of her mother. He rubbed his bristly beard with his right hand trying to regain control. "I l-loved her. It devastated me to come home to her grave knowing I wasn't there for her, to hold her, to say good-bye…"

His voice trailed off again, overwhelmed by the years of buried memories. Lizzie wiped the tears streaming down her cheeks.

"The people of Bath asked me to help get supplies into the colony. At first, it gave me a reason to keep going, but I was so busy I wasn't around. Luckily, ye mother's family took ye in. For the next few years, I delivered merchandise to other colonies. About two years ago, the *Boston News-Letter* printed an article about a Spanish ship wrecking off the coast of Florida. Men from all over headed south to seek the treasures the ship held. Bath's leaders chose me to lead a group of friends on a mission to retrieve some of the treasure. By the time we got there most of it was gone. We stopped at the islands of the Bahamas, where I met Benjamin Hornigold. Under his command, we did some privateering, a sort of legal piracy. The crew made me captain of my first privateering ship. We got information claiming that our rightful privateering was illegal in the eyes of the new king, which branded us as outlaws in defiance of the Crown."

"Can't you give up piracy? Don't you want to be with me?"

"My life is different now. I can't go back to the life I once had."

"What about the pardon? Doesn't it clear your name?"

"Not all governors accept it. Besides, it isn't just about losing ye mother. Martha fell off the wagon and lost our second child when ye were two years old. We wanted a son, but she could never have any more children. I've always blamed myself."

Lizzie stared at him in shock. She never knew anything about a sibling. Now she understood why he was avoiding her. Not knowing what to say, she was relieved to hear voices hollering below.

"Stop fighting!" Blackbeard yelled as he scurried down the wooden ladder.

Two pirates circled one another with swords drawn while the rest stood around. Lizzie was impressed by their footwork and expert fighting skills as their silver swords clashed in a flurry of movements.

Climbing down the ladder, Lizzie inched her way to the captain's cabin, trying to stay clear of the dueling pirates. Meanwhile, Blackbeard and his quartermaster tried to stop the swordfight. Things got worse as the rest of the crew started fighting. Suddenly, a loud bang echoed across the deck, causing Lizzie to jump. Thick smoke engulfed the air as Cookie held his pistol high.

"Put down ye weapon, Cookie," Blackbeard demanded.

"I will, when they put down their swords," Cookie spat, swinging his pistol at Israel Hands and John Martin.

"Ye heard him, drop the swords," Blackbeard ordered.

Lizzie held her breath, praying the dispute would end. Considering what she knew about Israel, she felt sure he started it. Thankfully, both pirates dropped their swords. Israel stomped off, showing disrespect for his captain. Furious, Blackbeard lectured the pirates on the rules. As Lizzie watched him display an outrageous temper, she couldn't believe he was the same man she was talking to. His change of behavior scared her. Until now, she considered her papa's alias to be a disguise, but being Blackbeard was more than she realized. He seemed to like this position of authority. Was it possible he could be both the fearsome pirate Blackbeard and her father?

CHAPTER NINE

BLOODSTAINED COBBLESTONES

August 11, 1718 ~ Monday

Shrill cackles filled the air as black-backed seagulls swooped over the *Adventure*'s deck. Lizzie listened to their laughter seemingly directed at the pirates as they prepared to anchor in the Pennsylvania channel. Excitement filled her heart as she waited for their arrival, an event prolonged because of all the ships in the harbor. With multitudes of English, French, and Spanish ships coming into the Delaware Bay and exiting into the Atlantic Ocean, it was remarkable how well the *Adventure* fit in. No one noticed a pirate ship in their midst, a tribute to the hard work to disguise it. Her papa stood at the ship's helm where he kept an eye on the heavy traffic of ships.

"Where's Cookie?" Jake questioned, coming up beside her.

"He's counting our supplies. I offered to help make a list, but he insisted I enjoy the view. It's pretty amazing."

"I haven't seen it either. The ship I apprenticed with traveled from New Bern to the southern colonies around Charles Town. One time we came up to Boston, but I didn't leave the ship. I hope we get a chance to go ashore with the crew," Jake declared, leaning on the rail.

"Where do you think they'll go? The tavern?"

"Probably. They're getting restless. Even I am. Being stuck on a ship can sometimes drive a person crazy," Jake pointed out.

"I'll be glad to get off, too. At least to get something more decent to eat. If I eat those awful hardtack things again, I think I'm going to go crazy myself," Lizzie mumbled, shivering at the thought of eating the stale bread for the last three days.

"I'm sure seeing all these ships is making the men agitated as well. It must be agonizing to be in the middle of so many prizes."

"What about the pardons? They swore to stop piracy."

"Yes, when they faced the hangman's noose, but they've been living this way for years. I'm beginning to see why it's appealing. JJ said they started seeking treasure after a hurricane wrecked a Spanish treasure galleon off the everglades in 1715. They served the government as privateers, attacking foreign ships for their cargo. At first it was an honest life, until it got out of control. There's no going back."

"Do you know why they wanted to come here?"

"Maybe they want to enjoy themselves before heading to the Caribbean for the winter. The cold months make traveling nearly impossible up here. It's too hot to be heading to the Caribbean in August."

"There are so many different ships. You said something about a Spanish treasure galleon. Are any of these ships similar?"

"I don't see one. They're huge, about 170 feet long. Those ships are brigantines, and the smaller ones are snows. Brigantines are the same length as the *Adventure*, sixty-five feet. Most of these vessels are fishing boats, barges, and periaugers. The *Adventure* is called a sloop."

"How about the ship with the flag of Great Britain heading to the ocean?" she asked, pointing at the vessel with its three masts.

"That's a frigate. See the name on the side boards near her bow? Those letters, HMS, stand for His Majesty's Service, meaning it serves in King George's Royal Navy. Frigates hold twenty or more guns for battle. It's good they're headed out to sea. The last thing we need is a run-in with the Royal Navy."

"Aye, it would be a problem," agreed a voice behind them.

Lizzie was glad to find the eavesdropper was her papa. Regrettably, her hopes for a better relationship with her father had faded as his behavior became irritable. Her fears seemed ridiculous as he leaned against the railing and spoke reasonably to Jake.

"Ye know a lot about ships and sailing, lad. I'm impressed."

Making sure no one was nearby, Lizzie decided to use this opportunity to question her papa. "Why are you called 'Blackbeard'?"

The suntanned creases around her papa's dark brown eyes relaxed as he chuckled in amusement. This sudden change caught Lizzie off guard, causing her to wonder what was behind his mood swings.

"My friend Sam 'Black' Bellamy died. We sailed together when I served under Benjamin Hornigold. He and Hornigold didn't see eye to eye, so the company split. Sam captained the largest pirate ship in history called the *Whydah*. He joined forces with another pirate captain named Paulsgrave Williams. On a stormy night near Boston, Massachusetts, Sam's ship wrecked off the Capes. Paulsgrave and his crew weren't nearby at the time. Most of the *Whydah*'s crew drowned, including Sam. The few men who lived hung for their piracy. I led a raid on the ships coming into Boston for the lives of Sam's men who hung. Pirates started calling me 'Black' as a memorial to Sam."

"Some call you 'Teach.' How does that fit in?" Jake piped up.

"I didn't want to tarnish my father's name so I went by Edward Thatch, a variation of the surname Thatcher. As a young man, I served as an apprentice under Father's friend, Richard Thatcher. He was a merchant who lived in the Thornbury Township of Pennsylvania and sailed out of the riverside town of Marcus Hook. Thatch changed to Teach because of the way people pronounced it."

"Then they called you 'Blackbeard,'" Lizzie mentioned.

"Pirates began calling me 'Black' after Sam died. My close friends who knew me as a young man joked about me being Blackbeard. They put 'Black' in front of my last name, Beard, which created 'Black Beard.' It was meant to be two words, but most sailors think the 'Beard' half referred to the beard I grew to conceal my identity."

A yell triggered Lizzie to jump. She watched the crew let down the heavy iron anchors, letting them sink into the greenish-blue water. Moments later, the anchors hit the bottom, causing the *Adventure* to jerk. The movement startled Lizzie, who gripped the railing to prevent going overboard. Now anchored, the crew uncovered the periauger.

"Welcome to Philadelphia!" Black Beard announced.

"Will Jake and I get to go into town?" Lizzie questioned.

"The crew will go ashore in shifts of three trips. I'm going with the first group and Cookie with the second. There may be a chance for ye to go when I get back," Black Beard confirmed.

"If I can't go, I would like for you to mail the letter for me."

"We'll see. Come on, Jake, the crew's moving the periauger."

The men hoisted the boat into the air with ropes. Swinging the twenty-five-foot canoe over the starboard side of the *Adventure*, they eased it into the water. Cookie came up wearing a navy-blue turban around his head as he carried a supply list and a pewter cup.

"Here's the cup ye asked for, Captain," Cookie declared.

"Gather around," Black Beard commanded. "Cookie has a cup of black and white buttons. There are twenty-one buttons. I'll be leading the first trip, and Cookie will go on the second. Those who draw a black button will row the periauger and help load the goods. The rest will protect the ship."

"What about our time ashore?" Owen Roberts protested.

"Ye will get a chance after the supplies are loaded."

The crew lined up to get a button. Lizzie was surprised to see pistols hanging from their waists. Black Beard announced that his quartermaster, Thomas, would join him on the first trip, along with

John Giles, Joseph Brooks, and an African named Richard Greensail. Cookie would lead the second group with JJ Brooks, Edward Salter, John Martin, and Jake. The third would include Israel Hands, Owen Roberts, Philip Morton, and two Africans, Thomas Gates and James White. Jake and Lizzie leaned on the railing to watch Black Beard and the first group climb down the rope ladder to the periauger.

Picking up the oars, the pirates rowed to the wharf while Black Beard sat in the back. The periauger made its way across the vast river as it meandered through the ships. Recalling their conversation, Lizzie had asked Jake to share more of his travels when a ruckus broke out. She stared as the crew fought like animals. Cookie tried to stop them, but no one listened. Husky and Garret Gibbons pulled men apart until they singled out one pirate. Not surprisingly, it was Israel.

"What ails ye?" Cookie snapped as Husky and Garret held Israel.

"He insulted Captain," John Martin said. "I told him to shut up, and he took a swing at me."

"Do ye have anything to say?" Cookie asked Israel, who spit in his face. "Take him below deck, Husky. Captain can deal with him."

Husky wrestled Israel, who shouted despicable words at John Martin. Stunned by his dirty language, Lizzie barely heard Jake say the periauger was back. The pirates went to help haul up the barrels of supplies. Finally, Joseph Brooks and John Giles boarded the ship.

"Get ready, Miss Lizzie. Ye are going with me," Cookie declared.

"Let me put my hat away," Lizzie answered as she hurried off.

Entering the captain's cabin, Lizzie retrieved the letter from under her bed. She left her tricorn hat behind as she stuffed the letter into her white stocking and returned to the deck where Jake waited.

"Come on, Lizzie," he urged, grabbing her elbow to escort her to the railing. "JJ's in the boat. I'll be right behind you."

Finding his behavior odd, Lizzie glanced at Cookie, who was talking to JJ's father, Joseph. "I was getting my letter. What's going on?"

"Owen thinks you shouldn't go ashore. Hopefully, Joseph and Garret can control things until Thomas gets back."

Goose bumps covered Lizzie's arms at the mention of Owen's name, despite the steamy August heat. Her mind slipped back to the day he held her in the storage hold. Not wanting to stay, she swung her leg over the railing and eased down the rope ladder trying not to look down. This was scarier for her than the night she climbed aboard.

Shaking, Lizzie was relieved to set foot on the periauger. With the assistance of Jake's new friend, JJ Brooks, she sat down on the center board. Jake climbed down next, followed by Cookie, Edward Salter, and John Martin. Once in the twenty-five-foot canoe, they picked up the oars and began the journey to shore. From down here, the *Adventure* looked huge among the other ships. Admiring them, Lizzie felt her excitement growing with every stroke of water. Soon the periauger reached the wharf full of boats tied to the long dock. The men tied the periauger to a wooden pole while Cookie helped Lizzie out.

"Let's find Thomas. JJ, stay with the boat," Cookie advised.

Following the cook, Lizzie walked down the dock. Unlike Bath, the wharf was full of sailors loading or unloading goods. The amount of people surprised Lizzie. Coming to the end of the dock, she noticed a sign nailed to a wooden pole with the words "Dock Street" written in black paint. The street was bricked with stones, a far cry from the dirt streets of Bath Town. Roaming the busy cobblestone street, they spotted Thomas Miller at a merchant near the wharf.

"Ye are here," the quartermaster said when he saw them. He motioned for Edward Salter and John Martin. "These barrels are ours."

As the two pirates picked up one of the barrels and carried it down to the dock, Cookie turned to Thomas. "Where's Captain?"

"He said he was going to see George Guest, but I just came from there. George spoke to him, then the next thing he knew he was leaving," Thomas responded, pointing to a building behind him.

Gazing at the building, Lizzie noticed a sign hanging by the door. The owner had painted a picture of a blue anchor on the sign along with the name George Guest's Blue Anchor Tavern across the top.

"Do ye think he went to—well, ye know what I mean," Cookie hinted, glancing awkwardly at Lizzie.

Thomas looked uncomfortable. "Possibly. What does it matter?"

"Israel started a fight. We got it under control, but Captain needs to get back and stabilize things," Cookie revealed.

"I'll handle things until Captain gets back," Thomas commented.

"Be careful, Thomas. Israel's jealous of ye position. Ever since *Queen Anne's Revenge* sank, he's been mad. Black Beard urged us to vote ye in after William Howard left, but Israel wanted to be quartermaster. Being a master pilot and third in command isn't enough."

"I'll keep an eye on him. He thinks because he was captain of one of the four ships back then it puts him above the rest of us. In the meantime, John Martin can find Captain," Thomas proclaimed.

"Okay, Miss Lizzie and Jake are going with me. They can help carry the smaller items on my list," Cookie mentioned.

Nodding, Thomas left them and disappeared into the crowd. With the men headed to the ship, Cookie led the way through the busy wharf and up a cobblestone street that another sign confirmed was High Street. Staying close, Lizzie took in the sights and sounds of the bustling atmosphere. High Street was full of carts and buggies pulled by different colored horses as their shoes clip-clopped on the cobblestone streets. Besides the businesses lining High Street, Lizzie noticed how big and beautiful the brick houses were in comparison to Bath's wood-planked homes.

Soon they arrived at the General Mercantile, which was about double the size of the store in Bath. Baskets of fruits and vegetables lined the storefront, beckoning those passing by. As they climbed the stairs and entered, Lizzie's senses came alive the same way they did when she walked into Harding's Store. The smell of freshly ground coffee beans filled the air, and the sound of creaking floorboards echoed as the customers walked through the three rooms of goods. Walking past a barrel of coffee beans, Cookie stopped at a large crate of lye soap. Surprised to see something made on the farm, Lizzie picked up a bar.

"Good eye, Miss Lizzie, we need ninety bars," Cookie remarked, filling a basket he got at the door. "We're about out of candles, too."

"Can't we make them?" she blurted out.

Cookie chuckled. "We can't make them on a ship. I never liked doing it in the first place. All sailors buy soap and candles."

"Can we buy scented soap? My aunt puts flowers in it to make it smell better. The soap you gave me stinks," Lizzie informed him.

"Flowers? I don't think so," Jake objected.

"Jake's right. We prefer the smell of the sea. Ye can have ye own scented soap. By the way, Captain wanted me to buy material for ye to make a new dress. Since ye are here ye can pick it out."

"A new dress?"

"Ye need something else to wear. He probably gave me enough money for two dresses. Jake can go with ye. I'll gather my list."

Working through the crowd, Lizzie and Jake walked to the sewing section as Cookie went about his shopping. Tables of brightly colored material were in stacks around the side room. Besides the bolts of cloth, there were baskets of thread, wool, and yarn already spun from sheep wool. There was even a basket of sewing, knitting, and crocheting needles along with brushlike cards to unknot the wool to prepare it for spinning.

"How many times are you going to circle those bolts of cloth?" Jake questioned as she studied the material.

Looking up at him with his arms crossed and eyebrow raised she replied, "I need a good material to work with."

Jake sighed. "Give me the letter you want to mail. I'll give it to the clerk while you finish here. I've seen enough cloth."

"Turn away," she said, not wanting him to see under her skirt.

When Jake turned, Lizzie made sure no one could see her before lifting her skirt and sliding the letter out of her stocking. Handing it to Jake, she watched him go up to the counter. After comparing the cloth, she chose a tan-colored cotton material and a light blue one. Taking them to where Jake waited in line, she convinced him to hold the cloth while she browsed the variety of hats in the front window. The hats were exquisite with satin brims and either a fancy bow or exotic bird feathers. Picking one up, Lizzie placed it on her head and looked at herself in a small looking glass on the table.

"You look beautiful, miss."

Startled, Lizzie put down the looking glass to remove the hat. She realized a young man was standing there staring at her. Getting an uneasy feeling, Lizzie decided to get back in line with Jake.

"Excuse me, my friend is waiting," she stated as she moved away.

Another young man stopped her. Although he was clearly standing in her way, none of the ladies or gentlemen in the store noticed. Realizing she had a problem, Lizzie prayed as she tried to leave.

"Miss, there's a coffee shop down the street. Will you join us for a cup?" the second one added.

"No, thank you. I really must be going," she insisted.

When she attempted to move, someone grabbed her. Panicking as her attacker wrapped his arms around her waist, Lizzie kicked him while screaming Jake's name. Despite her efforts, the two young men opened the front door as their friend carried her around the corner.

111

Fear overwhelmed Lizzie as they took her to the alley. She was surprised when someone hit her attacker, causing him to drop her. As she fell onto the cobblestones, she recognized Jake. Scrambling out of their way, she watched them fight like rabid foxes. Unfortunately, the young men teamed up on Jake with their long-bladed knives. Pulling out his own knife, Jake fought them. Begging God to help Jake, she gasped when one of them caught Jake off guard by stabbing his knife into Jake's side. Jake collapsed to his knees. Blood spilled out onto the brick cobblestones as a gunshot sounded through the alley.

Looking up, Lizzie spotted Cookie with a smoking pistol in his hand. The shot spooked the three young men, who ran down the alley to the street on the other end. Lizzie got up and ran to Jake.

Cookie knelt on Jake's other side. "Is it bad?"

Jake braced himself with his right hand while he held his injured side with the other. Removing his blood-covered hand, he looked at the place where the knife pierced his side. Grimacing at the bloody wound, Lizzie tried not to get upset. The wound looked deep.

"It needs stitches. Ye will have a better chance if a doctor fixes ye up. If it gets infected ye might see those pearly gates. Besides, it may have punctured ye insides. Can ye walk?" Cookie questioned.

"Guess I don't have a choice," Jake panted.

"Alright, Miss Lizzie," Cookie began as he removed the navy-blue turban on his head. "Help me wrap this around his body. Hopefully, it'll hold up until we can get him to the doctor."

"Don't forget the supplies," Jake reminded Cookie, wincing as he lifted his shirt so that they could wrap his wound.

"I'm sure Mrs. Bulah Coates will hold our supplies when I tell her what happened. The store has been in her husband's family for generations," Cookie answered, helping Jake walk to the store.

Waiting on the steps for Cookie, Lizzie glanced at Jake, who was holding his injured side while propping his forehead against his fist. Although he didn't complain, she knew he was in pain.

In no time, Cookie returned, and after helping Jake to his feet, the three of them crossed the cobblestone street. Continuing down a side street, they passed a beautiful stone church. Eventually they came to another street whose sign identified it as Vine Street. On the corner stood a quaint brick house. Walking around to the side porch, Cookie knocked on the door where a sign hung bearing the name Doctor Arnold Chadwick. Moments later a tall, black-haired man answered. Based on his fancy attire, Lizzie assumed he was the doctor.

"Joseph Curtice? It's been a long time. What can I do for you?"

"Doc, the lad is injured. Can ye look at him?" Cookie requested.

"Absolutely, take him into my examining room," Dr. Chadwick instructed. "How did he acquire this injury?"

"Three scoundrels grabbed Miss Lizzie in the General Mercantile. One stabbed Jake when he went to help," Cookie explained.

The doctor shook his head. "I heard there were some young men causing trouble. Have a seat. This may take awhile."

"Miss Lizzie will stay, but I need to find Captain Teach."

"You missed him by about forty-five minutes. He insinuated he was going to the Penny-Pot Tavern before he returned to the ship."

Cookie looked surprised. "He came here? I assumed he went straight to the Penny-Pot like he always does."

"Perhaps he's still there. I better check on your friend," Dr. Chadwick told him as he closed the door to the examining room.

Lizzie couldn't believe her ears. Why did her papa visit the doctor? Were they old friends, or was there something he was hiding?

"I'll be back soon, Miss Lizzie," Cookie promised as he left.

Sitting in one of the chairs, Lizzie replayed the attack in her mind. About thirty minutes passed, and still no sign of either Dr. Chadwick or Cookie. Suddenly the door opened, and in walked a woman wearing a lacy black shawl over a sleeveless, frilly red dress. Lizzie stared at the fancy blonde lady. She had never seen anyone like her.

"You must be Lizzie," the woman said. "How's your friend?"

Stunned to hear this stranger speak her name in an unfamiliar accent, Lizzie's mind raced. "How do you know my name?"

The woman smiled. "Cookie told me."

"You know Cookie?"

"Yes, he's a friend of mine. He told me what happened. I was concerned so I decided to come see how things were," she revealed.

"I don't really know. Dr. Chadwick hasn't come out yet."

"Do you mind if I sit and wait with you?"

Hesitating, Lizzie gave her a nod. If this lady knew her name, then she had to be telling the truth about knowing Cookie. Watching the lady sit down, Lizzie wondered how Cookie knew her.

"Forgive me for being rude, ma'am, but who are you?"

"Sorry, I should've introduced myself. I'm Margaret. I work at a place called the Penny-Pot. Cookie stopped by looking for Edward Teach. I told him Edward had just left and was headed to his ship."

"Edward Teach was at the Penny-Pot with you?"

"Like I said, I work there. It was good to see Edward, although it wasn't a good time for him to come to Philadelphia with Governor William Keith placing a warrant out for his arrest. He ordered a drink like he always does and asked for the *Boston News-Letter*, but he didn't seem quite right. We were discussing Stede Bonnet when John Martin came in. They left suddenly, something about an issue on the ship."

Before Lizzie could think of a response, the side door opened.

"M—Margaret?" Cookie stuttered. "What are ye doing here?"

"I wanted to see if everything was okay. Did you find Edward?"

Cookie's eyes darted to Lizzie. "Does she know?"

Lizzie realized they were hiding something. "Know what?"

"Uh—it doesn't matter," Cookie hesitated. "No, I didn't get to Captain in time. He and John hired a canoe to take them to the ship. I ran into Garret and Nathaniel on the docks with the last load of supplies. Garret said he'll get the items we purchased at the store while the others head back to the ship. They'll return for us."

"What are you keeping from me?" Lizzie persisted.

"I think she deserves an explanation," Margaret muttered.

"Nay," Cookie protested, shaking his head. "I've told Miss Lizzie everybody has skeletons. Captain will strangle me if I speak of his."

"Skeletons? I'm a friend of her father's. There's nothing wrong with her knowing about our friendship, Cookie."

The door to the examining room opened. Emerging, the doctor wiped his bloody hands on the white apron tied around his waist.

"His wound is severe, but I don't think any organs were punctured," Dr. Chadwick announced. "I've stitched him up and gave him pain medicine. Normally, I don't recommend my patients return to sea so soon, but this will have to be an exception. Like I told Edward earlier, it isn't safe to stay around with Governor Keith determined to arrest you. I'll show you what to do to the stitches, Joseph."

Cookie followed the doctor into the examining room, leaving Lizzie with Margaret. To her surprise, the lady grabbed her arm.

"Thank goodness he's okay. Look, dear, your father and I have known each other for years. Our friendship goes back to when I lived at Marcus Hook. He's told me about you. When Cookie came in and shared what happened I was concerned. It also gave me a chance to meet you. I tried to get word to Edward, but I guess he didn't get my warning to stay away. Pennsylvania is dangerous for pirates. Edward was acting odd, and I don't think it was because of Stede Bonnet."

Cookie and Dr. Chadwick exited the examining room supporting Jake. Standing, Lizzie and Margaret moved so that Jake could sit in a chair.

"Margaret, are you sick?" Dr. Chadwick inquired.

"No. Well, I came here on behalf of Edward," she admitted.

"Okay," the doctor responded. Looking at Lizzie he continued, "So, you're Edward's daughter. Your father mentioned you."

"Who is this lady?" Jake wanted to know.

"This is Margaret. She's a friend from the Penny-Pot. Doc, how long will Jake need to rest?" Cookie asked, changing the subject.

"A few weeks, so the stitches can heal," the doctor proclaimed. Handing Lizzie two large bottles of medicine he added, "Give him this for the pain three times a day. Change the bandages daily until you remove the stitches."

"Thanks a lot, Dr. Chadwick," Jake declared.

"Aye. We appreciate ye help, Doc," Cookie added.

"You're welcome. Joseph, it would be easier on Jake if you use my buggy. Come on, I'll help you hitch up my horse."

While Cookie and the doctor prepared the buggy, Lizzie bent in front of Jake who had closed his eyes as he held up his head.

"You're hurting, aren't you?" she whispered.

Jake nodded. "Yes, it's all I can bear. Doc said it might take a while for the medicine to relieve the pain. I'm light-headed, too."

Reentering the clinic, Dr. Chadwick and Cookie helped Jake stand and assisted him outside. Lizzie followed them with the medicine and bandages. Once Jake was in the buggy, the doctor spoke to Cookie.

"Remember, Joseph, he needs the pain medicine. It's crucial for his recovery. Hope you have safe travels."

"Are ye sure ye won't take any money?"

"I'm sure. Edward's a friend of mine."

"Thanks, Arnold. I'll get this buggy back to ye," Cookie promised.

"Don't worry about it," Margaret interrupted. "I'm going to ride with you to the docks. I can bring the buggy back to Dr. Chadwick."

"Sounds good. Be safe," Dr. Chadwick urged.

Cookie gave Margaret a weary look. Climbing into the back of the buggy, Lizzie waited for Margaret to join her. With Jake in the front seat, Cookie smacked his lips together and flicked the reins to coax the doctor's speckled horse onward. The black buggy lurched as the black and white horse clip-clopped down the cobblestone street.

Eventually, Lizzie spotted the sign for the Penny-Pot Tavern on the corner of Vine Street and Front Street. When her eyes saw the tiny building, she understood why her father went there. Unlike the chaotic area of Dock and Front Streets where the Blue Anchor Tavern was located, the Penny-Pot offered its guests a serene spot. Far from the busy wharf, the Penny-Pot was quiet, a perfect place for a wanted pirate to relax without the government coming to arrest him.

Passing the tavern, Lizzie wondered what secrets it held. Did her papa drink alone or was a lady friend always seated at his table? Glazing at Margaret's curly blonde hair and unusual outfit, she felt her mother wouldn't approve. Then again, maybe they were just friends.

By now, the buggy had reached bustling Front Street. Mingling with multitudes of sailors, they journeyed to the wharf, though it took awhile with all the people. Soon they came to the long wooden dock. Tying off the reins, Cookie helped Jake get down with Lizzie's assistance. They made their way down the dock with Jake while Margaret followed with his medicine and bandages. Nearing the end, Lizzie spotted Nathaniel and Garret waiting in the periauger. The two men assisted Jake into the boat as Cookie went back to the buggy. Retrieving a black-covered box, he rubbed the nose of the doctor's speckled horse and returned to the dock. Handing Nathaniel the box, Cookie shook Margaret's hand as she kissed him on his right cheek.

Turning, Margaret touched Lizzie's arm. "It was nice to finally meet you, dear. I hope your friend will have a quick recovery."

"Thanks. It was good to meet you, too, Miss Margaret."

Smiling, the mysterious lady walked away. Taking Cookie's hand, Lizzie climbed into the periauger and settled down beside Jake. Pushing the boat away from the dock, Cookie, Garret, and Nathaniel rowed toward the *Adventure*. Meanwhile, Lizzie gently pushed Jake's sweaty bangs out of his eyes, noticing that the pain medicine was beginning to have an effect. Watching him sleep, she thanked God he was okay.

Gazing back at the wharf, she could see Margaret maneuvering the horse-driven buggy through the crowd. She couldn't stop thinking about skeletons. What did Cookie mean? Was Margaret a skeleton of her papa's past? A while back, Cookie compared skeletons to sins. Were all skeletons equivalent to sins, or were some things you just wished to keep secret? It was all very confusing, and the fact her papa had seen the doctor was an even bigger puzzle. One thing was sure: her first trip to Philadelphia was certainly one she would never forget.

CHAPTER TEN

CRAFTY HANDS

August 15, 1718 ~ Friday

Raindrops beat against the windows of the captain's cabin as thunder boomed overhead, causing Lizzie to jump. The book she was reading fell to the floor. Bending to pick it up, she wondered if the storm was going to be bad and whether Cookie needed her in the galley. Earlier, Cookie insisted he had things under control, giving her time to finish sewing one of her new outfits. Completing it sooner than expected, Lizzie decided to read more of the book she found on her father's bookshelf. The worn, burgundy-covered book had been her companion while trying to get Jake's fever to break. Thankfully, he had recovered.

Turning the pages to where she'd stopped reading, Lizzie heard the door of the cabin squeak open, followed by Jake's voice calling her. Peeping around the door frame of her room, she leaned off her bed to get his attention. Seeing her, he walked over.

"Cookie didn't need me so I came to work on my new dress," she explained, sliding down to make room for him. "I finally finished it and decided to read for a while. I'm starting the blue dress next. Cookie said Mrs. Coates gave me the material after what happened. So, what are you up to? Is it raining yet? I heard thunder."

Sitting on the bed, Jake responded, "Yes, it's raining pretty hard. It drizzled off and on for over an hour. I was helping JJ fix some ropes, but when it started pouring, Black Beard told me to get inside."

"How's your side feeling?"

"The stitches are tender. Cookie thought they needed to stay in a few more days. The inside hurts when I bend to pick something up. At least I only have three more days of medicine. I'll be glad when I don't have to take it. The pain medicine makes me feel light-headed," Jake continued. "Is the book good?"

"Most of it is about life at sea, Spanish treasures, and the voyages of legendary buccaneers. It's entertaining, though I must admit rather gruesome. I found it on Papa's bookshelf," she answered.

"What's it called?"

"*The Buccaneers of America* by Alexander Exquemelin. He was a Frenchman who published it in English in 1684. From what I understand, the author sailed with several buccaneers. Supposedly it's true. Right now, I'm on chapter four of part two, reading about Sir Henry Morgan. If Papa read this when he was young, I can see how he got into treasure hunting. It's exciting to read about adventures."

"I've heard of it. There are many stories about Henry Morgan and other buccaneers like Henry Avery, Sir Francis Drake, and Captain William Kidd. In today's terms, they would be pirates. Captain William Kidd hung in London for his piracy crimes. On his first hanging the rope broke so they had to do it again. An old sailor shared with me the details of Captain Kidd's hanging. After he hung at the gallows, they tied his body to a post to wash in three tides before putting tar on him and placing his body in a gibbet or iron cage hanging over the harbor. This was done to warn other pirates," Jake informed her.

"Do they still tar pirates today?"

"There are rumors of it still happening, but rumors aren't always true. I've heard rumors about Black Beard. So far, they've been false."

"What rumors have you heard about Papa?"

"Never mind, I shouldn't have mentioned it," he muttered.

"You might as well tell me."

Jake hesitated. "I heard Black Beard tortures his victims by whipping them and cutting off their fingers or ears. Supposedly, he has murdered entire crews just for fun. JJ told me it wasn't true. Unlike many pirate captains, Black Beard has never killed anyone though he has been known to severely wound them. He prefers to scare his victims until they give up their possessions."

"Is that it?" she asked, feeling he wasn't telling everything.

"He's known to have fourteen wives," he said awkwardly.

"Fourteen wives?"

"After discovering you're his daughter, I find it hard to believe he has had thirteen other wives since your mother died. It's possible he married again or has girlfriends. Being out at sea for so long can make a man lonely. Still, I find it hard to believe."

"I can't believe it either. Papa told me Momma lost a child when I was little. He blames himself for the accident. You would think he wouldn't care if he had thirteen other wives," Lizzie declared, wondering if Margaret was one of the women in his life. Cookie's skeleton concept crept into her mind, reminding her of another possible skeleton this time in Jake's life in the form of nightmares. "I don't mean to be nosy, but when you were so weak you talked in your sleep."

"I probably snored quite a bit, too. JJ says I sound like I'm sawing logs," Jake chuckled. "What did I talk about?"

"You seemed to be in a nightmare since you were breathing hard. I was able to make out the name Gabrielle. Wasn't she your sister?"

The expression on Jake's face changed. He clearly knew what the nightmares were about.

"She was my youngest sister. Guess the medicine made me delirious. I haven't dreamed about the attack in years," he mumbled.

"I don't remember Gabrielle. Most of the time I played with Bridget. She and Trent were a year younger than me. Alice and Rebecca played with your sister Eleanor," Lizzie replied.

"Gabrielle was always with Ma. She turned one in May before the Indian attack in September."

"I know you miss them. Sometimes I forget how hard your life has been. I lost Momma, but you lost your entire family in one day."

"September will be seven years since the attack," Jake commented. "It took me a long time to sleep without nightmares. For a ten-year-old it was hard. I never felt like I could talk to anyone about it. Eventually I came to the assumption God didn't care because He allowed it to happen."

"Do you still believe God doesn't care?"

"I did until recently. Between the shark incident and what happened in Philadelphia I'm beginning to wonder. Every time something happens you talk to God. He seems to listen to your prayers like He did my mother's. I don't know what to think," he admitted.

"They say it helps to talk things out, especially if you've kept it bottled up for years. I'm a good listener if you need to talk."

Jake stared at the floor. Wanting him to know she was just offering support, Lizzie decided to rephrase her words.

"What I meant to say was I'm here if you need a friend."

"I know," he murmured. "Maybe you're right." Leaning forward, he propped his chin on his hands and took a deep breath. "I remember going to the barn that morning with Pa. The sun was barely up, but we were already outside feeding the animals and milking the cow. Ma was cooking breakfast. When I gathered eggs from the chicken coop, I saw something moving in the bushes by the outhouse. Pa had said bears were killing hogs, so I snuck back to the barn to get him. He told me to keep an eye out while he got his shotgun from the fireplace. After he left, I spotted an Indian hiding behind a tree."

Getting emotional, Jake paused to gather himself.

"I ran to the house to tell Pa. He helped Ma and the girls get into the attic. I got the gun Pa gave me to shoot squirrels and helped him close the window shutters. The Indians were circling the house, hollering like crows. We slid furniture in front of the door. Pa told me to hide. I ran and got under their bed, taking my gun with me. Then I heard the Indians come into the house. Pa started shooting, but there were too many. I climbed out the window to get help, but got scared and crawled under the house between the rock foundation," Jake recounted, stopping to wipe the tears from his eyes.

"I found myself sitting in my favorite hiding spot by the rock fireplace where I would go to avoid a spanking. From there, I could hear the Indians yelling and the screams of my mother and sisters. I sat frozen in fear, listening to the horrible sounds and begging God to save us. After the Indians left, I crawled out to find our chickens, hogs, horses, and cow butchered. They destroyed the garden and burned the barn. I called out to my family, but no one answered."

By now, Lizzie was wiping her own tears. She had no idea how terrible a burden Jake had been carrying.

"All of them were murdered. Those savages even killed our dog. Pa was on the floor with arrows through his chest while Ma was slumped in her rocking chair. They lined the girls up against the wall and put their rag dolls in their hands. It was like the Indians staged the scene for spite. I ran to the plantation where your uncle lived. He went to our house with a group of men to search the woods. There was nothing they could do except bury the animals. Mr. Lee also helped me bury my folks," he finished.

"After you stayed with Uncle Jared, who did you live with?" Lizzie inquired, as her mind drifted to her uncle's death, which was probably like the horrible deaths of Jake's family.

"I stayed with Mr. Lee three days before the second attack occurred. He sent the women and children up the Neuse River to the nearest fort in New Bern. The men who were too old to fight went with us. I ended up living with an older couple named Joseph and Elizabeth Bowden. Having no children of their own, they treated me like a son during the four years I stayed with them. The captain I apprenticed under was a friend of Mr. Bowden's. When we returned to port, I always visited them. Looking back, I suppose God put them there for me. In January when I turned seventeen and my apprenticeship was over, I went to see them. Mr. Bowden died last summer from heart trouble. Mrs. Bowden was glad to see me and begged me to stay, but I felt like I needed to go out on my own. I promised to come back to see her one day," Jake declared.

"So, you decided to come to Bath."

"Yes, and now I'm a pirate," he joked as his stomach growled.

Lizzie smiled. "Sounds like you're hungry. Let's go to the galley. Cookie should have dinner ready."

"Okay," Jake agreed, standing up.

"Oh, I forgot to return your shirt," she said, handing him the folded, cream-colored material. "I managed to get the blood out and stitched up the hole."

"Thanks, Lizzie, and thank you for listening."

Leaving the captain's cabin, Lizzie followed Jake out into the rain. Scurrying down the stairs to the galley, she could hear Cookie talking. Entering the room, she realized he was talking to his newest companion, the beautiful parrot he acquired in Philadelphia. As it turned out, the black-covered box Cookie got from the horse-drawn buggy contained this parrot. According to him, the bird had belonged to Dr. Chadwick, who received the parrot from an elderly lady as payment for his care. The parrot annoyed Dr. Chadwick's wife, Ethel, with its constant squawking, so he had to keep her in his horse shed. When Cookie went with him to the horse shed, he saw the parrot and asked about her. Dr. Chadwick offered the bird to him.

The green-feathered bird bobbed its bright red head up and down as it walked across the oak table. Lizzie couldn't stop laughing as Cookie mimicked her. Jake stood in the doorway shaking his head.

"Ye are a pretty girl, Reba," Cookie praised the bird.

"Reba pretty girl! Reba pretty girl!" squawked the parrot.

"Talking to your girlfriend, Cookie?" Jake teased, reaching out his finger to rub the parrot.

Surprisingly, the red and green parrot fluffed up her feathers as she attempted to bite Jake's finger. He pulled back just in time.

"It wouldn't be wise to rub her. She already nipped at JJ and got blood," Cookie warned. "She hasn't lashed out at me. I was amazed to discover she knows a few tricks. If I can teach her to do them by command, perhaps she can entertain us."

"What's for dinner?" Lizzie wanted to know.

"Corned beef, peas, and boiled cackle-fruit. Why don't ye get plates? Ye can eat with me before the crowd comes in. I'll join ye after I tell Captain dinner is ready. Don't let Tuffy mess with Reba," Cookie instructed as he started up the stairs.

Grabbing a pewter plate, Lizzie spooned corned beef and peas onto it. Picking up some cackle-fruit, better known as boiled eggs, she gave it to Jake. As he took the plates to the table, Lizzie filled pewter cups with water. She left Cookie's cup empty knowing he would probably drink his usual toddy for the body as he called it.

Sitting down, Lizzie prayed over the food. They began to eat as Cookie returned dripping wet from the rain. After drying off, he sat down in the chair beside Jake.

"Cookie, I've been meaning to ask you something. Jake's joke about Reba being your girlfriend reminded me that Miss Margaret kissed you on your cheek when we left Philadelphia. Are you and Miss Margaret just friends?" Lizzie inquired.

"Aye, she's a friend," Cookie replied, suddenly tensing up.

"A kiss? Sounds like a sweetheart to me," Jake blurted out.

"Sweetheart? Nay, nay, nay," Cookie said, shaking his head.

"Is she *just* a friend of Papa's, too?"

"I've said too much," Cookie mumbled.

"Miss Margaret talked about the governor's plans to arrest Papa. Her concern seemed to go beyond a casual friendship. I just want the truth. Is she Papa's girlfriend?" Lizzie persisted.

Cookie stared at his food. "I don't know. When we go up north, Captain always stops in Pennsylvania. Everyone on this ship knows he likes to visit the Penny-Pot Tavern and most of us have seen him in Margaret's company. There's a joke among the men about her being his sweetheart, but I'm not sure. They've spent many hours alone at the table in the corner of the tavern. She was born in Sweden but grew up at a place called Marcus Hook. Ye will have to ask him."

Marcus Hook sounded familiar to Lizzie. She struggled to remember where she heard it besides when Margaret mentioned it herself. Finally, she recalled her father talking about it when he shared how he got his nickname. He apprenticed under Richard Thatcher who sailed out of the township Marcus Hook. Did her papa have feelings for Margaret before he met her mother? Many questions filled Lizzie's mind as she considered how close her father was to this lady. She started to ask Cookie how long he had known Margaret when voices drifted from the stairs.

Turning, Lizzie spotted Jake's friend, JJ Brooks, coming down the stairs with a stream of crew members. As the men formed a line for their dinner, Cookie quickly finished his food so that he could serve them. Scraping her plate, Lizzie put the dirty dishes in the wooden bucket Cookie washed them in. Jake assisted Cookie with the food while Lizzie poured rum. She noticed her papa at the end of the line listening to his quartermaster, Thomas. Watching him, she realized how skinny he was getting. In fact, he looked sickly. Perhaps he was sick. After all, Dr. Chadwick had seen him.

Her mind drifted to the conversation they had when she returned to the *Adventure* after the events in Philadelphia. He had been concerned about the three young men who attacked her, but when she talked about arriving at Dr. Chadwick's office, he became disturbed. His reaction got worse when she mentioned Margaret and his visit to the doctor. He didn't share an explanation and had since been quiet.

By now, the line had dwindled as the pirates sat at the table to eat. When her papa came up, Lizzie offered him a cup of water.

"I'll have rum like everyone else," he requested.

Despite the fact his breath already smelled of rum, Lizzie poured him some. She knew he had been drinking more since they left Pennsylvania, but there wasn't much she could do about it. As he reached to take it from her, she noticed tiny red specks like a rash on the back of his hand. Although worried, she said nothing, promising herself she would talk to him about it later.

Soon, the crew had eaten their dinner. Before they returned to their duties, the black-haired Israel Hands stood up. Banging his spoon against his pewter cup, he got his comrades' attention.

"I have something to say!" he bellowed.

"What is it, Israel?" Black Beard demanded from his seat.

The room grew quiet as the men looked from Israel to their captain. Lizzie suddenly felt uneasy.

"As sailing master, my responsibility is the condition of this ship. She's in bad shape and needs careening. Others agree, it's time to fix her up," Israel proclaimed.

"True, but we don't have supplies," Black Beard countered.

"We can sail down to Bermuda and capture a ship," Israel shot back. "Then we'll take the *Adventure* to a remote place like Ocracoke Island to careen her."

Outbursts erupted, causing Lizzie to jump in fright. Seeing the commotion getting out of hand, Cookie pulled Lizzie aside as Black Beard stood up to regain control over his crew.

"Miss Lizzie, I think ye should go," he whispered.

"I'll go with you," Jake commented.

"Nay, ye need to stay here. Ye are a member of the crew," Cookie murmured, motioning for Lizzie to hurry.

Glancing at Jake, Lizzie started up the stairs leading to the main deck. When she was halfway up, she squatted on the stairs to eavesdrop on the conversation down below.

"Settle down, fighting is against the ship's articles," Black Beard yelled. The ruckus calmed down enough for the pirate captain to continue. "Israel, have ye forgotten the pardon ye signed pledging ye will no longer dabble in piracy? Breaking such an oath will put us in danger of hanging at the gallows."

"No one will know. It's a perfect plan," Israel urged.

"I don't like going against our pardons. It's too risky to challenge another ship with so little gunpowder. We can still go to Ocracoke and patch the *Adventure* with tar," Black Beard said.

"Don't be hardheaded, Captain. I motion to hold a vote. The articles state we're allowed a vote on such matters unless in battle."

Black Beard didn't respond right away, but when he did, Lizzie sensed uneasiness in his voice. "Very well, those in favor of Israel's idea say, 'Aye.' Those against it say, 'Nay.'"

A clamor of mixed voices answered their captain. Lizzie was unable to decipher between the two parties. Apparently, her father didn't have any trouble sorting it out.

"The nays have it. We'll keep a southwesterly course to Ocracoke," Black Beard resolved as chairs slid across the floor, signaling they were getting up.

"Wait," Israel stopped them. "I couldn't hear which side won. Captain, it's only fair to hold a written vote. A lot of ye can't write ye name, but a mark of x or o will do. Cookie, we need paper."

"I don't take orders from ye," Cookie snapped.

"Fetch the paper, Cookie," Black Beard grunted. "The outcome of the written vote will be the final decision."

Everything was quiet as the crew voted for the second time. Anxious to hear the results, Lizzie held out her fingers counting the votes as her papa read them off. After the last one, she looked down at her hands. To her horror, Israel won by one vote.

"Captain, looks like we're headed south," Israel mocked.

Instead of waiting for her papa's reaction, Lizzie got up and climbed the remaining steps. Trying not to slip on the saturated deck, she went inside the captain's quarters and found a rag for drying herself off. Hearing the door open, she looked up to see Jake coming in.

"I can't believe they voted to steal a ship," she blurted out.

"How do you know about the vote?"

"I overheard it from the stairway," she confirmed, handing Jake the rag as he shook his head.

"Couldn't resist, huh?"

"I thought it was important to listen. I assume you voted."

"Yes, I didn't want them to think I wasn't one of the crew. It's the first time I voted. I'm surprised so many agreed with Israel."

"Why did Papa allow Israel to take over? He's the captain."

"From what JJ has told me everyone gets a vote. It isn't like the merchant ships I served on or the Royal Navy ships where the captains make the decisions. Black Beard didn't have a choice. He could get demoted if he denied Israel a legal vote."

"What do you mean?"

"Usually, the crew votes with the captain. Black Beard made his opinion clear. Israel must have worked on the crew for days to get so many on his side. Because of the split, this could cause a dangerous situation. I'm concerned we might get killed if there's a battle."

"I haven't even thought about dying!"

"Israel could also convince the others to hold a vote for a new captain. My guess is he's preparing to take over. His plan to get most of the crew on his side was quite crafty, like a seasoned chess player. The good thing is he made the first move, which means your pa will be watching him. Some will stand behind Black Beard. They won't let him take command without a fight."

"There are twenty-two men on this ship, and half are willing to forfeit their pardons. I understand we need supplies, but stealing will make things worse. There will be people on the ship they're planning to capture. What will happen to them? Israel said no one will know."

"He probably plans to kill them. Just because Black Beard hasn't killed his victims doesn't mean Israel won't. Things have changed."

"But what about the pardons?"

"They're pirates, so they crave the excitement. The ones who voted with Israel are hoping to find treasure. Last night, JJ and I overheard Thomas and Garret talking about Stede Bonnet," Jake revealed.

"Wait. Miss Margaret mentioned him when she told me Papa went to the Penny-Pot Tavern."

"He was in the headlines of the *Boston News-Letter*. Thomas Miller must have read it. He told Garret about a reported sighting of Stede Bonnet's ship along with three others. They were capturing ships in the Delaware Bay. Governor Keith planned to stop him. We had to pass his ship during the night when we came into the bay."

"Stede Bonnet must be a pretty important person."

"JJ told me Stede Bonnet sailed with Black Beard before his flagship, *Queen Anne's Revenge*, wrecked. Stede had his own ship called the *Revenge*, but he wasn't much of a leader. Most of the crew thought he was crazy. He received injuries in battle and for the next few months stayed in his cabin. When he did come out, he was always in his nightgown with one of his books. He had a very large library onboard."

"Why is he so important if he no longer sails with Papa?"

"Because Black Beard purposely wrecked *Queen Anne's Revenge* to get rid of Stede and his followers. As soon as Stede realized they ran aground, he went to Bath with a group of his men to receive pardons from Governor Eden. While he was gone, Black Beard abandoned the rest of the crew and set sail on the *Adventure*. Stede was furious when he returned and has sworn to seek revenge on Black Beard."

"Thank God he didn't spot us in the bay. Sounds like Mr. Bonnet would've attacked. Still, I can't understand why half the crew doesn't care about the pardons," Lizzie replied.

"Maybe they don't want to change. Black Beard and his closest friends decided to go to Bath for the pardons. The question is why did he wait so long? JJ said they captured a ship near Puerto Rico last December. After interviewing the ship's crew, they learned about King George's recent pardon. Strangely, Black Beard ignored the information. They kept capturing prize ships until Black Beard decided to blockade Charles Town for a chest of medicine."

"That sounds strange. Do you think Papa is sick?"

"I don't know. It's odd he only asked for a chest of medicine when he could have had anything he wanted. JJ informed me there was a French doctor onboard from a captured ship. Something caused Black Beard to dump Bonnet before coming to Bath."

"Dr. Chadwick mentioned seeing Papa. He's been drinking more and appears to be losing weight. I noticed he has a rash on his hands."

"There are all kinds of diseases sailors get after prolonged voyages. Between the worms getting into the food and the bad living conditions, he was bound to get something. It might be scurvy, the disease caused from lack of fresh fruit. Those who suffer from it lose weight and sometimes lose teeth. Don't worry. I'm sure the doctor gave him some medicine if he's sick."

Thinking about her papa's illness, Lizzie sent up a prayer for him. She also asked God to protect and forgive them for the act of piracy the crew was planning under the leadership of the deceitful, but crafty Israel Hands. Jake was right: Israel Hands was dangerous.

CHAPTER ELEVEN

☠

DEATH'S HEAD

August 22, 1718 ~ Friday

Anxiousness caused Lizzie to feel as though butterflies were in her stomach. With each passing day, she felt worse knowing the *Adventure* would eventually cross paths with another ship, one the crew planned to capture. Besides the moral reasons for her edginess, Lizzie couldn't shake the comment Jake made. She fervently prayed the coming battle wouldn't result in their death.

"Are ye alright, Miss Lizzie?" Cookie questioned.

Blinking, Lizzie noticed him staring at her with concern. Deep in thought, she suddenly realized she had neglected her mopping.

"I'm sorry, Cookie, my mind keeps drifting."

"Ye should take a break. We've been working hard since dawn. I can finish," Cookie suggested as he looked around the galley.

"Maybe I should go get a little fresh air. Thanks, Cookie."

Putting her mop away, Lizzie grabbed her tricorn hat and climbed the stairs. As she stepped on the wooden deck, the bright sunshine beamed down from the cloudless blue sky. Gazing over the deck, she searched the faces of the crew members who were busily carrying out their duties. She spotted Jake sitting on a crate near the port side of the ship. His brown-haired friend JJ Brooks sat beside him. Walking over to them, Lizzie saw they were working with rope.

"Hello," she declared, causing them to look up. "I was just getting some fresh air. Would it be okay if I sat down?"

Jake greeted her with a smile. "Sure."

Sitting down beside Jake, Lizzie pointed to the round, wooden tool Jake was using to undo the rope. "What is that?"

"It's a fid. We use it to splice the individual pieces of hemp rope. Loops are made by rejoining the ends," Jake explained.

Lizzie watched them work the metal point of the fid into their ropes, noticing how young JJ was. "How old are you, JJ?"

JJ glanced up at her. "Um, I'll be eighteen in December."

"I turned seventeen in January," Jake mentioned.

"Aren't you sort of young to be a pirate?" Lizzie implied.

"Sailors start young. Ma died from having a baby when I was eight. She lost several children. At the time, we had just moved north of Bath Town. After she died, we sold our homestead and returned to Charles Town where Pa was originally from. He worked at the shipyard until everyone lost their jobs. The Royal Navy came looking for sailors, promising good pay. Pa got lucky and landed a job with the navy. They hired me as a cabin boy doing odd jobs. Life in the Royal Navy was rough. Food was terrible and they never paid us. The captain got mad and whipped me with a cat-o'-nine tails until I bled. When Pa tried to stop him, the captain whipped him, too," JJ revealed.

"Why didn't you leave?" Lizzie asked.

"We tried," JJ acknowledged. "Our ship was captured by a pirate fleet called the Old Flying Gang. Three captains named Benjamin Hornigold, Samuel 'Black Sam' Bellamy, and Edward 'Black Beard' Teach led the group. They captured three hundred ships, never killing a soul. We joined the Old Flying Gang, giving up our slavery for the freedom piracy offered. Hornigold split ways with Teach and Bellamy. That's when we joined Black Beard's crew. Turns out Pa knew Captain as a child and spent many afternoons fishing with him."

Lizzie's jaw dropped in astonishment. "What?"

"Black Beard likes to keep his previous life secret. Pa feels it's safer for us if the others don't know. He woke me last night and brought me out on deck to tell me ye are Black Beard's daughter in case something happened. I had no idea."

Before Lizzie could respond, someone yelled, causing the three of them to look up. Thinking the worst, Lizzie suddenly felt fearful. Thankfully, another voice calmed her pounding heart.

"There's a spout!"

"Somebody spotted a whale. Come on, maybe we can see it," JJ urged as he led the way to the bow of the ship.

Thrilled to see an animal she had only read about, Lizzie followed them as they leaned on the railing to look for the giant beast. Gazing into the greenish-blue water, she saw the majestic creature rise out of the waves. Nearly the same size as the *Adventure*, the gray whale sent up a spray of water from the hole on top of its square-shaped head. With a slap of its massive tail, the whale dove into the mysterious deep.

"Wow!" Lizzie breathed.

"Isn't it a beauty? Sperm whales are the most common whale, but I've seen a few other kinds. When they come up from the depths of the sea, they breathe out air, causing the big blow of mist from their blowholes. Have ye seen one, Jake?" JJ wanted to know.

"No, but I've heard about them."

A shout sounded from up in the sails. Holding up her hand to block the blinding sunshine, Lizzie gazed into the rigging. She spotted Israel Hands in his red shirt as he stood on a beam holding onto the mast. Below him, several pirates pointed at the southern horizon. Looking to the south, she saw two objects in the distance.

"We've got a prize!" Israel hollered, climbing down the ratlines.

Several crew members cheered as others exchanged looks of concern. Hearing the commotion, Black Beard walked out of his cabin. After Quartermaster Thomas briefed him, the pirate captain headed for the ladder leading up to the cabin roof. He pulled his spyglass out of his long black coat and studied the object in the horizon. Clenching his jaw, he put down the spyglass and addressed the crew.

"French flags are flying in their rigging," he announced, sliding the interlocking pieces of his spyglass together. "Prepare for battle."

The crew dispersed, scrambling around like ants. Climbing down from the cabin roof, Black Beard came over to JJ, Jake, and Lizzie.

"JJ, go tell Cookie about the French ships," he ordered.

"Aye, aye, Captain," JJ affirmed as he ran to find the cook.

Looking at Lizzie and Jake, Black Beard continued, "Come with me. We have some things to discuss."

Glancing at Jake, Lizzie followed her papa to his cabin. As Black Beard closed the door behind them, he went to a chest behind his desk. He pulled a key from his coat pocket to unlock it.

"Jake, how accurate can ye shoot?" he questioned.

"I've got decent aim. Pa taught me to shoot at the age of nine."

Black Beard handed Jake a pistol and a small box. Returning to the chest, her papa brought back a large belt covered with ammunition. Placing it on his desk, he went back for six more pistols.

"Good. Typically, the action stays on the captured ship, but if things get out of hand they'll come aboard. Have ye killed a man?"

Lizzie gasped. "This is crazy! It's bad enough you're stealing a ship and possibly committing murder. You can't expect Jake to kill, too."

"Lizzie," Jake began.

"What? You aren't a pirate!" she objected angrily.

"Ye don't understand, Lizzie. I need to know if he can kill a man should the need arise," Black Beard explained.

"I'll do whatever in self-defense," Jake proclaimed.

"Ye proved that in Philadelphia. Hopefully, ye won't have to. I try to capture ships without killing anyone, but I can't predict how they'll react. I haven't had to kill a soul yet, and I don't plan to start today."

"What should I do when the fighting starts?" Jake asked.

Black Beard rubbed his beard. "I won't ask ye to fight, but the others might question ye loyalty since ye signed on as a pirate. Ye life might be in danger if they think ye are a traitor. I know ye don't agree with this, and I'm sorry ye are involved. The best I can do is keep ye on the *Adventure*. Here's some black gunpowder and ammunition. As for ye, Lizzie, staying here in the roundhouse will be the safest place. I'm leaving ye with a pistol. Have ye ever learned how to shoot?"

"Uncle Thomas tried to teach me last year when he taught Trent. He thought it would be good for me to learn even though Aunt Grace was against it at first. It was hard to hit the blackberry-stained cloth we were aiming at," she answered.

"At least ye know the fundamentals. I hope ye won't need a pistol, but I don't like leaving ye unprotected," he commented as he slid back the chair behind his desk and knelt on the floor.

Intrigued by his bizarre behavior, Lizzie watched him pry up the board. Her papa extended his hand into a cubby beneath the floorboards and lifted out a small wooden box. Raising the box lid, Black Beard pulled out a silver flintlock pistol and handed it to her.

"This belonged to ye grandfather. I began carrying it when he died and keep it with some other personal things. It's sentimental."

"Uncle Thomas taught me how to shoot a shotgun, not a pistol."

"Alright, I'll fill ye in on the basics. First, set the lock to the safety position at half-cock. Pour black gunpowder from this flask down the barrel and pull out the ramrod from underneath the barrel. Take a bullet wrapped in patch cloth and ram it down the barrel with the ramrod. Next, put gunpowder into the priming pan. Close the pan cover and set the lock to full-cock position, aim, and pull the trigger."

"I don't know if I can remember all that," she mumbled, staring at the flintlock pistol in her shaky hands.

"If ye can't figure it out, whack ye enemy with the brass butt of the pistol," he encouraged. "Jake, I'm also giving ye a musket and a cutlass. When firing the musket don't push the ramrod with ye hand. Use ye pinkie. Men have lost their hands because the gun went off too soon. Losing a finger won't cripple ye. Do ye need a dagger?"

"No, sir, I have my hunting knife."

"While I put on my bandolier, look in the chest and bring me the *Adventure*'s flag," Black Beard requested.

As Jake walked to the chest, Black Beard put on a fancy red coat before adding the black leather bandolier. The broad belt crossed his body from his right shoulder to his left side and had small pockets where he put ammunition. He tucked six loaded flintlock pistols in the belt, strapped it in place, and grabbed his three-cornered hat.

Jake returned carrying a folded black cloth. "Is this it?"

"Aye," Black Beard confirmed, grabbing the pistol from Lizzie. "Ye can take it to Garret while I talk to Thomas about our strategy. Lizzie, I'm putting the pistol in the top drawer. Cookie may need ye help until we get closer to the ships."

Lizzie followed Jake and her papa out of the captain's cabin. Walking onto the deck, she could see the crew of pirates hard at work. She spotted Cookie coming up with an armload of weapons. Startled to see so many guns and swords, she approached Cookie cautiously.

"Wow," Lizzie breathed. "Where have you been storing all these? I didn't know there were so many weapons on board."

Dumping his load, Cookie looked at her. "Ever since the swordfight incident Thomas started keeping them in the storage hold. Ye look worried, Miss Lizzie. I'll do everything I can to protect ye."

"Thanks. Captain gave me a pistol, but I don't know if I can use it. I was surprised to see him with so many. Why does he need six?"

"Flintlock pistols were invented in France by Martin Le Bourgeoys about a century ago. They're effective when fighting at close range, but take too long to reload. Imagine being in a fight. Ye stop to refill ye gun with gunpowder, get a lead bullet out of the patch box, ram it down the bore, and pour more gunpowder in the priming pan. By then, ye enemy would've killed ye with his sword. Captain isn't the only one who carries multiple pistols. We do it so we can fire again with another gun. When we've shot each of them, we use the brass butt of the gun as a club. If all else fails, we draw our cutlass or small knife called a dagger," Cookie explained.

"Do you think it'll be a bloody battle?"

"Most battles result in injuries, but hopefully no one will get any serious wounds. We need their ships for repairs, which is why our gunner, Philip Morton, will use grenades. He'll move the cannons to the portholes on either side of the sleeping quarters as a decoy. A cannon blast would tear a hole in the side of their vessel. Although it wouldn't sink their ship, it may cause damage to parts we can use. Philip plans to shoot a few cannonballs into the water to scare them. We'll throw the grenades onto the deck. Later, Philip will load the cannons with swan shot, a mixture of old pieces of iron and nails."

"What are those for?" Lizzie inquired, pointing to a pair of arrow-shaped iron hooks attached to ropes.

"They're grappling irons. We use the hooks to pull the ship close so we can board it. The four barbed hooks grip the wooden hull."

"Won't we be in trouble if someone sees us attack the two French ships? What if the Royal Navy finds out?"

Cookie nodded. "We should be seven hundred miles off the Carolina coast. The main issue will be when we take it to Ocracoke. It'll be safer even though the nearest land is the island of Bermuda."

Inhaling deeply to calm her nerves, Lizzie watched Jake and Garret Gibbons as they unfolded the black flag. Once they secured the flag to the rope, the two of them hoisted it into the rigging.

"What kind of flag flies over the *Adventure*, Cookie?"

"Some call it Death's Head while others call it the Jolly Roger. We fly a black flag at the last moment as a warning to surrender or face death. Not all pirates fly the same flag, but almost all of them have a black background. Legend has it that the name Jolly Roger is a reference to Old Roger, a nickname for the devil. I heard it's from the French word *joli rouge*, meaning red flag. Death's Head flags are meant to strike fear in the hearts of those who lay eyes on it."

Lizzie noticed a white skull sewn on the black material. "Why is there a skeleton on it?"

"The skull and crossbones are a symbol of death."

"Cookie," JJ's father, Joseph Brooks, interrupted them. "Thomas told me to let ye know we're within shooting range."

"Come on, Miss Lizzie. Ye can tend to Tuffy and Reba. I'll be back as soon as I can, Joseph," Cookie responded.

"Captain said we're going to defend the *Adventure* while the crew boards the ships. JJ and Jake will help us. Don't take long with those animals," Joseph declared, grabbing his weapons.

Going downstairs behind Cookie, Lizzie tried to calm her nerves. Coming into the galley, Reba's unmistakable greeting filled her ears.

"Cookie! Cookie!" the red and green bird squawked.

"I'm here, Reba. Miss Lizzie will be taking care of ye."

"Reba pretty girl!" the parrot shrieked.

Cookie chuckled. "Ye are a pretty girl. Now where's Tuffy?"

"Here she is," Lizzie said, picking up the black cat, which came from underneath the table where she had been napping.

"Good, I assume ye are staying in Captain's cabin," Cookie stated, allowing Reba to climb on his shoulder.

"Yes, he said it would be safer," she replied.

Following Cookie and Reba, Lizzie carried Tuffy to the deck. By now, the crew was grabbing swords and guns in a frenzy. Without stopping, Cookie entered the cabin and put Reba on a chair.

"Stay safe, Miss Lizzie, and don't let Tuffy eat Reba."

"I'll do my best," she promised. Touching his sleeve with her fingertips she added, "I'm praying for all of you."

Cookie gave her a nod, obviously too touched to speak. Leaving, he went back on deck as Lizzie peeped out of the open door. Searching the familiar faces, she recognized Jake's light brown hair headed toward her. Looking past him at her papa, she understood why many feared him. Black Beard looked like a wild man with his long red coat, six guns strapped to his chest, and sword hanging from his belt. Lizzie suddenly felt worried as reality set in. Whether she liked it or not, she was Black Beard's daughter. His reputation for being brutal was something she may have to live with.

"Ahoy there!" Black Beard bellowed in his brass, cone-shaped speaking trumpet. "Who are ye and from whence have ye come?"

"Get inside and put a chair under the door latch," Jake muttered.

"I will. Be careful, Jake."

Backing away from the door, Lizzie propped a chair under the latch. She got Grandfather Beard's flintlock pistol out of the desk drawer. Picking up a box of ammunition, she coaxed Reba to jump on her shoulder. Entering her room, she let Reba hop on the chair in the corner and sat on her bed as Tuffy pounced up beside her.

"This isn't good, Tuffy," she sighed, rubbing the cat's ears.

Boom! Boom! Boom!

Cannon fire echoed through the cabin followed by a sudden shifting of the *Adventure*'s hull. The noise spooked Tuffy, who scratched Lizzie's arm as she bounded off the bed to go hide while Reba screeched in fear. Drawing up her knees, Lizzie inspected her injured arm as another round of cannons went off.

Praying with all her might, Lizzie listened to the gunshots, cannon fire, and men hollering as the ships fought. Her mind drifted to her family. More than anything, Lizzie wished she and Jake were at home instead of in this predicament. Lizzie hoped her aunt had gotten the letter she sent her from Pennsylvania.

Suddenly, everything was quiet. Tuffy slowly came out from under the bed as Reba started squawking again. Wondering if it was over, Lizzie went to the next room. Moving the chair from underneath the door latch, she opened the door and peeped through the crack. She noticed the grappling iron hooks connecting the *Adventure* and one of the French ships, but otherwise the deck appeared empty. Cautiously stepping outside, she closed the door behind her to keep the cat and bird from escaping. A man fell from the roof and landed in front of her. Screaming as he grabbed her, Lizzie tried to get away.

Asking God for help, she was relieved to see JJ and Jake jump the railings between the French ship and the *Adventure*. JJ drew his sword and fought the Frenchman, who withdrew his own sword.

"Get back!" Jake shouted as a loud bang echoed across the deck.

Gasping, Lizzie spotted JJ sprawled on the deck and the Frenchman standing over him with a smoking pistol. She covered her face, fearing the worst. Judging by the sword in JJ's hand, it looked like he won the swordfight, but didn't realize the Frenchman had a gun.

Jake snatched the loose sword from the deck. Armed with JJ's sword, the Frenchman attacked Jake with the same vigor with which he fought JJ. As their swords clashed in a flurry of clanging metal, Lizzie prayed Jake would win. She felt ashamed as she considered her motives. To win the battle, Jake would have to kill the Frenchman. Overwhelmed with conflicting emotions, Lizzie begged God to forgive her for the evil thoughts of revenge.

Moving to the center of the ship, Jake did a surprisingly good job keeping his more experienced opponent at bay. As they danced around with swords clanging, Lizzie scurried over to JJ's body. Falling to her knees, she placed her fingers against his neck to feel for a heartbeat. Amazingly, he was unconscious but still alive. Lizzie untied the navy-blue neckerchief he wore around his neck and used the cloth to put pressure on his wounded shoulder. She held it tight, trying to stop the gushing blood. Suddenly, sounds of cannons and pistols went off again as the *Adventure* rocked. Guessing the pirates had engaged with the other French ship, Lizzie wondered how many were dead. With her hands covered in blood, she prayed for God to spare their lives.

To Lizzie's horror, another Frenchman jumped over the railings between the ships. Glancing around for a weapon to protect herself, she was grateful when JJ's father, Joseph, came bounding over the railings after the intruder. The two men engaged in a wrestling match. Watching them fistfight a few yards from where she and JJ were, she noticed Cookie climbing back onto the *Adventure*. She waved at him to get his attention when Jake hollered.

Looking to see if he was okay, Lizzie's heart jumped when she saw him fall to the deck. Dropping his sword, Jake held the upper part of his left arm as he knelt on his knees in front of his opponent. The Frenchman prepared to slash Jake again when Cookie whacked the man on the back of the head with the butt of his pistol. Joseph also managed to clobber his challenger. With both Frenchmen knocked out, Cookie tied them up while Joseph and Jake came to check on JJ.

"Is he—?" Joseph mumbled, unable to finish his question.

"He's alive, but barely," Lizzie told him. "I've tried to stop the bleeding, but it's pretty bad."

"Cookie! Hurry! JJ needs you," Jake called out.

"I'm coming," Cookie declared, rushing over to them.

Bending down, the pirate cook checked his heartbeat again before lifting the cloth to check his wound. "Miss Lizzie, go boil some water and get the surgical kit. It's on the top shelf in the galley beside my chest of herbs. Help me get him up, fellows."

Going down to the galley, Lizzie filled the cauldron with water and started a fire in the coals. As she located the surgical kit, Cookie, Joseph, and Jake brought JJ in and put him on the table. Cookie told her to get some brandy while he inspected JJ's shoulder. Bringing him the brandy, Lizzie went back to the cook pit for a bowl of boiling water. Cookie removed JJ's shirt and poured brandy over his bloody wound. Removing a spoon and knife from the surgical kit, Cookie heated them and attempted to dig out the bullet. Not being able to watch, she turned her head until Cookie triumphantly announced the bullet was out.

"Cookie! We need help!" exclaimed Edward Salter as he came in.

"I'm in the middle of patching JJ up."

"Is he going to be alright?"

"Too soon to tell," Cookie grunted.

Edward sighed. "It was worse than we expected. Those Frenchmen don't give up. There are more injured men on their way. Black Beard wanted me to give ye an update. He's decided to keep the best ship with the plunder on it. We'll be taking down the sails and rigging from the second ship for supplies. Captain ordered the French captains and their crews to be released on the worst ship."

"Did any of the Frenchmen get killed?" Joseph questioned.

"Nay, but Israel came close to killing one of the captains. Black Beard had to threaten him. Israel made a foolish remark to Captain, saying he'd soon regret his decision to let the French live."

"Is Captain hurt?" Lizzie asked, catching a warning from Jake.

"He's fine. Captain and Thomas are interrogating the crews."

Two pirates entered the galley with an injured man between them. Cookie motioned for them to put the man in the corner.

"Edward, I need ye to pick out the worst injuries. I'm almost finished stitching JJ up," Cookie proclaimed.

Nodding, Edward set to work. Soon the galley was so full that Cookie decided to move some of the men into the sleeping quarters. While Jake, Joseph, and Edward helped him relocate the patients, Lizzie carried the surgical kit and brandy. Looking at the hurt men propped against the walls, she wondered if it was all worth it.

Evidently, the battle had gotten bad considering all those hurt. A couple had injuries from embedded caltrops, a sharp metal object like a tack. From what Lizzie understood, the Frenchmen were famous for throwing these objects—known to sailors as crowsfeet—onto the decks. Thankfully, most of the injuries were minor, though John Giles and Stephen Daniel were in serious condition. Cookie couldn't help them except to wrap their wounds and give them brandy.

Exhausted from assisting Cookie, Lizzie was relieved when he told her things were under control. Going to the galley, she grabbed a wash rag and began to scrub the bloody table. As she scoured the wooden surface, she noticed a lump of black material by her feet. She picked it up, realizing the material was the Death's Head flag.

Tears welled up in her eyes as she stared at the skull and crossbones. Recalling Cookie's words about the black flag being a warning, she couldn't help but think it was a warning for them, too. As she wiped tears, Jake came in from the adjacent room.

"What's wrong?" he urged.

A fresh wave of tears streamed down her cheeks. "I just found this flag. Cookie told me it's a warning to surrender or face death. Today we faced death, Jake."

"You can't dwell on it, Lizzie. Nobody died, and we're headed back to Ocracoke Island. Can you bandage my arm? Cookie stitched me up but didn't have time to wrap it."

Wiping her eyes, Lizzie went to the supply shelf. Knowing Cookie used most of the bandages, she searched for anything clean. Luckily, she found a clean rag at the back. Returning to Jake, she rolled up his sleeve so that she could wrap his wound. Although she was thankful his injury wasn't bad, her mind spun with all the things that could have taken place. Without realizing it, she started to shake. Jake grasped her hand. Startled, Lizzie glanced at him. He didn't say anything, but the understanding in his eyes reassured her. Jake was right; she couldn't dwell on the negative. After such an unnecessary battle, she had to hold on to the grace God had shown.

CHAPTER TWELVE

SECRETS IN INK

September 1, 1718 ~ Monday

Dense fog enveloped the *Adventure*, making it difficult to see anything beyond her bow. As Lizzie stood outside the captain's cabin gazing into the foggy abyss, she mumbled a prayer under her breath. Only God could guide the *Adventure* and the French ship behind her safely into the narrow inlet.

According to her papa's calculations, they were near Ocracoke Island, though with the inclement weather there was no way to know how close they were. Lizzie feared they would run aground on the sandy shoals of the inlet. She doubted they could survive long if the ferocious waves of the Atlantic Ocean threw them against the shoals.

Pulling a scrap piece of cloth around her, Lizzie was thankful she saved it from her new dresses. She originally thought the half-blue, half-tan shawl looked ridiculous but it was kind of pretty. It felt good today when the sun failed to shine through the fog.

The weather was changing as the last days of summer gave in to fall. Before long, the days would be shorter and the weather much cooler, but until then they would have to put up with nature's tug-of-war. This was why the fog had been so thick the past three mornings—the result of a contest between the humid afternoons and the nippy nights.

Looking up at the cabin roof, Lizzie could barely make out her papa's tall figure as he attempted to locate Ocracoke Island through his spyglass. The constantly moving fog suddenly lifted, giving her a clear view of her father. Just as quickly, the veil of misty clouds drifted back over the cabin, completely covering it. Hopefully, as the morning progressed the fog would disappear.

After seven hundred miles of travel from the warm waters of the Gulf Stream near Bermuda, Lizzie was looking forward to reaching Ocracoke. She wondered if her papa would take her and Jake home, though she doubted he would until they careened the *Adventure*. Jake told her the careening process was complex. Considering they stole the French ship, she felt sure the process would also be dangerous.

In her heart, Lizzie was ashamed to have been a part of such an ungodly sin. Even though she had no control over it, she still felt dirty inside. Just knowing they deliberately planned and executed an attack bothered her. She had lived with these men for forty-eight days, yet she forgot what united them. Beneath the lively music, hard work, and good-humored personalities, they had piracy in their veins.

Until now, she hadn't given much thought to God's point of view on piracy. In His commandments, God specifically listed stealing among the forbidden actions. Keeping their oaths to the king's pardon was the least of the pirates' troubles. They could mislead the governors, but God saw every move they made. Lizzie made up her mind to confront her papa, to plant the idea in his head of a holy God listening to his thoughts. She hoped he would listen to what she had to say; however, his mood had been sour lately.

Deciding to see if Cookie's stew was ready for dinner, Lizzie made her way downstairs. She saw Cookie bent over Tuffy's sand-filled box, scooping it out to throw overboard. Jake and JJ sat at the oak table teasing Cookie while they ate their stew. Lizzie grinned as she walked up to the pirate in his blue-striped britches.

"There's nothing scarier than a pirate armed with a bucket of cat droppings," she giggled as Jake and JJ laughed hysterically.

Shaking his head, the pirate tried to conceal his amusement as he filled the wooden bucket with lumps from the sandbox. Reba squawked from her cage while Lizzie got a pewter porringer bowl and dipped out some of the stew from the cauldron positioned over the coals of the cook pit. She placed it on the table before going back for a pewter cup of water. Sitting across from Jake and JJ, she blessed the food and began to eat.

"I'll be back. I need to take this out," Cookie sighed, holding up his bucket of cat droppings.

Watching the cook leave, Lizzie listened to Jake and JJ talk about JJ's shoulder. It had been ten days since he received his injury. The gunshot wound was healing, and he would be able to do light chores in a few days. Sadly, Stephen Daniel and John Giles were still in critical condition and in desperate need of a doctor. Lizzie hoped someone on the island could help them.

To everyone's surprise, Tuffy jumped down from the chair where she had been napping. Trotting over to her fresh sandbox, the one-eyed black cat squatted to do her business, much to their disgust.

"I'm going to thump ye good eye out," Cookie hollered at Tuffy as he entered the galley. "Couldn't ye wait before ye dirtied ye box again? If ye keep tinkling at this rate I'll have to ration ye water."

"Don't threaten her, Cookie. She can't help it," Lizzie pleaded while Jake and JJ cackled in amusement.

"*Meow!*" Tuffy wailed pitifully as her whiskers flared up.

"Oh no, she can't help it," Jake began, briefly pulling himself together. "The poor thing lives on rats and leftover beans. With that combination what do you think she's going to do?"

"Have you fed Reba beans, too? The air sure is stuffy between Reba and Tuffy!" JJ agreed as he and Jake burst out laughing.

"Really? I thought it was ye, JJ. Since ye both think it's so funny, I'll let ye take turns scooping her droppings," Cookie suggested with a chuckle. "Ye want some of those little cakes for dessert? They came from the French ship. It's supposed to be a delicacy."

"Why not? It sure beats beans!" JJ snickered.

Jake held his stab wound from Pennsylvania. "I've laughed so hard my side hurts. I guess it hasn't totally healed yet."

Cookie brought out a small box and picked up one of the French desserts. The cakelike delicacy looked delicious, but Lizzie wasn't sure she wanted to partake. Wouldn't tasting the sweet treat be like the sin of stealing them in the first place?

"Ye want one, Miss Lizzie?" Cookie asked.

"I—um," she stuttered uncomfortably.

"How many people get a chance to eat a French treat?" he urged.

"They're really good! Try one, Miss Lizzie," JJ commented as he finished the last bite of his.

"He's right. They're good," Jake added, biting his own cake.

Hesitating, Lizzie reached into the small box to get a French treat. Taking a bite, she was pleasantly surprised at how delicious the cake was. She understood why the French ship carried the confectionaries. Finishing her dessert, Lizzie cleared the table. Placing her empty bowl in the wash bucket, she turned to Cookie.

"I'll be back, Cookie. I need to use the outhouse," Lizzie informed him as she left the galley and started up the stairs.

Lizzie was nearly at the top as a shadow blocked the light in the doorway. Looking up, she saw Nathaniel Jackson and John Martin.

"Pardon me, Miss Lizzie," John mumbled, removing his tricorn hat to show respect. "Hope Cookie prepared something edible."

Lizzie smiled. "Yes, his stew was quite tasty."

"Great! I could use a good meal."

Moving past the pirates, Lizzie wondered how two decent men became rogues. Since JJ's injury, she had learned more about the

Adventure's crew. In addition to Cookie growing up north of Bath at Lake Mattamuskeet, several others lived in nearby areas, including Thomas Miller, Garret Gibbons, John Philips, Nathaniel Jackson, John Giles, Stephen Daniel, and John Martin. Out of all of them, John Martin was the only pirate from Bath Town. His father was the late Joel Martin, who owned the plantation bordering Grandfather Worsley's. Now knowing his identity, Lizzie saw the Martin family resemblance, but clearly the harsh lifestyle he chose made him age considerably. She recalled the gossip at Joel Martin's death in 1716 when his son didn't return home for the funeral. John's younger brother, William, had taken over the family sheep herd.

Reaching for the door latch of the captain's cabin, Lizzie was astonished to discover it ajar. Pushing the door open, her eyes focused on a man seated behind her papa's desk. The man was none other than Israel Hands. Looking up at Lizzie, the black-haired pirate scrambled to his feet as his face flushed red. Dropping what he was holding, he quickly slid handfuls of loose paper into a pile.

"What do ye want?" he snarled angrily.

Frightened to be alone with the unruly pirate, Lizzie tried to hide her true emotions. "I stay here, don't I?"

Israel's cold eyes penetrated hers. "Aye, but I don't understand why. Ye certainly don't seem to be Black Beard's lover. If ye were, I don't think he'd be too keen on ye spending time with Cookie."

A sickening feeling rose up in Lizzie's chest as she listened to his accusations. Israel wasn't naïve. He was obviously snooping.

"What's going on in here?"

Spinning around, Lizzie was relieved to see Jake standing in the doorway. Jake glanced at her and then back at Israel.

"It's none of ye business," Israel countered.

"Looks like you're trying to find something."

"I don't have to answer to ye," Israel snapped. "What business do ye have in Captain's office? It's suspicious for both of ye to be here."

Stunned by the change of subjects, Lizzie realized Israel was trying to catch Jake off guard by insinuating he was breaking the rules.

"Captain wanted the sounding weight," Jake replied.

Israel narrowed his eyes. "Get it then. Don't keep him waiting. I don't see the chart of Ship's Channel. Captain will have to find it."

Without another word, Israel left the desk. Moving out of his way, Lizzie and Jake watched him leave the cabin.

"I'm so glad to see you!" Lizzie blurted out.

"I can imagine. Was he really looking for a map?"

"It's possible, but he seemed skittish. When I first walked in, he moved the papers on Papa's desk. Then he started questioning me."

"Interesting," Jake mumbled, walking to the desk. He studied the papers on top. "These are maps. Maybe he was telling the truth."

Going into the room where she slept with her papa, Lizzie froze. The entire room was in a jumbled mess. Clothes were all over the place and the straight-backed chair turned over.

"Jake, come here."

"What is it?" he asked, entering the room. When he saw the disarray, his eyes widened. "Wow."

"Israel must have been searching for something in here, too."

"Looks like a hurricane came through here," Jake observed.

Returning to the main cabin, Jake went straight to the chest of weapons. Seeing the lock was still secure, Lizzie looked around the room, but nothing seemed out of place.

"Why do you think Israel was snooping around?" she questioned.

"I don't know. It's strange. I'll talk to Black Beard about it when I take him the sounding weight."

"What's a sounding weight?" Lizzie inquired as Jake walked over to the wall of books where Black Beard kept his navigational tools.

"It's a rope with an iron weight on the end to make it sink. Thomas has one on the French ship, but Black Beard wanted to check the water level from our side," Jake explained.

"How does it work?"

"The weight is dropped in the water and pulled up with the rope. Water depth is determined by how much of the rope is wet. The rope has leather straps every fathom, which is equivalent to six feet."

"We must be close to shore if he wants to measure the depth."

"Yes, they're preparing to lower the anchors. Are you coming?"

"I'll be out there shortly. With all the commotion over Israel, I didn't make it to the outhouse."

Jake grinned. "Okay, don't fall in."

Shaking her head, Lizzie picked up a corncob from the bucket by the door of the outhouse while Jake left the cabin. Making sure there were no rats inside, she entered the tiny room and pulled up her dress. Finishing her business, she exited the head, as Cookie called it. She was about to leave the cabin when an idea crossed her mind. Jake checked the chest to make sure Israel hadn't broken into it, but what about the secret place under the floorboards?

Walking to her papa's desk, Lizzie slid the chair back. Patting the floorboards, she realized one of them was loose. Wondering if Israel found the hiding spot, she pried it up using her fingertips. As she removed the board, Lizzie could see the small wooden box her papa had shown her and Jake prior to the battle. Pulling it out, she opened the lid and peered inside. Although it didn't look like Israel found the box, her curiosity got the best of her.

Grandfather Beard's flintlock pistol rested on top of a few letters and a Bible. Lifting out the worn, black leather Bible, Lizzie discovered it was a family Bible with names inscribed on the front page. The inscriptions had the same handwriting, including her own name and birth date, except for two. Someone else wrote them. Since the inscriptions were the death dates of her momma and Grandfather Beard, Lizzie guessed they were her papa's handwriting. Setting the Bible aside, she sifted through the other items, which included a compass, a clay pipe, and a necklace. Picking up the necklace, Lizzie saw it held three of the familiar skeleton crossbone pendants. These pendants were tokens given after the loss of a loved one. Three names were on them; Anne Beard, James Beard, and Martha Worsley Beard.

Tears welled up in Lizzie's eyes as she saw her momma's name. Just knowing her papa still carried her pendant touched her heart. Wiping her eyes, Lizzie felt the ship suddenly lurch, causing her to lose her balance. Hitting her head on the desk, she grabbed her forehead as she stared wide-eyed around her, wondering what happened. Deciding she better get the box back in its hiding place, Lizzie carefully put the Bible in first followed by the skeleton pendants. She was about to add the stack of letters when a word caught her eye. Among the letters bearing the names of Susannah Franck, Grace Lee, and both Thomas Worsley Jr. and Thomas Worsley, Esquire, was a letter addressed from Philadelphia, Pennsylvania. Stunned, Lizzie realized the letter was the same one her aunt received in Bath back in July. She unfolded the letter as someone opened the door to the cabin.

"Miss Lizzie?" questioned JJ's voice. "Jake said ye were in here."

"Yes," she replied, quickly sliding the letters into the box and placing her grandfather's pistol on top the way she found it.

"Where are ye?" JJ persisted, his voice getting closer.

Replacing the box, Lizzie sealed the floorboard and stood up as JJ peeped over the desk at her.

"What are ye doing on the floor? Goodness, ye head's bleeding! Ye must have hit it on something when the French Martiniqueman collided with the *Adventure*. I'll go get some bandages," JJ offered.

"I'm okay," Lizzie reassured him as she wiped blood from her forehead. "So, that's what happened?"

"Aye, the crew was lowering the anchor when something shoved the ship. Captain thinks the French ship ran into us. He's trying to confirm it with Thomas."

"Is there any damage?"

"Nothing visually, but who knows what's below the waterline."

"I guess we should go see what's going on," Lizzie mentioned.

Following JJ onto the deck, Lizzie was surprised to find the weather had changed considerably as the fog lifted. They went to the port side of the ship where the crew had gathered.

Seeing them, Jake came over. "What happened to your head?"

"I scraped it against the desk when the ship lurched," she recalled, self-consciously touching her forehead.

Black Beard shouted across the deck, grabbing everyone's attention. "Listen up! I don't know what damage we have, but we've anchored the *Adventure* and the French Martiniqueman. While Thomas surveys the situation, we're going to hoist the periauger boat off the side. John Giles and Stephen Daniel need a doctor. Nathaniel Jackson, Garret Gibbons, and John Martin will go ashore to find one."

"Captain, I should be heading up the group," Israel protested.

"Did ye not hear me? Nathaniel, Garret, and John are going."

"I hold a higher office than Garret. In fact, since ye chose Thomas to captain the French Martiniqueman I'm the second in command. It's only fair for me to lead the search party," Israel explained.

"My decision is made."

Everyone stared at them, anxious to hear Israel's response. He clearly had something to say but evidently decided now wasn't the time to confront him when most of Israel's loyal followers were on the French ship, a decision Black Beard likely made on purpose. Glaring at his captain, Israel spit on the deck before marching over to the stairs leading into the galley. As the pirate disappeared below deck, Black Beard turned to the rest of the crew.

"I spotted a ship on the sound side of the island. Looks like they're flying the flag of Great Britain. There may be other ships anchored at Ocracoke for food or water so keep looking for a doctor until ye find somebody. Keep ye identities secret," he ordered.

"What do we say if asked how they got hurt?" Garret inquired.

153

"Tell them a cannon broke loose during the journey and the men were injured," Black Beard instructed.

"A cannon? They'll be suspicious when they see their wounds are worse. What about the French ship? Won't they think it's odd for us to have a French ship when this one's Spanish?" Garret pointed out.

"We don't have a choice," Black Beard snapped at his boatswain. "The truth will send our necks to the gallows to be hung. Ever since we captured the French ship, I've been thinking of a cover story. If whoever ye bring back here doesn't believe us then we'll have to deal with it. My priority is to do whatever to save John's and Stephen's lives. I don't want to dig two holes on the beach by the end of the week."

"None of us do, Captain," Garret muttered.

"Stop standing around! Get the periauger in the water!"

Scrambling, the pirates uncovered the periauger in the center of the ship. They carried it to the starboard side of the *Adventure* while Lizzie and JJ watched from a distance. With Cookie, Jake, Black Beard, John Philips, and the African James White in the bow of the boat and Garret, Nathaniel, Philip, John Carnes, and John Martin in the aft, they managed to hoist the twenty-five-foot boat into the air. Working together, they lowered the periauger into the water. Then the three chosen pirates went down the rope ladder.

While they rowed ashore, the crew went to the port side of the ship. Lizzie realized they were trying to help the French ship come alongside the *Adventure*. After a lot of effort, the ships finally drew close enough so that the crew could throw the grappling irons onto the deck, locking the vessels together. Once the grappling irons were secure, several men came over from the French ship.

The first was Edward Salter. "Cookie, what do ye have to eat?"

"There's a cauldron of stew waiting for ye," Cookie replied.

"Great! I'm starving," Edward announced, heading to the galley.

Husky climbed over behind him, followed by James Blake and Thomas Gates, two of the Africans. As they started down the stairs to eat, they met someone in the stairway. It was Israel.

Gazing in Black Beard's direction, the black-haired pirate swung his leg over onto the French ship. Lizzie started to mention it to JJ, but he was no longer standing beside her. Looking around, she noticed JJ walking over to his father, who had just come aboard.

"Glad to see ye up walking!" Joseph exclaimed, hugging his son.

"I'm almost ready to start doing light work," JJ responded.

By now, Jake and Cookie had joined them as they listened to Joseph's account of his journey on the French ship. According to Joseph, the seven-hundred-mile trip had gone well until they accidently hit the *Adventure*. When the fog lifted, they realized the ships were close but were unable to keep them from clashing as the *Adventure*'s anchor pulled her to a stop. Thankfully, both ships were all right.

"What kind of cargo was on the ships?" JJ wanted to know.

"It was a paltry amount of plunder. Most of it was casks of sugar and sacks of cocoa. There are some barrels of cotton and indigo die, but we can't do much with them unless we can find a buyer like we did last year in the Bahamas. The only thing of value were the spare masts, riggings, sails, and anchors. We did find barrels of tar, pitch, and oakum, which will help us with the careening," Joseph revealed.

"Why was it sailing so light?" Cookie questioned.

"Thomas said the two French captains claimed they were headed home to France after a trading trip to Fort-de-France, Martinique. Evidently, they had a load of wine when they arrived at the island. There are a few bottles of wine in the captain's cabin along with more crates of French confectionaries," Joseph answered.

"Will you each get a portion of the plunder?" Jake asked.

"The pirate articles state we'll get a share of the plunder, but since there wasn't any gold or jewels, I'm not sure. We can't sell it at Ocracoke. If we do split it, ye will get a portion, too, Jake."

Jake looked surprised. "Oh, no, I only wanted to understand how the rules worked. I don't expect a share."

"Ye signed the papers like the rest of us," Joseph reminded him.

"Black Beard told me to sign them. I didn't want to be a—" Jake began but then stopped suddenly, not wanting to complete his sentence.

"Ye don't want to be a pirate," Joseph finished for him as Jake looked embarrassed. "There's nothing to be ashamed of. I understand the circumstances. Try not to show ye are against it. If Israel thinks ye aren't committed to piracy he'll cause trouble for ye."

"He's already suspicious about something," Lizzie mumbled.

"Yes, Israel was snooping around the captain's cabin. He acted strange and even went through Lizzie's things," Jake explained.

"We'll have to keep a better eye on him," Cookie warned.

"He claimed to be getting a chart for Captain," Lizzie continued.

"I mentioned it to Black Beard when I took him the sounding weight. He never sent Israel to get a chart. Israel lied," Jake told her.

"It doesn't surprise me," JJ said as Black Beard walked up.

"What are ye talking about?" the pirate captain inquired.

"We're discussing the problem with Israel," Joseph declared.

"Jake told me he was snooping," Black Beard grunted.

"Just so you know, I also spotted Israel sneaking aboard the French ship a few moments ago," Lizzie informed him.

"I'll handle it. I came to tell ye I spotted John, Garret, and Nathaniel rowing back to the ship. It appears they have two other men in the periauger. Lizzie, I want ye to stay in the roundhouse. We don't need word getting out we have a lady onboard. Jake and JJ can go with ye so they don't see JJ's wound. Obviously, they would notice ye wound being from a gunshot. Since Stephen's and John's injuries were from grenades, they hopefully won't figure out we were in battle. Cookie, inform Stephen and John that someone is coming. Joseph, tell the others to help pull up the periauger."

Cookie and Joseph descended the stairs as Lizzie entered the captain's cabin with Jake and JJ. The boys plopped down in the straight-backed chairs while Lizzie sat at her papa's oak desk. As the boys talked about Israel, Lizzie leaned her chin against her arm. Her mind drifted to what Jake said about Israel lying. If Israel wasn't looking for a chart of Ship's Channel, then why was he searching through her papa's papers? Glancing at the charts and papers in front of her, she picked one up. It appeared to be a scratch sheet of calculations.

After looking at several others, she concluded most of the papers were plats or maps. She was beginning to think Israel was looking for a chart for himself when her eyes caught something unusual. Peeking out from under a pile of charts was a black leather-bound book. As she pulled it out, she remembered seeing it before—her papa's private pocketbook diary. Did her papa leave the diary out or did Israel find it? If so, why was he interested in her papa's pocketbook?

Flipping through the pages, Lizzie could understand why Israel may have been searching for it. She yearned to read it herself. How did her papa feel when Israel outsmarted him by getting half the crew to vote in his favor? What were his thoughts about the capture of the French ship? Did he mention her name or how he felt about her being with him over the last forty-eight days? Was there any inkling of the sickness he had or his feelings for Margaret?

So many questions filled Lizzie's mind as she struggled to keep herself from reading the contents of the pocketbook. She desperately wanted to know the answers, but something was stopping her. Would she be trespassing into her papa's privacy if she read it? Wasn't it the same as Israel, even though her motives were different? Standing, Lizzie took her papa's pocketbook to her room. For now, the mysteries recorded in the diary would remain secret.

CHAPTER THIRTEEN

☠

OLD SLOUGH PREDICAMENT

September 13, 1718 ~ Saturday

Frustration drove Cookie to slam his fist on the oak table as he expressed his feelings to Lizzie. "I'm tired of being a mother hen! The men are always hungry and ye can't clean the dishes before they want the next meal. Like I have nothing else to do except cook. To top it off my pots and pans are scattered all over this tent!"

"It'll be okay, Cookie," Lizzie reassured him. "Eventually, we'll figure out where everything is, and I'm here to help you."

"There's more than cooking. While we're careening the *Adventure*, we're in a dangerous spot. Suppose one of the other ships on the island gets suspicious and starts poking around. I don't like it one bit. In the past, we careened our ship on abandoned islands."

Lizzie debated how to encourage Cookie, who was pouring freshwater from the island water hole into one of the two ceramic jars. This proved difficult since she didn't have an uplifting attitude herself. The morning started with her papa announcing his journey to Bath without her.

"How are Stephen and John?" she asked, changing the subject.

"Those doctors think they'll recover. I was glad to see their merchant ship head back to London, England. That prying Dr. William Briggs kept making comments about the wounds not looking like injuries from a loose cannon. Luckily, Dr. Thomas Taylor was more interested in helping them than how they got the injuries. It's nice not having to worry about covering up our way of life out of fear they may alert the authorities."

"There still must be something to worry about or Papa wouldn't be going to Bath. Do you think someone will tell Governor Eden?"

"Too many ships pass through Ship's Channel because it's the only route to the ocean. Someone will get suspicious," he responded, pouring one last cup of water into the ceramic jar.

Cookie sealed the jars and finished preparing the food needed for the trip across the Pamtico Sound. Handing him the cooked pork and hardtack, Lizzie watched him pack the items in a sack. He added them to a crate of French gifts for the governor, which included cocoa, loaf sugar, and sweetmeats, otherwise known as desserts. Once it was ready, he filled a jar with rum to go along with the bottle of French wine. Noticing a couple of boxes stacked to the side, she started to ask him what was in them when Jake entered the tent.

"Sorry I'm late, Cookie. JJ and I were trying to finish stitching the sailcloth so we can go search the woods for firewood," he apologized.

"We're behind, too. Is Captain ready to go up to the countryside?"

"Yes, the periauger is in the water. James Blake, Thomas Gates, James White, and Richard Stiles will be traveling with him," Jake proclaimed, referring to four of the five Africans.

"Is there anything else I can do, Cookie? I really need to hang up the wet clothes I washed," Lizzie inquired.

"Everything's packed. Jake can help me carry this to the water."

"Lizzie, can you help us gather wood? Thomas plans to begin tarring the masts and beams next. We'll need more wood to keep the fires burning to heat the tar and pitch," Jake declared.

"Sure, I'll meet you after I get the clothes on the line."

"Oh, can ye feed Reba and Tuffy?" Cookie added as he handed Jake the ceramic jars of water and rum. "I fed the chickens this morning but forgot to give them the leftovers from dinner."

"Not beans!" Jake joked.

"Don't tease me about feeding them leftovers again," Cookie warned, attempting to hide a smile. "Come on, Captain is waiting."

Cookie picked up the remaining goods as they left the galley tent. Meanwhile, Lizzie walked to the pot where he kept leftover beans. Scraping some into their own porringer bowls, she went to where the two animals stayed in Cookie's handcrafted wooden pens.

"*Meow! Meow! Meow!*" Tuffy begged, wanting to get out.

"Reba out! Reba out!" squawked Reba.

Lizzie's heart yearned to let the pitiful animals loose, but she knew it wasn't safe for them on the island. Opening the gate to each cage, she slipped the bowl of beans to them and locked it back.

"I know you're ready to stretch your paws and wings, but you'll just have to wait. When the careening is over, you'll be free again."

With the two of them satisfied, Lizzie grabbed her three-cornered hat and went to finish the laundry. Shielding her eyes from the intense sunlight, she rounded the corner where a rope hung from the galley tent to her father's tent. Until now, she had been staying with her papa. Since he would be gone for several days, Black Beard had asked Cookie to move into the tent so that she wouldn't be alone.

Lizzie picked up her wet blue dress from the basket and draped it over the rope. While she hung the soggy clothing, she watched her papa set sail on the double mast periauger with his black companions. She absentmindedly grasped the locket she had been wearing since they arrived on the island a week ago. It was clearly tough for Black Beard and his men to row against the short, choppy waves. They slowly made their way westward into the dark blue waters of the sound, beginning their forty-seven-mile trip up to Bath Town.

Hearing a flock of honking geese, Lizzie looked up just in time to see twenty dark brown feathered geese fly across the pale blue sky. The leader of the flock guided the V formation over Ocracoke to the island south of it on the other side of Ship's Channel. Lizzie admired them as they soared high above the *Adventure*.

Changing her attention from the geese to the ship, she noticed the crew was making progress with the careening. After twelve days of work, the *Adventure* was finally sitting upright in the water. The first few days of their stay on Ocracoke were busy unloading the ship, including their personal items, kitchen supplies, weapons, sailing gear, cannons, navigational devices, and furniture. In addition, the barrels of food, water, and rum were now under canvas tents on the island along with the stolen barrels of indigo, barrels of cotton, bags of cocoa, and ninety casks of sugar from the French Martiniqueman. They even removed the heavy ballast stones used to stabilize the *Adventure*.

Having lightened her load, the pirates pulled the *Adventure* on her port side with ropes tied from her main mast to the iron device on the deck of the French Martiniqueman. According to Jake, the device was a capstan and was not only a crank to haul up the massive chained anchors but was also useful to pull the *Adventure* to her side.

Positioning the ship, the crew began by scraping seaweed and barnacles off the bottom. Cookie explained the need to scrape the hull two or three times a year. It was amazing how the seemingly harmless barnacles and greenish-brown seaweed could reduce the ship's speed. Another detrimental creature was the clams or mollusks resembling worms. These teredo shipworms bore holes in the ship, causing damage to the boards made from white pine trees. Shipworms were destructive and could sink ships if not scraped off using an adz, a heavy tool like an ax with a chisel-like blade.

The next step was to use the broad-bladed ramming iron to split rotten seams and the angled-bladed jerry iron to hack off the old oakum between the boards. They replaced rotten planks with the stolen supplies. Pirates with carpentry skills caulked new seams while others brought them animal hair and oakum. The process was slow, requiring them to stuff the mixture between the seams by hammering a narrow-bladed iron tool with a wooden mallet.

Thankfully, the French ship had barrels of tar, pitch, and oakum, which Lizzie discovered was heated tar and the stringy fiber of the hemp plant. The crew sealed the bottom boards with hot tar. They ground paint in a stone pestle muller while the tar cooled. Once the crew painted the bottom of the ship, they slowly raised the *Adventure* back upright and replaced the boards on the deck. Now the men were working to secure the new mast.

Hanging the last of the clothing on the line, Lizzie took the empty basket to her father's tent. She placed the basket in the corner near her makeshift bed before walking to her father's desk. He told her to help Cookie keep an eye out for Israel Hands while he was gone. Additionally, he planned to lock the bottom drawer so that no one would have access to the important papers. Tugging on the drawer, Lizzie was glad to see he had locked up his private things including his personal diary and Grandfather Beard's box. Satisfied she wouldn't have to worry about Israel, she left to find Jake and JJ.

Returning to the sunlight, she searched for the group of men by the crescent-shaped beach on the sound side of Ocracoke Island. She spotted JJ sitting on the beach stitching sails. Walking to him, she passed the pile of ballast stones, noticing the men were heating another round of tar and pitch. The big, black iron cauldrons reminded her of candle making.

"Where are ye headed, Miss Lizzie?" JJ called out.

"Jake asked me to help you gather wood."

JJ looked surprised. "This gives me a chance to show ye more of the island. I told Jake we're going to Old Slough. We've gathered all the washed-up driftwood around here."

"Old Slough? Isn't that where Cookie gets the freshwater?"

"Aye, Old Slough is the Old Watering Hole near Springer's Point. Slough is another word for marsh or bog. With all the saltwater, it's one of the only places on Ocracoke Island where ye can find drinking water. Sailors stop here because of the freshwater."

"Are you ready to go?" Jake wanted to know as he walked up.

"I'm ready if ye are," JJ stated.

Placing the sailcloth aside, JJ removed a piece of leather from his palm. Lizzie remembered seeing Jake use it before. The leather had two holes, one for the thumb and the other to hold the long needle.

"What's that for?" she inquired.

"This palm grip helps push the needle through the stiff sailcloth without stabbing your hand," JJ said. "Come on, let's go."

As they headed for the woods, Lizzie noticed Jake was wearing a flintlock pistol on his side. "Why do you have a gun, Jake?"

"Captain wanted me to have one while he's gone."

Soaking in the scenery, Lizzie listened to the black, crowlike grackles chattering overhead as they left the sandy beach and began their trek through the tall, pointed marsh grass. The forest consisted of red cedar trees draped in Spanish moss and scraggly live oaks stunted by the salty air blowing off the ocean. Zigzagging through the green and brown marsh grass, Lizzie thought about those who traveled to this island over the ages. Each soul had undoubtedly made their way down this same path to the Old Watering Hole. Suddenly, Lizzie collided with Jake, who stopped to avoid knocking JJ over.

"This is it. This is Old Slough!" JJ announced.

Glancing around, Lizzie could understand how the place got its name. Everywhere she looked was marsh and woods. In the center of the small clearing, there was a rock-built well with a wooden lid to keep animals from falling into it and tainting the freshwater.

"Let's split up. We'll cover more ground," Jake suggested.

JJ nodded. "Ye go north, I'll go east, and Miss Lizzie can look around here. We'll make a pile for the others to help carry it back."

Both boys headed off in separate directions. Lizzie began her task by collecting fallen limbs. Trying not to get rotten ones, she soon realized the job was difficult. Gathering all she could find, she decided to go in the direction Jake had gone. Coming to a pile he had accumulated, she combined the limbs with her pile at Old Slough.

Dropping her last load, Lizzie went back to where Jake's pile of limbs had been. She expected to find another pile, but after prancing around in the marshy wilderness she found nothing. Not knowing where she was, she felt relieved when she heard Jake's voice. Her relief turned to curiosity as she recognized JJ's voice as well. Frozen in disbelief, she listened behind bushes as they talked about her.

"Did ye grow up together?" JJ questioned.

"Yes, we were childhood playmates. Her family moved to Bath before the Indian War. It's kind of weird how I ended up at Bath in July. I haven't seen her family since I was ten."

"How old is she?"

"She's sixteen, a year younger than I am."

"Are the two of ye close?"

"Why are you asking so much about Lizzie?"

"I value our friendship too much to let something come between us," JJ confessed. "I'll just spit it out. Is Miss Lizzie ye girl?"

"What? My girl? No way. I mean, we're…friends."

"Then ye won't mind if I pursue her."

Lizzie gasped. Realizing what she did, she covered her mouth.

"What do you mean by pursue her?" Jake pressed.

"If she isn't ye girl and ye aren't interested in courting her, then I'm going to pursue her. Miss Lizzie is a very smart and beautiful young lady. I just wanted to make sure ye were okay with it."

"Knowing Lizzie, I doubt she'd agree to be in a relationship with a—she's just different," Jake covered, quickly changing his words.

"A pirate?" JJ finished. "Why wouldn't she be okay with courting a pirate? Her pa's a pirate. I'll discuss the matter with Captain Black Beard. Surely, if I ask him for permission she'll be open to the idea."

"Just because you ask him doesn't mean she will."

Moving quickly, Lizzie made her way through the marshy undergrowth in the direction of the Old Watering Hole. Thoughts swirled in her head as she tried to make sense of what she overheard. Her heart beat fervently in her chest at the idea of JJ's interest in her, and his plans to ask her papa if they could court. Taking care of him had given them a chance to talk, but she didn't know it would lead to this.

Not paying attention, Lizzie tripped over a tree root. Thrusting out her arms, she caught herself. Sitting up, Lizzie halted as she spotted a beautiful white stallion lift his head from the marsh. She recalled Cookie telling her about a herd of wild ponies living on the island. To her horror, the male pony stood on his hind legs and kicked his front hooves, signaling she was a threat. Knowing how dangerous wild ponies could be, Lizzie sat still, praying the pony wouldn't attack. The stallion continued to buck and snort as a warning.

Easing to her hands and knees, Lizzie moved away from the pony. Pausing to glance back at the white stallion, she felt something bite her left arm. Jerking, she found herself staring at a rattlesnake showing its fangs. Reacting quickly, Lizzie crawled away from the snake while keeping an eye on the white stallion. With her back against a weathered live oak tree, she inspected her snakebite. Trying not to get upset she hollered, hoping Jake or JJ would hear.

"Lizzie, where are you?" Jake shouted.

"I'm over here. There's a wild pony and a snake," Lizzie yelled.

Jake and JJ arrived with pistols drawn. Seeing the snake about to strike again, JJ shot it with his flintlock pistol. The gunshot spooked the stallion, which reared his front hooves and ran into the underbrush.

Jake slid the pistol into the leather holster. "Are you okay?"

"The snake bit me. Do you think it was poisonous?"

"Aye, it's poisonous," JJ confirmed, picking up the dead snake. "It's a diamondback rattler. We need to get ye to camp."

"Let me look at your arm," Jake stated.

Turning over her throbbing left arm, Lizzie showed him the double fang marks imprinted on her wrist. Jake held it for JJ to see.

"We need something to wrap it with," Jake muttered, removing his long-bladed knife from the sheath.

"What are you doing?" Lizzie demanded.

"I've got to cut a place to relieve the poison," Jake explained.

She jerked her wrist out of his hand. "No way! You're crazy!"

"Ye are right, it'll stop the poison. I'll hold her," JJ offered.

"Nobody's cutting my arm," she insisted angrily.

"We don't have a choice. You'll have to trust us. Do you want to die?" Jake threatened. Lizzie shook her head. "Then give it to me."

Tears welled up in Lizzie's eyes as she allowed JJ to grasp her arm. Uncomfortable with him holding her hand, she tried to be brave through the pain as Jake cut her arm an inch above the snakebite. JJ handed Jake his navy-blue neckerchief to wrap around the bite.

With their help, Lizzie stood up, although she was dizzy. By the time they reached Old Slough, Lizzie felt her predicament was getting worse as the poison got into her bloodstream. Deciding she needed to rest, she stopped to sit on the stone structure of the well. Jake squatted in front of her. Lizzie tried to hide her fatigue, but there was no fooling Jake. She gazed at her arm, which was now twice its normal size and turning deep red.

"Her arm's looking bad. We've got to get her to Cookie. He'll know what to do," JJ declared. "Come on, Miss Lizzie, I'll carry ye."

"I can walk," she exclaimed, hopping up from the well.

The sudden movement caused her to feel light-headed, prompting her to sit back down. Holding her head, she tried to gather herself.

"Your shoulder isn't healed," Jake reminded him. "I'll carry her."

By the look on JJ's face, Lizzie could tell he was disappointed by Jake's idea. She was going to try walking again when Jake stood.

"Alright, Lizzie, let's go."

Glancing at JJ, Lizzie decided she better listen to Jake. She couldn't keep going, and under the circumstances she rather Jake tote her. Wrapping her right arm around Jake's shoulder, she held on as they journeyed through the marsh behind JJ. Lizzie tried not to worry as she held her snake-bitten arm against her and asked God for help.

Eventually, they made it to the sound side of the island where the landscape changed from marshy woodland to the sandy shore. Walking across the sand, they came to the pirate camp. JJ went ahead to find Cookie. When they returned from the galley Cookie instructed Jake to bring her to the captain's tent. Ducking under the flap, Jake placed Lizzie on the bed. Cookie began to unravel JJ's neckerchief.

"Looks like it was poisonous," he mumbled, feeling her forehead.

"Aye, it was a diamondback rattler," JJ confirmed.

"This is bad," Cookie sighed. "JJ, go boil water. There's catnip in my herb chest for tea. It's great for fevers. I'll get bandages."

Cookie found bandages and a jar of catnip. Washing off the blood, he wrapped her arm. He tied a knot in the bandage when JJ entered with a pewter cup of hot water. His father, Joseph, was with him.

"JJ told me what happened," Joseph said. "By the way, I found a bottle of French wine and a jar of rum on the beach."

"Captain won't be happy his wine and rum are missing. Oh, well, can't do anything about it," Cookie commented.

JJ mixed the catnip in the hot water and passed it to Cookie. Lizzie took it from the cook as she began to sip the awful-tasting mixture. Once she swallowed half of it, Cookie turned to Joseph.

"I think we're going to need the old Indian woman. The poison seems to be moving rapidly. Do ye remember where she lives?"

"It's been awhile, but I'm sure I can find it," Joseph replied.

"An Indian woman?" Jake questioned sharply. "Why do we have to get an Indian involved? Won't the catnip work?"

"Catnip is for fevers. There are herbs for snakebites, but I don't have any. The old Indian woman will know which native herbs are safe to use," Cookie responded as Joseph left the tent.

"Am I dying?" Lizzie wailed as tears streamed down her cheeks.

"Don't talk like that. Ye will be fine," Cookie encouraged her.

His reassurance didn't soothe Lizzie's nerves as she laid down on her bed. She wondered if the edginess was the snake venom pulsing through her veins. Knowing her survival relied on this elderly Indian woman, she felt a sense of despair come over her. Thoughts of home filled her mind as the venom made her weaker. She longed to see her family, to tell them how much she loved them. Realizing she might not get the chance, she tried to pull herself together.

"Jake, can you do something for me?" she begged. "If something happens to me…"

"Nothing's going to happen to you. Don't give up."

Wiping her tears, Lizzie tried to stay positive, knowing Jake was right. Tired, she closed her eyes to rest. At some point, she heard voices talking, but she was too exhausted to listen. All she could do was pray the old Indian woman was near and God would help her have a cure for the venomous snakebite.

CHAPTER FOURTEEN

☠

WHITE FEATHERS

September 15, 1718 ~ Monday

Leisurely placing one bare foot in front of the other, Lizzie walked the shoreline on the sound side of Ocracoke Island thankful to be alive. Fiddler crabs feeding in the tidal waters scurried sideways from her path waving their large claws like a fiddler making music. Smiling at the funny way they moved, she looked back, making sure she hadn't ventured too far from the pirate encampment. Deeming her journey far enough, she sat down to soak up the sunshine.

Glad to be away from the commotion, Lizzie let out a sigh. As she exhaled, she imagined the built-up stress leaving her. While she had been recovering from the snakebite, Quartermaster Thomas Miller struggled to keep the men motivated to complete the repairs of the *Adventure*. After a week and a half of constant work, the men were tired and it was certainly showing. Tensions were high due to exhaustion and Israel Hands' complaining. His sour attitude no doubt came from his anger over the authority Thomas held while Black Beard was away. The fact Israel was becoming defiant of Thomas' orders made Lizzie's concerns grow. She hoped her papa would return soon.

Watching the little brown and white sanderlings chase the gentle waves rushing ashore, Lizzie focused on her surroundings. Nature had a way of cleansing one's thoughts and reminding a person that the One who created all things was in charge. She recalled reading in the Bible about Jesus pointing out how God fed and cared for the fowls of the air. Gazing at the seabirds feeding on creatures in the tide, she understood she needed to let go of her worries and trust God. Digging her toes in the sand, she leaned against her knees, closed her eyes, and released her concerns in prayer.

As she prayed, a voice interrupted the sound of seabirds. Startled, Lizzie's brown eyes flew open as she found herself staring at an elderly woman dressed in a tanned deerskin dress. She recognized the brown-skinned woman as the elderly Indian who saved her life.

"You look better," she murmured, giving Lizzie a toothless grin.

Standing, Lizzie greeted her with a smile of her own. "Yes, ma'am, I'm doing a lot better. I'm grateful for everything you did. Those herbs you brought cured the poison from the snakebite."

"The mint plant does wonders for snake poison, but I cannot take the praise. The Mighty Creator makes the plants and roots of the earth. He has power over death," the Indian woman commented, resting her handwoven basket on the sand.

"So, you believe in God?" Lizzie inquired with curiosity.

"'God'?" the elderly woman repeated, obviously confused.

"I call Him 'God,' but I suppose He's the 'Mighty Creator,' too."

"My tribe worshipped the sun and moon when I was young. After the great sadness, I came to know of the Mighty Creator." Pausing, the Indian woman raised her hand and pointed in the direction of the pirate encampment. "Looks like your tribe has finished the repairs."

Gazing at the *Adventure*, Lizzie debated how to explain to the elderly woman her involvement with a group of men. It wasn't natural for a young lady to be on a ship, especially one full of pirates.

"Yes, ma'am. It was in bad shape so it's taking awhile to fix it," she started, hesitating as she heard a snorting sound nearby.

Searching the marshland, her eyes caught a glimpse of white. She realized it was the white stallion she saw two days ago at Old Slough. The pony grew tense as he blew air from his nostrils. Scared to move, Lizzie remained still, unsure what to do. To her amazement, the Indian woman raised her hand at the pony and mumbled words Lizzie didn't know. Moments later, the stallion shook his head and backed away. Trotting to his herd of twenty or more ponies feeding in the salt marsh, the white stallion pawed the ground with his right hoof.

"How did you get him to leave?" Lizzie asked.

The woman chuckled. "The white warrior is smart and he listens."

"I wonder what he's doing," Lizzie said, watching as the pony repeatedly pawed the ground.

"Certain areas have freshwater below the surface of the marsh. Ponies can sense these places. They use their hooves to dig a hole until the freshwater rises," the elderly woman proclaimed.

"You know so much. How long have you been here?"

"Since I was a little girl. The island has been my home for many winters. I am ninety winters old."

"What's your name?"

The elderly woman looked surprised. "They call me Medicine Woman, but my name is Waurraupa Soppe. It means White Feathers. My mother was given white egret feathers as a gift when I was born."

"That's a pretty name."

"People come to the island for water and leave. Will you be here long?" White Feathers wanted to know.

"I'm not sure. It depends on my papa. He's the captain of the ship and will make the decision to leave."

"Are you the only girl in your tribe? I did not see any others when I came to your hut. You are brave traveling with many men."

Lizzie felt awkward. "Yes, I'm the only girl. My papa and I haven't spent much time together. I live with my aunt on the mainland. This summer, I had a chance to go with Papa up north. It's good to be with him, but I'll be returning home."

"Is your mother in the Great Beyond?"

Guessing she meant heaven, Lizzie looked at her bare feet as she responded, "Yes, she's in heaven. When I was little, she got sick from yellow fever. Do you live here with your—tribe?"

"No, my people died from a sickness. We were the Woccon tribe. Each summer, we came from the mainland to feast on the creatures of the sea. One summer there were many men here. They were sick. Our people caught the sickness, too. When the leaves fell from the trees my family and most of our tribe had gone to the Great Beyond. Those who lived chose to join the Hatteras tribe on the island north of here. I chose not to leave. This island is my home. I wish to keep the old ways," White Feathers recalled.

"It's terrible to lose your family. I understand how you feel."

"You have your father."

"I'm not sure for how long. He hasn't said anything, but by the rash on his hands and the way he's been acting, I think he's sick. There's a sickness some sailors get from lack of fruit while they're on long voyages. They call it scurvy," Lizzie declared.

"I have heard of such a sickness. Many men have stopped on this island seeking fruits to cure it. We only have wild figs. The blessed thistle plant may help your father. Come, I have some growing near my hut," White Feathers offered, picking up her handwoven basket.

"Wait. I don't have shoes on."

"I will get it for you. Stay here."

Before White Feathers could make it to the well-worn footpath, something came bursting out of the nearby woods. Expecting to see the white stallion, she saw it wasn't the pony she anticipated. Lizzie stared at the beautiful gray speckled pony dashing across the marsh.

The majestic animal carried a rider on its back whose deerskin clothing and dark complexion were like the elderly woman's.

"Yicau! I looked all over for you!" the rider shouted, pulling the pony's mane to get it to stop running. Dismounting, the young Indian froze as his dark eyes fixated on Lizzie. "Who is she?"

"Red Wolf, this is Lizzie. She had the snakebite," White Feathers explained. "Why are you looking for me? I told you I needed sassafras."

Eyeing Lizzie, the Indian boy replied, "We must hurry, Yicau! The old sea guide came seeking your help. He says his wife is sick, much worse than before. You will ride with me."

"No, Red Wolf. Her spirit is too wild for me to ride."

"You have no choice. The woman could die unless we go quick. Come, let me help you climb on," Red Wolf insisted.

Turning around, White Feathers returned to the beach where Lizzie was still standing. Reaching into her basket, she pulled out a handful of what looked like tree bark and passed it to Lizzie.

"Boil this sassafras bark in water and spread it over the rash. Tea with the blessed thistle would do better. Come to my hut to get it. Several men in your tribe know where it is."

"Yicau! Yicau!" Red Wolf called urgently, though Lizzie wasn't sure what he was saying.

The Indian woman walked over to Red Wolf and his speckled pony. Helping her climb on its back, the young Indian mounted the pony behind her. Reaching around her to grab the tangled black mane, he gave his pony a kick, causing the beautiful animal to gallop away. Seconds later, they were out of sight, leaving Lizzie holding the handful of sassafras bark.

Deciding she should head back to camp, she began her trek down the sandy shoreline. Stepping lightly on the shell-scattered sand, she thought about her surprise visitors. Nearing the encampment, Lizzie noticed the men were no longer working on the *Adventure*. Curious to find out why, she quickened her pace. Her stomach lurched as she spotted the twenty-five-foot long periauger in the water, a sign of her papa's return. Slipping up behind Cookie, she dropped the sassafras bark on the sand and stood on her tiptoes to see her papa. Stretching as high as she could, she watched the captain talk. He sounded irritated.

"Until the court date we're staying here," Black Beard stated.

"That's all the advice Tobias Knight had?" John Martin wanted to know as others murmured in agreement.

"What did ye expect?" Black Beard snapped. "All he can do is talk to Governor Eden. Ye should've thought about it before ye stole the French ship. Tobias thinks we're foolish sheep! He put his name on the line. We knowingly violated our pardons."

"He didn't want to help?" JJ's father, Joseph, questioned.

"I'm saying he didn't have to do anything. He's giving us a second chance, but I'm warning ye this is the last time. This court hearing he's setting up will hopefully get the French ship cleared so that we can burn it. We must destroy the evidence," Black Beard reported.

"Let's burn it now," Israel proclaimed.

"Nay! We aren't doing anything until Governor Eden gives the approval. The smoke alone will raise alarm. I'll tell the court we found the ship drifting. Then Tobias is going to suggest we burn her to the waterline to keep her from blocking the inlet. The thing is, to get Eden to agree, we have to give him eighty casks of sugar."

Suddenly there was an uproar of protests, particularly from those who sided with Israel Hands during the vote.

"Handing over the plunder is better than hanging. I didn't tell Tobias how many barrels we stole. We can hide a portion of it on the island while we make the trips to Bath," Black Beard said. Motioning toward the periauger, he added, "Get this boat out of the water."

"Ye still have some explaining to do. Where did ye get this?" Israel challenged, pointing at the sand.

Not being able to see what he was talking about, Lizzie crouched down beside Cookie so she could peer between their feet. From this new vantage point, she could see her papa standing beside a barrel and an open wooden chest.

"I bought it up in the country."

"How did ye sword break?" Israel persisted.

"It broke when I pried open the chest to store the goods I bought. Tobias gave it as a gift but failed to give me the key. Now, get the boat out of the water," Black Beard ordered, heading to his tent.

Quickly standing, Lizzie noticed JJ following her papa. Wondering what he was up to, her attention turned to the chest as the pirates discussed its contents. Inside the chest was a box of tobacco pipes, a fifty-eight-yard roll of crepe fabric, a handful of government-issued scrip paper, and a unique silver drinking cup.

"What are ye looking at?" Cookie demanded. "There's work to do. Husky, take this half-empty barrel of brandy to the galley. Thomas, don't ye need to grind the paints so the crew can finish painting the *Adventure*'s deck? And Israel, don't just stand there. Get this periauger out of the water." Turning to Jake he continued, "Help me carry this chest to the galley. Then go find Miss Lizzie."

"I'm right here, Cookie," Lizzie spoke up, scaring the pirate.

"Ye know better than to sneak up on me," he grumbled, rubbing his forehead. "Where have ye been?"

"I went for a walk along the shore."

"The shore, huh? How long have ye been here?"

"Long enough."

"Ye heard it then," Cookie muttered, leaving her wondering what he meant. "Oh, well. Ye can help me and Jake sort this mess."

Lizzie walked behind Jake and Cookie as they hoisted the chest. Meanwhile, Husky picked up the half-empty barrel of brandy and followed them to the galley. Once at the tent, Husky put the barrel down and returned to the shore. Jake and Cookie took the chest inside to begin organizing the objects Black Beard supposedly bought in Bath Town. Lizzie knew for certain some of the items weren't available at Harding's General Store. The most striking was the silver drinking cup. It was a rare item only prominent families would have. Hoping her father didn't steal the goods, Lizzie tried to reassure herself that perhaps Secretary Knight gave them to him. After all, hadn't he just lectured his crew on the morals of living an honest life?

A sudden entrance startled Lizzie out of her daydreaming. She and Jake were standing at the table watching Cookie count the scrip paper, which the government used in place of hard currency. Glancing up, she recognized JJ's familiar face. Snatching the tricorn hat from his head, he gave her a grin before addressing the cook.

"Just came from Captain's quarters. Pa met me as I was heading back and gave me this bark. Ye must have left it by the shore," he announced, holding up the sassafras White Feathers gave Lizzie.

"It's mine," Lizzie blurted out. "You can leave it on the table. I'll deal with it when I get a chance."

As JJ placed the bark on the table, Lizzie caught him staring at her. Feeling uncomfortable, she tried to avoid his gaze by keeping busy. She could tell he was still watching her as she admired the silky crepe fabric from the chest. Worried he might misread her uneasiness and think she liked him, Lizzie told Cookie she would take the roll of fabric to the back of the tent where Tuffy's and Reba's cages were.

"Captain wants to see ye, Jake," JJ proclaimed.

"Me? What for?"

"Take it from me, lad," Cookie urged. "If Captain wants to speak with ye, then hurry—particularly when he's in a bad mood."

"Did I do something wrong?" Jake questioned, sounding nervous.

"Don't worry. Ye will be fine," JJ encouraged him.

Despite JJ's reassurance, Jake still looked anxious as he left the tent to meet his fate. Shortly after he left, Cookie spoke up.

"I feel for the lad; hope Edward isn't hard on him. He's done everything we've asked him to do."

"He only wanted to talk to him. It's no big deal," JJ stated.

The two of them continued to talk about Thomas and the men who were painting the railings of the ship. Not wanting to be in their conversation, Lizzie stayed at the back of the tent. As she replenished the water in Tuffy's and Reba's bowls, she listened to JJ's aimless chitchat. She couldn't help but wonder if he was postponing his time until Jake came back. Thankfully, it didn't take long for Jake to return.

"How did it go?" JJ wanted to know.

"I'm not sure. He wasn't mad."

"Good. Come on. Let's go paint. We might go fishing later!"

"Okay," Jake responded. "Captain wants to talk to you, Lizzie."

Lizzie came out of her corner. "So now he's asking for me?"

"Yes."

Judging by the awkwardness in his voice and how he sheepishly looked away, she knew something was going on. Gazing at Cookie, Lizzie headed out of the tent, pausing only to hear JJ's offer.

"After ye meet with Captain ye are welcome to join us fishing."

"I'll think about it," she replied, trying to be polite.

Leaving the galley, Lizzie crossed the short distance between the tents. Feeling the hot sand between her toes, she entered the captain's quarters. She spotted her papa standing at his desk holding a map in his left hand as he drank from a tall brown jug. He motioned for her to come in as he grabbed his desk for support.

"Have a seat," he greeted her enthusiastically. "How long has it been? Four days, perhaps five?"

Stunned by his loss of the sense of time, Lizzie sat in a straight-backed chair in front of his desk. "It's been two days. They've made a lot of progress on the repairs, and I got bit by a snake while gathering firewood. Cookie remembered the Indian woman. She gave me healing herbs."

"Jake told me. I'm glad ye are okay. They say Medicine Woman is crazy, but she's wise," he declared, taking another swig of brandy.

"Are you feeling well, Papa?"

"Sure! What makes ye think I'm not?"

"You seem tired, and with all the drinking I just figured something was wrong. While I was walking along the beach today, I saw the Indian woman, White Feathers. She gave me sassafras bark. It's a healing herb. I just thought—" Lizzie began as he interrupted her.

"Stop worrying! I don't need herbs. I'm enjoying a little dram. Since we left without my rum I'm making up for lost time. Brandy will cure all ailments. Now, it's time we talk about young Brooks."

Lizzie watched him put the bottle of spirits down and rub his calloused hand through his wiry black beard.

"JJ? Why do we need to talk about him?"

Black Beard chuckled. "Don't play coy with me, young lady. He told me all about his intentions to court ye."

"What?"

"Ye didn't know he had feelings for ye?"

"I overheard him talking to Jake but didn't think he was serious."

"Ah, 'tis the mystery of love. Poor lad was shaking like a newborn calf taking its first steps. I can't blame him for being nervous. Courting a man's daughter is one thing. When he's ye captain and a pirate to boot, well, JJ better be walking a straight line," he said.

"JJ is nice, but I'm not interested in courting him."

"Because of Gale's boy, I presume?"

"You mean Miles Gale?"

"Aye. The lad would make a good suitor for ye. He's educated in the traditional schooling of fine arts, literature, and social graces. I can see why ye captured his attention. Ye look like ye mother."

"How do you know about Miles? Did you see Uncle Thomas?"

"There wasn't enough time. I asked Tobias to let the family know ye are safe. He said when ye and Jake disappeared in July Thomas came to him wanting to know where I planned to go. They guessed ye were with me after finding the boats. Thomas later told him about the letter ye sent to Grace. We agreed it's best for ye to stay with me until the court hearing. Jake told me about the Gale boy. JJ said Jake wasn't pursuing ye, but I made sure. The last thing I need is two young bucks fighting over my daughter. It was in defending himself that Jake told me about the Gale boy. He assured me he was just a good friend."

Fuming at the thought of Jake sharing such private things, Lizzie stood up. "Papa, I have no desire to court. There are more important things, like the potential criminal charges looming over us."

"Aye, which is why I must prepare my arguments for the governor," he agreed, hoisting the bottle and downing another swallow.

Knowing she couldn't persuade him to stop drinking or try sassafras bark on his hands, she left her papa with his spirits, convinced he was sicker than he was letting on. As Lizzie's eyes adjusted to the sunlight, she spotted Jake by the covered pail of drinking water. She walked over as he kneeled to sip water from the wooden ladle.

"From now on, Jake Griffin, mind your own business. I don't appreciate you tattle-telling," she exploded.

Jake wiped his chin with the back of his hand. "What?"

"I thought we were friends. How dare you tell Papa about Miles!"

With her arms tightly crossed, Lizzie marched off, ignoring Jake's offer of an apology as she hurried to her private beach, wanting to be alone. Although she was furious with Jake, the trickle of tears dripping down her cheeks proved to be more hurt feelings than true anger. He wounded her in ways she hadn't expected and couldn't understand. Was it possible she could no longer trust him?

CHAPTER FIFTEEN

☠

THRASHERS' PREY

September 25, 1718 ~ Thursday

Gazing at the bouquet of wildflowers, Lizzie let out a sigh. The last thing she expected to see on the table was an empty wine bottle of red and yellow flowers. No matter how beautiful the daisylike wildflowers were in their green-tinted glass container, she couldn't stand them. This was more than kindness. It was trouble.

"Aren't they pretty?" came Cookie's voice as he entered the galley tent. "Now I know why the lad wanted an empty wine bottle."

Lizzie didn't need Cookie to tell her who the lad was. She knew it was JJ. He must have done it while she was washing plates outside.

"Those flowers are special," Cookie continued.

"Really, Cookie? You're reading more into it than you should," Lizzie interrupted, reaching for the basket of clean plates by her feet.

"What I mean is they're special to Ocracoke. They only bloom for a few weeks. By October, they'll be gone. I don't think JJ's feelings will be gone that fast, though," he said with a chuckle.

"Please don't encourage him."

"Captain encouraged him when he agreed to let him court ye."

Lizzie shook her head, hoping to rid her mind of the scene four days ago when her papa made his decision. She still couldn't believe he gave JJ permission even after she begged him not to. Then again, he hadn't been thinking clearly lately. Obviously, the stress of the court hearing had affected him, but his irrational behavior was due to his drinking and then the miserable hours getting sober. Amazingly, when he left for Bath Tuesday morning, he was acting like himself again.

At least the only ones who knew about JJ's interest in her were Cookie, Jake, and JJ's father, Joseph. To keep her identity secret, Black Beard made sure JJ understood the relationship had to be private. This aided Lizzie's efforts as she avoided being alone with him.

"I'm going to see White Feathers," Lizzie announced.

Cookie scratched his head. "Ye spend a lot of time over there."

"There's a lot to learn. Why should I sit around when I can learn about Ocracoke? Who better to teach me than a native islander?"

"We're not sitting on our hands. The fellows are trying to get the guns remounted. Then we've got to put the cannons back."

"The crew is doing that. I'm the one with nothing to do."

"Ye can polish the bronze bell."

Narrowing her eyes, Lizzie gave him a sarcastic look.

"Okay, polishing a bell isn't exciting. Be careful and keep ye eyes open for wild ponies. Husky said the white stallion chased him yesterday. He was getting water at Old Slough," he warned.

"Why is the white stallion mean?"

"He's the leader of the herd. To protect his ladies, he'll do anything. With more people coming to the island, their way of life has become threatened. People take them from the island. They should be left to run free like they've done for a hundred years."

"Haven't they always been on the island?"

"Legend has it that the Banker ponies are descendants of Spanish ponies stranded after a ship wrecked off the shoals during a hurricane. Supposedly, the ship was from Spain and the ponies were pureblooded animals of the finest quality, though shorter than average horses. Everyone on the ship perished, but the ponies swam to shore. Since the ship was on an exploration trip, no one came looking for them. Years passed and the ponies thrived on the island."

"I didn't know they had such an interesting history."

"Ye just remember they're dangerous. Captain left me responsible for ye, and I don't want to disappoint him."

"Don't worry. I'll be fine," she promised as she started to leave. Hesitating at the tent flap, she looked back. "Oh, and please move those flowers. We don't want anyone to ask about them."

Stepping into the sunlight, Lizzie looked around before hurrying away from the pirate camp. Hoping JJ wouldn't spot her, she walked to the small beach where she spent her time. She climbed the sandy embankment and started down the path to White Feathers' hut.

Walking through the woods of cedar trees and yaupon hollies, she made her way across the interior of the island. As she hiked the narrow path, she kept a lookout for snakes and wild ponies. Thankfully, her trek was uneventful and about twenty minutes later she emerged in a little clearing. A mud-built hut stood in the center of the clearing with a garden out back. Approaching the hut made of tree bark and moss, Lizzie spotted the old Indian woman sitting on a log.

"Hello, White Feathers!" she called, not wanting to scare her.

Without turning from her work, White Feathers welcomed Lizzie with her Woccon nickname. "Greetings, White Swan."

Smiling, Lizzie walked over to her friend as she recalled the reason for her new name. White Feathers had given her the name, which was Waurraupa Atter and meant she was graceful.

Drawing near, Lizzie noticed White Feathers was braiding a piece of leather. By her deerskin shoes was the largest dark green turtle shell Lizzie had ever seen. She sat down in front of the elderly Indian to show respect the way Red Wolf taught her.

"What are you doing?" Lizzie asked as she rearranged her dress.

"Making a basket."

"I didn't realize turtles grew so big. Where did you find it?"

"Sea turtles are bigger than land turtles. They come up from the ocean to lay eggs in the sand when the weather turns warm. Their eggs and meat are good. Turtles of the sea cannot hide in their shell. They have flippers instead of legs," White Feathers told her.

"Wish I could show my cousins back home. They would love coming to the island," Lizzie proclaimed.

"When do you go home?"

"It depends on Papa. I meant to tell you about the blessed thistle plant you gave me the other day. Papa refused to drink any blessed thistle tea and still won't try the sassafras on his rash. He insists he isn't sick."

"We cannot force man to do as we wish. All we can do is ask."

Lizzie slowly nodded, letting her wise words sink in. She was still thinking about her papa when White Feathers changed the subject.

"How did you like the figs you took back to your tribe?"

"They were delicious! We ate them for breakfast with biscuits, eggs, and ham. My friend Cookie says figs grow wild on the island."

"The island has nine kinds of fig trees and bushes. Some are hard to find. They ripen in the hot days of summer. Only one ripens now."

Just then, Red Wolf came trotting up on his speckled-gray mare. As the young Indian dismounted his pony, Lizzie saw he was wearing a leather pouch at his side. He also carried a long stick with a sharp stone tied to the end like a spear.

"Any luck catching fish?" White Feathers wanted to know.

"No luck, Yicau. The creek had no fish," Red Wolf grumbled.

Lizzie recalled her conversation with White Feathers when she told her what Yicau meant. It was the Woccon tribe's word for old woman or grandmother. Red Wolf's Woccon name was Yauta Tire Kiro, meaning he would be a great hunter like the rare red wolf native to Carolina.

After sipping water from a clay pot, Red Wolf came over to where his grandmother was making a handle for the turtle-shell basket. "I will try to fish in the ocean, Yicau."

White Feathers looked up from her work. "Be careful for the strong current. You know it is powerful. It will pull you out to sea."

"I remember," he replied, picking up his spear.

Thinking about the ocean made Lizzie's heart beat faster. She wanted to see it but would have to convince Red Wolf to take her. He was about to swing his leg over the pony when she got the nerve.

"Um, Red Wolf, can I go with you? I haven't gotten a chance to go to the ocean side of the island yet," she blurted out.

By the look on his face, she could tell he wasn't thrilled about it. Thankfully, White Feathers spoke first.

"Take her, Red Wolf."

Hesitating, the young Indian motioned for her to come over. Lizzie hopped up and hurried to where he waited. Once he mounted the gray mare, he reached to help her climb on. This was more complicated than Lizzie figured as she struggled to find a foothold. With Red Wolf's help, she straddled the pony.

"Hold on," Red Wolf instructed as he gripped the pony's black mane in one fist while holding the spear in his other.

Having nothing to hold on to, Lizzie wrapped her arms around Red Wolf's waist as he kicked the pony, causing them to take off. Desperately clutching the fringes of his deerskin shirt, she prayed she wouldn't fall. In her mind, she could hear Cookie telling her to be careful and to watch out for wild ponies. What would he say if he knew she was riding one? Even though Red Wolf had tamed the mare, she still had a lot of spirit, as White Feathers so often put it.

Cautiously lifting her head, she saw the forest blur by as it gave way to marsh and sea oats. The breeze through her hair felt exhilarating. Soon, she could sense the pony slowing down. Releasing her grip, Lizzie waited until it stopped before she dismounted.

"Now what?" she asked him.

"We walk the rest of the way."

"What about your pony? Won't she run away?"

"Black Star will be fine. She likes to eat the oats here," Red Wolf responded as he started to walk up a sandy embankment.

"Black Star? That's an interesting name," Lizzie continued, trying to keep the conversation going as she followed him. "We have two horses at home named Honeybee and Butterscotch."

"She has a black star above her eyes."

Glancing back at the pony, which was already munching on sea oats, she noticed the patch of black on her forehead.

"You have a really—" she began, stopping abruptly as she reached the top of the embankment. "Wow."

The scene was better than Lizzie imagined. It took her breath away. Nothing stood between them and the rolling waves crashing ashore except the gorgeous cream-colored sand. For miles in either direction, all she could see was sand and sea.

"Like it?" Red Wolf questioned, bringing her out of the trance.

Astonished he would ask something so ridiculous, Lizzie looked at him, realizing he was teasing as she caught him snickering.

"Yes, it's beautiful," she declared.

Shaking his head, Red Wolf descended the sand dune with his spear. Lizzie followed his lead. In no time, they were standing by the water's edge where the waves were washing up on the shore. Red Wolf rolled up his pant legs and started to search the water for fish. Meanwhile, Lizzie took off her shoes and stockings so that she could dip her toes into the nippy water. Quickly drawing back, she again tested it, this time dowsing her whole foot into the sea. Braving the cool late September waters of the Atlantic Ocean, she danced around in the waves, chasing the sandpipers. Seagulls squawked overhead, seemingly laughing at her. When she exhausted herself, she decided to look for seashells in the tide.

Collecting shells ranging from ridged ones to some shaped like a spiral, Lizzie delighted in finding the colorful treasures. She marveled at how amazing God was for creating so many unique creatures. When she bent down to pick up a rocky oyster shell, Red Wolf let out a shout. Whipping around, she spotted him holding his spear in the air with a fish flopping on top.

Grinning, Lizzie walked to where he was. "You caught one!"

"Yes, Yicau will be pleased," Red Wolf stated, removing the large fish from his spear. "Would you like to try catching one?"

Lizzie raised her eyebrows in surprise. "Me?"

"Thought you wanted to learn our way of life?"

"Okay, I'll try."

Leaving the fish and her pile of shells just beyond the reach of the incoming tide, Lizzie joined Red Wolf in the water. At first the waves didn't bother her, but as they waded deeper into the greenish-blue ocean she could feel a sense of panic creep up her body the same way the water was creeping up her dress.

"Red Wolf, I think this is far enough."

"Take my spear. Steady yourself and look hard for the fish. They will swim up to us. We must stand like a deer, still and alert."

Taking the spear, Lizzie tried to stand like a deer, which was difficult when the waves kept pushing against her. Fighting them, she watched and waited. Time passed slowly with nothing in sight but their own feet. She was ready to give up when a movement caught her eye—a swish of a tail perhaps, or was it her imagination?

"Did you see one?" she whispered, unsure if fish could hear.

"Wait for it. The bluefish will pass this way again."

Sure enough, the bluefish came into view, swishing its forked tail. Holding the spear with both hands, Lizzie stabbed the wooden pole into the water hoping she was aiming for the fish and not their bare feet. The motion triggered her to lose her balance as she collapsed in the water. Reacting quickly, Red Wolf grabbed her just in time to keep her head from going under. Holding onto him, Lizzie tried to straighten up but she kept slipping in the sand. With her legs thrashing in the water, she finally gained enough ground and was able to stand.

"Are you hurt?" Red Wolf panted, still grasping the speared fish with his left hand.

Someone yelled at them from the beach. Looking over Red Wolf's shoulder, Lizzie recognized Jake running toward them.

"Get your filthy hands off her, you savage Indian!" he shouted.

Letting go of Red Wolf, Lizzie darted out of Jake's way as he knocked the young Indian into the water. Grabbing the speared fish, she waded out of the water while they fought in the ocean.

"Stop it, Jake!" she pleaded. "He was trying to help me."

"White Swan speaks the truth," Red Wolf piped up.

"White Swan?" Jake spat, taking a swing at him.

"It's the name White Feathers gave me," Lizzie explained. When she saw Jake wasn't listening, she waded back into the water to try pulling him away from Red Wolf. "Jake, stop! This is crazy."

"Crazy? I'm trying to save you!" Jake protested.

"Save me? I lost my footing. Red Wolf was helping me."

Jake stopped fighting to look at her. Breathing hard, he pushed back his dripping bangs and eyed Red Wolf.

"Come on, Lizzie, you need to get back to camp. You shouldn't have come this far. I think you've had enough adventure," he grunted through gritted teeth as he made his way out of the water.

"I'm not ready," she countered. "He is White Feathers' grandson. I wanted to see the ocean, and he was coming here to fish."

"Cookie said you were visiting, but you failed to mention this Red Wolf Indian. The old Indian woman didn't say anything about him either when she said you were at the beach. You've been gone longer than usual, and Cookie was getting concerned. Let's go. It'll be getting dark in a couple of hours."

Glancing at Red Wolf, Lizzie gave him a sympathetic look. "I'm sorry, Red Wolf. I guess I should be heading back."

"You want your fish?" Red Wolf asked.

"Take it to White Feathers."

"Yicau will be grateful," Red Wolf responded, placing both fish in his leather pouch. With a grin he added, "Kittape?"

Lizzie smiled, knowing he was asking if she planned to visit them again tomorrow. "Kittape."

"What?" Jake interrupted, looking at her.

"It's just a Woccon tribe word."

Picking up her shoes and stockings, she was about to collect her stash of seashells when White Feathers appeared over the sand dune. Surprisingly, an old white man was with her.

"What's wrong, Yicau?" Red Wolf called out.

"A whale is stuck on the shoals," White Feathers announced.

"Someone needs to see if it's stuck or injured. I would go, but I'm not as spry as I once was. Years ago, I watched an Indian swim out to a whale. Medicine Woman thinks ye can," the old man said.

Hearing the old man talk in the sailor slang like the pirates, Lizzie guessed he was the pilot Cookie told her about. According to Cookie, Robert Farrow guided ships into the inlet, a duty given to him by the government of Carolina. Several other men lived on Ocracoke, but he and his wife, Louise, were the only ones living on the southern end. Lizzie assumed he was the same guide Red Wolf talked about when he came for White Feathers to help the guide's sick wife. She recalled White Feathers saying Mrs. Farrow was better.

"I will try. Where is it stuck?" Red Wolf wanted to know.

"On the point where the inlet flows into the sound," Mr. Farrow declared, guiding his brown horse down to the beach.

"Let me get my pony," Red Wolf commented as he whistled.

Responding to his call, the beautiful pony trotted onto the sandy beach. Once Red Wolf had retrieved her, he climbed onto her back and joined the old man, who had mounted his own horse. With a word of caution from White Feathers, they took off like the wind.

"I am going to see what can be done. Are you coming, White Swan?" the old Indian woman questioned Lizzie.

"Yes, ma'am."

"What?" Jake demanded, pulling her aside. "Lizzie, we need to get back to camp. There's no need to go look at a stranded whale."

"You said we've got a couple of hours before sunset. How many chances will we get to see a real whale up close?"

Jake ran his fingers through his light brown hair in frustration. Lizzie held her breath hoping he would agree while working on her next argument. Thankfully, she didn't have to keep nagging him.

"Fine, let's go."

Grinning, Lizzie stuffed seashells in her stocking-filled shoes before running over to White Feathers. Ignoring her saturated clothing, she walked beside the elderly Indian woman, trying to keep up with her surprisingly swift pace while Jake trudged behind. After what seemed like miles of endless sandy beach, they made it to the end of the island. Nearing the peninsula, Lizzie could see the giant, dark gray whale floundering in the tidal waters off the point on a sandbar. Amazingly, the creature was over half the size of the *Adventure*. The old man stood on the edge of the water, watching Red Wolf inch his way to the massive beast in what appeared to be bloody water.

"The great whale has lost his blood," White Feathers observed.

"Aye, it's a shame. The lad said he's badly injured, the bottom jaw and tongue are gone. He's trying to figure out a way to get on the beast so he can plug his blowhole," Mr. Farrow answered.

"Plug his blowhole?" Jake blurted out.

"There's nothing we can do to save it. Looks like the thrashers got a hold of him," the pilot confirmed.

"'Thrashers'?" Lizzie repeated. "I thought whales were the biggest animal in the ocean."

"They are, but all creatures have enemies. For sperm whales, those enemies are thrashers and swordfish. Both will fatally attack a whale. By the bites, I'd say this whale was the thrashers' prey. In most cases, both will eat the whale's tongue. Without his tongue, the whale will die. We need to put the poor beast out of his misery by plugging its air hole. Indians have done it for years," Mr. Farrow stated.

White Feathers nodded. "Warriors of my tribe took canoes out when they saw a whale. They plugged the blowhole and waited for it to wash up on the beach. Whales are used for many things."

Gazing at Red Wolf, Lizzie noticed he was wading toward them in the waist-deep, scarlet-colored water.

"I need a plug," he announced as he made it back to shore. "We must hurry. The sharks are already coming near."

"I have something," the old man replied, hurrying to his horse.

Loosening the cinch holding the saddle in place, the pilot removed the saddle from his horse's back and placed it on the beach. Snatching the saddle blanket off, he handed Red Wolf the navy-blue material.

"It is not big enough. The whale has a hole this big," Red Wolf reported, holding up his hands to show it was at least two feet wide.

"We don't have anything that big," Mr. Farrow pointed out.

"Give me all your shoes," Red Wolf requested.

"Our shoes?" the old man asked Red Wolf, who was spreading out the navy-blue saddle blanket. "What will ye do with them?"

"Put them in this blanket."

"You're crazy!" Jake snorted. "I'm not taking off my shoes so you can stuff them down a whale's blowhole."

Seeing White Feathers taking off her deerskin shoes and the old man removing his boots, Lizzie dumped her collection of seashells on the beach. Tying her stockings around her arm, she passed her shoes to Red Wolf while Mr. Farrow got a rope.

"We need all the shoes," Red Wolf mentioned, eyeing Jake.

"No way!" Jake objected.

"Please, Jake," Lizzie begged.

Blowing in frustration, Jake rolled his eyes. He took off his boots and threw them at Red Wolf. With all the shoes, the young Indian folded the corners of the blanket together and tied the rope around the bundle.

"I'm going, too. I may not be able to climb on him, but I can do something," Mr. Farrow proclaimed, joining Red Wolf in the water.

When they were halfway, the old man fell. Juggling the bundle of shoes, Red Wolf helped him get up. After arguing, the old man agreed to stay in the shallow water. Red Wolf waded across the sandbar and up to the massive, dark gray beast. Avoiding the animal's large tail as it splashed the bloody water, Red Wolf climbed up on one of its paddle-shaped fins, which was the size of a canoe. Shuffling toward its large, square-shaped head, he reached the blowhole, where he shoved the bundle of shoes. The whale heaved forward, tossing him off its back. Clambering, the young Indian grabbed the paddlelike fin.

"Red Wolf!" White Feathers gasped, holding her cheeks.

Watching Red Wolf straining to pull himself up, Lizzie debated what to do. Although Mr. Farrow was trying to reach him, she knew he wouldn't be much help. Looking around, she concluded there wasn't anything they could do to help him unless…

Lizzie's gaze shifted to Jake. "You've got to help him, Jake."

"What? I don't think so."

"He might drown if you don't do something."

"Do what? Risk my life? Drown myself?"

"Just try. Please, for me."

Shaking his head, Jake waded into the water and made his way to the dark gray whale. The whale must have sensed his presence as he showered Jake in bloody seawater. Praying for them, Lizzie stood beside White Feathers, who was whispering Woccon words under her breath. As Jake regained his foothold, the whale lurched again, this time sending both boys underwater. Horrified, Lizzie tried not to panic as she prayed to God for help.

Jake and Red Wolf resurfaced. Holding on to each other, they attempted to remount the massive whale. This time, with Jake's help, Red Wolf made progress and minutes later he was hovering over the blowhole for the second try. Grabbing the bundle of shoes barely hanging from the opening, he forced it downward, plugging the two-foot-wide hole. Once in place, Red Wolf slipped off the whale's back and with Jake's assistance landed in the bloody, waist-deep water.

"Praise the Lord!" Lizzie breathed, relieved they were both okay.

"Red Wolf is all I have," White Feathers admitted. "Many warriors have braved the waters. I am proud of him. He could have died."

"Well, thankfully he didn't."

"You do not know the truth about him. He is not my blood. You think he is my grandson. It is not so. His parents died in the Great Sickness when he was a babe. I raised him as my own. Red Wolf does not know he has different blood."

"I don't think it would matter. Red Wolf loves you."

White Feathers didn't respond as Jake, Red Wolf, and the old man reached the shore. Behind them, the whale squirmed on the sandbar. Waiting for the great whale to breathe its last breath, Lizzie looked to the western horizon. The sun lingered above the dark blue waters of the sound, casting the sky in hues of pink, orange, and deep purple.

After no activity, Red Wolf waded back in the water to check the whale. Confirming it had taken its last breath, he climbed on its back to retrieve the bundle of shoes. The task of removing them from the blowhole was difficult. Surprisingly, Jake offered to help. Scrambling on top of the dead whale, Jake used his hunting knife to cut the hole bigger while Red Wolf pulled the bundle free. Shouting, they dismounted the dark gray creature and waded ashore.

"Even though the tide is coming in I don't think the beast will go out to sea. It'll be dark soon. We'll butcher it in the morning. Ye are certainly brave, lad. I'll see ye at daybreak," Mr. Farrow praised Red Wolf as he got his boots, rope, and blanket.

Saddling his brown horse, the old man mounted it and galloped away. Lizzie put on her stockings and shoes before picking up the handful of seashells. She looked at the giant whale again. Having seen a whale from the *Adventure*, she couldn't shake the feeling of deep sadness. Gazing at its huge, glazed-over eye, she wondered what horrible experience the whale felt during its final hours of life.

With White Feathers' riding astride Black Star, they walked the sandy beach. Eventually they made it to the marsh and sea oats. From there they trooped through the woods, arriving at the hut where they said their good-byes. Red Wolf thanked Jake for risking his life to help. This shocked Jake, who offered his hand in a handshake of peace.

Watching them, Lizzie thought about how hard it was for Jake to accept Red Wolf after all Jake went through seven years before. Each year on September 22, the colony stopped to remember the lives lost during the Indian attacks. Lizzie had noticed a change in Jake's attitude three days ago when the date rolled around. She hoped that Jake's meeting Red Wolf would help Jake move forward.

Leaving the clearing, Lizzie and Jake meandered through the cedar trees and yaupon hollies. Ear-piercing cries from locusts in the trees gave the woods an eerie feeling. With the fading daylight, it was difficult to see. They were halfway across the densest part of the forest when a shriek sounded through the woods. Terrified, Lizzie grabbed Jake's elbow. Two shadows came around the next bend. She recognized the figures as JJ and his father, Joseph.

JJ eyed Jake. "Where have ye been? Cookie's worried."

Jake yanked his arm away from her. "I found Lizzie with the Indian, but the old pilot came up. He said there was a stranded whale at the end of the island on a sandbar. We went to look at it."

Realizing JJ was jealous of seeing her holding Jake's arm, Lizzie spoke up. "I wanted to see the whale."

"Ye father returned half an hour ago," Joseph revealed.

Trudging onward, Joseph told them what happened in Bath at the court hearing. Secretary Knight opened the floor for Black Beard to speak. After telling the governor and officials how his crew found the French ship stranded, he mentioned the dangers of leaving it near the inlet. He asked Governor Charles Eden what he should do. Several council members questioned this story. Governor Eden referred to Tobias Knight for options, giving him the opportunity to offer the plan he and Black Beard cooked up. The governor approved, giving Black Beard the right to burn the ship to her waterline.

Coming out of the woods, the group descended the sandy embankment that led to the sound side of the island. From here, Lizzie could see the *Adventure*'s outline against the dark purple sky. Although the sun had disappeared beyond the horizon, there was enough light to see the French ship anchored close to land. Approaching the camp and its soft glow of lantern light, Lizzie could hear the men talking. They had almost reached the galley tent when Cookie came running over.

He pulled her into a hug. "Ye scared the daylights out of me!"

"I'm sorry, Cookie," she mumbled, both surprised by his hug and delighted he cared about her. "I didn't mean to worry you."

"What happened to ye? Never mind. Ye can tell me later. Captain ordered the men to burn the French ship."

"Let's go see what we can do," Joseph commented.

Watching them join the rest of the crew, Lizzie stood alone on the crescent-shaped beach, swatting mosquitoes. The pirates started the fire, and in no time the remains of the French ship burned in bright orange flames, taking with it the skeletons or secrets Black Beard acquired from its stolen plunder. Staring into the inferno, Lizzie's mind wandered as the blaze reached into the night's sky, sending smoke drifting up to the evening's first stars.

CHAPTER SIXTEEN

☠

COLD HEARTS

October 1, 1718 ~ Wednesday

October arrived, bringing with it the first dry weather in three days. Lizzie was glad to see the sun again as she fed the chickens and thought about the storm they endured. The rainy weather put a strain on the pirates, who spent their time drinking, competing in games, and getting on each other's nerves. Out of the twenty-three men, only Jake, Cookie, and JJ remained sober. This gave them many hours of idle chitchat, much of which Lizzie tried to keep Jake and Cookie involved in so that she wouldn't be alone with JJ.

On Friday afternoon before the storm, Lizzie and Jake went to see the whale. Red Wolf, White Feathers, and Mr. Farrow worked hard to salvage what they could. By Saturday, Mr. Farrow had the blubber and oil moved to his place. He planned to trade it with merchants for supplies. They finished the hardest work when the rain started Saturday night. Mr. Farrow thought it would take several days to strip the whale to its skeleton. They intended to use the bones, too.

To Lizzie's surprise, the whale had a fifteen-pound brain and had swallowed a giant squid. It reminded her of Jonah's ordeal in the Bible. The prophet disobeyed God, and as a result, a big fish swallowed him. After three days he prayed for forgiveness, and God caused the fish to spit him out. Jonah ended up preaching God's word.

Getting her mind off the whale, Lizzie gathered eggs from the chickens. Meanwhile, the pirates picked up the limbs left by the storm. Grabbing leftovers from breakfast, Lizzie headed to Tuffy's and Reba's cages. They greeted her with squawks and meows.

Unlocking the latch, her eyes caught a glimpse of some dark purple skin on her right wrist. A chill went through her as the memories of how she acquired the bruise came flooding back. It began with a simple mistake that caused a knockdown, drag-out of a mess.

The situation started when Husky challenged John Martin to an arm-wrestling match. Of course, Husky easily beat him. Eventually, the exciting game had every pirate entertained. Hours passed while the world outside the galley tent whirled with wind and rain. Finally, Israel dared Black Beard to a match, saying he couldn't hang with the crew. Intoxicated and determined to prove himself, the captain accepted the dare. Black Beard was stronger than Israel anticipated.

The wrestling match didn't excite JJ like it did the rest of the pirates. Instead of joining the others in cheering, JJ cornered Lizzie in a conversation. When she heard her papa ask for someone to refill his cup with brandy, she jumped at the chance. Focused on fulfilling her papa's request, Lizzie went to pour the brandy when her eye caught JJ winking at her. Not paying attention, she missed her papa's cup and poured brandy all over the table. Furious, Israel jumped up and grabbed Lizzie's wrist, making her scream.

His brutal action caused an uproar as Black Beard sprung to his feet and JJ attacked Israel from behind. In a flurry of fists, the situation escalated to a fight that ended with a shot from Cookie's flintlock pistol. The ordeal was something Lizzie wouldn't forget.

After feeding her friends, Lizzie walked back to the table to wash the bowl the leftovers were in. Cookie entered the galley, bringing with him brass weights.

"What are you up to?" she asked.

"Captain wanted these French weights. He needs to weigh—well, I guess I shouldn't say," he muttered, acting sheepish.

"Weigh what?"

Looking around, Cookie leaned forward and lowered his voice. "He wants to weigh the gold and silver coins."

"Gold!"

"Shhh!" he gasped. "Not so loud!"

"I'm sorry. Can I come with you?"

"Suppose ye could."

Trailing behind Cookie, Lizzie entered her papa's tent. As they closed the flap, Black Beard greeted them in a gruff voice.

"I'm busy. Whatever ye want will have to wait."

"Captain, I found it," Cookie announced, capturing his attention.

"Great! Bring it here," he exclaimed as he took the brass weights from Cookie. "What are ye doing here, Lizzie?"

"Cookie said you were going to weigh something."

Black Beard eyed Cookie. "He did, huh? Well, have a seat."

Pulling a key from his coat pocket, the bearded captain opened the bottom drawer where he kept his prized possessions. Lizzie sat down in front of her papa's desk, noticing how her papa seemed to be somewhat sober. Curious to know why he hadn't been drinking as much, she watched him place three tan cloth sacks on his desktop. Opening one of them, Black Beard dumped out silver "cob" coins. The next sack was full of gold coins, and the third held a bunch of broken coins commonly called pieces of eight. Weighing each pile of coins, he made notes in a black leather book that Lizzie recognized as his pocketbook diary. Suddenly there was a shout.

"What's going on now?" Black Beard questioned with a sigh. "Go look, Cookie. Those men are worse than children."

With a nod, Cookie left the tent as Black Beard looked up at her.

"I'm sure ye are wondering about all this," he acknowledged, waving his hand over the piles of coins.

"Yes, I have to admit I'm curious to know how you got it."

"I think ye already know. I've told Cookie in case something happened to me. Ye can never say a word to the crew, including JJ."

"You don't have to worry about me telling JJ."

"I've noticed the two of ye spending time together."

"Only because I had to."

"Or because ye are realizing he's a good, hardworking lad."

Cookie returned before she could object. She forgot what she was going to say when she saw his concerned face.

"Captain, we have a problem. Nathaniel was in the rigging fixing sails torn in the storm. He saw a ship off the southern coast. It appears to be coming into the inlet. Thomas took him a spyglass."

"So? Ships go through the inlet all the time. What makes this one important?" Black Beard wanted to know.

"Nathaniel thinks it's worth looking into."

Black Beard slowly nodded. "I'll be there in a moment then."

Cookie headed outside while Black Beard slid the coins into their cloth sacks. Placing them in the drawer, he locked it and stood up. Leaving the tent with her papa, Lizzie saw the pirates had gathered at the edge of the water staring at the *Adventure*. Nathaniel Jackson was high in the rigging holding onto the mast with one arm while he peered through the spyglass with his free hand. Quartermaster Thomas Miller stood on the deck below with his hands propped on his hips. Putting down the spyglass, Nathaniel said something to Thomas, who relayed the information to Black Beard.

"Captain, Nathaniel says it's a brigantine. There's no flag in her rigging. What do ye want to do?"

Black Beard looked concerned as he rubbed his wiry beard. "No flag? That's not good. We need to check it out. Prepare to set sail."

Surprised by his command, the pirates looked at each other before scattering. As they went about their duties, Lizzie ran to catch up with her papa, wondering what he wanted her to do.

"Um, Captain, what should I be doing?" she asked him.

Stopping in his tracks, Black Beard whipped around to look at her. "I'm sorry, I hadn't even thought about ye. Ye don't need to go with us. In fact, Cookie should stay here, too." Raising his voice, he called out to the men. "Cookie, come here."

Cookie hurried over. "What is it, Captain?"

"I want ye to stay here with Lizzie. There's no telling what will happen, but I don't want Lizzie there in case it gets nasty. Stephen Daniel and John Giles can help JJ and Jake guard the plunder."

"Do ye think the ship is a threat?" Cookie questioned in alarm.

"Since they aren't flying a flag, I'm thinking they're pirates."

"Aren't pirates friendly to each other?" Lizzie inquired.

"Most of us are rivals competing for the same prize ships. We need to get going. Cookie, keep ye pistol near and cover the casks of sugar with limbs. We must protect the plunder. It's our leverage to clear ourselves with Governor Eden," Black Beard pointed out.

"Maybe Miss Lizzie would be safer with the Indian woman."

Black Beard glanced uneasily at Lizzie. "It might be a good idea. We don't need them to find out that we have a lady in our company or that I have a daughter. Also, find her a shirt and some britches. Do whatever ye can to make her look like a young man."

The pirate captain walked to his tent. He soon returned wearing his fancy red coat and the bandolier strapped to his chest. There were six pistols tucked under the leather bandolier and a sword hung from his side. Coming over to Lizzie, he handed her a flintlock pistol.

"Do ye remember how to use ye grandfather's gun?" he grunted.

"Not really, except for hitting the enemy with the handle. Cookie gave me lessons with his pistol," she replied, taking the gun.

"Whatever works. Be careful."

Moving to the water's edge, Black Beard helped the others launch the periauger full of weapons and men. On the second trip, he joined the group as they rowed the periauger to the *Adventure*.

"Come along, Miss Lizzie, we've got to hurry," Cookie urged.

Fearful of what was going to happen, Lizzie hurried to catch up with him. Inside her papa's tent, the cook located the chest where he kept spare clothes. Lizzie recalled the first days of her adventure when he gave her items from this chest. Rummaging through it, Cookie pulled out a shirt, pants, and a pair of shoes.

"Change into these," he instructed as he left the tent.

Taking the clothes, Lizzie changed her outfit. Tying up her curly, dark brown hair in a bun, she pulled down her tricorn hat to hide it. Thoughts rushed through her mind as she hid her belongings among the clothing in Cookie's chest. Touching the locket hanging around her neck, she tucked it under her shirt and prayed for God to help. She couldn't shake the panic she felt. Could this be another battle? If they were pirates, she doubted it would turn out well.

Exiting her papa's tent, she said good-bye to Cookie before setting out for White Feathers' hut. She looked around for Jake but realized the camp was empty. In the distance, she could see the *Adventure* sailing away from Ocracoke Island and into the channel.

Sighing, she walked to the small beach where she spent so much of her time. Wrestling with feelings of fear and worry, Lizzie headed into the woods of cedar trees and yaupon hollies. She held tightly to her grandfather's pistol, praying as she hiked to her destination.

Boom! Boom! Boom! Boom! Boom! Boom!

Startled, Lizzie instinctively ducked as she wondered if the noise was cannon fire echoing in the distance. Suddenly, a second round reverberated through the trees.

Boom! Boom! Boom! Boom! Boom! Boom!

Terrified and overwhelmed, she fell to her knees and called out to God. With tears streaming down her cheeks, she fought with feelings of wanting to return to camp even though it could be dangerous. Picking herself up, Lizzie dusted the sandy dirt off her pants and grabbed her grandfather's pistol. Forcing her better judgment aside, she headed back to the sound side of Ocracoke. In no time, she could see the crescent-shaped beach. Approaching the camp, she ran across the sand to the galley tent as Cookie emerged carrying a spyglass.

"Why are ye back?" he demanded. "Ye shouldn't be here."

"I heard the booming and decided to return. What's happening?"

"It sounded like friendly fire. Pirates have a tradition when we encounter fellow pirates. Each ship fires six cannon shots in salute to the other captain. Then the crews will raise their black flags."

"What are you doing?"

Cookie held the spyglass to his eye. "I'm trying to see who it is." After a few minutes he lowered it and scratched his chin. "Looks like Calico Jack on deck. He's the only pirate I know who owns a calico jacket. Best I remember, he's Captain Charles Vane's quartermaster."

"Calico Jack?" Lizzie blurted out.

"His real name is John Rackham. He got the nickname 'Calico Jack' from his colorful patchwork clothing. There are quite a few men aboard their brigantine, about eighty to a hundred, if I had to guess. Most likely, they'll come ashore. Ye need to hurry up and get to the Indian's hut. Vane's crew is a rowdy bunch. They're coldhearted men, Miss Lizzie, and I know this because we've had men among us who were just as bad. I need to tell the others who it is."

"I can go."

"Nay, ye need to get to safety." Looking back at the galley tent, he sighed. "I don't know how we're going to feed them."

"Stay here and get ready for them while I go tell the others what's going on. I know the way to Springer's Point."

"Alright, but ye better go to the hut from there," Cookie agreed.

Leaving her grandfather's pistol in the tent, Lizzie took off for Springer's Point. Zigzagging around water holes, she went through the marsh to higher ground. The pirates moved the sugar and cocoa so that the floodwaters wouldn't ruin the plunder. Coming to an area of live oak trees, she spotted Stephen and John as they finished putting the last limbs on the hidden loot. Hearing her footsteps, someone grabbed Lizzie from behind and held a knife up to her.

"Who is it?" called JJ's voice as Lizzie tried to free herself.

"It's me, Lizzie!" she quickly responded, knowing they wouldn't recognize her in sailor's clothing.

"Lizzie? Why are ye here? Put ye knife down, Jake," JJ stated.

Letting go of her, Jake put his knife back in its leather sheath. "Why are you dressed like a pirate?"

"Cookie sent me," she announced, aware of the strange look on Jake's face. "He looked in his spyglass. It's Captain Charles Vane. There's about eighty to a hundred pirates on board the ship."

"Vane, huh? Haven't seen him in months. Stephen and John can stay here to guard the plunder. We'll go see if Cookie needs help. Let me go update them," JJ declared, returning to the live oak trees.

Once they were alone, Lizzie apologized for not speaking up as she approached and explained why she was wearing sailor's clothes. Jake also expressed regrets for holding a knife to her. When JJ came back, the three of them started for camp. Walking through the marsh, JJ talked about Charles Vane. Listening to his description of the vicious pirate captain, Lizzie kept in step with Jake. Drawing near to the pirate camp, she saw the *Adventure* with another ship beside her. The brigantine, as Cookie called it, was the same size as the *Adventure* and had a black flag flapping in the breeze from the topmast.

"We're going on to camp, Lizzie, but you need to get to White Feathers' hut. Cookie said you'd be safer there. When he gives the okay, we'll come get you," Jake instructed as they departed.

Walking away, Lizzie felt drawn to the pirate camp, though she tried to fight her urges to return. Turning around, she went back. After reaching the encampment, Lizzie could see a group of scraggly looking men already on the beach while another load of pirates rowed ashore on two periaugers. Shocked by the number of pirates intermingling with Black Beard's crew, Lizzie scurried to the back of the galley. Praying no one would see her, she hunkered down behind the tent. Thankfully, she found a loose area of the canvas where she could crawl underneath, coming out on the inside near Tuffy's cage.

The cat greeted her with whiskers flared. *"Meow!"*

"Shhh," Lizzie hushed her.

Above Tuffy's cage, Reba began to squawk. Not wanting to draw attention to herself, Lizzie moved to the edge of the tent. She carefully lifted the flap to take a peep outside. The first thing she saw was Cookie standing by the cook pit turning an iron spit with a piece of meat roasting over the fire. Her papa came walking up with another man behind him. The other man wore a long gray coat with frills around the cuffs like the ones Governor Charles Eden wore. His long brown hair hung down to his shoulders, and he had a scar on the left side of his neck partially covered by a bright red scarf.

Figuring the man was Charles Vane, Lizzie watched him follow Black Beard into his tent. She could hear her papa offer the other pirate captain a little dram of brandy, which Vane gladly accepted.

"I can't believe it, Charles," Black Beard confessed. "To think Benjamin Hornigold would stoop so low as to start hunting pirates. He was one of us, for goodness sakes!"

"Aye, Edward, 'tis a shame. He's not the only traitor. My former captain, Henry Jennings, turned out to be a deserter, too. It's all Woodes Rogers' fault. Ever since he came from Bristol, England, to reside at Nassau, he's been meddling with our friends and taking over our island. Nassau has always been a safe haven for us, a place we could go without worry of the authorities. Well, ye can forget going back because Rogers has cleaned out the place. In fact, I've set up a new base for operations at Green Turtle Cay. Henry Jennings found us a couple of fortnights ago, so we came up here for a little excitement. We managed to capture a few ships on our way up from the south. Got some good plunder, I might add," Charles Vane replied.

"We've been in the northern waters most of the summer. In May, we blockaded Charles Town and later ran *Queen Anne's Revenge* aground at Old Topsail Inlet near Fish Town. I convinced the foolish Stede Bonnet to go see the government at Bath while I stayed with our four ships. When he and part of the crew left, I stranded all but a hundred of the remaining men and departed on the *Adventure*. By the time Bonnet returned, we were up at Bath Town getting our own pardons," Black Beard revealed.

"So, ye are free men?" Vane asked.

"We were until the fellows outvoted me and attacked a couple of French ships on our way back from Pennsylvania. Now we've got to pay a fine to Governor Eden."

"Did ye happen to see Margaret while ye were in Pennsylvania?"

Lizzie leaned forward to hear her papa's answer. Before he could speak, someone entered the tent calling out for his captain. Not recognizing the voice, she presumed he was from Vane's crew.

"What's wrong?" Vane demanded.

"Calico Jack said to come get ye. Several fights have broken out."

"I'm not surprised. There has been a lot of tension lately. With ninety men cooped up on a ship, it was only a matter of time before things exploded. The pirate articles say quarrels will be settled onshore, so let them get it out of their systems," Vane responded.

"This is more serious, Captain. Normally it's a fistfight, but this time they're using weapons. Calico can't stop them," the man urged.

"Alright, I'm coming. Sorry for the interruption, Edward. Ye know how it is with an unruly bunch of scoundrels."

Lizzie watched the three men leave her papa's tent to see what the commotion was about. Curious to see things herself, she eased out of the galley tent and went around to the back side of her papa's quarters. Making sure her hat covered her hair, Lizzie snuck behind some barrels of rum that stood outside the tent.

A throng of pirates stood cheering as men fought each other. From her hiding place, Lizzie could see Charles Vane forcing his way through the crowd while Black Beard called his men together. With Vane's eighty-nine pirates and the eighteen in Black Beard's crew, the crescent-shaped beach was rather crowded. Being so close to Vane's crew gave Lizzie a new outlook on what defined a pirate. These men were clearly ruthless and had encountered many battles. Some even had a missing leg and were walking on a wooden peg.

As the mob parted for their captain, Lizzie spotted an African man bigger than Husky straddled on top of a crewmate. The white man struggled under his attacker's weight, but the tight grip around his throat quickly strangled the man to death. Once his body went limp, the broad-shouldered African pulled out a long-bladed knife and stabbed the deceased pirate in the chest. This infuriated those nearby who tried to stop him. By now, Vane had ended the other fights. All the attention was on the African who sliced open the dead man's chest. Horrified, Lizzie watched in stunned silence as the African pulled out the man's bloody heart.

Feeling sick, she covered her mouth as she hurried back to the galley. Behind her, a gunshot echoed through the angry crowd. Back in the galley, she threw her hat to the ground and found an empty bucket to gag in. Sitting behind some crates, she overheard voices a few feet from her.

"What's going on, Cookie?" Jake wanted to know. "JJ and I split up to cover more ground hunting. I heard a gunshot."

"Several fights broke out within Vane's crew. There's a six-foot-tall African in his crew named Big Reuben. He was fighting another man named Shorty, who is a mouthy showoff despite his small size. From what their crewmates told me, Shorty wanted the African beads Reuben wore around his neck. Everyone knows Africans prize these beaded neckpieces as a symbol of pride. It's a part of their heritage. Well, Shorty got it in his head he was going to steal them. Reuben waited for the first opportunity to get on land and take back what was his. He choked Shorty to death and cut out his heart. Then Shorty's brother Rooster shot Reuben to avenge his brother's death."

"Cut out his heart? Why?" Jake blurted out.

"Because Shorty brought shame to Reuben. African beads are a symbol of honor, and by taking them Shorty was taking his honor. The only way to win his honor back was to take Shorty's heart. I know it sounds crazy, but it's like an unspoken law. Enough about them. Leave those rabbits ye killed right there," Cookie declared.

"Two pirates dead and they just got on the island. Doesn't sound promising to me. We have our own problem. While I was hunting, I ran into White Feathers' grandson. He hasn't seen Lizzie."

"She's missing? Captain's going to be upset about this! We must find her. She could be hurt," Cookie stated, his voice full of panic.

"Lizzie could be anywhere. I didn't tell Red Wolf why she was supposed to be at his grandmother's so he's not out looking for her. Do you think we need him for his tracking skills?"

Conflicting thoughts bombarded Lizzie. The last thing she wanted was them to worry, but if she gave away her secret, they would know she disobeyed both her papa and Cookie. Not knowing what choice to make, she found herself crying as scenes of the murder flashed through her mind. Her crying got the attention of Cookie and Jake, who pulled back the tent flap. Still sitting behind the crates, Lizzie hugged her knees as tears flooded down her cheeks.

"Miss Lizzie?" Cookie called out as he knelt in front of the crates.

Seeing Cookie staring at her, Lizzie threw her arms around his neck. She wept into his shoulder while he gently patted the back of her head, trying to comfort her.

"I'm sorry, Cookie. Please don't be mad. I should've listened to you. Those pirates are horrible. He cut out his heart," she sobbed.

"I wish ye hadn't seen it. Being a pirate makes a man change. Some even turn to the dark side. Those men are the ones who have endured hardships and personal losses. They allow the devil to work on their cold hearts and dark souls. It gives the rest of us a bad name. Shorty got what he asked for when he stole the beads, which meant heart and soul to Reuben. In return, Reuben stole his literal heart and his life. Now Rooster will have to watch his back. I know he was taking revenge on his brother's killer, but Reuben has friends, too. They're a brutal bunch. We must figure out what to do with ye. It isn't safe, especially since they're fighting among each other."

"Should I take her to White Feathers?" Jake questioned.

"The men will be drinking heavily tonight. For now, Miss Lizzie can hide here. Let's keep this between us. I need to go check on the roast. Why don't ye clean the rabbits ye killed, Jake? Be careful coming and going," Cookie instructed as he helped Lizzie stand up. "Stay here, Miss Lizzie. Jake can bring ye something to eat."

"I'll be back, Lizzie," Jake added, leaving the tent behind Cookie.

Moving to Reba's and Tuffy's cages, Lizzie bent to rub Tuffy as the one-eyed cat brushed against the wooden pegs of her cage. Fresh tears filled her eyes while guilt swept over her. Cookie had been so good to her. How could she deliberately disobey him? Not only were his feelings hurt, but now he had to face her father. Why had she put him in such a predicament?

The image of Reuben holding the heart in his blood-soaked hand came to her mind again. She doubted the image would go away. Like Cookie said, these pirates had cold hearts. They weren't just pirates, they were murderers. Nobody on the island was safe.

CHAPTER SEVENTEEN

☠

PIRATE BANYAN

October 4, 1718 ~ Saturday

Smells of burning cedar filled the air, giving off a smoky aroma as it seasoned the meat hanging over the cook pit. Lizzie stood by the fire occasionally turning the iron spit to rotate the slab of pork meat. Across the camp, Vane's men were preparing meat on another cook pit. Reaching up, Lizzie self-consciously pulled down her tricorn hat to make sure no one noticed she was a girl. She had been wearing her disguise since the pirates arrived Wednesday.

During the last three days, Charles Vane ordered a dozen of his crew to stay aboard his brigantine after more fights erupted. Shorty's brother, Rooster, was among those detained. A hearing took place on the ship. Vane's crew voted to release the men with a warning of punishment. Lizzie learned from Cookie that Vane's punishments were brutal. Cookie also told her Vane kept Big Reuben's beads for himself, a move some of his crew didn't like.

While Captain Vane dealt with his unruly crew, Black Beard and Quartermaster Thomas Miller arranged for the plunder to be under guard. They divided the job into three shifts assigned to JJ, Stephen, and John Giles. The rest of the crew mingled with Vane's men as they shared stories of captured ships and sipped on bottles of rum.

With such edginess in the air, Lizzie had been spending her days with White Feathers. In the evenings, she stayed away from her papa so that Captain Vane's crew wouldn't get suspicious. Not knowing where Vane's men would go on the island, Cookie suggested Jake go with her to White Feathers' hut.

Despite the concerns at the pirate encampment, Lizzie enjoyed her time with White Feathers. Jake and Red Wolf were now friends and strangely had a lot in common. Red Wolf's parents died from the Great Sickness that infected the Woccon tribe because of careless white men. On the other hand, the revenge-seeking Tuscarora Indians killed Jake's family. Both had harbored deep-rooted anger.

As Jake discovered the best way to make and set hunting traps with Red Wolf, Lizzie went with White Feathers to pick fox grapes. Having gathered seven bushels, they had been boiling them down. Today, Lizzie helped the elderly Indian stomp the remaining grapes to make grape juice. It was so much fun, she talked about it on the way back to camp, hardly giving Jake a chance to tell her about throwing tomahawks and shooting a bow and arrow.

When they returned mid-afternoon, Cookie informed them Black Beard was hosting a pirate banyan, which he explained was a party. Hunting groups went into the interior of the island to kill enough meat for the feast. Captain Vane sent some of his crew with Black Beard's men on the hunt, but most stayed to see how Rooster would react to seeing his brother's grave.

The pirates buried Shorty and Reuben on higher ground sewn up in their sailcloth hammocks. This was the customary seaman's burial before tossing the body overboard. Since Vane didn't care what they did with the bodies, it was up to their crewmates to make do without a coffin. According to Cookie, no one spoke over the bodies. In his opinion, every man deserved a few words spoken, even if it wasn't the ritual the colonists did from the Book of Common Prayer. It sounded like pirates didn't receive a Christian burial on land or at sea.

Having so much to do for the feast, Cookie put Lizzie and Jake to work preparing the hog that Garret and John Martin killed.

Vane's crew had also killed a cow. To Lizzie, the situation was wrong. The meat came from open-grazing livestock owned by planters on the mainland. Cookie explained how the animals roamed free on the island. Until now, Black Beard insisted on eating wild animals and seafood native to Ocracoke, but with so many to feed he agreed with Vane to allow hunting parties to kill some of the livestock.

"How's the pork roast coming, Tiny?" Cookie asked.

Hearing her new nickname, Lizzie turned to see Cookie walking up carrying a cast-iron cauldron and a bucket. The name had been a clever idea of his to keep her identity secret. His joke of her being a tiny little thing for a pirate had literally became her new disguise.

"It's getting close," she replied.

Cookie grinned as he put the iron pot by the fire. "Good. I've got a surprise. We're going to make hoecakes and false chocolate."

"So, that's why you wanted to see if White Feathers had any extra cornmeal. How do you make false chocolate? Surely, you aren't using the cocoa plunder," she continued.

"I know better than to take the loot. I picked up a bucket of live oak acorns while the men were hunting. Boiling them makes the nuts soft enough to grind. Indians get the oil out of the nuts, but ye can also make false chocolate. It's good stuff, even if it isn't sweet."

Cookie dumped acorns into the cauldron of water. Leaning over the pot, Lizzie wrinkled her nose. The floating acorns didn't look appetizing, and she doubted Cookie could make them into chocolate. Going to the galley tent, he returned with a bowl of cornmeal and an empty bowl. He added boiling water to the cornmeal to make it thick. Stirring the mixture, he dropped a spoonful into a seasoned cast-iron frying pan. Soon, the empty bowl was full of golden-brown hoecakes.

Looking into the smoke-filled sky, Lizzie noticed the sun had nearly disappeared beyond the western horizon. Streaks of color illuminated the pink clouds as a flock of geese honked overhead.

"I've got your table, Cookie," Jake commented as he came over. "I found the boards you kept from the French ship and got four empty barrels. Where do you want it? I already fixed Calico Jack's."

"How about over here?" Lizzie suggested, pointing behind her.

"Nay, put it near the fire. Those gallinippers will be out with all the rain we've had. The smoke keeps them away," Cookie advised.

"'Gallinippers'? What are they?" Lizzie wondered.

"He means mosquitoes," Jake informed her as he moved the barrels to where Cookie wanted them.

Once they finished setting up the table, she placed the bowl of hoecakes on top. She went to the galley tent, found a basket, and filled it with pewter plates and cups. Back at the cook pit, Jake strained the soggy acorns while Cookie ground them in a bowl. In no time, the false chocolate was ready to eat with the hoecakes and pork roast. Seeing Black Beard's men gathering, Cookie urged them to eat so that the others wouldn't recognize Lizzie. With plates full, they sat on short barrels on the opposite side of the fire. Mumbling a prayer, Lizzie dipped the hoecake in false chocolate. Surprisingly, it tasted like sweet roasted chestnuts.

"Well, does it taste like chocolate?" Lizzie questioned Jake.

"I don't know. I've never had chocolate. Have you?"

"Yes, but only a few times, so I'm not sure. It's expensive."

"Now you know how to make the fake kind," Jake laughed.

Gazing at the pirates, Lizzie noticed that some had started playing music while others enjoyed their feast. One of her papa's men, Richard Greensail, played a tune on his long trumpet. She recalled Jake talking about the African's talent. Listening, she had to agree that the long trumpet made a beautiful sound. From here, she could see her papa eating with Charles Vane at their campfire. By the way they interacted, she wondered how her papa could be friends with the cruel man.

"Looks like Captain Vane's men are eating fish along with their beef," Lizzie mentioned as she picked up a piece of pork.

"They probably haven't had fish. JJ said they've been at sea trying to outrun the authorities and terrorizing ships. When I was over there it looked like they caught some mackerels and were roasting oysters."

"Nasty! They can have all the slimy oysters they want."

Jake chuckled. "Oysters aren't bad. It's how you cook them."

"If you say so," she answered, swatting a mosquito biting her back. "Cookie was right. The gallinippers are already swarming."

"It's the rain. They thrive on wetlands. Without a breeze, they'll tote us away. They aren't as bad as the black biting flies."

"I can't stand any of them," she added, hitting one biting through her sleeve.

"Guess Black Beard's getting tired of the bugs, too."

Lizzie looked across the camp at her papa. The pirate captain had jumped to his feet and was madly swatting the biting insects. Holding onto the smoking clay pipe, he danced around cursing as those around him laughed at his drunken performance. Embarrassed, Lizzie watched as he tripped over one of the rocks around the cook pit. Luckily, he managed to keep from falling into the fire.

"I see Captain is entertaining us," JJ said, causing Lizzie and Jake to look up.

JJ moved another small barrel to where they were sitting. Placing it close to Lizzie's, he sat down with his plate of food. Although she was uncomfortable with him seated so close, Lizzie tried to hide it.

"It's quite a party," Jake muttered, shaking his head.

Black Beard tied strips of paper to his wiry beard before lighting the slow-burning fuses. The flames illuminated his face, casting shadows over his features to make him look like the most fearsome pirate alive, if not the devil himself.

"I think he's lost his mind," Lizzie sighed.

"Captain sets his beard on fire since the smoke keeps the mosquitoes away. He does it to scare captives, too," JJ informed them.

"Black Beard and Vane are both drunk," Jake stated as the captains did a jig to the sounds of spoons, flutes, and a four-stringed cittern.

"I'm glad I got a chance to enjoy myself. Sitting alone at Springer's Point for eight hours is miserable. So, what did ye do today, Liz—" JJ began, stopping when Jake loudly cleared his throat. "What?"

"You mean 'Tiny,'" Jake reminded him.

"'Tiny'? I haven't even been around her," JJ remarked sarcastically.

"'Him,'" Jake corrected. "You haven't been around *him*."

"If somebody hears ye, there could be trouble," Cookie warned as he walked up. "Let's talk about my chocolate. How was it?"

"Chocolate?" JJ repeated, looking at his plate.

"I thought it was good," Lizzie admitted with a smile.

Cookie grinned. "Thank ye. Wait a minute. They're playing one of my favorites. Come on, JJ, ye know the words. Sing it with me."

The music changed to a fast-paced song Cookie called "Coast of High Barbary." As Richard Greensail led the other musicians with his long trumpet, the entire pirate banyan erupted in shouts. Dancing wildly on the sandy shore, the pirate clan belted out the words in unison as a few of them added an occasional "Arrrr!" in their pirate slang.

Look ahead, look a stern, look the weather in the lee,
Blow high! Blow low! and so sailed we.
I see a wreck to the windward and a lofty ship to lee,
A sailing down all on the coasts of High Barbary.

JJ and Cookie convinced Lizzie and Jake to sing the chorus of "Blow high! Blow low! and so sailed we" while they recited the rest of the song with the pirates. Lizzie had to admit it was kind of fun. Six verses later, they were nearing the end of the song.

With cutlass and gun, O we fought for hours three,
Blow high! Blow low! and so sailed we.

The ship it was their coffin and their grave it was the sea.
A sailing down all on the coasts of High Barbary.

When the song was over, the pirates held up their cups of brandy in a toast to their captains. One of Vane's men who knew Cookie and JJ walked up, causing their private party to end. The pirate looked scary, wearing a patch over his right eye.

"Hey, why don't ye join in on the fun?" the man asked.

"Go ahead, JJ. I've got to clean up," Cookie said.

"I don't believe I've met the two of ye," the pirate added to Jake and Lizzie. "How long have ye been with Black Beard?"

Nervous, Lizzie glanced at Jake, who quickly spoke up. "We're new to the crew, joined Captain back in July."

"What about ye?" the pirate addressed Lizzie.

Lizzie tried to calmly respond in what she hoped sounded like a manly voice. "Aye, joined in July."

"We have work to do, JJ. Go have a good time," Cookie stated as he narrowed his eyebrows at the young man.

Getting the signal, JJ handed Jake his empty plate. As the other pirate turned to leave, JJ gave Lizzie a wink.

"I'll see if I can get them to play 'A-Roving' for ye, Tiny."

Confused, Lizzie watched him join the partying pirates while Cookie chuckled. "Whew! It sure was a close one. Ye did good, Tiny. If I didn't know better, I'd say JJ was jealous of ye, Jake."

Jake shrugged. "I don't know why."

"I do. Ye have been spending too much time with you-know-who. His song choice makes it as clear as day."

"What do you mean?" Lizzie wanted to know.

"Here's the main parts of the song," he replied. "In some fair land there lived a maid. Her eyes are like two stars so bright. Her face is fair, her step is light. Her cheeks are like rosebuds red. There's wealth of hair upon her head. I love this fair maid as my life. And soon she'll be my little wife."

Feeling her cheeks flush with embarrassment, Lizzie quickly stood as she snatched the plates from Jake. "I've heard enough."

Cookie laughed in amusement. "Well, ye asked."

Grabbing the basket, Lizzie raked dirty pewter plates and cups into it before taking them to the galley tent. She placed them on the table and started to leave when she heard voices. As Lizzie drew closer to the rear of the tent where Tuffy and Reba were, she recognized Israel's voice.

"I know just the place, Calico. There's a live oak tree on the way to Springer's Point with twin trunks," Israel explained.

"Good. Let's go, the sooner we bury this, the better. Did ye get the shovels?" Calico inquired in a hushed voice.

"Aye, Cookie was so busy he didn't notice."

Calico snickered. "This little plan we've cooked up might work out after all. I'll meet ye in five minutes."

Silence filled the air, leaving Lizzie to conclude the men had dispersed. Knowing whatever they were up to was important, she hurried to tell Cookie. Unfortunately, Jake was the only one by the fire.

"Where's Cookie?"

"Vane's cook wanted to borrow his cauldron. Sounded like they can't get enough of those oysters. Cookie thought he'd take it over there himself to make sure it comes back. Why? What's wrong?"

"I overheard Israel and Calico Jack talking. They're headed for Springer's Point to bury something under a twin live oak tree."

"When did you see Israel? I thought you were putting up plates?"

"I was. There were voices behind the galley. When I got closer, I heard Israel talking. Israel called the other man Calico. He told him about a twin live oak tree and said he took some shovels. Calico made the statement their plans might work. They're burying something, Jake, or maybe someone. Israel's got a thirst for power, and if Calico Jack is involved, then it must be serious. We've got to tell Cookie."

"What do you expect Cookie to do about him?" Jake asked.

Lizzie sighed. "Forget it. We'll follow Israel and Calico. At least we'll know what they're up to. We can tell Cookie about it later."

"'We,' huh? I don't recall agreeing to go with you."

"I doubt you're going to let me go by myself."

Jake hesitated. "Okay, we'll go, but to make sure we aren't spotted, let's take these bowls and pans to the galley."

Grabbing a few bowls, Lizzie followed Jake, who took a cast-iron frying pan. Leaving the items inside, they snuck under the canvas at the back of the tent and scurried unnoticed into the dark. Without a lantern, the walk through the marshland was tough. Above them, the quarter moon gave little light, but with the glowing stars they would be able to find their way back to camp. The darkness gave Lizzie an eerie feeling. Realizing how hard it would be searching for a twin live oak in a forest of shadows, Lizzie began to wonder if her idea was crazy. She started to suggest turning back when Jake touched her arm.

"Hold on a second," he whispered. "Might be voices. Come on."

Sticking close, Lizzie could hear voices, too. Jake stopped and motioned for her to crouch down. Now on their knees, they crawled behind some bushes. When they were close enough to hear the voices clearly, Jake put his finger to his lips. There was no mistaking who they were: Israel and Calico Jack. Peeping out from between the bushes, they watched two figures in the light of the quarter moon throwing sand from their shovels as they worked to dig a large hole. Behind them was a twin live oak tree.

"What's up with Teach? Have ye done what we talked about?" Calico questioned, pausing to lean against his shovel.

"I've tried, but Black Beard's smart," Israel answered as he wiped his brow with his sleeve. "He keeps his chests and desk locked."

"Why can't ye take the whole thing?"

"Can't be sure which is the communal plunder. I'm not stealing multiple chests and risk Black Beard catching me."

"We had an agreement. I held up my end," Calico insisted.

"Captain's got the keys. I'll get them. Don't worry," Israel promised, going back to his digging.

Calico started shoveling again. "Edward Teach may be smart, but no more than Vane and he's going down."

"It's all about timing. Once I drop Black Beard in Bath, I'll have it all. Ye are the one who has to have a plan," Israel responded.

"I've got one. I just need to pick an island to maroon Vane on and decide who joins him. Can ye overthrow Teach?"

"I think so. Seven weeks ago, half the crew was on my side. We outvoted his loyal friends and stole the French ships," Israel replied.

"How many casks of sugar did ye capture?"

"Ninety. Eden gets eighty casks to clear us. If Black Beard doesn't take the sugar, I can't get rid of him and his followers," Israel added.

"Vane's got enough plunder to keep us going for a while. I can't figure out why Teach doesn't have more. Where's the gold and jewels? He's famous for mounds of loot," Calico asserted.

"We've captured many treasure ships. When the company split in July, those retiring got their share. The remaining is supposedly in safekeeping. Black Beard has no idea how much I know. Ever since we left Bath, we've had this girl onboard."

"A girl?" Calico blurted out. "I haven't seen any girl."

"Captain must be hiding her from Vane. The crew found her and her brother a few days after we set sail. I think Black Beard took them for ransom. It was clear when Captain returned from Knight's place with gifts. He claimed to have bought them in Bath, but most likely Eden gave him the gifts in exchange for their safe return."

"Why give Eden the sugar then?"

"Maybe he lied to the crew and is selling it. My guess is Eden will finish paying the ransom once we arrive in Bath with the captives. For now, Black Beard can continue to think he has the upper hand," Israel stated. "What about Vane? Will he notice his treasure's gone?"

"Nay, thanks to Teach he's been too drunk to see anything. This pirate banyan has been the perfect cover," Calico confirmed.

"Can ye trust the man who helped ye sneak the chest off the ship?"

"Aye, he's a friend. He'll take my place when I become captain. Grab the end of the chest. The hole is big enough," Calico declared.

Squinting, Lizzie saw Calico and Israel climb out of the hole. They grabbed a medium-sized chest, moved it to the hole, and began to dump sand on top. Suddenly, Lizzie felt the urge to sneeze. She tried to hold it back, but it came out anyway. Jake covered her mouth as he looked at the live oak tree. Israel and Calico stopped to stare at their hiding place behind the bushes. A noise echoed through the woods, causing goose bumps to cover Lizzie's body.

Whooo…whooo…whooooo!

"Did ye hear something?" Calico asked Israel.

"I thought so. Guess it was only an old hoot owl. He's making a fuss in the trees," he grunted, filling his shovel with sand.

"It didn't sound like a hoot owl the first time. I'll look around."

Jake let go of Lizzie's mouth as he helped her scramble to her feet. Zigzagging through the trees, she tripped over a tree root. Getting up, she realized she hurt her left ankle. Luckily, Jake looked back and saw her hobbling. Hearing leaves crunch as someone walked toward them, Jake picked her up. Eventually, they made it back to the marsh.

Not daring to talk, Lizzie kept silent. She shuddered at the idea of Israel telling Calico Jack about her. His guess of why she and Jake were with Black Beard was wrong, but it was better for him to keep believing it. If he found out that she was Black Beard's daughter, her life would be in danger. This was more than two rogue pirates bucking their captains. They weren't just stealing treasure. They were planning a takeover.

CHAPTER EIGHTEEN

CAPTAINS' PARLEY

October 9, 1718 ~ Thursday

Each passing day heightened the chances of someone noticing the grand pirate banyan at Ocracoke. Ships were going in and out of the inlet on such a regular basis that Lizzie figured they must be transporting tobacco. With the crops shipping out of the colony, the potential for outsiders to see the two pirate ships increased. Lizzie couldn't help but think about her own family. No doubt, they were working hard to get their own tobacco, corn, cotton, and sweet potatoes out of the fields. She wondered how things were going with the African slaves her papa brought to the colony.

Other than the ships traveling through the inlet, things had been quiet, with a few exceptions. Along with the constant drinking of both pirate crews, several of Vane's men had gotten into another fistfight. Today, the men were back to being friends. They sipped brandy as they played card games and checkers while a hog roasted over their cook pit. Watching them from the galley tent, Lizzie shook her head.

Ducking back inside, she hobbled over to Cookie, who was busy slicing potatoes. Her left ankle was still achy, but she had learned to shift her weight to keep from making it hurt. Over the last few days, Cookie insisted she soak it. He also had some stern words for her and Jake, though he was glad to know about Israel. So far, he hadn't gotten a chance to get alone with Black Beard to fill him in on the buried treasure chest or Israel and Calico Jack's planned takeover.

"Cookie, how much longer do you think Captain Vane will stay? They've been here ten days," Lizzie asked, sitting across from him.

"He'll leave the first of next week. We only have enough spirits to last the weekend. From what I heard, Vane's supply is low, too."

The flap to the galley tent opened, and in walked Jake carrying a musket. She could tell he was in a happier mood than when he left. Cookie assigned him the job of going hunting with JJ's father, Joseph. Jake had been upset since they were supposed to be killing another hog from the open-grazing livestock. Cookie had the hog Philip Morton killed yesterday roasting on the cook pit for dinner.

"Guess what? We're going to have deer stew!" Jake exclaimed.

"Deer? I thought ye were hunting hogs?" Cookie questioned.

"We tracked the hogs through the marsh at Old Slough when we spotted a buck drinking from the creek. I was closer, so I took the shot. Joseph and I carried him back to the live oak tree where they have been skinning the meat. When we came to get supplies, Captain called him. Can you come help me skin it, Cookie?"

"Somebody has to keep the pork turned and the fire going. Tiny doesn't need to be by the cook pit with Vane's men nearby. Can ye wait for Joseph?" Cookie answered, pausing to scratch his head.

"I can help you," Lizzie suggested.

"Are you sure you can help me butcher the deer? It's gruesome."

"I've seen hogs butchered before."

"Watching isn't the same as participating. I need help holding the rope, which means you'll have to stand beside me and the carcass."

"Just let her go, lad. She can handle it. She's a pirate," Cookie chuckled as he went back to cutting potatoes.

"I didn't say I was a pirate, Cookie. I'll always be a girl, you know."

"There are some female pirates sailing the Caribbean."

"Really? I thought all pirates were men. Didn't you, Jake?"

Jake shrugged. "I figured if women couldn't be sailors, then they certainly wouldn't be pirates. Don't the pirate rules forbid it?"

"Aye, but some still become pirates. I've heard they dress like men and learn to survive from their fathers or husbands," Cookie replied.

"Grab a bucket to put the meat in. I'll get the rope and meet you at the back," Jake announced, leaving the musket with Cookie.

Finding a bucket, Lizzie said good-bye to Cookie on her way out. Once Jake joined her with the rope and a small handsaw, the two friends took off for the woods. Five minutes later they were standing by a live oak tree where the antlered deer was waiting. The first thing Jake did was tie the rope to the deer's back hooves. Throwing the opposite end of the rope over a tree branch about two feet over his head, Jake hoisted the deer into the air so it hung upside down.

With the rope tied to a limb, Lizzie kept the tension tight so that Jake could butcher the deer. Using his hunting knife to cut a notch around the deer's ankles, he pulled its furry, tan-colored hide down little by little until it hung over its antlered head. Next came the disgusting task of cutting off the pieces of meat. When he removed the meat, he lowered the carcass and started to saw the deer's forehead.

"What are you doing?" Lizzie blurted out.

Jake stopped to look at her. "Lots of people keep deer antlers. He's got a wide rack for a six-pointer. The brow tines are long, too. I thought you could handle it."

"I know they do. We're getting the meat, not his skull," she mumbled, turning away so she didn't have to watch.

Shaking his head, Jake went back to sawing. "I saw Red Wolf. He said White Feathers misses you."

"Maybe we can go tomorrow. Why was Red Wolf so close to camp? We told him it was dangerous with all the pirates."

"He's tracking raccoons. They feed in the marsh where they wash their food before eating. Raccoons have odd eating habits.

Red Wolf wants a few for food, and White Feathers needs a coonskin hat."

"Did Joseph see him?"

"No, we split up to locate the hogs. After an hour, we met at the watering hole. To be honest, I'm glad we didn't spot them. I don't feel right about killing animals who belong to someone else. I'll be glad when Vane leaves so we can eat wild things," Jake commented.

"Cookie says they'll leave next week. The supply of rum is low."

Jake untied the rope, saying he and Joseph would bury the carcass. He picked up the antlers and a ham while Lizzie carried the rest of the bloody meat in the bucket. Toting it to the galley, they gave it to Cookie, who soaked the deer in water and seasoned it with herbs.

"I'm going to go see if Joseph can help me bury the carcass. Surely he's finished helping Black Beard by now," Jake remarked.

"Don't be long. The pork roast was nearly done the last I checked. Tell Captain to call the men together," Cookie told him. Once he was gone, Cookie looked at Lizzie. "Fill a bucket with water and meet me by the cook pit. I've got to get my cauldron."

Nodding, Lizzie grabbed a clean bucket on her way out. Going around to the side, she opened the lid to the water barrel and dipped the bucket into the water. When it was full, she replaced the cover and carried the water to the cook pit. Cookie was already removing the pork from the iron spit hanging over the fire.

"Dump ye water into the cauldron, Tiny. It needs to be a third full to cook the deer meat," Cookie instructed, cutting the pork in pieces.

Pouring water into the cauldron, Lizzie went back for more. On her third trip, Cookie told her that was enough and asked for the deer meat. When she returned, he took the seasoned meat from her.

"Thank ye. I'll take over while ye go get the plates. I think the potatoes are ready to eat as well. This deer will be supper."

Heading inside the galley, Lizzie found the basket of pewter plates and cups. As she returned, she heard her papa telling the crew dinner was ready. She walked to the makeshift table to fill her plate. Settling on a barrel, she had just finished praying when the pirates began to trickle in. Across the camp, Vane's men passed out plates of food to their own crew. Lizzie had eaten half her meal when JJ walked up.

"Hey, where's Jake?" he asked, sitting on the barrel beside her.

"He and your father are burying a deer carcass they killed."

"I can't wait until Vane leaves so I don't have to guard the sugar and cocoa," he muttered, taking a bite of roast.

"The rum is about out, according to Cookie. He thinks they'll be leaving soon. Aren't you on the next watch?"

JJ sighed. "Aye. I'll relieve Stephen after I eat." Pausing to look around, he leaned closer. "I've been wanting to talk with ye, Lizzie, but with Vane's men and my duties I haven't had a chance."

"JJ, I don't think we should be talking about—"

"No one can hear us," he interrupted softly. "I want to know ye better. Maybe once Vane leaves, we can go for a walk by the ocean."

Uncomfortable, Lizzie debated how to answer. Thankfully, she saw Jake and Joseph returning to camp. The two of them grabbed a plate when someone in Vane's crew yelled.

"Captain! Captain!" called the cook as he hobbled over, dragging his wooden peg leg across the sand. Stopping in front of Captain Vane and Quartermaster Calico Jack he relayed the message. "William just sent word from our ship. There's a brigantine coming into the inlet flying a Death's Head flag in their rigging."

"Death's Head?" Captain Vane repeated as Black Beard came to hear the news. "It's pirates then. Who do ye think it is, Edward?"

"Could be LeBouche or Williams," Black Beard suggested.

"What about Worley or Bonnet?"

Black Beard's demeanor tensed at the sound of Stede Bonnet's name. "Any of them are possible. If they've already sent up their black flag, they must know we're pirates. Who knows ye are here?"

"No one as far as I know."

"Wait. We passed Worley's ship on our way here, remember?" Calico Jack commented. "He was headed south toward Fish Town."

"I forgot about Worley. We didn't talk much, just through our speaking trumpets. He would've seen us headed north. I don't think he's a threat. He hasn't been a pirate long," Vane proclaimed.

"How many are in Worley's crew?" Black Beard questioned.

"About twenty-five."

"Well, we can't do much until they get here," Black Beard said as he motioned for his quartermaster. "Thomas, prepare for visitors."

Thomas Miller nodded as he walked over to Garret Gibbons and John Martin. Meanwhile, Vane gave his own men instructions. As the pirates started their preparations, John came to speak to JJ.

"Ye need to get to the sugar and cocoa, JJ. Tell Stephen to stay with ye until we know what's going on," the Bath native told him.

"Okay," JJ responded as he handed Lizzie his plate.

Taking it, she watched him leave before going over to the table where Joseph and Jake were gobbling down their meals.

"Help me carry these plates to the galley, Tiny. Some are still eating, but these dirty plates can be cleaned," Cookie requested.

Lizzie followed him to the galley tent. While she cleaned cups and plates, Cookie brought in another load before going back out. As Lizzie washed, her mind drifted to the coming pirates. It was interesting this new pirate captain's name was Worley. Although it was very similar to her family's surname, Worsley, she doubted there was a connection. Still, she was curious to know what kind of pirate he was. There was a big difference between Charles Vane and her papa.

Suddenly, Jake entered the galley with a bucket. "The ship is anchoring near Vane's brigantine. Cookie says we need to stay in here."

"I know what we'll do. We can watch from the back of the tent."

"The back of the tent? What if we're spotted?"

"We won't be," she declared as she moved to the back corner and crouched down. "I did it when Vane arrived."

Jake hesitated before kneeling beside her. Lifting the flap, Lizzie leaned over so that they could peep out without drawing attention. From this vantage point, she could see a periauger on the sandy shore with two barrels and six men. As they stepped on land, one of them stood out from the rest. He was an average-sized man wearing a dark green coat and a tricorn hat with a large white feather stuck on its right side.

Vane shook his hand first. "Welcome to Ocracoke, Worley."

"Thanks," the pirate captain stated, removing his feathered hat.

"Worley, I'd like ye to meet my comrade, Captain Edward Teach, otherwise known as Black Beard," Vane continued.

Worley shook Black Beard's hand. "It's a pleasure to meet ye, Captain Teach. I'm Captain Richard Worley. I've heard about ye treasure-hunting adventures. Both of ye are pirate legends."

Black Beard chuckled. "I don't know if ye can call us legends."

"It sure sounds good!" Vane laughed as he slapped Worley's shoulder.

"What brings ye to the island?" Black Beard inquired.

The grin on Worley's face vanished. "I'm here to bring bad news. Stede Bonnet was captured."

Shocked mumbles broke out among the pirates. Lizzie wondered how her papa's men felt about their former crewmate's capture.

"Let's discuss this in my tent," Black Beard prompted.

"While we talk, my men are going to fill our water barrels. We aren't staying around," Captain Worley proclaimed.

"Alright. Thomas, help them get all the water they need," Black Beard instructed his quartermaster as he led the way to his tent.

Watching the three captains coming closer, Lizzie felt she had seen Richard Worley before. His facial features seemed familiar, but she couldn't place him.

"Looks like they're going to have a tense parley," Jake whispered.

"A what?"

"It's a serious talk," he muttered as the captains entered the tent.

Even with the tent flap closed, Lizzie could hear her papa offer his guests a cup of French wine. Both captains eagerly accepted.

"So, what's this about Bonnet's capture?" Charles Vane asked.

"We captured a ship loaded with cargo and passengers a mile off Ocracoke. When we questioned them, they told us about Stede Bonnet's arrest. They had no reason to lie," Richard Worley explained.

"Where was he caught?" Black Beard wanted to know.

"Captain William Rhett found him near the Cape Fear River. He blockaded Charles Town for supplies. The government had a grudge against Stede. They're looking for ye, too. After three blockades in a matter of months by both of ye as well as Bonnet, the people of Charles Town are angry. We spotted ye ships from off the coast. Knowing Captain Vane headed this way, I decided to see if ye were here. Ye need to watch ye backs," Worley replied.

"Bonnet never was one to put up a fight," Black Beard mentioned.

"He fought for a little while, but Rhett trapped him. I heard Stede grew a backbone after the two of ye split. He's been all over the place. There was a rumor he was tracking ye down," Worley informed him.

"Hmm," Black Beard snorted. "What will ye do? Ye can't hide in the Bahamas. Vane says Woodes Rogers controls Nassau."

"With winter coming, we discussed laying low someplace tropical. My men have treasure fever, though, so I can't pass any opportunities on the way to tropical bliss. What about the two of ye?"

"I'll have to talk it over with my men. Like ye said, with the winter coming, someplace warm would be nice," Vane acknowledged.

"Excuse me, Captain, the water is loaded," declared a new voice.

"I'm coming," Worley said. "Watch ye backs, fellows. Take care."

"Ye do the same," Black Beard responded.

"Thanks for bringing the news, Richard," Vane added.

Replacing his feathered tricorn hat, Captain Richard Worley joined his men as they stepped into their periauger and started rowing to their ship. Inside the tent, Captain Charles Vane spoke up.

"Perhaps we can reignite the Jacobite movement. We could get a couple of diehard Jacobites to join us, like Oliver LeBouche, Edward England, or Paulsgrave Williams. I thought about Worley. He hasn't been a pirate long, though, and I'm leery of his loyalty to the cause. With our combined men and cannons, we'll easily take the Bermuda Islands and set up a pirate empire of our own."

"It's a lost cause. We can't fight a losing battle. King George might be an illegitimate king and a German ruling Great Britain and Scotland, but he's in control. Bringing back a small group of men loyal to the Jacobite cause won't make a difference. We can attack every ship in the Royal Navy and still be outlaws," Black Beard reminded him.

"Just a small group, huh? I'm sure there are plenty of men who continue to be loyal to Queen Anne's half-brother, James."

"Aye, and at one time I was one of them."

"What do ye mean *was*?" Vane exploded. "George wrongfully took the crown. James should be king. I refuse to accept his pathetic paper he calls a pardon. He's not my king, and I intend to do all I can to prove it."

"Don't be stupid. Do what we did and surrender to a governor."

"So ye won't join me?" Vane persisted.

"Nay. Tobias Knight has assured me our pardons are still valid."

"There's talk of war against Spain. We can be privateers again."

"Aye, my informant in Bath says the same. I hope it's true. My men would enjoy raiding Spanish sloops. It's been a long time since we did any legal piracy," Black Beard remarked.

Vane sighed. "Fine. We'll be heading to our base at Green Turtle Cay in the Abaco Islands. If we're trapped like Bonnet, I'll go to my powder room and blow up the ship, sending all of us to hell. I'll do anything to avoid the hangman's noose. Where will ye go?"

"I don't know. We don't have a base like ye do."

"Ye are welcome at Green Turtle Cay, at least until spring. Just remember to raise ye black flag or we might blow ye down to the devil's lair," Vane warned with a chuckle.

"I appreciate the offer. When will ye be leaving?"

"As soon as we get packed up. Sounded like Rhett is out for blood. With Bonnet and his men awaiting trial and most likely a hanging, Rhett will be hunting us. Ye would be wise to leave, too."

"We've got to take the sugar to Eden first," Black Beard stated.

"If ye say so. I've got to tell my men to pack," Vane concluded as he left the tent and gave out orders.

"Whew! What a change in events," Jake breathed as he stood up.

"I know. Do you think Mr. Rhett will come looking for Papa?" Lizzie asked, getting up from the ground.

"It sounded like he was. Either way, we're better off with Vane leaving. Twenty-two pirates are better than 112. At least it won't look like we're trying to start a pirate colony."

Peeking outside, Lizzie watched Vane's men pack. It didn't take them long to haul their belongings to the ship. Others toted buckets of freshwater from Old Slough to fill water barrels. Soon they were saying good-bye to Black Beard's crew as they rowed boatloads of men to their waiting brigantine. Even with 90 men, it only took an hour for them to pack up. In the distance, Lizzie spotted Calico

Jack talking to Israel. She figured they were making last-minute plans. With nothing left on the island, Vane approached Black Beard to shake hands. He then climbed aboard their periauger with Calico and a few others. Watching them from the beach, Black Beard's crew waved as Captain Charles Vane and his rogue pirates left Ocracoke.

Cookie suddenly entered the tent. "Worley and Vane have left. Sorry I didn't get here sooner, but Vane's cook needed help. Stede Bonnet has been captured and everyone's in a panic."

"We overheard," Jake confessed.

"Ye did?" Cookie blurted out. "Well, never mind how. We've got to talk to Black Beard. He needs to know what's going on."

"What is going on?" questioned a voice.

Startled, all three of them spun around to see Black Beard standing in the back entrance to the galley tent.

"Captain, we've got a major problem with Israel," Cookie revealed, as he told Black Beard what Lizzie and Jake had seen five days prior.

Black Beard rubbed his wiry beard. "Well, this is a challenge, isn't it? I'm glad we found out, but ye could've gotten shot."

"It's my fault. Jake wouldn't have gone if I didn't insist. What can we do to stop Israel?" Lizzie urged.

"I have an idea, but we must hurry. I told Thomas to fill our water barrels. As soon as Vane's ship has sailed, the men will begin stocking the *Adventure* and bring forty casks of sugar from Springer's Point."

"I thought Governor Eden requested eighty casks," Jake observed.

"He did. I'll have to make two runs. The *Adventure*'s keel will have a hard time in the shallow waters with the weight of all eighty casks. We'll take the first shipment to Tobias, then return for the rest. My plan is to leave both of ye with Cookie. I don't think many ships will come ashore, but we still need to guard the remaining plunder."

"What about the communal plunder? Israel plans to steal it from ye," Cookie reminded him.

"He won't because I'm putting it in a barrel and leaving it with ye. After we're gone, ye are going to dig up Vane's treasure."

"Are ye sure it's wise to steal Vane's treasure?" Cookie protested.

"It isn't his anymore. Wouldn't it be better for us to have it instead of Israel or Calico Jack?" Black Beard pointed out.

Cookie shook his head but didn't say a word. Lizzie didn't think he was disagreeing with her papa. He just seemed bewildered.

Peeping out of the tent, Black Beard added, "Vane hoisted his anchor. It's time to make our move. Let me talk to Thomas. He needs to keep an eye on Israel. In the meantime, start packing everything except this tent and the supplies ye need while we're gone."

Black Beard left the galley while Cookie started packing. Trying to help, Lizzie gathered the plates, cups, and bowls. Beside her, Cookie sorted his iron cooking pots and utensils as he sent Jake to get the deer meat out of the cauldron. Fifteen minutes later, her papa returned, asking her to bring a bucket to his quarters. When she went next door, Lizzie found him unlocking a wooden chest.

"There ye are. Bring the bucket," he instructed as he lifted the lid of the chest and began removing items.

Setting down the bucket, Lizzie decided to ask about Richard Worley. "Papa, how well do you know Captain Worley? He didn't act like Captain Vane. I know it's strange, but he looked familiar."

"He's ye mother's cousin. Richard's father and ye grandfather are brothers. I met him years ago, but back then I didn't wear a beard so of course he didn't recognize me. He isn't too clever, though. For some reason, he thinks changing his name from Worsley to Worley makes a difference. It certainly isn't the best disguise."

"I can't believe Momma's cousin is a pirate."

Black Beard snorted. "I doubt he has what it takes. If he's the same man I remember, he won't be able to maintain the pirate life."

Lizzie looked at the scattered objects on the sand, including the bandolier, several weapons, spare clothing, a fancy red coat, and the notorious black flag with its white skull and crossbones. Wondering why her papa was dumping the chest, she was shocked when he pulled out the wooden bottom. He grabbed a sack, and dumped the contents into the bucket. A stream of gold coins fell from the bag.

"Is this the communal plunder?" Lizzie inquired.

"Nay, it's my personal stash. Take these keys and open the bottom desk drawer. I need those sacks of coins. It's the communal plunder."

Walking to the desk, she unlocked the drawer. Once it was open, she pulled out the three tan cloth sacks, allowing her eyes to linger on his black leather diary. Locking it back, Lizzie brought the sacks to her papa, who was still dumping gold in the bucket.

"Is this all of the plunder or did you bury some?" she asked.

"Nay, burying plunder on islands isn't smart. We spent most of it at taverns and buying supplies. The last ship we raided had African slaves, but no gold or jewels. We split them in Bath, which I guess is like a treasure within itself," he revealed, taking the sacks from her.

"So, this is it? There's nothing left of your treasure except these?"

"Sort of. In July, the men who left our company received several Africans instead of gold and silver. John Martin decided to take the same deal, choosing to give his slaves to his mother and brother. The remaining crew who didn't originate in Bath or didn't need the Africans chose to split the money among them whenever we return to land," he explained, filling the empty sacks with sand.

"What are you doing now?"

"I'm putting sand in these sacks so the chest will keep its weight. If it's too light the men will notice."

With the sacks of sand in the chest, Black Beard put the contents back inside and locked it. He carried the gold to the galley tent. Lizzie followed and watched him locate a small empty rum barrel before dumping the gold into it. Once the barrel was full, he replaced the lid and went to see how Cookie's packing was coming. Cookie was giving him a review of the food when Thomas Miller entered the tent.

"The water is loaded, Captain, and the men are almost finished hauling the casks of sugar to the ship."

"Good. Load everything in my tent," Black Beard ordered.

Bowing his head in acknowledgment, Thomas exited the galley. Meanwhile, Black Beard, Cookie, and Jake toted crates outside. Lizzie picked up lighter items and took them to the pile. Twenty minutes later, the only things remaining in the galley were the essentials needed for the three of them. Going to her papa's tent, Lizzie grabbed her personal belongings and moved her makeshift bed to the corner of the galley beside Reba's and Tuffy's cages. After putting away her belongings, she went outside to watch the men finish loading.

By now, only four pirates were collecting materials onshore while their comrades rowed the periauger to the *Adventure*. JJ was among those still on the island. Seeing Lizzie emerge, he quickly came over.

"I'll be leaving. Captain said all of us have to go, though I don't know why I can't stay," JJ grumbled as Black Beard walked up.

"Because ye are needed," Black Beard snapped. "Now get going."

Although JJ clearly didn't like the circumstances, he did as his captain commanded. When he left, Black Beard turned to Lizzie.

"I know ye want to go home, but it's safer for ye to stay here. Ye can go when we take the second load. It'll take several days to get there, a few to unload in secret, and a couple to return."

"Okay. Be careful," she told him, as her papa slowly nodded.

For a moment, Lizzie saw a flicker of emotion in her papa's eyes like he wanted to hug her. As he turned and walked away, she let out a sigh. Standing alone by the cook pit, Lizzie watched the few remaining pirates climb aboard the periauger with her papa. Picking up the oars, the men began to row. The island looked deserted with only a single tent on the crescent-shaped beach. Out on the water, the men boarded the *Adventure* before hauling the periauger up on the deck. They hoisted the anchor and rearranged the sails to catch the little bit of wind blowing out of the northeast. In no time, the wind filled the sails and the ship lurched forward out of the cove.

"The sun will set soon," Cookie announced. "Get the buckets."

Glancing at the dark silhouette of the *Adventure* against the setting sun, Lizzie took a deep breath, wondering if what they were preparing to do was a sin. Although it was her papa's idea to take the treasure from Israel and Calico, it was still stealing. Would God punish them, even though they were doing something good by getting it out of evil hands? Pushing her feelings aside, she grabbed a basket and followed Jake and Cookie, who each toted a shovel and two buckets.

The hike through the marsh was exhausting, but the remaining sunlight made their efforts much easier. Eventually, they found the twin live oak tree that marked the spot. Lizzie stood to the side while Jake and Cookie started to dig. After what seemed like forever, Jake's shovel hit something. Several more shovelfuls of sand revealed the hidden wooden chest. Having uncovered the treasure, Cookie grabbed one of the handles and with Jake's help lifted the chest. Dusting off the sand, the pirate opened the lid. Lizzie's eyes widened in shock as she saw the gold and jewels piled high.

"Wow!" she breathed in amazement.

"I've never seen so much treasure in my life," Jake added.

Cookie chuckled. "Ye finally got to see real pirate treasure."

Lizzie noticed a string of beads. "Are those Reuben's, Cookie?"

"Nay, those are a different shade of blue. I heard Vane got Reuben's beads. He usually gets what he wants. It'll be interesting to hear how Calico Jack demotes him and takes the ship. Hand me a bucket."

Lizzie passed a bucket to Jake, who held it while Cookie scooped handfuls of necklaces, pocket watches, and beautiful pieces of jewelry decorated with stones of deep red, brilliant blue, and dark green. The bottom half of the chest held gold and silver coins in addition to sacks of gold dust. According to Cookie, the plunder was worth more money than Lizzie could wrap her mind around.

With the chest empty, Cookie closed the lid and dumped sand back on top. Soon, he and Jake had buried the empty chest. As they picked up their buckets and shovels, Lizzie grabbed her basket of gold dust and trudged behind them. So much had happened she could hardly believe it. The captains' parley had certainly changed the course of events. She couldn't stop thinking about Stede Bonnet and the horrible fate he and his crew were facing at the end of a hangman's noose. His skeletons or past sins had certainly caught up with him. What kind a fate was waiting for other pirates—like Charles Vane, Richard Worley, and even her papa?

CHAPTER NINETEEN

SCUTTLEBUTT

October 23, 1718 ~ Thursday

Sunlight sparkled off the greenish-blue water of the Atlantic Ocean. The shimmering waves rushing ashore made the ocean look alive. Lizzie soaked in the scene, trying to savor God's beauty and knowing her time on the island was short. Today would make ten days since the *Adventure* left Ocracoke. If Cookie's predictions were right, her papa would be arriving before dark.

Breathing in the salty sea air, she walked in the ankle-deep water, pausing occasionally to pick up a stray seashell. The blustery breeze off the water blew against her, causing her blue dress to flap in the wind. Pushing stray hair behind her ears, she spotted a brown pelican swooping into the ocean to scoop up fish with the large pouch hanging from its throat. In the background, she could hear the waves crashing a few feet from her and the shrieks of seagulls overhead. It was a special sound she wanted to hold on to and never forget. Part of her wished she could stay in this moment forever.

"Lizzie, are you about ready?"

Jerking her head, Lizzie turned to Jake, who came with her to see the ocean for what she figured would be the final time. Sighing, she walked to where he was resting on the beach with his pants rolled up and toes dug into the sand.

"I guess. Wish we could stay, but I want to visit White Feathers and Red Wolf for a little while," she mumbled.

"Me, too. I wonder if Cookie has caught any fish. He was going to get a bath and shave first."

"I was surprised he decided to get a bath. I've been after him for days. You look better too without that scruffy beard. The way it was growing, you were fitting in with those pirates," she teased.

"Well, you look better in a dress."

"Cookie sure has enjoyed himself. He's been fishing every day."

Jake laughed. "I imagine he's also taking a few naps. Who knows? He might retire from piracy."

"I wish he and Papa would both retire and stop treasure hunting. Speaking of treasure, what do you think Papa will do with Vane's?"

"I doubt he'll share it with the crew."

"Israel sure is going to be mad when he finds out," she muttered.

"How about Calico Jack or Vane? Black Beard's going to have his hands full," Jake declared. "Look what I found for Hannah. It's a conch shell. You can hear the ocean roaring."

Amazed to see the large seashell, Lizzie held it up to her ear. "Wow! You really can hear the ocean. She's going to love it. Where did you find such a big shell?"

"Against the dunes. The tide pushes shells up there."

Dusting sand from his feet, Jake slid on his boots while Lizzie bent to put on her shoes. As Jake picked up the seashell for Hannah, she looked at the ocean once more before following him across the sandy beach. Soon they were walking through the sea oats, leaving the shining ocean behind. The worn path to White Feathers' hut was a familiar one by now. Lizzie couldn't stop thinking about the times she walked the sandy path learning from her Indian friends.

Nearing the clearing where the hut stood, she spotted the live oak tree Red Wolf had shown them three days ago. He said there was an ancient Indian legend about trees and friendship. Supposedly, if you made your mark on a live oak tree your friendship would live on forever. Making the legend a reality, Red Wolf carved a feather and a wolf figure into the tree bark to symbolize him and his grandmother. Then he gave the knife to Jake, who carved his initials JG. Finally, Lizzie carved LB into the bark, sealing their friendship for eternity.

"Welcome!" White Feathers greeted them.

Smiling, Lizzie wondered how the elderly woman always knew they were near. Hearing his grandmother speak, Red Wolf looked up from his work. The young Indian was tying off the ropes holding up a freshly tanned deerskin between two live oak trees.

"Where did you go today?" Red Wolf asked, coming over.

"Bet you can't guess," Jake joked back.

"The ocean?" Red Wolf answered dramatically.

Knowing they were teasing, Lizzie interrupted their game. "Stop rubbing it in. I love the ocean. Besides, we'll be leaving soon."

"Has your father returned?" White Feathers spoke up.

"We're expecting him anytime. What are you doing?"

"Getting ready for winter. Red Wolf is drying meat. I am helping him tan skins. The animal furs keep us warm on the cold nights."

"Yenrauhe, I want you to see my buck antlers. I killed one yesterday. They are bigger than the ones you have," Red Wolf urged, calling Jake by his nickname, which meant "brother."

Once they had gone around the hut, White Feathers looked at Lizzie. "Red Wolf has enjoyed spending time with Yenrauhe. His happiness has made me think what is best for him. Here he has no one. Maybe it is time for him to go north to join the Hatteras tribe."

"What about you?"

"One day I will go to the Great Beyond. He will be alone."

"He'll be fine. He's smart. The Mighty Creator will be with both of you," she insisted, pausing as Jake and Red Wolf returned.

Obviously trying to change the subject, White Feathers hastily pointed to a large clay pot. "We boil tree bark to tan the skins."

Peering into the clay pot, Lizzie could see the dark brown solution swirling in the boiling water. She was about to ask White Feathers how the tanning process worked when a sound captured her attention. Turning, she spotted Cookie coming into the clearing.

"What are you doing here, Cookie?" Jake called out.

"I spotted a ship. It's ye father, Miss Lizzie," he replied. "They'll probably be here within the hour."

Thanking White Feathers for helping Lizzie, Cookie said good-bye. Lizzie watched him leave the clearing with sadness in her heart. This was the moment she had been dreading. She fought surging emotions as Jake shook Red Wolf's hand.

"Let's say our good-byes in case we leave today," he suggested.

"Wait," Red Wolf proclaimed as he ran into the hut. He returned with his bow and arrow, offering it to Jake. "May it bring you luck."

"I can't take your bow and arrow."

"It is a gift. You can remember your time on the island."

"Get the gift for White Swan," White Feathers requested.

Moving quickly, Red Wolf brought out several items, the largest being one of the turtle shell baskets White Feathers made. As he gave the basket to Lizzie, she could see there was also a seashell necklace and a white object cradled in the bottom of the dark green turtle shell.

"Yicau made the necklace and basket for you. I carved a pony on the whale bone to remind you of the wild ponies," Red Wolf said.

Overwhelmed with gratitude, Lizzie threw her arms around his neck. She then gave White Feathers a hug too, telling her she would always remember their friendship. With gifts in hand, she and Jake left the clearing, waving to their Indian friends. Walking through the woods, they made their way to the sound side of Ocracoke Island.

Eventually, the woods of cedars and yaupon hollies gave way to marsh. In no time, Lizzie could see the small beach leading to camp. On the water, a ship sailed across the sound headed for Ocracoke. Back on the crescent-shaped beach, Cookie was fishing.

"I'm going to sit here until Papa arrives."

"Okay. I'll let Cookie know we're back. Give me your turtle shell basket. I can take it to the galley," he offered.

Lizzie handed him the gifts. Sitting on the little beach, she watched him meander his way to the camp. Gazing back at the ship, Lizzie inhaled the salty sea air. As she leaned against her knees, she stared absentmindedly at the gentle waves pushing ashore. Farther up the beach, fiddler crabs hid in underground holes while brown and white sanderlings ran to avoid the incoming tide.

"Cookie says we'll pack when they get here," Jake informed her, walking up. When she didn't respond he added, "Are you alright?"

Sighing, Lizzie nodded. "It's just sad leaving the island."

"I thought you would be happy to go home."

"I am, but I'll miss White Feathers and Red Wolf."

Jake sat on the beach and began drawing pictures in the sand with a stick. Not paying attention to him, Lizzie went back to her personal thoughts as she listened to the soothing slushing of water.

"What are you going to do when you get back?" Jake asked.

Confused, Lizzie looked at him. "What do you mean?"

"Things have changed between you and your papa."

Lizzie placed her chin on her arm as she stared at the *Adventure*. "I'm not sure how life will be with Papa. I'm afraid he'll leave again."

"He'll be back. What about JJ? He's not going to give up wanting a relationship with you."

"You know as well as I do Papa won't stay in Bath long. Not with Mr. Rhett trying to capture pirates. Papa and the crew will unload the sugar and leave for a tropical island. Naturally, JJ will go with them."

"Are you so sure?"

"What? You think he'll stay in Bath?" Lizzie blurted out.

"For you he would," Jake mumbled, still drawing in the sand.

Lizzie had never considered JJ giving up piracy to be with her. "He can't. He's a pirate."

"When JJ sees how much Miles likes you, he'll stay. He's serious."

"JJ will have to get over it. What about you? In July you had plans to get a job in Pennsylvania. Are you still going there?"

"I don't know."

His response was so sad, Lizzie wondered if he was depressed about leaving the island or if something else was bothering him. She considered inviting him to stay in Bath but decided it wasn't her place. When they returned home, he would go back to being a hired hand. At this thought, Lizzie felt bad. Jake had become more than a hired worker. They had gone through a lot in the last three months.

"They're setting the anchor," he observed.

Looking up, she saw men hurrying around the deck as the massive iron anchor dropped into the water with a splash. The *Adventure* lurched as the anchor set and the crew uncovered the periauger.

"Come on, let's go help Cookie," Jake urged as he scrambled to his feet and offered his hands to help her.

Reaching for them, Lizzie pulled herself up. Still holding his hands, she stood frozen as he stared at her with such concentration, she suddenly felt uncomfortable. The moment lasted for a few seconds, but the grip of his hands lingered in her palms even after he let go and turned away. Feeling breathless and confused, she watched him walk back. Had she imagined it, or did something just happen?

Stunned, Lizzie blindly made her way across the sand as she asked God to help her sort through the feelings bombarding her. In her mind, she could see the attentiveness in Jake's eyes.

"What's the matter with ye, Miss Lizzie?" Cookie inquired.

Blinking, she looked at him and realized she was now standing by the cook pit where he was removing his cauldron.

"I—I'm fine," she stuttered. "Where's Jake?"

"He's fetching water from Old Slough. We'll need to refill the barrels," he responded, setting his cauldron down. "They're here."

Turning, Lizzie saw the periauger stop at the water's edge. Black Beard got out first, followed by John Martin and Edward Salter. James White and Richard Stiles, the Africans, unloaded two empty barrels while their captain approached Cookie and Lizzie.

"How did things go, Captain?" Cookie greeted him.

"It went well. We unloaded at Tobias Knight's during the night to keep suspicions low. Where's Jake?" Black Beard questioned.

"He's getting water. I thought we'd get a head start refilling our water barrels," Cookie revealed.

"Good idea. Did ye have any trouble while we were gone?"

"Nay, we've been enjoying ourselves, haven't we, Miss Lizzie?"

"Yes, the weather's been nice."

Black Beard glanced over his shoulder at his men. "I assume ye didn't have any trouble with—well, ye know."

"It's taken care of. We moved it to an empty rum barrel. There was enough sparkle to make ye eyes water," Cookie assured him.

"I'd like to see it. When Joseph and JJ get here, I'll have them put it in my cabin. In the meantime, keep filling the water barrels. John and Edward are going to Springer's Point to get the sugar while Richard and James row the periauger back to the *Adventure*."

"I'm surprised Israel didn't come," Cookie remarked.

"Oh, he's on his way. He insisted on helping."

"What if he goes by the twin live oak tree?"

Black Beard shrugged. "It doesn't matter. He can't see anything."

"So, we're leaving today?" Lizzie asked.

"Aye, the sooner we get the second load to Bath, the better. I'm hoping to get everything on board the *Adventure* before the sun sets. We have two or three hours of daylight left. Ye will have to come up with something for supper, Cookie. The men aren't happy with Joseph's cooking," her papa reported with a chuckle.

"I'm not surprised. My cooking is fit for a king," Cookie laughed.

Lizzie giggled as her papa let out a snort. "I'm not sure it's that good, but it's definitely missed. Why don't ye pack what's left in the galley tent? I'll have someone kill a few rabbits before we leave."

"There's no need. I've caught enough fish to make a fish stew. They're swimming in a barrel of seawater. We ran out of potatoes and onions, but Jake purchased some from the old pilot yesterday. We've got a list of supplies we'll need once we get to Bath. Everything's out except eggs. Those chickens are producing eggs like crazy. I think the pirate banyan disrupted their output," Cookie announced.

"Sounds good. Looks like the others are here. I'll be back to look at the goods," Black Beard grunted, giving them a wink.

Leaving them, Black Beard walked toward the arriving pirates, including Owen Roberts, Israel Hands, Joseph Brooks, and JJ. The four of them received their orders as John Martin and Edward Salter appeared with the first cask of sugar. After loading the sugar into the periauger, their African crewmates started rowing it to the *Adventure*.

Jake returned with buckets of freshwater. Once he dumped them in an empty barrel, he and JJ set out again. John, Edward, Owen, and Israel headed to Springer's Point for two more casks of sugar. Seeing Israel and Owen acting like friends, Lizzie couldn't help but wonder if Owen was his recruit. Remembering how Owen treated her in the storage hold back in July, she could envision the two pirates working together. As they left camp, Israel looked in her direction. His eyes narrowed, causing goose bumps to cover her arms.

"Hey, Cookie!" Joseph exclaimed. "How have ye been?"

Lizzie changed her focus to JJ's father, who had walked up to them. Glancing back at Israel, she was glad to discover he was leaving camp.

"We're good. I heard ye took my place in the galley. Looks like I might be out of a job," Cookie answered, snickering.

Joseph laughed. "I don't think so. There's news ye will be interested in, though. The scuttlebutt is Israel's recruiting for a takeover."

"A takeover, huh?" Cookie repeated casually, eyeing Lizzie.

"Aye. I know it's gossip, but from what I hear he's been holding secret meetings with certain members of the crew."

The pirates continued to talk, but a hissing sound coming from the galley tent got Lizzie's attention. Looking back, she saw her papa motioning for her. Leaving the conversation, she went inside the tent.

"I need ye to show me the hidden treasure," her papa stated.

Moving pieces of canvas, she showed him the barrel where Cookie and Jake hid Captain Vane's treasure. The pirate captain looked inside, grinning as his eyes glimpsed the abundance of gold and jewels.

"This is better than I guessed. There must be a fortune in here. Vane will be furious when he finds out it's gone!"

"What will you do with it?" she wanted to know.

"I don't know yet. I'll have to think things through."

"Papa, Joseph was telling Cookie about scuttlebutt. What is it?"

"Scuttlebutt is what sailors nicknamed the barrel where we dip out water. It also means gossip, and Israel has been spreading a lot of it."

"Guess you haven't told anyone about Captain Vane's treasure."

"Nay, it's best to keep it to ourselves. Do ye have any rags? I'm going to cover the treasure before replacing the lid."

Digging out some rags, Lizzie gave several to her papa. He had just secured the lid when Cookie popped his head into the tent.

"Captain, four more men are here. The fellows are back with another load of sugar as well," he reported. "By the way, Miss Lizzie, can ye take this cauldron? Ye can put my cooking supplies in a crate. I'll be there shortly to help, but first I need to dismantle the iron spit."

Walking over to the cauldron, Lizzie carried it to the makeshift table while her papa joined Cookie outside. With the real table on the ship, Cookie had moved the other one inside. Picking up cooking utensils and a handful of bowls, she had just located a crate to put them in when a voice spoke. Looking up, she found Israel staring at her.

The grin on his face gave her chills. "Well, the last time I saw ye, we were sailing to meet Vane. Where has Cookie been hiding ye?"

As he spoke, Israel took several steps toward her. Not wanting to be near him, Lizzie backed away, keeping her eyes fixated on his every move. Her heart beat faster as she debated what to do.

"What's the matter? Are ye scared?" he taunted her. "Ye look like a scared baby rabbit. Guess what? Black Beard doesn't know it yet, but things are about to change."

Fearful of what he would do, Lizzie almost fell backward as she tripped over something on the sand. "Get away from me."

"Or what? Are ye going to scream? I could cut ye tongue out," he mentioned, patting the leather sheath holding his knife.

The pirate inched closer until he was standing in front of her. With nowhere to go, she leaned against the table. She could see the stubble of his unshaven chin and the eerie twinkle in his dark eyes.

"What are ye doing? Leave her alone!"

Relief flooded over Lizzie as Cookie entered the tent. The sneaky pirate backed away when he saw Cookie.

"Are ye okay, Miss Lizzie?"

"She's fine. We're discussing where she's been," Israel snapped.

"Captain is looking for ye. We've got work to do."

"I don't take orders from ye, and I know there's work to be done. Ye are just a cook and a servant."

"What?" Cookie exploded.

"Ye heard me," Israel spat as he left the tent.

Cookie let out a blow of frustration. "That low-down, no-good rat! No wonder there's scuttlebutt about him. He is a butt if ye ask me. If he keeps it up, I'm going to beat the tar out of the rascal."

"I'm so glad you came. He scared me," Lizzie mumbled. "I feel bad for the crew. Papa said scuttlebutt was gossip, but this scuttlebutt is true. If only they knew what Israel was planning."

"Aye. It was hard listening to Joseph debate if this takeover business was only rumors. We've been friends for a long time, but if Israel were to hear us talking, we would lose the upper hand."

Sighing, Lizzie helped him finish packing the cooking supplies. Next she moved the chicken eggs to a basket lined with cloth while Cookie made sure their cages were secure for the transfer. Finally, he checked Tuffy's and Reba's cages. Lizzie smiled as she observed the pirate cook talking to his pets as if they were babies. With everything ready, Cookie led the way outside. The pirates were busy loading two more casks of sugar into the periauger. Black Beard walked over as the Africans rowed to the ship.

"The men have two casks of sugar left. Afterwards, we'll load the water barrels and what's left in the galley tent."

"What about the remaining plunder?" Cookie remarked.

"I'm going to leave it at Springer's Point. We'll have 10 casks of sugar left and 140 sacks of cocoa. When we come back, we can stop to get it. Do ye have everything packed up?"

"We do."

"I'll have the tent taken down, then," he added, turning to leave.

"Wait, I need to tell ye something," Cookie started as he grabbed Black Beard's arm. "Israel cornered Miss Lizzie a little while ago. He scared her to death and said some nasty things to me."

Black Beard looked at Lizzie. "Are ye alright?"

"I'm a little shaken, but okay."

"I don't know how he slipped away without anyone noticing," he acknowledged as he gave his men orders to dismantle the tent.

Black Beard, Cookie, and seven of the pirates removed the contents of the tent while two others loaded the final casks of sugar into the periauger. Lizzie stood beside Tuffy's and Reba's cages with the basket of eggs. Holding her personal things and the gifts from White Feathers, she watched the men drag out crates and barrels. Jake and JJ returned carrying their last buckets of freshwater.

"Whew! I'm exhausted," JJ panted as they dumped them.

Setting down his empty buckets, he put his hands behind him to stretch his back. Jake wasn't as dramatic. He seemed uneasy as he placed his buckets beside JJ's. She considered if it had anything to do with the awkward moment between them earlier.

"It's good to see ye. Wish we could've gone to the beach. I heard ye enjoyed the ocean this week," JJ said.

Lizzie looked at Jake. "Yes, the weather was great."

"Don't stand around. There's work to do!" Black Beard ordered. "They are halfway back to shore. Get those chicken cages ready."

The reddish-brown chickens clucked wildly as JJ and Jake loaded two of the four cages into the periauger. After they were secure, the Africans rowed the feathered fowls to the *Adventure* where the crew dropped ropes and pulled the chickens aboard. When they returned, JJ and Jake placed the last two cages of chickens in the periauger for the second trip. Soon, they were back for Tuffy and Reba, who made such a fuss that Lizzie felt sorry for them.

Once the animals were on board, the pirates loaded the water barrels, crates of cooking supplies, the cauldron, canvas tent, and the barrel of live fish Cookie caught for supper. Lizzie bit her lip as she watched the men carry the barrel containing Vane's treasure and the smaller one with her papa's stash of gold. Joseph teased Cookie about putting rocks in the largest barrel, not knowing it held the treasure. Thankfully, the others laughed at his joke as they took it to the periauger.

Eventually the crescent-shaped beach was empty. With the goods loaded, the pirates returned to the *Adventure*. Staying with her papa, Lizzie was the last to leave the island, along with Cookie, Jake, and JJ. Cookie got into the periauger first with the basket of eggs. Lizzie handed him her belongings before attempting to climb aboard. Taking her papa's hand, she swung her leg over the bow while Jake and JJ kept the boat steady. Settling at the stern beside her papa, she held her things as Jake and JJ started rowing.

Before long, the sandy shore was in the distance as they drew near the towering *Adventure*. Watching JJ and Jake scamper up the ladder, Lizzie prepared for her turn. When her papa gave the signal, she took a deep breath and put her foot on the first step. Placing one foot after the other, she avoided looking down at the faces of her papa and Cookie. As she clambered over the railing, she moved out of the way and waited for Cookie and Black Beard to climb up.

The men hauled up the periauger with ropes and swung it around to the center deck. Cookie retrieved the eggs and Lizzie's belongings. Telling her he was taking them below deck and starting the fish stew, the cook descended into the belly of the ship. Meanwhile, the crew scurried across the deck as Black Beard shouted commands to get the sails turned. Jake was busy helping haul up the anchor.

Overwhelmed with all the commotion, Lizzie leaned against the railing to look at the island one last time. In her mind, she thought about all the things she had done on the island. Between meeting White Feathers and Red Wolf to experiencing a pirate banyan with over a hundred pirates, it had been quite an adventure. Thinking about Captain Vane made her remember Calico Jack and Israel. She couldn't help but worry about what Israel would do next. Clearly, the scuttlebutt wasn't rumors. He was currently making moves toward a takeover. The question was, what exactly would he do? Surely he and Calico Jack made other plans that she and Jake didn't hear. Staring at the shore of Ocracoke, Lizzie wondered what secrets the island held.

CHAPTER TWENTY

☠

SMOKING GUN

October 25, 1718 ~ Saturday

Rays of sunshine streamed across the horizon as daylight drew to a close. Streaks of orange and purple outlined the puffy, dark pink clouds hanging low in the western sky. The colors punctuated the black silhouettes of towering trees lining the Pamtico River. Lizzie enjoyed the sunset from the *Adventure*'s deck. Overhead, three white tundra swans made a whooping sound with their wings as they flew north to the large Mattamuskeet Lake, where thousands of swans flocked in early December.

In the two days it took to cross the sound and travel up the Pamtico River, they hadn't passed any merchant ships, which was a good thing. Even Israel seemed to be on his best behavior. Jake had been avoiding her for some reason, while JJ tried to get her attention. She couldn't count how many times he got in trouble for neglecting his duties to talk to her. As the *Adventure* sailed up the river, she could see Bath Town Creek ahead as it forked off to the right.

Hearing the shuffle of boots on the roof, Lizzie turned to see her papa descending the ladder propped against the captain's cabin. He carried a spyglass in his right hand from surveying how close they were to Bath. Once he was back on deck, he joined her by the ship's railing overlooking the greenish-blue water.

"We're close. I know ye want to go home, but we need to transfer the sugar first. I'll take ye home in the morning," he told her.

"Sounds like we'll be anchoring near the mouth of the creek."

"Aye, it will make it easier to haul the sugar to Tobias' place. He's taking inventory for Eden. It'll take about ten trips."

"Why not take it to Tunnel Land? I've heard there was a secret tunnel running from the wharf to the cellar of the big house."

Her papa laughed. "There is a hidden brick tunnel, but it isn't a secret. It would be stupid to use it since everyone has heard the legends. We've been taking the sugar to Eden's storehouse in town. He needs twenty more to make a total of sixty. The remaining twenty hogsheads will go to Tobias."

"I'm surprised Governor Eden didn't want to hide his sugar at Tunnel Land. I know he sold it to Mr. Lillington in April, but with it being vacant it makes the perfect hiding place. No one would think to look in all those outbuildings."

"There's no reason to hide it. The men at the hearing heard Eden order me to pay a tax to the government with the sugar we supposedly found. Besides, he doesn't own Tunnel Land anymore. Tobias told me John Lillington sold the land in early September. The new owners are Stephen Elsey and James Robins. Both were members of my crew who chose to stay in Bath when we split in July. They swapped a few African slaves for the land," he explained.

"Wow, there sure have been a lot of changes since I left Bath."

"Three months is a long time. Going back will be hard. It was always difficult for me to return after a voyage. Things change in the colony, but it's the changes in ye soul which are challenging."

Lizzie slowly nodded, letting his words sink in. He was right. She didn't feel like the same person.

"Do ye see the gator?" her papa asked, changing the subject. "He just popped up out of the water. Here, look through my spyglass."

Reaching for the spyglass, Lizzie noticed his hand was shaking. As she took it from him, he quickly clasped his hands together to stop the trembling. Concerned it was a sign of his sickness, she considered saying something but decided against it. He was clearly trying to hide his symptoms from her. She held the spyglass to her right eye. Sure enough, she could see the large eyes of an alligator staring back at her from the edge of the marsh lining the banks of the river. Although submerged, the gator was obviously big, judging by the length of its long snout.

"I recall my father telling a funny story about an alligator. When he first came to Bath, he met a man named John Lawson. He died in 1711, but ye should know his daughter," Black Beard proclaimed.

"Yes, Isabella and her mother, Mrs. Hannah, still live in the house he built at the corner of Front Street and Bay Street. It's the best lot in town with a beautiful view of Bath Town Creek."

"John was one of Bath's founders, so naturally he got the best pick of land. He was an interesting man who enjoyed trying new things. For years, he traveled creeks and rivers all over Carolina, documenting nature and Indian tribes. Lawson authored a book detailing all he saw. Some say he'd rather live among the savages than the English."

"Grandfather said he died in the Tuscarora Indian War."

"Aye. He was the first casualty. I heard he was visiting a tribe, and after they killed him, they started attacking the colonists. The tribe he was with ended up being the worst. Not all Indians were mean. Some had nothing to do with the attacks. Others were seeking revenge for the abuse some Englishmen did to their families. They captured another man named Baron Christoph Von Graffenried. Susannah's husband, Martin Franck, had dealings with the baron. Martin helped him establish a settlement near New Bern on the Trent River."

"Did Uncle Martin go exploring with him and Mr. Lawson?"

"Nay. Christopher Gale was supposed to go on the same trip they got captured on but couldn't due to sickness in the family."

"I didn't know Miles Gale's father was involved with Mr. Lawson. So, what happened with the alligator?" she wanted to know.

"I'm sorry, I lost track. Father told me Lawson was staying in a house he made by the Trent River. His Indian guide had gone to visit relatives near New Bern. There was a strange sound coming from underneath the house. The noise scared both him and his dog. He sat in his chair with the shaking bulldog wondering what kind of huge animal was under the floorboards. When the Indian came back, he told him what happened. His Indian friend laughed and said it was an alligator. The next day, they looked under the house. Just like the Indian said, an alligator had dug out a tunnel to live in."

Laughing with her papa, Lizzie felt a surge of happiness come over her. It was good to be sharing a funny moment with him. As she gazed into his smiling face, she could see the weathered creases around his eyes. Up close, he looked tired and pale beneath his wiry beard, but the grin on his lips proved he was happy, too. As four more white tundra swans flew over the *Adventure* making their signature *oo-ou-oo* call, he tilted his head to watch them.

"The tundra swans are coming in. Did I ever tell ye about the time ye grandfather and I went hunting for one?" he questioned.

"I don't think so."

"Well, it was a few days before Christmas, and he wanted one for Christmas dinner. We went to Lake Mattamuskeet to kill one. It was so cold I thought we were going to freeze to death, and the wind off the lake made things worse. Ye know, there's an odd thing about swans. They're smart and graceful birds. When a tundra swan picks a mate, they'll stay with each other for the rest of their lives."

"White Feathers called me White Swan. She said I was graceful."

"Interesting. Another thing about them is if their mate dies, the other will mourn. Sometimes they'll even die from heartbreak."

"So, they're like people?"

"Aye."

A call from Thomas interrupted their conversation. "Captain, we're ready to let down the anchor whenever ye give the signal."

"Duty calls, Lizzie," Black Beard said as he joined Thomas. Clearing his throat, the captain bellowed, "Let down the anchor!"

In a rush of movements, the crew released the anchor. As it sank into the water with a splash, several pirates climbed into the rigging to tie off sails while others uncovered the periauger. Four of the Africans—James Blake, Thomas Gates, Richard Stiles, and James White—went down to the storage hold in the front of the ship to retrieve two casks of sugar. Securing the sails, the pirates hoisted the periauger and swung it over the railing on the starboard side.

Once in the water, John Martin and Joseph Brooks climbed down the rope ladder to help maneuver the casks of sugar as their crewmates hoisted them on ropes over the same pulley. With the sugar ready, Nathaniel Jackson and Stephen Daniel descended the ladder as Black Beard gave Thomas instructions for the rest of the crew. Finally, the pirate captain climbed down the rope ladder.

Lizzie watched them row the periauger toward Tobias Knight's dock. The men were surprisingly quick, moving swiftly with the incoming tide, which aided their efforts. When they were halfway across the mouth of the river, a bell rang from the Knight plantation. Seeing someone short standing by the bell post, Lizzie figured Scripo was the one ringing it to let Secretary Knight know visitors were coming.

A commotion caused Lizzie to peer over her shoulder. Israel Hands was behind her swearing loudly. At first she thought he was cursing her, but she quickly realized Tuffy was on the receiving end of the verbal abuse. The one-eyed cat arched her back as she let out a hiss, giving Israel a taste of his own medicine. Irritated, the pirate waved his hands as the cat lunged at him and bit his arm.

"I'll kill ye!" Israel screamed, slinging Tuffy against the ship.

Gasping, Lizzie rushed to see if she was hurt as Israel turned on her. The fury in his eyes made her shrink against the railing in fear.

"Don't ye touch that pest! She's going to the gators," he spat.

"No!" Lizzie shrieked as he made a grab for the cat.

"Leave my cat alone!" Cookie yelled.

Whipping around, Israel grinned. "It's about time ye came up. Ye cat is going to die, and there's nothing ye can do about it."

Cookie jumped on Israel, knocking him on the deck. The two pirates fought with each other as members of the crew stopped what they were doing to watch. Quartermaster Thomas Miller came up from below deck as the four Africans hauled up two more casks of sugar. Thomas stopped the fight by pulling Cookie off Israel.

"What's going on?" he demanded.

Israel pulled out his knife. Raising it over his head, he jumped on a nearby crate as his red shirt flapped in the wind. The rogue pirate shouted something to his supporters about a takeover, which triggered a fight as those still loyal to Black Beard tried to regain control. Terrified, Lizzie asked God for help as she crawled over to Tuffy. The poor cat meowed pitifully as she rubbed her head against Lizzie's hand. It appeared she injured her leg and was in a lot of pain. Gently picking her up, Lizzie tried to make it to the back of the ship. Once she was a safe distance away, she looked for Jake but couldn't spot him on the crowded deck. She was about to take Tuffy to her room when a voice echoed from nearby. Recognizing her papa's voice, she ran to the railing with Tuffy and peered down at the greenish-blue water.

"What the heck is going on up there?" he bellowed.

"Israel started a fight."

"A fight? I can't leave those scallywags for thirty minutes! Who took the ladder? Get someone to pull us up."

Running to the captain's cabin, Lizzie left Tuffy on her bed before returning to the deck. Searching the faces, she made her way to the bow of the ship. Eventually, she found Jake trying to get away from one of the Africans, who was apparently on Israel's side. He managed to escape by crawling between the fighting pirates.

"Are you okay?" she asked as he scrambled to his feet.

"Yes, I wasn't expecting to fight for my life," he panted.

"Pa—I mean, Black Beard is back," she continued, barely avoiding saying Papa. "The ladder is missing. If we can't find it quickly, he wants somebody to pull them up."

"Israel must have moved it on purpose."

Lizzie felt relieved when he reached behind a crate and pulled out the rope ladder. Jogging back to the railing, Jake tossed it overboard while Lizzie stood by his side watching the fight. Seconds later, her papa was swinging his leg over the railing. Drawing a pistol from his belt, he held it up and let it rip. The loud bang echoed across the deck, capturing everyone's attention. Being so close to the gunshot, Lizzie held her ringing ears as Black Beard's angry voice growled at his silent crew. The only one who didn't stop fighting was Israel, whom Husky grabbed with his strong arms, leaving the scrawny pirate powerless.

"Stop! There is no fighting on the ship. Do ye hear me? Ye signed papers swearing to abide by the rules. I won't tolerate an unruly crew. Punishment is coming to whoever started this as soon as we've transferred the sugar. Now, load this periauger," he ordered.

The four Africans descended into the hold for two more casks while the rest of the men tied ropes to the other casks of sugar. Thomas Miller came over with a concerned look on his face.

"No disrespect, Captain, but Israel should've been restrained."

"We need all hands on deck until we get the sugar ashore."

"How can I deal—" Thomas began, but Black Beard interrupted him.

"I'm going to deal with Israel. From now on, ye are supervising the shipments. Tobias isn't feeling well so ye will be working with a guest of Mr. Knight's named Edmund Chamberlayne. Tobias has entrusted matters of finance to him. Just make sure everything goes smoothly. We've got to get this unloaded before the sun goes down.

I'm putting ye on the periauger in case another boat stops ye. Tell them ye are going ashore for water."

"Aye, aye, Captain."

Thomas climbed down the rope ladder as Cookie came up. He seemed to be as upset as Thomas was about not restraining Israel.

"Don't ye think Israel should be locked up?" he suggested.

"My mind is made up," Black Beard snapped. "We need everyone to get the sugar moved. Do something useful: start supper."

Cookie stared at him, shocked by how blunt he was. Lizzie had to agree. She had never heard her papa speak so sharply to Cookie. His mood swing made her wonder how he could act like two different people. When the Africans returned with the sugar, Black Beard walked over to the crew as they tried to hoist it over the side.

"Well," Cookie grunted. "I guess I have my orders."

"I'll help, but we should look after Tuffy first," Lizzie replied.

"My goodness, I forgot about my cat! Is she okay?"

"She hurt her leg. I took her to my room before I found Jake."

"Why don't both of you go to the galley? I'll get Tuffy. Something tells me we should get off the deck," Jake offered as he glanced over at Black Beard, who was yelling at the crew.

"Alright, I'll get a chicken," Cookie agreed. "I planned to make chicken pastry, but I'm not sure how good it'll be with one chicken. The rest will have to fatten up. Go boil the water, Miss Lizzie."

Lizzie descended the stairs. Once in the kitchen, she could hear Reba's squawks while moving the cauldron to the cook pit. Positioning it over the coals, Lizzie filled it with water and lit a fire. As she got things ready, Lizzie thought about all she had learned. Three months ago, she had no idea how ships worked, and here she was starting a safe fire like a true sailor. Cookie had taught her so much.

Jake came down the stairs carrying Tuffy. Moments later, Cookie joined them, dropping a headless chicken on the oak table. Lizzie plucked the chicken's reddish-brown feathers while Jake held Tuffy for Cookie to examine her. Sadly, Israel broke the cat's back left leg. Cookie made her a splint, but he wasn't sure how she would heal.

Putting Tuffy in her cage so that she wouldn't move around, Cookie started getting his chicken pastry going. Soon, the meat was boiling as the inviting aroma filled the room. Lizzie got out the flour and began rolling out the dough as Cookie dropped the strips into the cauldron. When it was in the pot, Cookie announced his plans to eat on the deck. Deciding to construct a makeshift table, Jake helped Cookie carry empty barrels and a board upstairs. While they were gone, Lizzie gathered bowls, pewter cups, and spoons into a basket.

Finally, the chicken pastry was ready. Coming back to the galley, Cookie told her the last four casks of sugar were on their way to shore. He grabbed a rag as he removed the cauldron from the coals and carried it upstairs. After putting out the fire, Lizzie picked up the basket of bowls. As she passed through the doorway at the top of the stairs, she felt a light breeze against her face. The soft glow of candlelight that the lanterns emitted reminded her of the first time she peeped over the railing in July. Oh, how far she had come!

"Get some pastry, Miss Lizzie," Cookie instructed as he put down the cauldron. "I don't care if those scoundrels ever eat again."

Grabbing a bowl, Lizzie spooned out some of Cookie's famous chicken pastry and filled a cup with water. She found a stool to sit on, prayed over her meal, and took a bite.

"Well?" Cookie asked as he sat down beside her.

"It's delicious."

The pirate grinned. "I'm going to miss having ye help me."

"I know. I'm going to miss you, too."

"Let's not start our good-byes tonight. Ye have one more night, so let's make it memorable. Israel has ruined the day enough."

"Do you think he'll try something again?"

"Nay, Captain's watching him. Israel scared me. Not for myself, but for ye. If he hurt ye…well, I would've killed him," he said.

"I don't think you would've actually killed him."

"I would if he hurt ye. The thought did cross my mind. Guess ye could say it's one of the skeletons in my cellar. Ye do remember me talking about them, don't ye?"

"Yes. I think everyone has a few skeletons. God promises to forgive us, though. He's willing to pardon you just like King George did, except when God pardons you, no one can change it. When you truly turn from your sins, He wipes the slate clean," she proclaimed.

Cookie didn't say anything else as JJ and Jake joined them with bowls of chicken pastry. They sat down on the deck to eat their meals while several other members of the crew filled their bowls.

"Ye were stingy with the chicken, Cookie," JJ teased.

"I should've known ye would be the first to complain. We only had one fat enough to season the pastry."

"It tastes good," Jake commented.

"Smells good, too," JJ's father added as he came over.

The conversation turned to the transfer of the sugar. Joseph filled them in on everything from Tobias Knight's sickness to the new man, Edmund Chamberlayne. Cookie told him about Israel's actions, the fight, and Black Beard's promise to punish him.

"Guess the scuttlebutt was true," Joseph stated. "Wonder how Captain will punish him? Ye know Israel will get revenge."

Boom!

"What was that?" Lizzie gasped as they looked at each other.

"Sounded like a gunshot," Cookie declared, scrambling to his feet.

Lizzie's heart lurched as she wondered who had shot the gun. She realized she hadn't seen her papa or Israel. Praying her papa was okay, she tried to stay calm. Jake must have been thinking the same thing.

"Where's Black Beard? I haven't seen him lately."

"He was headed to his quarters, said he wanted to make notes in the ship's logbook while things were fresh on his mind," Joseph revealed.

Everyone got up as Thomas Miller walked over to Black Beard's private domain where the noise came from. Curious faces gathered in a semicircle to see what happened. Thomas was two steps from the door when it suddenly opened, sending smoke into the night air. Black Beard stood in the light glowing from the doorway. In his right hand was a smoking gun. The backlight illuminated his black attire, making him look like the fierce pirate he was presumed to be.

"Where's Cookie?" the pirate captain demanded.

"Right here, Captain," Cookie announced, taking a step forward.

"Get in here. Mr. Hands has been shot."

"What?" Cookie exclaimed.

"Don't just stand there! The man's bleeding all over my floor."

Cookie turned to look at Lizzie. "Get my surgical kit."

Taking off, she went to the galley. Going to the shelf where the surgical kit was, Lizzie stood on her tiptoes to retrieve it. She was searching for a bucket to put water in when Jake and JJ entered.

"Captain's getting mad. We've got to hurry," JJ informed her.

"Take this to Cookie. Tell him I'll be there shortly. If there's blood all over the floor we might need some water," she said.

Grabbing the surgical kit, JJ scurried up the stairs. Lizzie put water in the bucket and found bandages. She followed Jake, who toted the bucket, noticing the weary looks on the faces of those on the deck. Once inside the cabin, JJ closed the door. Israel was on the floor in a pool of blood, moaning as Cookie knelt by his side. Thomas and Joseph stood in the corner mumbling while Black Beard paced back and forth, rubbing his wiry beard. Eventually, the cook stood up.

"Well?" Black Beard prompted.

"I'm no doctor. Sawing it off will keep him from bleeding to death," Cookie answered bluntly.

"Get away from me, ye old goat! Ye aren't going to saw off my leg!" Israel spat as he attempted to get up.

The movement caused the rogue pirate to drop his head on the floor as he rolled on his side in pain holding his bloody right leg. As Cookie moved out of his way, Lizzie saw his wounded kneecap. It was so awful she turned her head and tried not to gag.

"Ye heard him. He doesn't want my help. Let him lay there and die," Cookie proclaimed unsympathetically.

"Die? Ye can't leave me like this. There's bound to be a doctor in town," Israel groaned in misery.

"A doctor? Why waste money on a fool?" Cookie countered.

"Thomas, get the periauger ready, but don't put it in the water," Black Beard ordered. "Mr. Hands will be needing to see a doctor."

Everyone stared at each other in shock.

"What? The last thing he deserves is mercy!" Cookie exploded.

"I give the orders. He's going ashore. Get the periauger ready."

Thomas quickly left the cabin with Joseph. Before JJ and Jake could follow, Black Beard called them back to talk privately.

"Under the circumstances, it's best if ye and Lizzie go home, Jake. Things might get out of hand once the men find out what happened. JJ, ye can help me and Cookie with Israel."

"I don't want to help Israel," Cookie objected as he came over.

"Cookie, I know ye are angry, but ye need to stop challenging my authority. Bandage him up. Lizzie, go pack," Black Beard instructed.

JJ and Jake exited the cabin. With her papa helping Cookie bandage Israel's leg, Lizzie went to her room. She grabbed the turtle shell basket and started tossing items into it on top of the shell necklace and carved whale bone. Gathering her spare clothing and tricorn hat, she reached under her bed for the dingy blue handkerchief that covered the snuffbox. Opening the small silver box, she pulled out her oval-shaped locket and put it around her neck. With everything packed, she carried the turtle shell basket to the doorway, pausing to look at her bed once more.

"Are ye ready, Lizzie?" her papa inquired.

"Yes, I'm ready."

Following her papa out of the cabin, she peered over her shoulder at Cookie, who was roughly tying the bandage in a knot. Israel's protests of pain didn't deter the cook from being forceful with him. As they walked out on the deck, Thomas Miller met them.

"The periauger is ready, Captain."

"Good. Tell Husky and Owen to put Israel in the boat before ye lower it in the water," Black Beard requested.

Bowing his head, Thomas found the two men as Black Beard gave out orders. JJ and Jake took Lizzie's belongings and put them in the periauger with Jake's few personal items and the bow and arrow. The three of them stood near a lantern while Husky and Owen carried Israel to the waiting boat.

"JJ, did you hear what happened?" Lizzie whispered.

JJ glanced at Black Beard before answering. "Thomas told Pa that Captain shot Israel with a blank, otherwise he would be missing a leg at such a close range. Israel threatened him with a gun."

Stunned, Lizzie watched the pirates load Israel, thankful her papa hadn't killed him. Once the moaning pirate was on board, the crew hoisted the periauger. Cookie was the first to climb down the ladder, followed by JJ and Jake. Holding tightly to the rope ladder, Lizzie tried to keep her balance in the darkness. At last she made it. Looking up at the *Adventure*'s hull, she sat at the bow of the boat while her papa descended with a lantern. JJ and Jake started rowing.

From the lantern light, Lizzie could see the pain on Israel's face, yet she couldn't feel sorry for him. She despised that bright red shirt. Wondering if she had become hard-hearted, she reasoned her feelings were understandable. Hoping God would forgive her if she was in the wrong, she thought about her papa's decision to take Israel ashore. Part of her was surprised he was going to this extreme. The other part wondered if he still had a tiny piece of care in his heart. Was this choice Edward Beard's instead of Black Beard's?

Staring at the black outline of the towering ship, Lizzie could see the glowing lanterns surrounding the deck. A sliver of the moon shone in the night sky. Soon they were in the mouth of Bath Town Creek. No one spoke except Israel, who moaned and complained constantly.

"Shut up!" Cookie threatened, kicking Israel's good leg.

"Ouch! Don't kick me. I'm hurting," Israel shouted.

"Captain, his fuss will wake the town," Cookie yelled.

"Give me ye neckerchiefs," Black Beard demanded.

JJ untied the navy-blue one he always wore and passed it to him. Black Beard tied it around Israel's mouth while Cookie tied his neckerchief around his wrists. With his hands tied and mouth gagged, the rest of the journey went much more smoothly. Lizzie listened to the gentle slap of water against the periauger as her mind drifted to what she was going to say to Aunt Grace. So much had happened in the last three months, some of which she wasn't sure her aunt needed to hear. Were things such as Margaret in Pennsylvania, stealing the French ships, and the pirate banyan best left secret? Other things also crossed her mind. What would happen to Israel? And what about the gold? Would those who went rogue get part of the communal plunder?

By now Lizzie could see the outline of Bath's landing. Luckily, it was so late no other boats were at the dock. Moments later, they were close enough for JJ to tie off and step on the dock. With Jake holding the lantern, Cookie helped Black Beard lift Israel to his good foot. They assisted the gagged pirate as he limped into JJ's arms. Stepping on the deck, Black Beard and Cookie juggled Israel between them.

"How far is the doctor's house, Captain?" JJ inquired.

"It's across the street from the store. Keep ye eyes open."

JJ got back in the periauger while Black Beard, Cookie, and Israel went ashore. Candlelight lit up the darkness as the door of Doctor Patrick Maule's house opened. A man stood in the doorway motioning for the pirates to enter. The street went dark again until the door reopened. Cookie hurried back and climbed in the periauger. Untying the rope, they rowed to the opposite shore and located the dock Grandfather Beard built. Grabbing a pole, JJ tied the rope as Cookie helped Lizzie get out and passed Jake their belongings.

"Are you coming to the house?" Lizzie questioned Cookie.

"Nay, Captain will be waiting for us. We'll be in touch."

Standing with Jake, Lizzie waved to them as they pushed away from the dock. Walking to the house, her eyes spotted the fenced-in barnyard and the two-story home facing the waterfront. They were halfway across the yard when the family dog ran to them barking.

"Shhh! It's just us, Killer," she muttered, stooping to rub the little brown and white dog's head.

Killer pulled away from her as she sniffed her hand.

"It's been three months, Lizzie. She might not know you."

"Here, take my things so I can pick her up."

Jake held her belongings while she grabbed the little dog, which tried to lick her face. Lizzie rubbed her fur as they walked up to the house. Once on the front porch, she took a deep breath and knocked on the door. She felt nervous even though she couldn't explain it. Knocking again, she heard something moving on the opposite side.

"Who is it?" came Aunt Grace's unmistakable voice.

Lizzie's heart thumped harder. "It's me, Lizzie, and Jake."

The door opened slowly. Aunt Grace stood in the doorway in her nightgown with a shotgun in her hands. Upon seeing them, she lowered the gun as she raised her hand to her face.

"What's going on, Momma?" Trent's voice urged from within.

"It's Lizzie!" his mother shouted, handing him the gun.

Letting go of Killer, Lizzie hugged her aunt with tears streaming down her cheeks. Everyone exchanged hugs as Killer barked excitedly at their feet. It was so good to be home!

CHAPTER TWENTY-ONE

☠

FAREWELL, ADVENTURE

October 31, 1718 ~ Friday

Adjusting to life back in Bath hadn't been easy. Upon Aunt Grace's insisting, Jake had been sleeping on a pallet in Trent's room. Sunday morning started with a delicious breakfast of sausage, eggs, and a cup of fresh milk from Betsy followed by the usual Divine Service. Jake joined them in hearing God's word before going to Grandfather's house. After dinner, Uncle Thomas; his wife, Sarah; Uncle John; Aunt Charlotte; Aunt Mary; her fiancé, Thomas Bustin; Aunt Grace; and Grandfather Worsley all gathered to hear the highlights of the adventure. Even the children listened on the floor as they passed around Hannah's conch shell.

Lizzie felt bad after hearing how worried the family had been when they discovered she and Jake were missing. Thankfully, Uncle Thomas and Uncle John found the boats before they got a search party started. With their pirate brother-in-law just leaving the colony, they guessed Lizzie and Jake were with him.

Monday began the workweek as everyone kept busy canning vegetables and planting the fall crop of collards. Luckily, Aunt Grace had been lenient with Lizzie, who spent time with her papa, though she still had to catch up on her schoolwork in the evenings. With the days dwindling to his departure, Black Beard made daily trips to the house to spend time with her. This was an issue for

Aunt Grace who wasn't too happy about her pirate brother-in-law telling his adventures to Trent, Alice, Rebecca, and Hannah. Sadly, time was running short. Today the *Adventure* would be leaving Bath.

Lizzie had dreaded this moment for days. Part of her wanted to go with him, though she knew it was crazy. Her life was in Bath with her family, not on a pirate ship. Still, thoughts of being without her papa made her heart ache. How could she say good-bye when she finally had a relationship with him?

Sighing, Lizzie crossed the yard from the outhouse. While she went to do her business, Aunt Grace finished stitching the six-foot-long material for Jake's new mattress. Walking up to the back porch, Lizzie watched her aunt stuff the mattress as Hannah, Rebecca, and Alice passed her handfuls of cornhusks.

"Jake's going to be so surprised!" Hannah announced.

"He's family now. I don't know how long he'll stay, but he'll have a bed. Thomas is getting a bed frame," Aunt Grace said.

"When are we giving it to him?" Alice wanted to know.

"Tonight. He can sleep on it until we get the frame. We'll have to rearrange Trent's room," Aunt Grace answered.

"Momma," Hannah interrupted. "Someone's coming."

Looking up the path, Lizzie spotted a cream-colored horse pulling a wagon. As the rig came closer, their dog, Killer, started barking. A man sat on the bench flicking the reins. His striped britches, blue shirt, and the navy-blue turban on his head were an instant giveaway. It was Cookie. Delighted, Lizzie ran to meet the wagon. Since the pirates were keeping a low profile, she had only seen him twice. Both times had been with her papa at Tunnel Land.

"Hey, Cookie!" she shouted, waving as he pulled the reins, coaxing the cream-colored horse to stop. "It's so good to see you."

"Can't stay long. I was heading to town for supplies. I'm sure ye pa told ye we're leaving today," he stated while getting down.

"Yes, I'm afraid so. Let me go get Jake. He's helping Trent patch the fence. I know he wants to see you before you leave."

"We'll talk later. Captain is meeting Tobias. He wants to see ye and Jake at Tunnel Land in an hour. I should be back about the same time. The men are waiting to load the supplies by James and Stephen's dock. I borrowed their rig," Cookie proclaimed, referring to Tunnel Land's new pirate owners.

"I'll tell Jake. Do you have time to meet my aunt and cousins?"

"Aye, but I have something to tell ye first."

Going to the back of the wagon, Cookie slid out a cage with Tuffy in it. Surprisingly, the cat was standing on her injured leg.

"You brought Tuffy! She's doing so well."

"She's hobbling around a bit. I've come to a sad conclusion, Miss Lizzie," Cookie revealed, pulling out another cage. "I think it's best if they both stay here with ye."

"What?" Lizzie gasped as he set Reba's cage on top of Tuffy's.

By now, Aunt Grace was walking up with the girls. Rebecca and Alice stood by their mother as Hannah shyly peeped out from behind her. Lizzie realized they had only seen him in July at the store.

"Aunt Grace, this is Cookie."

Cookie shook Aunt Grace's hand. "It's nice to meet ye, ma'am."

Hannah giggled at the sound of his nickname. Stooping to her level, the pirate cook gave her a wink.

"It's a pleasure to meet you, too. Lizzie told us a lot about you. I heard you are a great cook," Aunt Grace responded.

"What kind of bird is that?" Hannah asked.

"Come take a look," Cookie insisted. "Tuffy was a crew member until a recent injury. She's having a hard time keeping the rats off the ship. Her friend Reba is a parrot. I got her in Pennsylvania."

Hannah smiled. "She's so pretty!"

"If it's all right, ma'am, I'd like to give my pets to Miss Lizzie. A ship is no place for a bird like Reba, and Tuffy is too weak to fight rats. She needs to enjoy the rest of her days. I'll pick up another cat in St. Thomas. So, what do ye say?" Cookie questioned Aunt Grace.

"Uh, well, I guess."

"Thanks. It means a lot knowing they're here with Miss Lizzie," he muttered, bending down to rub Tuffy's cheeks.

Reba seemed jealous of Tuffy. "Reba pretty girl! Reba pretty girl!"

"Aye, ye are a pretty girl," Cookie chuckled, touching her green tail feathers. "Good-bye, my loves."

Letting out a sigh, the pirate climbed into the wagon. "Don't mean to rush, but I need to go. Captain will wonder where the supplies are. It was good to meet ye. I'll see ye later, Miss Lizzie."

He flicked the reins, sending the horse forward. Lizzie waved before bending to peer into Reba's cage.

"Where will they sleep, Momma?" Rebecca wanted to know.

"Can they stay in my room?" Lizzie pleaded. "I'll look after them."

"The bird is kind of loud," Aunt Grace observed.

"She'll settle down when she gets used to things. Please, Aunt Grace," Lizzie begged, not wanting them to have to be in the barn.

"They're animals. They'll be fine outside."

"It's too cold," Hannah objected.

"Please let them," Lizzie urged as her cousins joined in.

"Alright, but if they get rowdy they're going outside."

Picking up Reba's cage, Lizzie led the way to the kitchen. Behind her, Alice carried Tuffy while Rebecca and Hannah helped their mother find bowls for water. After getting the pets settled upstairs, Lizzie and her cousins went back outside. They just walked out on the porch when Grandfather Worsley rode up on a brown horse.

"Well, this is an unexpected visit," Aunt Grace greeted him.

"I came to tell you Mary and John are missing," he stated grimly.

"Missing?" Aunt Grace blurted out. "What do you mean?"

"I went to have Thomas look at some papers. Charlotte came saying Mary never returned from the cellar. She looked for John, who was fixing the feed trough, but couldn't find him either."

"Perhaps she rode into town with John to see Thomas Bustin."

"She would've told Charlotte. Thomas is heading into town to ask around and get a search party started. Maybe all of you should come with me. Charlotte and I could use some help looking around the plantation. Girls, go tell Trent and Jake to hitch the wagon."

Rebecca and Hannah took off running. Alice offered to take Jake's new mattress inside. Once they left, Grandfather spoke up.

"We need to be careful, Grace. Neighbors have lost hams, links of sausage, vegetables, and even chickens. We've lost a few ourselves. I thought a fox was in the henhouse, but Thomas has heard others making the same complaints. Someone is stealing the food."

"You think this has something to do with their disappearance?"

Another horse came trotting up the path with Uncle Thomas in the saddle. As he pulled the reins, the black horse came to a stop.

"What did you learn in town?" Grandfather asked.

"No one has seen them. Thomas Harding is getting the word out. I'm headed to Secretary Knight's so he can sign orders for the rangers to search. Governor Eden is at a council meeting in the Chowan Precinct and won't be back for a couple of weeks. Harding thinks Indians took them. John Porter heard noises last night at their place on the edge of town. He saw an Indian running off with meat from the smokehouse. While I talked with Harding at the shipyard, Thomas Bustin came up. He's upset about Mary and is headed to your house."

"What's going on, Momma?" Trent inquired as he and Jake walked up with the girls. "Rebecca said to hitch the wagon."

"We're going over to your grandfather's. I'll explain on the way. Get your bonnets, girls," Aunt Grace instructed.

Rebecca and Hannah went inside the house while Trent jogged to the barn to get Honeybee. Uncle Thomas told Jake what happened when Lizzie suddenly remembered Cookie's visit.

"Wait, we can't go. Jake and I are supposed to go to Tunnel Land. Cookie came by and said Papa was meeting with Mr. Knight. He wants to see us before he leaves," she declared.

"I'm not sure you should go, Lizzie," Aunt Grace said.

"Jake will be with her, Grace. We don't want to hold Edward up. Things are already difficult for him as it is," Grandfather insisted.

"I can ride with them to Tunnel Land," Uncle Thomas added.

"Alright, but be careful," Aunt Grace agreed.

Following Jake to the barn, Lizzie helped saddle Butterscotch and his horse, Buckwheat. When they returned, her aunt and cousins had locked the house and were climbing in the wagon. Grandfather rode alongside while Uncle Thomas joined Lizzie and Jake. Holding the reins, Lizzie nudged Butterscotch's belly with the saddle stirrups to coax the light brown mare into a trot. They traveled down the path and over the property line, passing empty fields. Soon Lizzie could see the gorgeous two-story mansion surrounded by outbuildings on the four-hundred-acre plantation. Uncle Thomas left them as he continued to Tobias' place next door.

Without the green-leafed tobacco standing in the fields, the house seemed larger. Even though she had come to this house twice in the last week, she had yet to sneak a peek inside the stately home. Her time at Tunnel Land had been on the dock. Dangling her feet in the water, she had listened to her papa while he fished. His stories of her mother and his boyhood were memories she would treasure forever.

Coming to a stop, they dismounted their horses and tied the reins to a wooden post. Out by the dock, she could see an empty periauger, but otherwise the place seemed deserted.

"Guess everyone's inside," Jake muttered.

Walking up the steps, Lizzie stood beside Jake as he knocked on the door. The view of Bath Town Creek was breathtaking. When the door opened, a tall, black-haired man peered out.

"We're here to see Black Beard," Jake stated. "I'm Jake Griffin."

The man opened the door wider as he extended his hand to shake Jake's. "Nice to meet ye. I'm James Robins." Glancing at Lizzie he continued, "Ye must be Miss Lizzie. Come in. Captain isn't here yet, but most of the others are. Thomas Miller and Philip Morton are the only ones on the *Adventure*."

Slowly nodding, Jake stepped inside. Lizzie stayed close to him as James shut the door and led them to a room on the right. She glanced at the staircase and furniture in the hall. The stairs brought back a childhood memory. Years ago, she played on those steps with Trent, who fell and cut his forehead. Aunt Susannah had taken them to see Grandfather Beard's widow, Elizabeth, after she married the former owner of Tunnel Land, William Masten. Lizzie couldn't recall the last time she saw her step-grandmother, Elizabeth, but Aunt Susannah had kept in touch with Elizabeth's family through letters.

"There ye are! We were wondering when ye would show up." JJ's voice greeted them as they entered the crowded room.

Jake told the pirates about the abduction while Lizzie looked around the parlor at the familiar faces. She assumed the only stranger was Stephen Elsey. Just like James said, Thomas and Philip weren't there. Israel was missing as well. Studying the room, she noticed an oak desk in the corner and several nice chairs. In the center of the parlor was a delicately carved table surrounded by four decorated straight-backed chairs. Burgundy coverings hung at the windows, allowing sunlight to stream in. A huge fireplace stood to the left. Taking in the beauty, Lizzie figured Governor Eden sold the contents along with the house. The two pirate owners didn't have the taste or means to purchase such fancy things in the short time since they bought it.

"Doesn't sound good," Joseph Brooks commented when Jake finished. "Could be another Indian war ahead."

"I hope not. The last one was bad enough," John Martin declared.

"Stop talking about bad news. Would ye like something to drink, Miss Lizzie? Some wine perhaps?" James Robins offered.

"I'm fine," Lizzie responded.

"Cookie's back. Let's help him unload the wagon," Edward Salter announced as he stood staring out the window.

The pirates left the parlor to help Cookie. Lizzie and Jake lingered on the porch with JJ and his father. The men started moving barrels when hollering came from the backyard. Joseph leaned on the rail to investigate as someone ran around the side of the house.

"Shut your eyes!" Jake blurted out as he jumped in front of her.

Confused, Lizzie stared at him. "Why?"

"Husky's running around without pants!" JJ reported, laughing.

"Have ye lost ye mind? Pull up those britches!" Joseph shouted over the cackles, as the pirates made fun of the tough-natured man.

"There's a skunk in the outhouse!"

"I don't care if there's a dozen skunks in there. Get ye pants up!"

"But he sprayed me!"

"Don't come over here. We'll have to get ye some fresh clothes."

Husky must have pulled up his pants while Cookie got the men refocused. The periauger was nearly full when Black Beard arrived on a gray horse. As he dismounted, Stephen Elsey and James Robins followed Husky to the outhouse with a shotgun.

"What's going on?" Black Beard asked, climbing up to the porch.

"Husky got sprayed by a skunk," Joseph informed him.

Black Beard chuckled. "A skunk? He'll have to wash in tomato juice before he gets back on the ship."

"He might have to sleep on deck," Cookie joked.

"Are the supplies loaded?" Black Beard inquired.

"They're working on it. While I was in town, I heard there might be another Indian uprising. Two people are missing."

"Lizzie's uncle told me at Tobias' place. Her mother's brother and sister are the ones missing," Black Beard answered.

"Grandfather came after you left, Cookie. Everyone is looking for them," Lizzie acknowledged.

"Tobias is organizing a search party of rangers. Hopefully they'll find them soon. I wasn't planning to leave until this evening, but

I've decided to go early. If there's another Indian war getting ready to break out, I want to warn Susannah and Martin," Black Beard stated. "Let's get the men together for a meeting. I know we're missing three men, but I already know where they stand."

Wondering what he meant, Lizzie watched her papa call his men over. Everyone gathered at the base of the steps. James and Stephen Elsey sat on the bottom stoop while Husky stood downwind from the others. Lizzie and Jake sat on the top step as Black Beard spoke.

"Israel is leaving the crew. When Cookie and I dropped him off in town, he got his part of the communal plunder. I know some of ye don't think he deserved it, but the articles are clear. Each of ye gets a portion. There's been a lot of scuttlebutt going around. I gave ye forty-eight hours to decide to stay with the crew or leave."

John Martin stepped forward. "Captain, I've enjoyed being part of the brotherhood, but my family needs help with the sheep herd."

"I understand. It's been good to have ye onboard, John," Black Beard replied. "Anyone else?"

"I'm going to leave, too, Captain," Edward Salter chimed in.

"So am I," Stephen Daniel piped up.

"It's time for me to go as well. Israel's mess didn't turn out right, and I'm tired of working the sails," Garret Gibbons mentioned.

"Aye, the back-breaking work has taken a toll on me. I think I'll spend some time at the Salty Sailor Tavern getting to know important people. Who knows, I might be governor one day," John Giles said as his fellow crewmates snickered in amusement.

"Ye will all be missed. Thanks for ye loyalty," Black Beard began.

"Captain," JJ interrupted. "I'm leaving, too."

Lizzie's eyes widened in surprise. Her mind drifted back to Ocracoke Island when Jake raised the possibility of JJ staying in Bath. Was JJ's decision based on his feelings for her?

"What do ye have to say about this, Joseph?" Black Beard asked JJ's father.

"We talked last night. It's his choice. He's got a good head on his shoulders and will do well at whatever he chooses."

"I agree. We will miss ye, JJ," Black Beard remarked. "Well, if there isn't anyone else, let's get the wagon unhitched, the supplies to the *Adventure*, and help Husky out. I've always heard tomato juice does the trick. I will separate the plunder for those leaving."

Stephen Elsey and James Robins went around to the cellar for jars of tomatoes while the others split up to do their duties. Black Beard walked over to the gray horse he borrowed. He grabbed a leather bag hanging from the saddle horn as he told JJ he wanted to speak with him. Figuring the bag held the gold, Lizzie slid over so they could pass through. Minutes later, JJ called Jake inside. From the look on Jake's face, Lizzie could tell he was surprised. As the door closed behind them, JJ's father, Joseph, came over.

"I've been meaning to talk with ye, Miss Lizzie. I'm not sure if ye have feelings for JJ, but give him a chance. If ye can't see past his life as a pirate, then I ask ye to let him down gently. He has his mother's kind soul and doesn't do well with rejection."

Stunned, Lizzie jumped when the door to the mansion opened. Jake and JJ each carried a cloth sack, though JJ's was bigger. Joseph called JJ down, saying he wanted to talk before he had to leave. Once they were gone, Jake sat on the steps and showed her the small sack of gold coins. Apparently, Black Beard felt he earned some of the plunder. He also gave him the pirate articles Jake signed when he joined the crew. Jake had just slid the handful of gold coins back into the sack when Black Beard appeared.

Descending the stairs, he distributed medium-sized sacks of gold to Stephen Daniel, Garret Gibbons, John Giles, and Edward Salter. John Martin received a smaller sack presumably because he already had Africans. After shaking hands with them, Black Beard asked Jake to help Cookie take the horses to the barn.

"I guess this is it, huh? The moment we've both been dreading," her papa said as he sat beside her on the step.

Looking at his trembling hands, Lizzie noticed his breath smelled like brandy. "Do you have to go, Papa? I wish I could go with you."

"Ye can't live on a pirate ship, and I can't stick around. There's talk of the pardons not being legal, at least not for us. Tobias says the courts could rule against them because of the French ship. Eden signed off on it, but several men didn't believe me. Supposedly, a new pardon is on the way, but we don't know when it'll reach the colonies. Besides, I should warn Susannah about the Indians," he explained.

"Can't you wait and see? We could write to Aunt Susannah."

"Tobias tried to get me to stay a fortnight, but I don't feel good about it," he stated. "I've enjoyed spending time with ye and will always remember our recent talks over briarberry pie. The men are restless. There are rumors of an early winter. We'll probably go to St. Thomas. It's a small tropical island."

Knowing she wouldn't convince him if Tobias couldn't even get him to stay two weeks, Lizzie decided to try another approach. "Will you come back in the spring?"

Her papa sighed. "A lot has changed with ye coming back into my life. I want to return, but I can't make any promises."

"I guess being in the Caribbean will be good for you. With the warm weather and less responsibilities, you can relax and get well."

"Get well?" he responded in surprise.

"I know you've been sick since we left Pennsylvania. I heard fresh fruit is good for scurvy, so eat plenty when you get to St. Thomas. By April, you can come back to see me. Joseph will want to visit JJ, and Cookie will be begging to see me, Tuffy, and Reba."

Black Beard chuckled. "I suppose they will. Speaking of JJ, he's pretty determined to court ye."

"Just because he's staying doesn't mean I'll court him."

"That's up to ye. I do approve of him, which is more than I can say about the Gale boy. I can't speak on behalf of his character.

Jake is also a good choice. Whether or not ye choose to court, I'm proud of ye and I know ye mother would be, too."

"Thanks, Papa," she whispered, trying not to cry.

"I visited ye mother's grave yesterday. The sun shone through the pines on her tombstone as I told her about our summer. I miss her."

"I miss her, too," Lizzie mumbled, wiping tears from her cheeks. "Papa, what's the deal with you and Margaret? She obviously cared about you, and well, I've heard the rumors…"

Black Beard took a deep breath. "No one could replace ye mother, if that's what ye mean. Margaret was there for me in the dark days. Life is full of choices, Lizzie, and they have consequences. My choice to be a pirate means sacrificing relationships, be it Margaret or ye."

Just then, Cookie walked up. "Captain, James White and Richard Stiles are back with the periauger. Husky has washed off and is putting on the clean clothes they brought from the ship."

"Alright. Tell the men to start boarding the *Adventure*."

Cookie went back to the men as Lizzie and her papa stood up. "Papa, there's one more thing. I'm trying to accept you're a pirate, but being a pirate goes against God. If you can sign a paper promising to stop piracy, then why can't you ask God to forgive your sins and start over?"

Her papa rubbed his wiry beard. "Ye have a good point, but I'm not sure if I can. Life is like the changing tides. Ye make good choices like the high tide and bad choices like the low tide. It's hard for me to admit I may have done bad things. Let's just say I have some—"

"Skeletons in your cellar?" she finished as he narrowed his eyes in confusion. "Cookie told me the same thing."

"I see. Well, Cookie's in the same boat as me."

"Will you at least promise you'll think about it?"

He chuckled. "Ye never give up, do ye?"

Lizzie grinned. "No. I'm a Worsley and a Beard. Determination is in my blood."

Walking to the dock with her papa, Lizzie could see the pirates boarding the *Adventure*. As the two Africans rowed back to the dock, Black Beard said good-bye to the six men staying behind. Meanwhile, Lizzie approached Cookie.

"I'm going to miss you," she confessed, hugging him.

Cookie squeezed her and kissed her forehead. "Same here, Tiny. Take care of my pets, and don't do anything I wouldn't do."

"I'll do my best. Look after my papa. I love you, Cookie."

"Of course I will. I love ye, too, Miss Lizzie."

"Come on, Cookie, it's my turn," Black Beard interrupted.

Letting Cookie go, Lizzie hugged her papa. She fought tears as he held her close. When it was time to go, he released her and gently wiped tears from her cheek with his rough, weathered thumb.

"No crying, my dear. I love ye," he murmured.

Lizzie tried to grin but hearing him finally say those three special words caused her to lose it. "I love you, too."

Black Beard stepped into the periauger with Cookie, Joseph, and Husky, who had already climbed in. Joseph pushed off from the dock, waving at his son as Richard Stiles and James White picked up the oars. They began their journey to the *Adventure* while those on shore waved good-byes. After a few minutes, James Robins suggested they go inside for a drink of brandy. The seven former pirates went inside, leaving JJ, Jake, and Lizzie standing on the dock.

Crossing her arms, Lizzie stood frozen as tears trickled down her cheeks. Her eyes stayed focused on the periauger until she could no longer see her papa's bearded face.

With a heavy heart she whispered, "Farewell, *Adventure*."

CHAPTER TWENTY-TWO

SPINNING LIES

November 8, 1718 ~ Saturday

Fastening a hairpin to hold back her curly, dark brown hair, Lizzie reached for the looking glass. Studying her appearance, she played with her hair by tucking it behind her ears and then pulling strands of hair down again. Sighing, she put the mirror back on the basin stand, reminding herself she didn't have all evening to get ready. She brushed the front of her new dark-purple dress, making sure there were no wrinkles. Aunt Grace surprised her with the long-sleeved dress, saying she needed a new one for the occasion.

All the fuss over this year's Harvest Day made Lizzie nervous. The event was always an exciting night of food, games, and dancing that highlighted the end of the flax harvest. Every year, planters spent weeks gathering flax. First, the men separated fiber from the plant's woody stem by crushing it in a flax breaker over wooden rollers. Next, the women spun the flax on small spinning wheels, making linen thread. Later, they wove the threads on a loom to make clothes and bedding.

On the second Saturday of November, they gathered at a home chosen by the Harvest Day Celebration committee. While the men competed to see who could harvest the remaining flax the fastest, the ladies spun it into thread, showing off their skills. Afterward, there was a feast followed by games and dancing.

Unlike in years past, Lizzie wouldn't be playing with the children. Having turned sixteen in May, everyone would expect her to compete in the spinning and participate in the social dance. Her family had been teasing her about Miles Gale, who no doubt wanted to dance with her. Lizzie dreaded the party, but it was a town event and someone would notice her absence. Nervously fixing her hair once more, she opened the door of Aunt Charlotte's room and went into the hall.

For a week, the Worsley family worked at Grandfather's harvesting the flax and spinning it into thread. The work was much easier with the African slaves her papa brought into the colony. Since they spent all day finishing the harvest, they decided to get ready for the party at his house before going over to the Martin plantation.

Thankfully, the rangers found Uncle John and Aunt Mary two days after their disappearance. They managed to escape their captors and were trying to get back home. Although the Indians didn't hurt them, Aunt Mary hadn't been acting like her normal self. So far, the Indians hadn't attacked the town or taken anyone else captive. The rangers had searched for Grandfather's Indian servant, Pompey, who was also missing. With the Harvest Day Celebration and Sunday's Divine Service, the rangers wouldn't be going back out until Monday.

Going downstairs, Lizzie went to Grandfather's study. The room held 1,050 books donated to Bath by Reverend Thomas Bray, a representative of the bishop of London, England. In addition to religious books read during Divine Services, it also included books on geography, history, grammar, biography, medicine, sports, law, poetry, and classical literature. Every two years, the library moved to another home. Grandfather received the honor of housing the only collection of books in the colony back in January's council meeting. Anyone could borrow a book to read or study for schooling, provided they brought it back. Lizzie had enjoyed reading many of them.

Approaching the partially open door, Lizzie heard her grandfather talking. Peeping inside, she saw Aunt Grace standing near her father wearing a light blue dress. Grandfather wore his navy-blue suit with ruffled white sleeves and fashionable knee-high white stockings.

"Don't you think it's time to wear a pink ribbon?" Grandfather asked as he tied a blue ribbon to Aunt Grace's left wrist.

"Pink ribbons are for single ladies, Father. You know that."

"Yes, but married women wear blue ones. It's been seven years. Jared would want you to move on. Widows typically remarry."

"Because they need a man. I have plenty of men in my life."

Grandfather sighed. "I only want what's best for you, my dear."

"I know, Father. I love you," she replied, kissing his cheek.

"Look at Lizzie," Grandfather said as he noticed her at the door.

Lizzie entered the study as her aunt smiled. "You're gorgeous!"

"Thank you," Lizzie mumbled, grinning.

"Hold out your hand, dear. I've got a special pink ribbon just for you. I picked it out myself," Grandfather instructed.

Extending her left wrist, she watched him tie on the light pink ribbon. During the spinning competition, most ladies sixteen years old or older wore either a pink, purple, or blue ribbon. Some fifteen-year-olds chose to wear a pink one as well, but it was a personal choice for them and their families. Pink symbolized they were eligible to court, purple was for engaged ladies, and blue for married ones. Lizzie didn't wear one at fifteen, but this year was different. Just seeing the pink bow on her wrist made Lizzie's insides churn.

"You're all dressed up!"

Turning, Lizzie saw Aunt Charlotte enter the room. The nineteen-year-old wore a green dress, although unlike her older sister, Grace, she wasn't wearing her straight, dark brown hair up in a bun. Lizzie noticed she was already wearing a pink ribbon on her wrist.

"Doesn't seem like you're old enough to join in on the fun. You might snag a fellow," Aunt Charlotte teased, giving her a wink.

Aunt Mary came in wearing a burgundy dress and a frown. Her cheeks were red as if she had been crying.

"What's wrong?" Grandfather questioned in a concerned voice.

"I'm not going to the party."

"Why not?" Aunt Grace pursued.

"Thomas Bustin is picking you up," Aunt Charlotte pointed out.

Aunt Mary burst into tears. "It's all a lie. I can't face those people knowing we lied to them."

Stunned, Lizzie watched her grandfather hug his crying twenty-one-year-old daughter. She wondered what her aunt lied about.

"Calm down," Grandfather hushed her. "What's this talk about lying? You would never do such a thing."

"John and I lied about getting captured by Indians."

"You did what?" Grandfather blurted out, pulling away from her. He motioned toward a chair. "Sit down and tell us what happened."

As Aunt Mary sat in the cushioned seat, Aunt Grace moved a chair nearby so that her father could sit beside her sister. Meanwhile, Aunt Charlotte gave her a white-laced handkerchief to wipe her tears.

"When the rangers found us, John made up the story to protect Pompey. He stole our chickens and everyone's food. Nathaniel and I caught him stealing again. He knew about it, but didn't think there was anything wrong with it based on his reasons. Pompey told me there are servants in the community with barely enough food. Children are starving, Father," she sobbed.

"Why didn't you come to me?" Grandfather inquired.

"Because John didn't think you would do anything about it. How could you when Pompey broke the law? He's been with us for years and practically grew up with John. After all he went through as an orphan of the war, it's hard not to feel sorry for him. John couldn't see letting him get punished for providing food for the families."

"I wish the two of you came to me first. Where's Pompey?"

"He went into Tuscarora Indian territory. What happens now?"

"You and John must tell the truth. Governor Eden isn't due back for another week. Until he returns, Tobias needs to know about the situation. Whatever happens, we'll face it as a family."

Aunt Mary dabbed her eyes with the handkerchief. "I'm sorry."

"Everything will be alright," Grandfather promised. "Lizzie, bring me the purple ribbon on my desk."

Picking up the dark purple ribbon, she carried it to her grandfather, who tied it to Aunt Mary's left wrist. Once it was secure, he suggested they go to the parlor where Uncle Thomas' wife was waiting with the children. Following him, they left the study.

Aunt Sarah Bonner Worsley sat in a rocking chair in front of the fireplace with her twenty-one-month-old son, John. Three-year-old Little Thomas played with Hannah on the rug by his mother's feet while Alice and Rebecca twirled around in their new dresses.

"Thomas just came in saying the carriages are ready. They're going to the Martin plantation with the flax and spinning wheel. Thomas Bustin is helping Trent load the food," Aunt Sarah proclaimed.

"We better get going. Are you ready to go, children?" Grandfather asked as Alice, Rebecca, and Hannah cheered in excitement.

"Yay!" Little Thomas giggled, clapping his hands.

Everyone laughed as Aunt Grace took her nephew's hand and headed out the door. With Thomas Bustin taking Aunt Mary, the rest of the family split up to ride with Grandfather and Trent, who were wearing identical navy-blue suits. Lizzie rode up front with her grandfather. Aunt Charlotte sat behind them holding Little Thomas so that Aunt Sarah could hold baby John. In the other carriage, Aunt Grace sat next to Trent, while Alice, Rebecca, and Hannah sat in the back. Flicking the reins, they started out for the Martin plantation.

By now, the sun was low in the sky and there was a slight chill in the air. As the horses pulled them to their destination, Lizzie's mind drifted to Aunt Mary's confession. She couldn't believe they lied to help Pompey escape punishment. It was hard to picture Pompey stealing in the first place. Even Grandfather's white servant, Nathaniel Ming, was guilty of keeping it secret. Thinking about the false alarm of another Indian attack, Lizzie realized her papa had gone to see Aunt Susannah for nothing. She made a mental note to remind Aunt Grace to send her a letter explaining it was a fictitious claim. Her papa would just have to keep believing the lie. Chances were, he had already been up the Neuse River to see his sister and was on his way to Ocracoke. Lizzie wondered what he was doing right now. Cookie was probably cooking supper. Oh, how she missed them.

Soon the Martin homestead was in sight. The home was occupied by Joel Martin Sr.'s widow, Elizabeth Martin, and their grandson, fourteen-year-old Joel. Sadly, Joel's parents died when he was little. Miss Elizabeth had two more sons besides Joel Jr. and four daughters. Each of the daughters were married, with the youngest, Ann, getting married last year. Their son William was also married and helped his mother run the plantation and the family's large herd of sheep. With his older brother, John Martin, returning to the colony after two years of piracy, William's workload would no doubt be a lot easier.

Lizzie could see wagons and carriages lined up behind the house. Joining those who had already arrived, Grandfather pulled on the reins to get his horse to stop. Stepping out of the carriage, Lizzie self-consciously touched her locket. She wished her papa could be here to share in this special occasion. Trying to push away her emotions, Lizzie took baby John so that Aunt Sarah could step down. Once Aunt Sarah took the little boy, everyone grabbed baskets of food and went to the barn. Elizabeth Martin came to meet them.

"It's good to see all of you. Make yourselves at home. William is entertaining guests by the barn. Bring the food over here, ladies."

Grandfather went to talk to the other men. The rest of the family followed Miss Martin to a long table where ladies were unloading food. Lizzie helped her aunts set out bowls of green beans, boiled potatoes, and sweet peas as well as a black walnut cake and a sweet potato pie. Trent took the empty baskets back to the carriages before going to see his friend Joel Martin. With nothing else to do until the spinning started, Aunt Grace and Aunt Sarah joined several mothers in conversation. Little Thomas and baby John had fun chasing children their age. Aunt Mary walked off with her fiancé, Thomas Bustin, while Aunt Charlotte looked for her current beau, John Barrow.

"We're going to go play. Are you coming, Lizzie?" Alice inquired.

"You go ahead. I'm going to make sure everything's set up."

Lizzie watched Alice and Rebecca head over to a group of young girls playing scotch-hopper as Hannah skipped behind them. Sighing, she walked to the barn where the spinning took place. Peering in the open barn doors, she could see rows of twelve small spinning wheels. Most had a stool in front of them. Walking to Aunt Grace's spinning wheel, she touched the wooden wheel, causing it to turn.

"Did you come to see if we set it up right?"

Turning, Lizzie spotted Jake holding a small stool. Shocked to see him dressed up, she couldn't help but stare. Like the other men and boys, he wore a navy-blue jacket, matching britches, and white knee-high stockings. Noticing her staring, he looked down at his outfit.

"This wasn't my idea. Your uncle insisted on it."

"Well, it's nice," she muttered.

"Thanks. You look nice too…I mean pretty," he replied uncomfortably. "I'll put the stool here. JJ will be coming to look for me."

"That's fine. How is JJ?" she asked.

"John has worked him to death to get ready for the party. Garret, Stephen, John Giles, and Edward have been working here, too.

With the crops in, JJ will be the only one staying. Stephen and Edward got a job with the cooper in town, and Garret is working for the blacksmith. I don't know what John Giles plans to do."

"Has anyone heard from Israel?"

"John Giles saw him drinking at the Salty Sailor Tavern. He's walking with a cane, but he'll have a limp forever."

The sound of a ringing bell filled the barn. Knowing it signaled the start of the event, Lizzie followed Jake outside. William Martin stood on a wooden platform in a circle of hay bales where the dancing would take place. Once everyone gathered, he welcomed the guests and called up Tobias Knight. As the secretary stepped forward with a cane to shake William's hand, Lizzie noticed how feeble he was. Her papa said he was sick when they unloaded the sugar.

"Greetings, friends," Mr. Knight proclaimed, pausing to cough into a white handkerchief. "It is a pleasure for me to begin this year's Harvest Day festivities. Governor Charles Eden's council meeting took longer than expected. He wishes he could be here."

Again, Secretary Knight got into an uncontrollable coughing fit. A man stepped up, but Mr. Knight waved him off, saying he was fine. Bowing his head, the dark-haired man retreated. He stood beside a beautiful woman whom Lizzie knew was Mrs. Katherine Knight. She figured he was their house guest, Mr. Edmund Chamberlayne.

"Edmund Gale, will you bless the food?" Tobias requested.

Edmund was the younger brother of Christopher Gale, Miles' father. Unlike his brother, who had been a former chief justice of the court, Edmund studied law and religion. He often read from the Book of Common Prayer during Divine Service. Asking everyone to bow their heads, Edmund prayed and turned it over to Tobias.

"Thank you, sir. Without further ado, let the competition begin!"

Shouts of excitement erupted from the residents of Bath. Men and women walked to the barn while others lined up to eat. Lizzie joined her aunts and cousins as they went to Aunt Grace's spinning wheel. Jake and Trent went to see the men's flax crushing contest.

Aunt Grace was the first of their family to show off her spinning skills. Lizzie watched her aunt spin the flax with expert speed. She was just as talented as the other experienced ladies. A group of elderly women inspected the work, making notes on texture, speed, thickness of the thread, and overall durability of the final product.

Soon it was time to switch off as Aunt Sarah handed baby John to her sister-in-law, Mary, and prepared to take Grace's place. Holding Little Thomas' hand to keep him from running off, Lizzie tried to pay attention while he played with the pink ribbon on her wrist. Eventually, it was Aunt Mary's turn. Lizzie studied the way Aunt Mary worked the thread. She was almost as good as Aunt Grace. Out of the corner of her eye, she caught Thomas Bustin observing his fiancée. Seeing him so intrigued with Aunt Mary's work made Lizzie wonder what he would say when he found out about the lie. He was devastated when she and John were missing. How would he feel knowing she was part of a conspiracy? Aunt Mary hadn't just been spinning flax for the last week, she had been spinning lies. Would he break off the wedding set for the end of December?

Twenty minutes later, Aunt Charlotte swapped seats with her older sister. Lizzie's nerves were churning as she waited beside Aunt Grace, who had taken Little Thomas. When it was finally her turn, she switched seats with Aunt Charlotte. Patting the foot pedal, Lizzie worked the flax in one hand as she kept the newly made thread aligned on the small wooden wheel. Everything Aunt Grace taught her flooded into her mind. The hardest part was keeping the thread tight while picking up more flax from the pile at her feet. For twenty minutes, Lizzie kept the pace until a bell sounded, ending the contest.

"My hands ache. I don't think I've ever spun so fast," she said.

Aunt Grace laughed. "Mine did, too. Let's go eat. Charlotte and Sarah went to find a table. The little ones were getting fussy."

Following Aunt Grace, Lizzie grabbed Hannah's hand as they meandered through the crowd. By now, a host of stars and a creamy full moon helped light up the yard. In addition to the moonlight, the Martins had lanterns on the tables and around the dance floor. Getting in line behind Alice and Rebecca, she helped her seven-year-old cousin fill her plate so that Aunt Grace could get one for Aunt Sarah. Aunt Mary ate with Thomas Bustin's family. With plates of food, they sat down with Aunt Sarah and the children while Aunt Charlotte stood in line. Lizzie savored her delicious meal of salted ham, sweet potatoes, butterbeans, and halved boiled eggs with a glass of tea. For dessert, she had a slice of apple pie with a flaky top crust.

Scraping the crumbs from her plate, Lizzie looked up just in time to see Grandfather walking toward their table. He stooped to tickle baby John's foot as he whispered to Aunt Grace.

"Thomas and I talked to John about the situation Mary shared. He's talking to Tobias. John went with him to give his account. We debated on waiting until Monday, but legally speaking Thomas felt it would be best if John told Tobias the truth tonight."

Just then, Uncle Thomas walked up with his twenty-three-year-old brother, John. Both men favored their father, with their tall stature and short black hair, but Uncle Thomas shared his father's straight posture. Uncle John stood beside his older brother with shoulders slumped as if the weight of the world was literally on him.

"Well? What did Tobias have to say?" Grandfather prompted.

Uncle Thomas sighed. "He was understandably upset and plans to send word to Governor Eden Monday. Tobias considered telling the rangers and the provost marshal but didn't want to disturb the evening. He'll tell them Monday before they continue searching for Pompey. We'll have to wait for Governor Eden's ruling."

"The town shouldn't be involved. He's our servant," John stated.

"They wouldn't if you came to me first. Those rangers went out under false assumptions. I don't want to talk about it anymore, at least not in public," Grandfather snapped as another bell rang.

Looking at the circle of hay bales, Lizzie saw Mr. William Martin standing on the wooden platform ringing a bell. Once the neighbors quieted down, he revealed the winners of the flax crushing and spinning contests, giving each a blue ribbon. Aunt Grace won the competition for the second year in a row. Mr. William announced that the first dance would be for fathers and unmarried daughters. He called the four musicians forward with their instruments, which included a violin, two flutes, and a six-stringed viol. As the music started, fathers escorted their daughters to the wooden platform. Watching girls walk by, Lizzie's heart ached. She wished her papa was here to dance.

"Come along, Lizzie."

Startled, she gazed up at her grandfather, who had extended his hand to her. Aunt Charlotte stood beside her father wearing a smile.

"What about Aunt Charlotte?"

"Who says I can't dance with both of you?"

Overwhelmed with emotion, Lizzie fought back tears as she took her grandfather's hand. Holding his elbow, she walked with him and Aunt Charlotte to the circle of hay bales. Joining the other dancers, they formed a circle. Lizzie held up her dress as she skipped to the beat. Aunt Charlotte locked arms with her father and twirled in a circle. He then locked arms with Lizzie and spun her around. Grinning, Lizzie enjoyed every moment of the dance until at last the music faded. Grandfather bowed as she and Aunt Charlotte picked up their dresses and dipped in a curtsy. As they left the dance floor, Grandfather pulled Lizzie aside while Aunt Charlotte returned to the table.

"I'm proud of you, my dear. Your father came to see me. He felt bad about not being able to be here tonight. We haven't always agreed, but he loved your mother. You look a lot like her. She loved you very much. Her love lives on. Never forget that."

Wiping tears from her eyes, Lizzie hugged him. "I love you."

"I love you, too," he murmured, squeezing her tightly.

On the way back to the table, Miles Gale stopped them. Lizzie suddenly felt nervous as she saw the delight on his face.

"May I have this dance, Lizzie?" he requested.

Glancing at her grandfather, Lizzie knew she couldn't say no. He looked almost as excited as Miles. It was quite an opportunity to dance with the son of a prominent family. Faking a smile, she grasped Miles' elbow, allowing him to escort her to the dance floor. Luckily, the tune was a lively jig in which all the dancers participated. Standing with other ladies, Lizzie skipped to the beat. Occasionally she had to spin around with Miles, but for the most part she didn't have to get close. At the end of the line, she spotted Aunt Charlotte and Aunt Mary dancing with their beaus, John Barrow and Thomas Bustin.

For two songs, Lizzie danced across from Miles. Surprisingly, she enjoyed herself. Looking around, she recognized several other people she knew, including Miles' stepbrother, Thomas Harvey; both of his sisters, Penelope and Elizabeth; and the storekeeper's son, Philip Shute. In addition to those her own age, other members of Bath enjoyed the dancing. There were Giles and Charity Shute; the Harding family; both Porter families; Sarah Gale; John Lawson's widow, Hannah; and Dr. Patrick Maule and his wife, Elizabeth.

After the second song, they announced the next dance would be a minuet. Lizzie recalled Aunt Mary talking about the fancy dance. Not wanting to do the minuet with Miles, Lizzie started to leave.

"Wait," Miles blurted out, grabbing her arm. "If you don't know the steps, I can show you."

Lizzie opened her mouth to object when someone put an arm around her. Whirling around, she found herself staring at JJ Brooks.

"Lizzie, they're playing our song," he proclaimed.

"We are dancing," Miles stated firmly.

"She promised me a dance. Excuse us," JJ countered.

Stunned, Lizzie allowed JJ to carry her away. Peering over her shoulder at Miles, she noticed the furious look on his face. The music started as those around them began to dance. Skipping to the beat of the flutes, Lizzie stepped forward to take JJ's elbow as he spun her.

"Where did you learn the minuet?" she asked him.

JJ chuckled. "I'm winging it."

"Oh, really? Well, I don't recall promising you a dance."

"Nay, but Mr. Prim and Proper doesn't know it."

"So, you lied?" she prompted, already knowing the answer.

"Let's say I stretched the truth. Pirates are known to do it, ye know," he commented with a wink as they separated.

Picking up her dress, Lizzie swished her long purple gown from side to side like the other ladies. As she danced, she thought about what JJ said. Although she liked him more than Miles, she didn't know if she trusted someone willing to lie. Then again, her own aunt and uncle had lied. Was it any different? When it was time to spin around again, she tucked her hand around his elbow.

"I thought you were giving up being a pirate."

"I'll stop my bad habits if ye will be my girl," he challenged her.

"JJ, I'm not interested in a relationship right now."

"Mr. Prissy must think ye are. He sure looks jealous."

Separating, Lizzie stole a glance at Miles. It was strangely satisfying to see him jealous of JJ. If he only knew JJ was a former pirate! The minuet dance ended, and Lizzie curtsied to JJ as he bowed. Another song started the second round of fast-paced group dancing. JJ offered to dance it with her, but Lizzie declined, saying she wanted to catch her breath. Although he wasn't happy, he escorted her to the sidelines. Seeing Miles making his way toward them, Lizzie got an idea.

"JJ, I'm thirsty. Let's get some apple cider."

His eyes lit up. "Sure."

Avoiding Miles, JJ escorted her to the wooden tub of apple cider. After standing in line for a few minutes, he picked up two cups from the table and poured apple cider into them with a wooden ladle. He had just handed the cup to her when Miles came up.

"Do you want to dance again, Lizzie?" he questioned, eyeing JJ.

"We're sort of busy," JJ mentioned, holding up his cup.

Miles ignored him. "I could've gotten you some cider, Lizzie."

"Thank you both for the dance. If you will excuse me, I'm going to go be with my family," she answered, leaving them behind.

Finishing the cider, Lizzie put the cup down and went to where Alice and Rebecca were playing hoops. The group of girls were competing to see who could roll an old iron barrel hoop to the finish line first. She was almost to the girls when JJ caught up with her.

"Hold up," he panted. "Are ye mad with me? I got the feeling ye didn't want me around, or was it just to get rid of Gale?"

"I enjoyed the dance, but need to spend time with my cousins."

"There ye are!"

Turning, Lizzie spotted John Martin jogging toward them.

"I've been looking for ye. My sister Ann told me she saw ye dancing with Miss Lizzie. William wants more peach brandy from the cellar. They like brandy as much as our old comrades did!" he laughed.

"I'm busy with Lizzie," JJ protested.

"We don't want our guests to run out of refreshments. Nothing's worse than a disappointed guest, unless ye count my angry mother."

"Alright, I'm coming," JJ grumbled. "I'll be back, Lizzie."

The former pirates walked away. Looking at her cousins, Lizzie realized Hannah was missing. Wondering where she was, she spotted several of Hannah's friends, including Isabella Lawson, playing hide-and-seek. She debated telling Aunt Grace when her eyes caught Hannah and Jake sitting on a hay bale. Worried, she went to the barn to see if the little girl had gotten hurt.

"Why aren't you playing with Isabella? Did you get hurt?"

Hannah shook her head. "No. I was talking to Jake. He's lonely."

"What?" Jake blurted out. "You said you wanted to talk."

"I did. You looked so lonely sitting here all alone."

"Hannah, I wasn't lonely. I'm enjoying the music," Jake revealed.

"Wouldn't it be more fun to enjoy it with other people? It's boring to sit by yourself with no one to talk to," Hannah pointed out.

"Where's Trent?" Lizzie piped up.

"He's talking to a girl. Wait until Momma finds out! Jake wouldn't have gotten lonely if Trent hadn't dumped him and you weren't dancing with his new friend, JJ," Hannah informed her bluntly. "I have an idea! Why don't you dance together while I play hide-and-seek?"

"Hannah, I—I don't think it's a good idea," Lizzie stammered.

"Why not? You've danced with Miles and JJ."

Speechless, Lizzie tried to figure out how to explain the situation. She was searching for the right words when Miles Gale walked up.

"Well, I've got to go," Hannah concluded as she slid off the hay bale and patted Jake's knee. "Have fun, Jake."

The little girl skipped away, leaving Lizzie and Jake with Miles.

"Are you ready to dance again?" Miles asked.

"I can't. I'm dancing the next one with Jake."

Lizzie didn't give Miles the opportunity to insist or Jake a chance to decline. Grabbing Jake's arm, she led him to the dance floor.

"I don't like dancing," Jake mumbled.

"I'm sorry, but I've had enough of Miles. Please do this for me."

Joining the other dancers, Lizzie picked up the rhythm. Despite Jake's inexperience, he finally caught on. As Lizzie danced, her mind drifted to the trouble her aunt and uncle would be facing in the days ahead. What would happen when the lies they had spun unraveled in front of the governor's council? The longer she dwelled on the situation, the worse she felt. Finally, she released her worries to God.

When it came time to spin, Lizzie locked arms with Jake. Seeing him having fun, she suddenly felt guilty for ignoring him. More guilt bombarded her as she considered her motives for getting him to dance to avoid Miles. Glancing at the pink ribbon on her wrist, she recalled the last conversation she had with her papa. He mentioned Jake's name when he spoke of Miles and JJ liking her. Lizzie realized how much she enjoyed Jake's company. She would never admit it, but other than dancing with her grandfather, this was the highlight of the evening.

CHAPTER TWENTY-THREE

☠

PAINFUL VERDICT

November 13, 1718 ~ Thursday

"Are you okay, Lizzie? You're acting strange. It's like your mind is a hundred miles away," Jake declared. Startled out of her daydreaming, Lizzie looked at him as he continued, "Is it your aunt and uncle? I know your family is worried about the outcome of the court hearing."

"No," she mumbled, gazing at the greenish-blue water below.

The two of them were crossing the old wooden bridge spanning Bath Town Creek with a loaded wagon of corn. This was the first time Lizzie had been to town since July, and for some reason she felt anxious. Jake had the task of taking the first load of corn to the horse mill to grind into cornmeal. He and Trent spent the day before hauling wheat to town to make flour. Lizzie rode with Jake so that she could mail a letter to Aunt Susannah explaining about the false Indian attacks.

"If it's not about today's hearing then what's wrong?" Jake urged.

"I don't know exactly. I just feel uneasy."

"It's probably your nerves. Everyone's been on edge."

"Maybe," she replied, looking at the letter in her hands.

Jake was partially right. With the hearing for Aunt Mary, Uncle John, and Grandfather's servant Nathaniel Ming starting in an hour, the Worsley family was tense. Tobias Knight called a council meeting Monday morning before the rangers went out. The council decided to arrest them until they heard from Governor Eden. Since Bath didn't have a jail, they were under guard at the Blue Heron Inn. Due to the seriousness of the situation, the governor's council reviewed the case in the Chowan Precinct on Tuesday the eleventh. When Governor Eden arrived late Wednesday, he ordered Grandfather to pay a bond of five hundred pounds to release Aunt Mary. Uncle John and Nathaniel stayed at the inn chained to their beds. Earlier, a messenger came to Grandfather's informing them a hearing was set for noon.

Uncle Thomas, acting as their attorney, suggested that the rest of the family who heard Aunt Mary's confession attend the hearing. Trent was taking his sisters over to Uncle Thomas' house to stay with Aunt Sarah. Although he wanted to go to the hearing, his mother wouldn't let him, stating he needed to help Jake get the corn to the horse mill.

Jake coaxed Grandfather's old white mule, Maude, to turn right on Bay Street. As they passed the Blue Heron Inn, Lizzie saw several horses already tied to the hitching post. Bath Town had plans for a church and courthouse with a jail, but the funds were short. Since it would be awhile to get one built, the council held court in the Blue Heron Inn that Mr. Thomas Unday rented from Governor Eden.

"Looks like Mr. Thomas is here," Jake commented, nodding at Uncle Thomas' black horse tied to the post.

"Aunt Grace said he's worried Uncle John will say something out of line. He's pretty sympathetic to Pompey's point of view."

Jake pulled up to the horse mill. Once the wagon stopped, Lizzie climbed down. Holding the strings of her pale blue handbag, she went next door to Harding's General Store to mail her letter. Lizzie grabbed the rail and scooped up her light green dress to keep from falling on the steps. She paused to look down Craven Street at the

Salty Sailor Tavern. For a moment, she envisioned the warm July day when she saw her papa and his crew walking to the alehouse.

Sighing, Lizzie stepped on the porch and opened the door. As she entered the store, smells of peppermint candy engulfed her. She looked at the room as if seeing it for the first time. In her mind, she made comparisons to the Coateses' store in Pennsylvania, which was a lot bigger. One of the things different was a crate of lye soap. Smiling as she remembered Cookie's comments, Lizzie realized she had seen things most people in Bath would never experience.

"Can I help you?" Mrs. Shute asked as she came out from the back room.

"Hello. I need to mail this to my aunt in New Bern."

Mrs. Shute took the letter. "I see you wrote 'urgent' on the outside."

Lizzie tried to choose her words carefully. Most people in town thought she spent the summer with relatives, which was partly true.

"Aunt Grace wanted to make sure she got it. Aunt Susannah said she was planning a visit for the holidays," Lizzie answered.

"Tell her to come to see me. How long is she staying?"

"I don't know. She's bringing my cousins."

"Good! I know you enjoyed spending time with them. Forgive me for prying, dear, but how is Mary? Do you know if she plans to carry on with the wedding? It's only six weeks away."

"She's doing okay. As far as I know, the wedding will still take place, but it really isn't any of my business. I've got to go. Have a good day."

"Uh...you too, dear," Mrs. Shute stammered, clearly stunned by Lizzie's subtle reminder about the wedding being no one's business.

Leaving the store, Lizzie thought about what Mrs. Shute said. It was hard not to feel frustrated with the questions. She knew everyone was talking about their family. Walking to the horse mill, she noticed Jake had company. As she approached the other wagon, she saw JJ Brooks talking to Jake as he unloaded the last crate of corn.

"Hello, Lizzie!" he exclaimed cheerfully, removing his three-cornered hat.

"Hello, JJ. How are you?" she greeted him politely.

"I'm tired, but doing great. John and I have been working hard to get his family's corn ground into cornmeal. Miss Martin has been sweet. She treats me like a son."

"JJ was telling me about Garret Gibbons," Jake informed her.

"John needed horseshoes so I left him at the blacksmith's forge where Garret works. Garret told us Tobias Knight's house guest, Edmund Chamberlayne, came this morning to ask him to go on a mission. Tobias is planning to send a letter to Black Beard Monday. He's sending his slave, Caesar, but needed two more men. James Robins already offered. Both James and Caesar were crew members before we dispersed in July. Garret agreed to go with them," JJ explained.

"That's odd," Jake pointed out. "Wonder why he asked Garret."

"Maybe Garret wants to set things right with Captain. John Martin says Garret left due to his disagreement with Captain, not because he wanted a new life. James Robins had a similar situation. He left in July because of the way Captain deserted Stede Bonnet," JJ declared.

"Why did Caesar leave the crew?" Lizzie questioned.

"Caesar was one of Black Beard's original crew members, but two years ago he was Tobias Knight's African slave. When ye father started his first voyage, John Martin and Garret Gibbons chose to go with him along with others in the community like William Howard and Cookie who lived near Lake Mattamuskeet. Tobias sent Caesar with them to help dive for the gold trapped in the famed sunken treasure ship."

"I hope Tobias explained the false Indian attack," Jake said.

JJ shrugged. "I would think so. Edmund told Garret another pardon is due by mid-December. This one will clear our names for sure. Tobias wants Captain to know about it. Hopefully, they'll get to Ocracoke before the crew loads the remaining sugar and cocoa. There's a chance they'll catch them before they set sail for St. Thomas."

"I need to get back to Mr. Worsley's plantation. Trent's probably wondering where I'm at," Jake mentioned.

"Aye, John was hoping to bring another load before the verdict," JJ responded, suddenly looking sheepish. "I'm sorry, Lizzie."

"I'm sure a lot of people will want to hear the verdict. I better start heading down to the Blue Heron Inn. Aunt Grace will be looking for me. See you later," she concluded as she turned to leave.

"Do you want me to take you down there?" Jake called after her.

"No, I'll walk."

Leaving them at the horse mill, Lizzie passed Harding's shipyard and Bath Town's wharf. She spotted Stephen Daniel and Edward Salter making barrels under the cooper's shelter. The former pirates were adjusting to their new life. It sounded like Garret was doing well with the blacksmith, Collingswood Ward. John Giles did exactly what he told Black Beard he planned to do. Since the end of the flax harvest, he had been at the Salty Sailor Tavern. Israel wasn't much better. He was renting a room at the tavern. There were rumors he ran out of money and was working for Roger Kenyon, the man who ran the place. Lizzie wondered if Colonel Maurice Moore knew about Roger hiring a former pirate. Mr. Moore owned the land and rented the building to Mr. Kenyon. Considering the tavern had a reputation for being rough, it wasn't surprising Mr. Kenyon hired Israel.

As Lizzie walked the dirt road, she passed houses belonging to Dr. Patrick Maule, Miles Gale's family, Mr. Maurice Moore, and Mr. and Mrs. Sigley, as well as two rented homes. Finally, she came to the two-story Blue Heron Inn, which was blue and had a porch. Governor Eden also owned the vacant lot between the inn and the Sigleys' home, which served as a place for wagons to park. The lot had two big oak trees, a maple tree, and a dogwood tree that bore white blossoms each spring. Governor Eden sometimes used it to host outdoor parties as well. He lived up the street past the general store.

Stepping on the porch, Lizzie was about to sit in a rocking chair when her family came over the old wooden bridge. Grandfather was up front with Aunt Mary while Aunt Grace and Aunt Charlotte rode in the back of the carriage. Flicking the reins, Grandfather steered his brown horse into the vacant lot. As they climbed down, Lizzie noticed they had grim faces. Her heart sank as Aunt Mary burst in tears.

Aunt Grace hugged her. "Pull yourself together, Mary. Thomas will do his best to lighten the verdict, but you must stay strong. We're all here supporting you and John because we love you."

"I know, I love you, too," Aunt Mary mumbled as she patted her eyes with a white handkerchief and took a deep breath.

The Worsley sisters followed their father up the steps as several men rode up on their horses. Lizzie didn't have a chance to see who they were as Grandfather opened the door and ushered them inside. Staying close to Aunt Charlotte, she got her first glimpse of the inn's interior. Aunt Grace never allowed her to go inside since it was an alehouse. To her amazement, the inn was already full.

A counter stood against the back wall where Lizzie figured they served the rum and brandy. There was a room to the right of the counter and a staircase on the left. Two chairs and a table were situated in front of the counter while a smaller table sat to the side with two more chairs. Another table and chair sat on the left side of the room facing the center, with five chairs against the wall. The right side was similarly set up except there were four chairs behind the table.

Meandering through the crowd of men, Lizzie followed her family to the right side of the room. She recognized Uncle Thomas sitting behind the table with Uncle John and Nathaniel Ming, who wore chains on their wrists. Seeing them, Aunt Mary abruptly stopped walking. Grandfather tried to keep her moving, but she just stood frozen.

"Mary, go sit beside Thomas," he instructed.

"I can't," she gasped as someone came up behind them.

Turning around, Lizzie realized it was Thomas Bustin. The tall, brown-haired man was wearing a dark gray suit with white knee-high stockings. He whispered something to his fiancée. Aunt Mary wiped her eyes with her handkerchief as she looked up into his face.

"Come on, Lizzie, let's sit down," Aunt Grace urged.

Aunt Charlotte led the way to the seats against the wall. She sat in the farthest one. Lizzie took the next seat, with Aunt Grace on her left. Grandfather sat beside Aunt Grace while Thomas Bustin took the last chair behind Aunt Mary. Uncle Thomas turned to speak with his father as a loud banging erupted from the front of the room. Lizzie spotted Governor Charles Eden sitting beside Tobias Knight at the center table. The governor wore a dark green suit and his signature shoulder-length white wig. He banged a wooden mallet on a square block of wood to quiet the crowd.

"Attention! Find your seats. Anyone who wishes to remain in court are to stand behind the council members," he announced.

Across the room, Thomas Harding sat at the table while William Sigley, John Porter, Simon Alderson, John Harding, and William Martin took up the five seats against the wall. There were six chairs behind two tables positioned in front of Governor Eden. Edmund Porter, Richard Rigby, Colonel Maurice Moore, Giles Shute, and the retired doctor Edward Travis filled five seats. The current doctor, Patrick Maule, was also sitting at the table. Other prominent men of Bath stood behind them, including Thomas Unday and Roger Kenyon from the Salty Sailor Tavern. Among the familiar faces, Lizzie recognized Thomas Roper, the bricklayer, as well as the blacksmith, Collingswood Ward, and John Lillington, the real estate appraiser and friend of Governor Eden. Even the former pirate John Martin was in the crowd with John Penny, his sister Elizabeth's husband.

Again, Governor Eden hammered his mallet to get everyone's attention. Once the room was silent, he motioned to his left where two men were sitting. One of them was John Colleson, who served as the court's clerk. In addition to keeping Bath's records of wills and land transactions, he was also a copyist, scribe, and notary. The other man was John Hatton, the appointed registered deputy. His job was to guard prisoners and to help Mr. Colleson maintain the records.

"This court hearing is now in session. Mr. John Colleson will record everything. During court proceedings, Secretary Tobias Knight acts as chief justice of the court. Chief Justice Knight, please read the charges against the accused," Governor Eden requested as he turned to Tobias Knight, who looked pale in his navy-blue suit.

Lowering his head, Tobias stood and began to read from a piece of parchment paper. "On the thirty-first day of October in the year of our Lord 1718, Mr. Thomas Worsley Jr. reported his brother, Mr. John Worsley, and sister, Miss Mary Worsley, missing to the government official, Secretary Tobias Knight. After hearing of their disappearance, a group of rangers went to find them. It was later discovered an Indian servant of Mr. Thomas Worsley Sr. was also missing."

Mr. Knight paused to cough into a white handkerchief. Gathering himself, the sickly secretary of the colony continued to read.

"Provost Marshal Thomas Harding and the rangers found Mr. John Worsley and Miss Mary Worsley on the second day of November. Mr. Worsley claimed Indians abducted them. The rangers have continued to look for Pompey, the servant belonging to Mr. Thomas Worsley Sr. Days later, Mr. John Worsley informed Secretary Knight these allegations were untrue. Secretary Knight sent letters with Mr. John Harding to Governor Charles Eden in the Chowan Precinct and called a meeting of the town council on

Monday, the tenth of November. The allegations against the accused are as follows: fabricating abduction, lying to a deputized officer, falsifying information, helping a fugitive escape punishment, allowing a fugitive to go unpunished, and endangerment of the colony. Mr. Nathaniel Ming, the servant of Mr. Thomas Worsley Sr., is charged with having knowledge of criminal acts and not alerting the authorities."

As Mr. Knight sat back down, Lizzie took a deep breath. Just hearing all the charges made her feel sick.

"Thank you, Chief Justice Knight," Governor Eden declared. "Mr. John Hatton, please unlock the chains and swear everyone in."

Mr. Hatton took a small key out of his coat pocket and unlocked the chains. Once they were free, the registered deputy picked up the Bible from his table and walked over to Nathaniel and Uncle John.

"Put your right hands on the Bible and raise your left hands," he ordered. "Do you swear to tell the truth, so help you God?"

"I do," they promised.

Moving down the line, the registered deputy asked Uncle Thomas and Aunt Mary the same question. He also swore in Thomas Bustin, Grandfather, Aunt Grace, Lizzie, and Aunt Charlotte. Next, Mr. Hatton walked across the room to swear in the witnesses.

"It is very serious to claim an Indian abduction considering the severity of the Tuscarora Indian War," Governor Eden proclaimed. "Another war could have started based on this false accusation. The governor's council in the Chowan Precinct wants immediate actions taken. We heard from one of the rangers, Mr. Simon Alderson, who was present at the retaking of Mr. Worsley and Miss Worsley on November the fourth. He had grave reservations about the abduction. Although the council ruled on the matter, we felt it necessary to hold this hearing before administering the recommended punishment. If the testimony reveals new insights, the ruling may change. The court recognizes Provost Marshal Thomas Harding as the first witness."

Mr. Harding gave his account of what happened when the rangers discovered John and Mary. He led the search party, but it was Simon Alderson and William Sigley who found them. All three heard John's story. In his description, Mr. Harding spoke of Mary's strange behavior, which they assumed was due to trauma. William Sigley recounted the same story, adding that John and Mary's clothes were torn.

Next, Governor Eden asked Simon Alderson, John Porter, and William Martin to speak. The men talked about the stolen food, although William looked uncomfortable testifying. Lizzie figured it was because they were close neighbors. During Mr. Alderson's testimony, he also gave reasons for his suspicions about the abduction. John Porter described the Indian he saw stealing cured meats from his smokehouse. Finally, it was Aunt Charlotte's turn. Her testimony was short and to the point, just like Uncle Thomas coached her to do.

"Mr. Thomas Worsley Sr. was there when Miss Worsley revealed the truth. Do you have anything to add?" Governor Eden inquired.

"I do. A week after the incident, Mary told us she and John lied about the abduction. She and Nathaniel caught Pompey stealing from us. After questioning him, she told John. Apparently, Nathaniel had caught Pompey stealing before but chose not to tell anyone."

"Very well. What do the defendants have to say?"

At this point, Uncle Thomas stood up. "If it pleases the court, I would like to speak on behalf of my clients."

"So granted."

"John, Mary, and Nathaniel understand the gravity of the situation and take full responsibility for their actions. They didn't intend to put others in danger, nor did they wish to scare their neighbors. All of them would like to publicly apologize."

Uncle Thomas sat down as Aunt Mary addressed the court. "I'm sorry for all the trouble I caused. My actions were uncalled for."

As she returned to her seat, Nathaniel gave his apology. When it was Uncle John's turn, he stood and looked at his older brother.

"I'm sorry for making everyone worry about another Indian war; however, I will not pretend to be sorry for helping Pompey escape."

Outbursts erupted as Governor Eden tried to gain control. Uncle Thomas grabbed his brother's arm and forced him to sit down. Fearful of what would happen, Lizzie fumbled with the strings of her handbag. Her brown eyes darted from her uncles to the governor, who was banging the mallet on the wooden block.

"Settle down or all of you will be charged with disrupting court!" he shouted angrily. When the men finally calmed down, he continued, "Mr. Worsley, are you saying you don't regret your actions?"

Uncle Thomas whispered something to his brother, but by his reaction Uncle John didn't heed his advice. "I have no regrets."

Again, the room exploded. Governor Eden slammed his mallet down so hard, Lizzie winced. Registered Deputy John Hatton jumped to restrain the men, but Governor Eden told him to sit down.

"You are the ones who done wrong!" Uncle John yelled. "Pompey had to steal because people were going hungry."

"Sit down! One more outburst and I will clear the court," Governor Eden spat. "The jurists will decide if the charges are justifiable. If they are, the council's punishment will follow; however, if they decide they are not, then we will adjourn until more evidence is available. Jurists, please write the defendants' names on the paper along with your decision. Mr. Hatton will bring the verdicts to me."

Edmund Porter, Richard Rigby, Colonel Maurice Moore, Giles Shute, and the retired doctor Edward Travis picked up a turkey feather quill and dipped them in ink before writing their decisions. Mr. Hatton brought the papers to Governor Eden, who looked over each one as he passed them to Chief Justice Knight.

"Defendants, please stand," Governor Eden began. "Nathaniel Ming, Mary Worsley, and John Worsley, on all accounts the men of the council find you guilty. Do the jurists have anything to add?"

"I would like to speak," Giles Shute commented. "Based on the testimony of the witnesses, Miss Worsley acted under the direction of her brother. Should she receive punishment if he was the one who lied? From my understanding, she didn't say anything at all."

All four council members murmured their agreement.

"Your concerns are noted. The rangers will continue their search for the missing fugitive, Pompey. He's wanted dead or alive for stealing and escaping punishment. Given the questionable behavior of Miss Worsley's actions, I feel we should take up her case after the rangers have a chance to locate the fugitive. Mr. Thomas Worsley Sr. has paid the bail of five hundred pounds so she will again be in his custody. He is to appear with his daughter at the council meeting in March. She must remain in the colony or will face charges of fleeing. Mr. Hatton, please bring me the Bible," Governor Eden requested.

The registered deputy delivered the Bible. Opening it, Governor Eden flipped pages until he found what he was looking for.

"Nathaniel Ming, you are guilty of the charges against you. The governor's council recommended you get twenty-nine lashes laid on your bare back. John Worsley, you are guilty of the charges against you. Since the colony could have been in danger because of your actions, the governor's council feels you should receive the full punishment. I considered reducing it due to this being your first offense, but it appears you have no remorse. Therefore, I sentence you to thirty-nine lashes laid on your bare back. The sentence will be immediately carried out. Chief Justice Knight, please read the scripture from Deuteronomy chapter twenty-five, verses one through three."

Tobias picked up the Bible. "If there be a controversy between men, and they come unto judgment, that the judges may judge them; then they shall justify the righteous, and condemn the wicked. And it shall be, if the wicked man be worthy to be beaten, that the judge shall cause him to lie down, and to be beaten before his face, according to his fault, by a certain number. Forty stripes he may give him, and not exceed: lest, if he should exceed, and beat him above these with many stripes, then thy brother should seem vile unto thee."

"The law states a man must be healthy to ensure lashing doesn't result in death. I direct Dr. Patrick Maule to examine Mr. Worsley and Mr. Ming. Court will resume by the whipping post," Governor Eden said as he swung his mallet down on the wooden block.

Hushed voices echoed as the room emptied. Standing, Lizzie followed her aunts outside. Thomas Bustin went with them, trying to console Aunt Mary. Grandfather waited with Uncle Thomas while Dr. Maule examined Uncle John and Nathaniel in the back room.

Stepping out on the porch, Lizzie wasn't surprised to see a large crowd in the side yard where the whipping post was located. As they gathered around the nearly bare oak trees to watch, she could hear pieces of conversation swirling about Aunt Mary despite the sounds of crunching leaves underfoot. She noticed there were quite a few women and children in the crowd as well. Many parents wanted their children to watch to keep them from breaking the law in the future.

"What are you doing here?" Aunt Grace questioned.

Curious to see who her aunt was talking to, Lizzie turned around. To her surprise, it was Trent and Jake.

"We came over to find out what happened," Trent responded.

"John was sentenced to thirty-nine lashes. Nathaniel will receive twenty-nine. Dr. Maule is checking them before they administer the punishment. There's no need for you to see the lashing. Did you and Jake get finished with the corn?" Aunt Grace wanted to know.

"No, ma'am, but—" Trent started.

"No buts about it. I don't want you to see this," she snapped.

"Let him stay, Grace," Grandfather spoke up, as he and Uncle Thomas joined them.

"I should be getting whipped," Aunt Mary wailed.

"We're blessed you didn't receive the same punishment, Mary. Let's get closer to show them our support," Grandfather replied.

Following her family, Lizzie walked with Trent and Jake as the crowd moved out of their way. From the looks on their faces, no one wanted to be near them. Governor Eden walked out the back door of the Blue Heron Inn. Thomas Unday was with him, along with the clerk, John Colleson. Tobias Knight limped on his wooden cane while the provost marshal, Thomas Harding, accompanied him. Dr. Patrick Maule came out next with Nathaniel and Uncle John. The registered deputy, John Hatton, concluded the processional.

Taking Uncle John to the whipping post, Mr. Hatton removed his gray suit coat and unbuttoned his white shirt. Meanwhile, Thomas Harding stripped Nathaniel, leaving the white servant to stand shirtless before the people. Mr. Hatton tied Uncle John's hands together with rope and fastened them above his head to the whipping post. As Mr. Hatton finished, Governor Eden spoke to the crowd.

"John Worsley was convicted of six charges and will receive thirty-nine lashes on his back. Nathaniel Ming is guilty of two crimes and will get twenty-nine lashes. Although Deuteronomy chapter twenty-five, verses one through three states a man shall lie down to receive his lashes, we erected the whipping post for this purpose. Dr. Maule has testified they are in good health. Chief Justice Tobias Knight will now read a passage of scripture as dictated by our law."

"I will read a psalm of David from chapter fifty-one, verse one," Mr. Knight proclaimed as he opened the Bible. "Have mercy upon me, O God, according to thy lovingkindness: according unto the multitude of thy tender mercies blot out my transgressions."

"To make certain we do not go over forty lashes, I ordered thirty-nine lashes. The clerk of the court, Mr. John Colleson, will count. Mr. Hatton, begin the punishment," Governor Eden instructed.

With his bare back facing the crowd, Uncle John waited as Mr. Hatton pulled back the leather whip and brought it down hard on his back. Uncle John's knees buckled beneath him from the strike. A loud crack sounded as the whip blistered his bare skin, causing a red mark to appear. Wincing, Lizzie watched Mr. Hatton hit her uncle as the clerk counted. After the tenth lash, Aunt Mary burst into tears. Beside her, Aunt Charlotte buried her face in Aunt Grace's shoulder.

Soon, the lashes were up to twenty. The whip broke skin as blood seeped from the wounded flesh. Each time the whip crossed his back, Uncle John nearly collapsed, but he never hollered. Seeing the blood running down his uncle's back, Trent turned away. Closing her eyes, Lizzie could still hear the crack of the whip and the clerk's voice.

"Twenty-eight…twenty-nine…thirty…thirty-one…"

Tears dripped from her eyes as she listened to the slap of leather against the flesh. Turning away, Lizzie leaned against Jake's shoulder. Suddenly realizing what she was doing, she quickly straightened as she wiped her face with the palm of her hand.

"I—I wasn't thinking," she stammered as someone touched her.

JJ was standing behind her, offering his navy-blue neckerchief. "Take this. I feel sorry for ye uncle. The whipping I got in the Royal Navy wasn't as bad as this. Even Pa didn't get thirty-nine lashes."

"Thanks," she whispered, wiping her cheeks with the neckerchief.

"Where have you been?" Jake asked him.

"I had a run-in with Israel. Stephen and Edward rode with me from the horse mill. When we got here, Eden was speaking."

"Is Israel here? We can't risk him seeing Lizzie," Jake declared.

"The last I saw him he was over by the big oak tree. It might be safer if ye leave before the crowd disperses."

"We can't leave yet, we have to wait for Uncle John and Nathaniel," Lizzie objected.

"I'll tell Miss Grace you and Trent are taking the carriage to the bricklayer's shed. At least Israel won't see you," Jake suggested.

Lizzie handed the neckerchief to JJ as she got Trent's attention. Drawing him away from the crowd, she explained the plans while keeping an eye out for Israel Hands. Reaching the carriage, Lizzie could hear Mr. Colleson's voice as they started whipping Nathaniel. With Trent at the reins, Grandfather's horse jolted forward. Lizzie sat beside him as he directed the horse to the bricklayer's shed.

While they waited, Lizzie's mind turned to something Cookie said about skeletons. This was a skeleton she wished had remained in the cellar. It would be weeks before Uncle John and Nathaniel physically recovered from the beating. The council's verdict was painful for everyone in the family, and only God could heal the inner wounds.

CHAPTER TWENTY-FOUR

☠

THE HUNT

November 24, 1718 ~ Monday

Moving a bowl of brown eggs to the kitchen counter, Lizzie picked one up as she tapped a knife against its shell. For some reason, she had never been able to crack an egg on the side of the mixing bowl the way Aunt Grace did, at least not without making a mess. Pulling the shell apart, she dumped the yellow yolk and gooey egg white into the mixing bowl. With Aunt Grace at Grandfather's house, it was her job to make sure her cousins ate breakfast, did their chores, and arrived at Grandfather's for the hog killing.

The last eleven days had been rough for the Worsley family. In addition to dealing with Aunt Mary's spontaneous crying spells, both Uncle John's and Nathaniel Ming's wounds were still raw. Grandfather decided to move Nathaniel from his servant's quarters to the house to make it easier on the family to look after him and Uncle John. Neither of them had talked much since their beatings. As if seeing them in pain wasn't bad enough, the people in town shunned their family at the last two Sunday Divine Services.

Ever since the beatings, Aunt Grace had gone over to help change the bandages every other day, per Dr. Patrick Maule's instructions. The process was extremely painful, and the medicine Dr. Maule gave them barely touched the misery. They weren't sleeping either, which made them irritable and difficult to deal with. This was particularly true of Uncle John, who refused to get a much-needed bath. After pleading with him, Uncle John finally agreed to let Aunt Grace help, but by then it was late in the evening. Concerned Uncle John would change his mind, Grandfather asked Aunt Grace to stay the night.

The journey home the previous night had been uncomfortable for Lizzie. Although she assured her aunt everything would be okay, Lizzie was nervous about being in charge. Despite her misgivings, it was comforting to have Jake in the house. He had been staying in Trent's room since they returned to Bath.

Around midnight, a pack of wolves came howling through the yard. The chilling sound woke everyone and caused fifteen minutes of chaos as the family gathered in the hallway wide awake. Taking control of the situation, Jake went outside with a shotgun to see what was going on. Trent went with him to make sure Killer was okay. Thankfully, the little whimpering dog had crawled under the back porch where the wild wolves couldn't reach her. Jake scared off the wolves before they could attack or kill any of the livestock. After the wolves were gone, everyone tried to go back to sleep, but it was difficult. Poor Hannah had the hardest time and ended up sleeping with Lizzie.

As Lizzie whisked the eggs in the mixing bowl, the back door squeaked open. Looking over her shoulder, she spotted Jake coming in the door with an armload of firewood.

"Thanks for bringing some more in, Jake."

"You're welcome. Trent's milking Betsy. He shouldn't be long. Is there anything else you need before I feed the livestock?"

"No, Rebecca will feed the chickens and gather the eggs."

"Sounds good. Send Hannah for the milk pail if you don't need her. I could use Trent's help as soon as he gets finished."

Jake left as the sound of stomping feet echoed from the stairs. Seconds later, Alice, Rebecca, and Hannah entered the kitchen.

"Morning, girls. Rebecca, please go feed the chickens and gather the eggs from the chicken coop. I need Alice's help if we're ever going to get out of here on time. Oh, and don't forget your coat."

"Sure," Rebecca agreed as she put on her coat, slid her feet into the oversized work boots, and grabbed the egg basket.

"Can I help, Lizzie?" Hannah questioned, picking up an egg.

Lizzie reached for the egg, but it was too late. Hannah had already cracked it on the edge of the table, busting the shell and splattering the gooey mess all over the wooden floorboards.

"You're in trouble now," Alice scolded her little sister.

"I'm sorry. I didn't mean to make a mess," Hannah apologized.

Sighing, Lizzie bent down to clean it up with a rag. "I know you didn't mean it, Hannah. Please put your coat on and bring in the milk pail for Trent so he can help Jake feed the animals."

Hannah grabbed her coat before heading out to get the wooden milk pail. Meanwhile, Alice rolled out dough for biscuits. Taking the bowl of scrambled eggs to the already hot fire, Lizzie poured the mixture into the frying pan positioned on the coals of the fireplace. In no time, breakfast was ready. Alice called everyone inside while Lizzie set the scrambled eggs, biscuits, and strawberry preserves on the table in the adjoining room. Once they sat down, Lizzie asked God to bless the food and thanked Him for His blessings.

Trying to hurry, Lizzie kept reminding her cousins to stop talking and eat. By the end of the meal, Trent was calling her "Grumpy," to everyone's amusement. Lizzie instructed him and Alice to help her clear the table while Rebecca and Hannah went upstairs to get Tuffy's sand-filled box. Picking up several plates, she took them to the kitchen and started to wash them when Jake came up behind her.

"Don't you think you're being hard on them? Lighten up a little, Grumpy. We'll be there on time," he declared as Trent and Alice brought the remaining plates. "Come on, Trent. Let's finish feeding the livestock and hitch the wagon."

Thinking about what Jake said, Lizzie tried to relax but for some reason she couldn't shake her uneasiness. Not sure where her feelings were coming from, she finished washing the dishes while Alice put them away. As they worked, Rebecca cleaned out Tuffy's sand-filled box. The one-eyed black cat stood in the doorway to watch.

"Rebecca, where's Hannah?" Lizzie inquired, suddenly realizing the seven-year-old hadn't come back downstairs with her sister.

"She wanted to play with Reba."

Before Lizzie could respond, a shriek erupted from the next room. Wondering what it was, Lizzie walked to the doorway as Hannah came running into the kitchen gasping.

"Reba's flying all over the house!" she panted.

"What? How did she get out of her cage?"

"I let her out. She looked so sad, like she wanted to fly. You let her fly around your room, so I thought it would be okay. I forgot to make sure the door was closed," Hannah explained.

Something crashed in the parlor. Panicking, Lizzie rushed to the front room fearful that the bird was breaking things. She felt relieved when she spotted Aunt Grace's rocking chair on the floor. From the looks of things, Tuffy climbed up on the rocker in pursuit of Reba, who was teasing the one-eyed cat. Tuffy's formerly injured leg didn't seem to bother her as she pounced on the chess table in the corner of the room. She meowed as she tried to trap Reba, but the red and green parrot outsmarted her opponent. Squawking loudly, Reba flew across the room and landed on the fireplace mantle. Lizzie cautiously walked toward her as Reba strutted around the various items. Seeing Lizzie coming, Reba turned around, nearly knocking off a vase with her tail feathers. Horrified, Lizzie lunged forward as the bird took flight, this time flying into the kitchen.

"We have to catch her. Your momma will be furious if something gets broken. Rebecca, will you and Hannah please take Tuffy outside while we corner Reba?" Lizzie requested as she sat the rocker upright.

Eventually, the girls successfully ran Tuffy to the kitchen, but as soon as she spotted Reba on the table, Tuffy's light green eye focused on her target. Again, Lizzie tried to sneak up on Reba. She was inches away from the bird when the back door opened. As Trent and Jake entered, the bird soared through the air toward the open door.

"No!" Lizzie yelled. "Close the door!"

Startled, Jake managed to close it just in time to keep the bird from escaping. Reba flew around the kitchen near the ceiling before landing on top of the cabinet where they kept Grandmother Worsley's china.

"What's going on?" Trent asked.

"Hannah let Reba out and now we can't catch her," Alice revealed.

"I didn't mean to," Hannah piped up.

"It doesn't matter," Lizzie interrupted. "Get Tuffy out of here."

Trent helped corner Tuffy while Lizzie got a straight-backed chair from the table. She was about to climb on it when Jake stopped her.

"What are you doing? You can't grab her. You know she bites."

"Do you have a better idea?" she countered.

"Give me your apron and move out of the way. I'll catch her."

Curious to see how he was going to catch the bird, Lizzie untied her apron and handed it to him. Behind her, Trent coaxed Tuffy outside. Positioning the chair beneath the cabinet, Jake slowly stood up on it and eased the apron into the air. Surprisingly, Reba stayed still, watching Jake's careful movements. The red and green bird bent her legs to fly as Jake dropped the apron on top of her. Screeching in protest, Reba fought the apron as Jake grabbed her body. Stepping down, he held her tightly in both hands so she couldn't escape.

"You caught her!" Hannah exclaimed as she ran over to him.

"I wasn't so sure it would work. I need some help taking her back upstairs. Why don't you come with me while everyone gets ready to leave, Hannah?" Jake replied as he led the way.

Lizzie put out the fire in the kitchen as Alice and Rebecca grabbed their coats and straw hats. Retrieving her own hat and coat, Lizzie followed them outside where Trent waited on the back porch. He was watching Killer run Tuffy around the yard. The little brown and white dog barked at the black cat, but Tuffy was too fast for Killer.

"Should we leave Tuffy outside, Lizzie? Between the wolves and Killer chasing her, I don't know if it's a good idea," Rebecca observed.

"She can climb a tree if she needs to escape," Lizzie assured her as Jake and Hannah came out wearing their coats.

"Are you ready?" Jake questioned, locking the door behind him.

"Yes, let's go," Lizzie proclaimed.

Approaching Butterscotch and the wagon, Trent picked Hannah up to help her get in while Rebecca and Alice quickly clambered in the back.

"Sit up front, Lizzie. Trent's riding in the back," Jake suggested.

Stunned, Lizzie didn't know what to say. To her surprise, Trent swung his leg over the side of the wagon and settled down beside Hannah. Feeling uncomfortable, Lizzie climbed up on the front seat. Sliding over, she made room for Jake, who sat down beside her and picked up the reins. Smacking his lips to get Butterscotch's attention, he flicked the reins, causing the wagon to jerk forward.

With the blustery winds blowing from the north, it was impossible to keep her straw hat on her head. Holding it in her lap, Lizzie tried to enjoy the ride to Grandfather's house, but she just couldn't motivate herself. The chilly November wind and gray sky didn't do much for her spirit either. Behind her, Hannah sang a children's song. When it was time to sing the chorus, she invited everyone to join her. At first Lizzie didn't sing, but after Jake nudged her, she joined in on the fun. Staying on the dirt path, they crossed the little wooden bridge spanning Glebe Creek, which bordered Grandfather's land and their own. Soon, Grandfather's two-story gray house was in view. Moments later, they came to a stop in the yard. Noticing they had arrived, Grandfather and Uncle Thomas walked over.

"Good morning!" Grandfather greeted them, helping Hannah down from the wagon.

"Where's Momma?" the seven-year-old inquired.

"I'm right here," Aunt Grace announced as she left the back porch to hug her daughter. "Did you sleep well last night?"

"No, ma'am. Wolves woke us up. Jake and Trent ran them off, and Lizzie let me sleep with her so I wouldn't be scared. It just wasn't the same without you, Momma. I missed you a bunch."

Aunt Grace smiled. "I missed you, too, honey."

"How many wolves were there, Jake?" Grandfather asked. "They were here, too. By the time I got outside, my Plott hounds were howling. Thank goodness the servants scared them away from the livestock."

"I'm not sure. Probably about ten or so. Don't you think, Trent?"

"Yes, at least ten."

"I'll check with the neighbors," Uncle Thomas commented.

"Well, we've got work to do first," Aunt Grace reminded him. "Come with me, Hannah. Aunt Charlotte is boiling tallow so we can make candles. You can go with me to the cellar for the string."

Walking hand in hand, the two of them went around the house where the cellar went underneath it. Meanwhile, Uncle Thomas unhitched the wagon so that Trent could take Butterscotch to the pasture with Grandfather's horses.

"Let's go to the beehives, Jake. I need help gathering beeswax for the candles," Grandfather said.

As Lizzie followed Rebecca and Alice to the old sweetgum tree, Grandfather took Jake behind the barn to the beehives. Across the yard, she noticed Grandfather's servants working to butcher a hog stretched out on the table used for the hog killings. Seeing the group of men working hard, she felt grateful she didn't have to help. The process of killing a hog and butchering the meat was disgusting. In the past, the women and children had to help, but since her papa had acquired the new workers they wouldn't have to assist.

Thinking about her papa made Lizzie's mind wander. It had been three weeks since the pirates left Bath. She thought he would have returned to town after receiving Tobias Knight's letter. She assumed the secretary mentioned the pardons due to arrive in mid-December along with the false Indian attack. Strangely, Garret Gibbons, James Robins, and Tobias' African slave, Caesar, had yet to return as well. A week had passed since they left Tobias Knight's dock. They were traveling on a periauger owned by James and his business partner, Stephen Elsey, so nothing could be traced back to the secretary of the colony. Lizzie couldn't understand what was taking them so long. Her papa had traveled to Bath from Ocracoke to see Tobias and again for the hearing regarding the French ship. Both times only took a couple of days.

Lost in thought, she followed Alice and Rebecca to the other side of the house. She jumped when someone tapped her on the shoulder. Surprisingly, she discovered JJ Brooks behind her.

"What are you doing here, JJ?"

"Ye uncle, Thomas, mentioned a hog killing to John when they talked yesterday. John offered to help. So how have ye been?"

"I'm fine," she mumbled as John Martin yelled across the yard.

"JJ! Get over here. We've got work to do."

JJ sighed. "I've been summoned. Maybe we can talk at dinner."

Jogging back to the other men, JJ joined John Martin, who was putting salt on the hams to keep the meat from spoiling. Later, they would hang them in the smokehouse to dry.

Eager to start the candle making, Lizzie walked to where Aunt Charlotte worked. Standing with Alice and Rebecca, she watched

Aunt Charlotte stir the cow fat in a large iron cauldron using a wooden paddle. Steam rose from the cauldron as smoke drifted into the air from the burning wood. To the right of the cauldron was a circular rack about waist high. The rack resembled a wagon wheel turned up on its side and could spin around. All six of the wheel spokes had a hook on them. A wooden plate-sized disk hung from the hooks by their handles. Candles hung on five smaller hooks on the underside of the disk.

Aunt Charlotte had just announced the tallow was ready when Hannah and Aunt Grace returned carrying spools of string made with braided hemp fibers. The timing was perfect as Grandfather and Jake came over with buckets of beeswax. Grandfather collected honey and beeswax from the wooden containers he built for them.

Lizzie was fascinated by the winged insects and enjoyed learning about them in a library book in Grandfather's study. It was amazing how God made such a small, hard-working creature that was so beneficial.

The wax made by the insects created the honeycomb where they kept their honey. Adding wax to the tallow made the candles smell sweet like honey. They also burned longer and cleaner without smoking up the room. Grandfather dumped the beeswax into the cauldron of tallow. Lizzie watched him and Jake join the other men while Aunt Charlotte mixed the tallow and wax.

Hannah rolled out the string for Alice, who cut off two-foot pieces with a knife and passed them to Rebecca. Taking the strings, Lizzie tied them to the hooks under the disks. Next, Aunt Grace grabbed the handle and dipped the strings into the boiling tallow. Lifting it, she let the pork fat drip into the cauldron before placing the disk back on the hook. Moving the wheel, Aunt Grace repeated the process.

The method of making candles was slow. While Aunt Charlotte stirred the tallow to keep it from sticking, Aunt Grace dipped the strings over and over. With each dip in the boiling tallow, the candles grew thicker and more durable. After twenty-five dips, the candles were ready to take off the rack. Using another knife, Lizzie cut the strings in half, making two candles. She stacked the new candles in a basket as Rebecca took her job of tying on the strings. Although the candles started piling up, Lizzie knew they needed a large supply for the winter. Unfortunately, a single candle lasted for only one evening.

Even with the windy weather, the Worsley girls made considerable progress by dinner. When it was time to eat, Aunt Mary came out of the house to ring the bell on top of a wooden post. At the sound of the clanging bell, everyone stopped working. They gathered at the back of the house where a table was set up. Once Grandfather prayed for the meal, Aunt Mary filled bowls with vegetable soup. Hog-killing day wouldn't be complete without the special soup made from the recipe Grandmother Worsley always used.

After Lizzie got her soup and cup of water, she found a place to sit under the old sweetgum tree. Sitting among the prickly, brown sweetgum balls with her cousins, she was surprised when JJ sat down.

"Mind if I sit here?" he questioned, not giving her time to object. "This soup is good. Miss Mary said it's ye grandmother's recipe."

"Yes, Grandmother loved cooking."

"Speaking of food, Miss Martin invited me to the Divine Service and to join her family for dinner. Jake told me he's been going with ye family to the services. I was thinking ye could go with me. We can eat dinner with the Martins afterward," he suggested eagerly.

"Miss Martin invited you, not me."

"I'm sure she'd be happy to have ye," he pointed out as someone announced they had visitors.

Looking up, Lizzie noticed five men had arrived on horseback. She recognized several of them, including Mr. Thomas Harding, Miles Gale, and his older stepbrother, Thomas Harvey. They dismounted as Grandfather and Uncle Thomas walked over to meet them. Meanwhile, the servants went back to work.

Grandfather spoke first, addressing Thomas Harding, who was leading the group. "Hello, Thomas. What can we do for you?"

"I came to warn you about wolves terrorizing the community over the last couple of nights," Thomas Harding declared.

"The wolves were here last night, but I didn't see them. Jake and Trent saw about ten at Grace's house. They never went to Thomas' place," Grandfather said.

"They've killed several cows, but they seem to be preying on sheep and goats. Governor Eden wants to form a scouting group. I don't know where they're bedding down in the daylight, so we'll have to hunt them on their terms. We're setting up hunting parties tonight. William Martin agreed to let us use some of his sheep as bait. I also spoke with Simon Alderson this morning. He can't help since we're still searching for your servant Pompey, but he did suggest setting traps at some of the places they've been. Hopefully, we'll be able to stop this slaughtering," Thomas Harding explained.

"If ye plan to use our herd as bait, ye need to make sure there's plenty of men with shotguns ready," John Martin spoke up.

"John's right. Father and I will help," Uncle Thomas agreed.

"We can't spare any of the servants, though," Grandfather added. "Someone needs to guard the livestock just in case they outsmart us."

Thomas Harding nodded in agreement. The other men spoke of their experiences with the wolves, but Lizzie was no longer listening. Her focus had shifted to Miles Gale, who was walking over to her. With her family listening to the conversation, no one except JJ noticed Miles.

"Hello, Lizzie. I wanted to invite you for dinner this Sunday after the Divine Service. My mother is really looking forward to it. Would you give me the honor of escorting you?" he wanted to know.

318

"I asked her first," JJ interrupted.

"What?" Miles gasped. "You're going with a common sailor?"

"A common sailor!" JJ blurted out, leaping up from the ground.

"Calm down," Lizzie urged as she stood and tried to keep JJ from saying what he really was. "Everyone knows the last Sunday in November is set aside for a day of thanksgiving for God's blessings. I plan to spend the day with my family like I always do."

"I can still pick you up for the Divine Service," Miles countered.

"She's riding with me," JJ spat.

"No, I'm going with my aunt and cousins."

"What about the following Sunday?" Miles pursued.

"Right now, we're busy working. I'll have to think about it, Miles."

"Alright. I'll be seeing you, Lizzie," Miles declared as he and the five men mounted their horses.

As they left the yard, everyone put away their bowls and went back to work. JJ tried to talk to Lizzie, but she gently pushed him away. To make matters worse, Grandfather mentioned they needed help cleaning the hog chitterlings. Since Aunt Mary offered to help finish making candles, Aunt Grace volunteered herself and Lizzie.

Cleaning hog chitterlings was another disgusting chore. They turned the hog intestines inside out with a stick, wiped them off, and submerged them in hot water in order to make link sausage. After stuffing the hog meat in the casings, the long strands of sausage hung in the smokehouse to dry. Although Lizzie loved eating link sausage, the process of cleaning the casings made her wonder how such a nasty thing could turn out so delicious.

Rolling up her coat sleeves, Lizzie grabbed one of the sticks on the butchering table and began to carefully turn the intestines inside out. She wasn't as fast as Aunt Grace, but she managed to flip the chitterlings without tearing the thin casing. Soon, they had two strands of chitterlings ready for the cauldron of boiling water. As

Lizzie added hers to the cauldron, she noticed a horse and rider trotting up.

"Aunt Grace, we have company."

By the time Aunt Grace had gotten her father's attention, the new arrival was dismounting his horse. Lizzie recognized him as John Giles, one of the former pirates in her papa's crew.

"Can I help you?" Grandfather offered.

"William Martin told me I could find his brother John here."

"What's going on?" John Martin remarked as he wiped the salt from his hands and came over.

"I've got important news to tell ye," John Giles started, glancing over at Grandfather. "It involves Captain."

"Then the Worsleys might need to listen."

"Hold on," Grandfather spoke up. "Everybody, take a break."

The servants looked at each other as they walked away. When they were out of earshot, John Martin turned to his friend.

"Alright, go ahead."

"Have ye heard about the wolves and the scouts hunting them?"

"Aye. What do they have to do with Captain?"

"The wolves aren't the only ones being hunted. This morning, I walked over to the cooper's shed with Stephen and Edward. When we got there, Colonel Maurice Moore was at the shipyard asking if anyone would be interested in going on a scouting expedition. Another man was with him wearing the navy-blue uniform of an officer in the Royal Navy. The officer needed to hire six men and two periaugers to row into the Pamtico Sound to see if they could locate two Royal Navy ships due to arrive anytime."

"What? This isn't good," John Martin replied.

"It gets worse. After hiring the men, Moore took the officer to the Salty Sailor Tavern. Since Edward and Stephen had to work, I followed them. I got a beer like I always do and chose a chair where I could hear part of their conversation. They kept their voices low, but I heard Moore introduce the officer to Roger Kenyon, the owner of the alehouse. The officer is Captain Ellis Brand from Virginia. He and his servant are staying at the Blue Heron Inn. Brand mentioned the words 'Maynard,' 'Black Beard,' 'Spotswood,' and 'capture.'"

John sighed. "Sounds like they're trying to capture the crew."

"The best thing you can do is stay out of it. I've heard about this Spotswood fellow from somewhere," Grandfather mentioned.

"I'll see if I can find out about him," Uncle Thomas stated.

"How about Garret, James, and Caesar?" JJ inquired.

"They'll just have to deal with the scouts," John Martin said.

"Don't ye think we should at least warn the crew?" JJ urged.

Lizzie's heart sank as she listened to the concern in his voice. She knew he was thinking about his father. Part of her agreed with JJ.

"Mr. Worsley had a good point. I think it's best if we keep a low profile. We can't risk it," John Martin continued.

"Forget about Israel keeping a low profile. The idiot volunteered to go on the scouting party!" John Giles exclaimed.

Lizzie made eye contact with Jake. Had Israel lost his mind, or was he trying to get to Ocracoke for his buried treasure? She couldn't help but wonder if Calico Jack had returned to the island. If they only knew the treasure was in Black Beard's cabin aboard the *Adventure*.

"To be fair, Israel didn't hear Brand say they're looking for the crew," John Martin reminded him.

"None of us did when we were offered the job, but we aren't idiots. Ye can't trust anyone in a Royal Navy uniform. Before this is over, Israel will say something stupid. Brand is here for a reason. He may be keeping his plans secret, but the real reason he's here will surface. There's also news about Black Beard's old quartermaster, William Howard. He was found guilty of piracy a few weeks ago in Virginia and is waiting to hang at the gallows."

John Martin shook his head. "If they arrested him, then we're all in danger. We've got to keep Israel from talking to Brand."

"We can't stop Israel from running his mouth," Jake pointed out.

"Nay, but we can keep an eye on him," John Martin suggested. "John, ye already have a perfect cover since ye spend a lot of time at the Salty Sailor. The rest of us can watch him outside the tavern."

"I still think we should consider warning the crew," JJ insisted.

"Weren't ye listening? It's too risky. We don't know if our pardons will hold. If we're caught trying to warn them, we might put our own lives in jeopardy. John can watch Israel and keep him from talking."

"Guess I should head back. There's no telling who Israel is talking to. I'll send word if I hear anything," John Giles promised, mounting his silver-gray horse.

As the former pirate headed back to Bath Town, JJ walked away with his hands clutched into fists. Jake went after him, but JJ wouldn't listen. When Jake returned, Grandfather was giving out instructions to finish the butchering. Motioning for Lizzie, Jake lowered his voice.

"You need to talk to JJ. He's going to do something stupid and won't listen to me. He's determined to warn his father and the others about Brand."

"I agree with him. They need to be warned," Lizzie countered.

"Do you want him to get caught? This is a bad idea. You're the only one who can change his mind," Jake pleaded. "He's our friend, Lizzie. Please try."

Crossing her arms, Lizzie took a deep breath. She knew Jake was right: she had to try. Reluctantly walking to the fenced-in pasture, she located JJ, who was saddling the Martins' light brown horse.

"JJ, I don't think you need to go," she began.

Whipping around, JJ looked at her with hurt in his eyes. "Ye should understand why I want to warn Pa. Don't ye want to give ye father a warning? I'm not just going for myself. I'm thinking of ye, too, Lizzie."

"Of course, but there's no sense in risking your life. Let's see what Uncle Thomas finds out. Can you wait a day or two?"

JJ leaned against the saddle as he stared at the ground. Concerned he was going to say no, Lizzie was surprised when he slowly nodded.

"Okay, Lizzie, I'll do it for ye. But just so we're clear, in two days I'm going, regardless of what ye or anyone else says."

Leaving him to remove the saddle, Lizzie walked across the yard thinking about her papa. The uneasiness in her stomach grew despite her attempts to give her worries to God. She couldn't believe men were hunting her papa and his crew like wolves. Then again, their way of life threatened others the same way the wolves threatened the livestock. They chose to be pirates and therefore would have to outsmart the hunters. All Lizzie could do was pray they didn't get stuck in the trap.

CHAPTER TWENTY-FIVE

☠

HIGH TIDE

November 26, 1718 ~ Wednesday

Ominous black clouds collected on the eastern horizon as they threatened a chance of rain. Looking up at them, Lizzie considered if they were an omen of bad luck or a warning from God. Despite her efforts to let it go, she couldn't stop comparing the hunted wolves to her papa's crew. Since Monday, the community had killed most of the wolves. She was glad the wolves were gone, but she also knew their fate could become the fate of her beloved papa.

Like the gathering rain clouds, the anxiousness in the air mounted with each passing day. According to Uncle Thomas, everyone in Bath Town was on edge as they waited for the return of the scouts hired by the Royal Naval officer, Captain Ellis Brand. Things weren't looking good for Garret, James, and Caesar either. No one had seen any sign of the three former pirates.

During the last two days, Captain Brand had interviewed whoever was willing to speak with him. John Giles reported numerous people talking to Brand at the Salty Sailor Tavern. Thankfully, Israel Hands hadn't been one of them. There was no way of knowing what people were telling Captain Brand, but Lizzie had a feeling the information wasn't good for her papa. Most everyone saw the crew arrive in July. The rumors of them being pirates had spread like wildfire.

Clearly, the rumors had reached far beyond Bath Town. Someone alerted the Virginia government and sent its Royal Navy to take care of it. Between Captain Brand waiting for him in Bath and the two Royal Navy ships coming through Ocracoke Inlet, the chances for the *Adventure* to escape were slim. Still, Lizzie hoped they had already left the inlet and were on their way to the island of St. Thomas.

One of the reasons for Lizzie's hope was the letter Uncle Thomas brought back from town the day before. The letter was a response to the one Lizzie wrote to her aunt about the false Indian attacks. Aunt Susannah mentioned having a relative she hadn't seen in years come to visit, saying it was wonderful to see him. Knowing the visitor was her papa, Lizzie was glad to hear he made it to see his sister. By the dates Aunt Susannah gave her, she guessed he would've arrived at Ocracoke with plenty of time to load the remaining casks of sugar and sacks of cocoa. If her timeline was right, they should have left Ocracoke days before the Royal Navy showed up. There was an issue she couldn't figure out, though. Where were Garret, James, and Caesar?

Lifting her chin, Lizzie stared into the dark gray clouds, trying not to worry. She closed her eyes to pray for her papa and his crew.

"What are you doing?"

Blinking, Lizzie realized Hannah was standing in front of her with a look of curiosity on her face. "I was praying."

"Why?"

Not wanting to put her grown-up worries on Hannah's innocent heart, Lizzie debated how to explain her concerns. Thankfully, Aunt Grace interrupted so that she didn't have to justify her actions.

"Come on, girls, we need to get started before the rain comes."

Lizzie tried to forget her worries as she joined her cousins around the large, black cauldron in Grandfather's backyard. Today, the Worsley girls were making lye soap. Jake and Trent offered to help, but when they arrived, Grandfather had another task planned for them.

With the temperatures dropping below freezing for the previous three nights, the colony experienced an early cold spell. The sudden change of weather triggered an unusual occurrence. Trout rose to the surface of the water as they came in with the high tide around daybreak. There were so many fish floating as if dead on the surface of the Pamtico River, all you had to do was scoop them up in buckets. This provided the perfect opportunity to gather the trout and salt them in barrels. With the water temperature warming up as the day progressed, time was short to collect the trout, which were quickly recovering from the shock of chilly water. The good thing about the warmer weather was it made the family's efforts much easier. At least they could work outside without being so cold.

As men from all over the colony flocked to the water, Grandfather arranged for Trent and Jake to help Uncle Thomas and four slaves gather the trout. The three periaugers brought in the fish while Grandfather kept the rest of the servants busy removing scales, cutting off heads, cleaning out the guts, and salting them in barrels. JJ showed up mid-morning to help since John Martin and his brother William didn't need his assistance gathering fish for their family. Grandfather put him to work stacking the trout belly-side up in the barrels so the salt would preserve the meat.

Glad that JJ was too busy to talk, Lizzie watched her three aunts set to work on the next phase of soap making. As expected, the first phase took Aunt Grace, Aunt Mary, and Aunt Charlotte all morning to complete. While they labored to get the lye ready, Lizzie and her cousins worked on preparing for winter. Many of the vegetables and fruits had finished drying out, so the girls were rearranging them in the cellar. One of the hardest things to deal with was stringing up the beans called leather britches. The girls also placed potatoes and turnips in a hole lined with straw, which preserved them through the cold months. Before long, it was time to eat dinner. After a meal of beef stew, they were ready to start the second phase of soap making.

The key ingredient required to make soap was lye. It came from wood ashes. Each of their homes had a barrel where they kept gathered ashes from the fireplaces after the hardwood had burned down. Periodically, they would dump the ashes into one of Grandfather's wooden, V-shaped troughs called a hopper lined with straw. Over time, the rain would separate the ashes from the potash otherwise known as lye. Some people used a barrel bound with tough hickory switches and packed with straw and water. Instead of the lye coming out of the trough under the hopper, the barrel had a small hole to let it drain out of the bottom.

Aunt Grace poured buckets of lye into the cauldron while Aunt Mary poured in the pork fat grease they had been collecting. Aunt Charlotte stirred the mixture with a wooden paddle as steam rose into the air. When the cauldron was full, Aunt Charlotte continued to stir in one direction, making sure to be consistent as Aunt Grace added the lavender to take away the greasy smell. Eventually, the mixture was thick enough to transfer to one of the soap molds spread out on the dormant brown grass. Each wooden soap mold was three feet wide, four feet long, and two inches deep. It held the mixture until it became solid.

Using a wooden dipper, Aunt Grace spooned the mixture into a bucket and passed it to Lizzie. Taking the heavy bucket, Lizzie walked over to a soap mold and poured the thick mixture of lye and grease into the wooden box. Beside her, Alice and Rebecca did the same with their buckets. Going back for more, Lizzie took turns taking the soap to the molds until the cauldron was empty. Then, Aunt Grace and Aunt Mary started the process all over again with a new batch.

While they worked, Lizzie's mind drifted to Cookie's comments about lye soap when they were in Pennsylvania. He said he never liked making soap and wasn't going to wash with the flower-scented kind. Lizzie smiled at the thought of her dear friend.

By early afternoon, the men had scooped up all the fish they could. With so many fish to clean, the work onshore continued. In addition to the cleaning and packing of the trout, several men started taking the barrels of salted fish to the smokehouse. As the men transferred the fish, the Worsley girls cut the hardened soap and kept the wooden molds full. Sometimes there was a lull in the soap making, giving them a break. It was during one of these periods of rest that Uncle John and Nathaniel Ming came out of the house.

"Looks like you've been busy," Uncle John commented, peering into the cauldron.

"Yes, we're pretty tired," Aunt Grace answered.

"I guess Father and Thomas are trying to get the trout in the smokehouse before it rains."

Uncle John glanced at Aunt Mary, who was taking a turn at stirring the mixture with the wooden paddle. Lizzie had noticed how her aunt seemed to avoid her older brother. Thankfully, Uncle John and Nathaniel had recovered since their beatings two weeks earlier. Although they weren't strong enough to help with the preparations for winter, they had come a long way. Nathaniel had even moved back into the servants' quarters since he no longer needed care. As far as Lizzie knew, neither of them had mentioned the lashing.

Hannah distracted Lizzie by tugging on her left arm. Shifting her attention, Lizzie was astonished when Hannah alerted her to the arrival of visitors. Several men had tied their fishing boat to Grandfather Worsley's dock and were walking up to the house. When the three men came closer, Lizzie recognized them as the former pirates John Martin, Stephen Daniel, and Edward Salter. Stopping their work, Grandfather told his servants to take a break while he spoke to them.

"Hello, John. I'm sure you and William are as tired as we are after dealing with these trout. Thanks for sending JJ over. He's been a big help."

"Glad he could help out," John Martin replied as he rubbed his jaw with his right hand. His eyes darted to JJ. "There's no easy way to say this. Stephen and Edward just came to tell me the scouts are back with news from a man named Lieutenant Robert Maynard. The scouts told Captain Brand and everyone on the docks the pirates are dead."

Lizzie's jaw dropped as she tried to absorb what he was saying.

"What?" JJ blurted out. "Ye mean my father…my pa…he…he's gone? It can't be! I refuse to believe it!"

"They're all gone, JJ. I'm sorry," John muttered.

They're all gone…They're all gone…They're all gone.

John's words echoed over and over in Lizzie's head. Her heart beat faster as reality sunk in. Finding it hard to breathe, she backed away from the others, unable to grasp the awful truth.

"This can't be," she whispered as tears trickled down her cheeks.

"Oh, Lizzie," Aunt Grace began, her voice full of emotion.

She took a step toward Lizzie to offer comfort, but Lizzie shook her head. Not knowing what she was doing, she took off running. Behind her, she could hear JJ's voice calling out her name.

"Let her go, lad," Grandfather advised.

Blinded by tears, Lizzie ran as fast as she could. Overwhelmed with emotion, she finally came to a stop, gasping as she collapsed to her knees on the pine-straw-covered ground. The chilly air burned the back of her throat, but she barely noticed. Looking at the forest of pine and oak trees, she realized she had been running to the back of Grandfather's property. Up ahead, she could vaguely make out the cluster of tombstones marking the Worsley family cemetery.

Scrambling to her feet, Lizzie wiped her wet cheeks with her coat sleeve as she hastily made her way to the graves. Although her eyes were blurry from crying, she located her mother's resting place with ease. Crouching down in front of it, she brushed away the fallen leaves and reached out to touch the words chiseled into the stone.

MARTHA WORSLEY BEARD
DIED 1711
AGED 25 YEARS

Fresh tears welled up in her eyes as she sobbed into the palms of her hands. She felt so helpless and alone. Her heart ached, knowing she would never see either of her parents again. Wanting to be close to her mother, she crawled forward. Placing her cheek against the tombstone, she cried tears of sorrow and pain.

The sound of crunching leaves startled Lizzie, who looked up to see Aunt Grace stooping to sit beside her. Without a word, her aunt gently pushed loose strands of Lizzie's tear-drenched hair away from her face. Lizzie wrapped her arms around her aunt as she sobbed into her shoulder. Aunt Grace held her tenderly, rocking her back and forth like she did years ago when Lizzie grieved for her momma.

After a few minutes, Aunt Grace spoke up. "I'm so sorry, honey. I wish there was something we could've done."

Lizzie cried harder as she recalled her papa's last words to her at Tunnel Land. She could almost feel his beard rubbing against her.

"Thank God you found her!"

Pulling away, Lizzie wiped her eyes upon hearing her grandfather's voice. The lanky, dark-haired man got out of his carriage and walked over, wearing a look of concern.

"I brought the carriage. Mary's putting on some herbal tea."

"Are you ready to go back to the house?" Aunt Grace inquired.

"No. I want to go home. I can't face everyone right now. I need to be alone for a while," Lizzie replied as her bottom jaw quivered.

"Okay, honey, we can go home."

"I'll take you over there," Grandfather offered.

Standing up, Lizzie held Aunt Grace's hand as they climbed into the backseat of the carriage. The ride home was a blur. Lizzie tried to stop crying, but she couldn't pull herself together. Before she knew it, they had arrived in their own yard. With Grandfather's help, she got out of the carriage and stepped up on the back porch. Aunt Grace opened the door and walked with her upstairs. As she entered her room, Tuffy and Reba greeted her. Ignoring them, Lizzie sat down in the straight-backed chair in front of her desk while Aunt Grace pulled back her quilt. Staring at the desktop, Lizzie caught a glimpse of the oval-shaped locket bearing her initials. Just the sight of it brought more tears to her eyes.

"Lizzie, why don't you rest for a while?" Aunt Grace suggested as Grandfather entered the room.

"Is there anything I can do before I head back to the house? Perhaps the children should spend the night with us," he hinted.

"I don't know, Father. Hannah's been having nightmares ever since the wolves scared her. For the last two nights, she's been sleeping in my room," Aunt Grace revealed.

"We'll see how things are in a few hours then," he stated. Walking over to Lizzie, he gave her a big hug. "I love you, my dear. My heart aches for the pain you're going through."

"I love you, too," she managed to choke out.

Kissing the top of her head, Grandfather left the room. Once he was gone, Lizzie went to her bed. As she sat down and looked at the quilt her mother made, another wave of tears streamed down her cheeks. Aunt Grace handed her a white handkerchief to dab her eyes with.

"Why did Papa have to be killed? I prayed for God to help him. Wasn't God listening?" she questioned, looking up at her aunt.

Sitting beside her, Aunt Grace clutched Lizzie's hand. "Honey, God always listens. Sometimes His answer isn't what we want."

"I can't believe God allowed those evil men to murder Papa."

"We don't know if it was murder."

"What?" Lizzie exploded, yanking her hand from her aunt's grasp as she stood up. "I can't believe you think he deserved this."

"Lizzie, I didn't say he deserved to die. You know he was a pirate. It was only a matter of time before he got himself in trouble."

"Papa isn't like Captain Vane or Calico Jack. He never killed a soul. There are worse pirates in the world. I've seen them. Why couldn't the Royal Navy attack them instead?" Lizzie pointed out.

Stunned, Aunt Grace stared at her. "You never mentioned any other pirates. I thought you went to Pennsylvania and Ocracoke."

Realizing she told too much, Lizzie scolded herself as she murmured, "Captain Vane came to Ocracoke to talk to Papa."

"I see. Is there anything else I should know?"

Lizzie let out a sigh. "I'm really tired. Can we talk about it later?"

From the look on her aunt's face, Lizzie could tell she didn't like that answer. Taking a deep breath, Aunt Grace stood up. Lizzie removed her shoes and stretched out as her aunt pulled up the quilt.

"If you need anything, holler. I'll be in my bedchambers writing a letter to your aunt. Susannah needs to know about Edward as soon as possible. Father can take the letter to town first thing in the morning," Aunt Grace declared as she started to walk away.

"I love you, Aunt Grace."

"I love you, too, dear."

Watching her leave, Lizzie shifted her focus to the design in the quilt. Tracing the stitches with her fingers, she thought about the hard work her momma put into making it. Her mind drifted to Aunt Susannah and the horrible news she would receive about the loss of her brother. Weeping into her feather-stuffed pillow, Lizzie cried herself into a restless sleep.

In her dreams, she found herself walking beside a river. The sky was black as if it were night, but the birds were chirping overhead. Confused, she spotted a dock near the bend in the river. She felt an urge to go there. As she approached the dock, she stepped out on it. With each step, the dock grew longer. At some point, she looked in the direction she had come. There was nothing but darkness.

Falling to the dock, she crawled on her hands and knees, keeping the wooden boards in sight so they didn't disappear, too. She finally saw something white in the darkness. The figure bobbed up and down below the dock. Leaning closer, she nearly fell in the water as she realized what she was looking at. Two empty eye sockets stared back at her. Again, the tide came in, completely covering the skeleton. When it subsided, she noticed a rope tied around the skeleton's neck. It held the skeleton to the dock like a hangman's noose. On the third tide, the skeleton grabbed her arm. Screaming, she tried to pry open the boney fingers, but their grip tightened. As the skull lifted out of the water, she saw a pirate's flag wrapped around its shoulders. The next thing she knew, the skeleton grabbed her other arm and was pulling her into the water. Terrified, she fought back.

Jerking in the bed, Lizzie fought her quilt until she woke herself. Sitting up, she gazed wildly around her, soon realizing she was safe in her room. Relieved to know she had been dreaming, she scooted back to lean against the wooden headboard. Wiping sweat from her forehead, her ears picked up the sound of raindrops pounding on the tin roof. The sound accompanied rumbling thunder.

A sudden knock on the door made Lizzie nearly jump out of bed. Seconds later, Aunt Grace's face peeped around the door. As she entered the room, Lizzie noticed she was carrying a wooden tray of food.

"I hope I didn't startle you," she said as she crossed the room and placed the tray on the nightstand. "How are you feeling?"

"I'm fine. I just had a bad dream."

"You look pale," Aunt Grace commented, feeling her sweaty forehead. "Are you hungry? I brought up your supper."

"Is it suppertime already? How long have I been asleep?" Lizzie asked as another round of thunder echoed through the room.

"You've been sleeping for hours, though I don't see how with this storm. Try to eat. I'll be back after I wash the dishes."

Lizzie didn't respond as her aunt left. Glancing at the tray, she stared at the plate of butter beans, collards, and ham. She started to turn over when the door opened again. Expecting to see Aunt Grace, she was surprised to discover Jake standing in the doorway.

"I promised Miss Grace I would coax you into eating," he commented. "The collards were particularly good after the frost."

Walking to her desk, Jake picked up the straight-backed chair and carried it to her bedside. Sitting down, he grabbed the plate of food and started scooping some collards on the spoon.

"I can feed myself."

"Good. Here you go," he stated, handing her the plate.

Letting out a blow of frustration, Lizzie sat up and took the plate from him. Snatching the spoon from his hand, she took a bite of the dark green, leafy vegetable. For the first time in her life, she purposely failed to pray before her meal, though deep down she felt sinful. She couldn't bring herself to talk to God when she felt He had betrayed her.

"Aren't you going to bless the food?"

"Why? God apparently doesn't listen to any of my prayers."

Jake crossed his arms as he leaned back in the chair. His narrowed eyes made Lizzie feel uncomfortable. He knew her too well.

"I recall someone else who felt the same way. He became friends with this girl who showed him he was wrong about God."

Knowing he was referring to her, Lizzie ignored him as she took a bite of ham. She felt irritated when he didn't stop talking.

"This friend gave me some advice. She said it sometimes helps to talk about things instead of keeping them bottled up inside."

Sighing, Lizzie put the food back on the wooden tray and sipped some of the apple cider. "You can't stop me from being mad with God. He could've helped Papa, but now he's dead and I'm alone."

"I know it's hard for you to deal with losing your papa, Lizzie, but you aren't alone. You have a family who supports you. I wish I had a family like yours. For many years, I was angry with God and the Indians who killed my parents and sisters. You've taught me to look at the good things and to be thankful I had people like Mr. and Mrs. Bowden. No one can take away the memories you have of your parents. Be thankful for the time you got with your papa this summer."

"Why did he have to die?" she whimpered, wiping her tears. "Did Stephen or Edward have any details explaining how he died?"

"Not really. Lieutenant Maynard is the one in charge of the two Royal Navy ships. He's supposed to be coming to town after he gets his affairs in order. There was a battle, but we haven't heard who started it. Tobias Knight's house guest, Edmund Chamberlayne, was in town with Governor Eden when the scouts came in. He heard the news along with the rest of the town and rushed back to tell Tobias, who can't leave his house due to his illness. A few hours ago, Tobias sent him and Scripo over here to tell your family what he heard. Both Tobias and Governor Eden are very upset about the situation."

"Do you think they hung him?"

"Since there was a battle we won't know until Maynard arrives."

"I had this dream earlier where I was on a dock. The next thing I knew, a skeleton grabbed me and started pulling me in the water. There was something odd about the dream. The water covered the skeleton three times. Didn't you tell me about a pirate who was hung and tied to a post to wash in three tides?"

"Yes. William Kidd was."

"Between the fish coming in with the high tide this morning and my dream about tides, I'm beginning to think about them more. Papa talked about the changing tides before he left. He compared the high tide to the good choices we make and the low tide to the bad ones. I hope those men didn't wash him in three tides."

"It sounds like he died in battle with the rest of the crew."

Lizzie lifted her head. "What did you say?"

"Uh…that he died in battle with the rest of the crew."

"I can't believe I didn't think about this!" she gasped. "They're dead, Jake. They're *all* dead. I was so upset over Papa I didn't think about the others. How could I forget Cookie?"

She paused as tears surfaced in the corners of her eyes. Across the room, Reba started squawking in her cage.

"Cookie! Cookie! Reba pretty girl, Cookie!"

Despite her tears, a smile crept onto Lizzie's face as she listened to the bird. "Cookie sure loved Reba and Tuffy."

Jake smiled. "He treated them like royalty."

"You know, I thought about how Cookie made fun of me liking flower-scented soap. He was such a kind soul. I loved him like an uncle. How's JJ?"

"JJ's taking it hard. He wanted to talk to you, but your grandfather didn't think it was the right time. John finally convinced him to go back with him. I couldn't get him to talk. He kept saying it's his fault he didn't go warn them about Captain Brand."

"I should've let him go the other day."

"It wouldn't have done any good. The crew would've been gone before he got there. He's just going to have to let it go."

"What about Garret, James, and Caesar? Are they dead, too?"

"I don't know. John Martin thinks it's possible they never made it to the *Adventure* with the letter. If they spotted the two Royal Navy ships, they may have turned around. They also could've delivered the letter and saw the ships on the horizon on their way back."

"Are the others worried about their lives?"

"If Brand wanted to kill them, he would've done so already. For now, John suggested they continue to keep a low profile. I just hope Israel keeps his mouth shut. The last thing we need is him getting drunk and spilling his secrets to the Royal Navy. JJ and the others aren't the only ones in danger. Israel knows another secret: us."

CHAPTER TWENTY-SIX

FLICKERING CANDLELIGHT

November 30, 1718 ~ Sunday

Hushed voices reverberated through the room as everyone waited for the Divine Service to begin. Sitting half-dazed on a wooden bench between Rebecca and Alice, Lizzie really didn't want to attend the service, but Aunt Grace insisted. Since today was the Day of Thanksgiving, Lizzie couldn't argue. After all, even Uncle John had joined the family for the special service.

A bell rang, signaling the start of the Divine Service. The room grew quiet as Miles' uncle, Edmund Gale, stepped forward wearing a black robe. He took his place behind a stand where he propped up the Bible and the Book of Common Prayer. Although Bath didn't have a preacher, Mr. Gale filled the position unless someone asked to do the reading. Occasionally, Bath had a visiting preacher who did the service. Because Bath didn't have a church, the service took place in the homes of the residents in town. John Porter was the current host. He sat on the front row with his family and Governor Eden.

"Good morning," Edmund Gale began. "Today is our Day of Thanksgiving. The Lord has richly blessed us. May we humble ourselves and earnestly thank Him for His provisions. Ushers, please light the three candles on behalf of the Father, Son, and Holy Ghost."

Uncle Thomas joined John Porter and Giles Shute in the corner of the room. They each lit a candle on the wooden table and returned to their seats. Lizzie admired the flickering candlelight, remembering how beautiful the *Adventure* looked surrounded by glowing lanterns. All she thought about lately was her time with her papa and his crew.

Opening the Book of Common Prayer, Mr. Gale began to read, causing Lizzie to snap out of her daydreaming. Everyone listened as he started the morning prayers by quoting a series of twelve Bible verses. He then read a section on the confession of sins and invited everyone to kneel. Lizzie knelt on the floor with the others as Mr. Gale continued to speak. Eventually, he got to the Lord's Prayer, given by Jesus in Matthew 6:9–13.

With eyes closed and head bowed, Lizzie repeated the familiar prayer along with everyone else. "Our Father which art in heaven, Hallowed be thy name. Thy kingdom come. Thy will be done in earth, as it is in heaven. Give us this day our daily bread. And forgive us our debts, as we forgive our debtors. And lead us not into temptation, but deliver us from evil: For thine is the kingdom, and the power, and the glory, for ever. Amen."

The sound of shuffling feet echoed as everyone stood. Mr. Gale led the congregation in singing Psalm 95 aloud. As they sat down, Mr. Gale started reading the first proper lesson from the Old Testament. Each day had assigned Scriptures for the Old and New Testaments. Since today was the last day of November and Saint Andrew's Day, the lesson was from Proverbs 20.

Once Mr. Gale read the Scripture, the congregation sang a hymn of praise, acknowledging God as Lord. The second lesson, from Acts 1, came next, followed by Psalms 144 through 146. He went on to read from the section dedicated to Saint Andrew, explaining how he became one of Jesus' twelve disciples. The account took place in the Gospel of Matthew. Andrew and his brother, Simon Peter, were casting fishing nets into the Sea of Galilee when Jesus walked up. Lizzie was listening to the account of Jesus telling the men to follow Him and He would make them fishers of men when something grabbed her attention.

A stranger was sitting with Colonel Maurice Moore and his wife, who were on the other side of the room. With the Porters' parlor so crowded, she hadn't noticed him. His navy-blue jacket was a giveaway. He had to be Captain Ellis Brand. Something inside her lurched. The blonde-haired man had ordered her papa's death. It didn't matter if he was at Ocracoke or not. He and his officers worked together for the same purpose, determined to get rid of Black Beard. Hurt and anger gnawed at Lizzie as she clenched her fists and tightened her jaw. Trying not to show resentment, she attempted to calm herself.

Shifting her gaze in his direction, Lizzie could see Colonel Edward Moseley and Captain Jeremiah Vail sitting behind Captain Brand with their wives. The ladies were sisters to Mrs. Moore. Lizzie remembered Uncle Thomas saying the three brothers-in-law were deeply involved with Captain Brand, though his inquiries into the matter didn't uncover much. On Friday, Uncle Thomas visited Tobias Knight, but the sickly secretary didn't have anything to add. Even Governor Eden was trying to find out why Captain Brand was there.

Before Lizzie knew it, the Divine Service had ended. Realizing she hadn't been paying attention, she felt bad when Rebecca asked her why she was still on the bench. Jumping up, she tied her black, hooded cloak around her neck. Taking Hannah's hand, she followed her cousins and Jake out of the Porters' home. Once outside, the Worsley family mingled with friends despite the chilly air. Several men spoke to Uncle John, including Thomas Harding, Giles Shute, and the blacksmith, Collingswood Ward. Meanwhile, Uncle Thomas and Aunt Sarah took their little boys to see her family, the Bonners.

"Where did Mary go?" Aunt Charlotte asked.

"She told me Thomas was going to take her home," Aunt Grace responded. "I have a feeling she's going to break the news to him."

Aunt Charlotte shook her head sadly. Aunt Mary's decision to call off her wedding set for the fourth Saturday in December had affected the whole family. Since the episode with Pompey, she had made comments about her fiancé, Thomas Bustin, deserving someone better.

"I wish we could change her mind. Maybe Thomas can talk to her," Aunt Charlotte continued, stopping to wave at someone.

Looking across the yard, Lizzie spotted Aunt Charlotte's beau, John Barrow. He motioned for her to join him and his family.

"John wants me to come over. I shouldn't be long," she stated.

"Katherine Knight came with Mr. Chamberlayne. I'm going to ask her how Tobias is doing. Thomas said he was pretty sick on Friday," Aunt Grace proclaimed. "I'll be back in a few minutes."

The sisters zigzagged through the crowd, leaving the three girls with Lizzie, Trent, and Jake. As Lizzie watched Aunt Grace hug Mrs. Knight, she caught a glimpse of her grandfather, who was talking on the porch with Colonel Maurice Moore. It looked like Colonel Moore was introducing him to Captain Ellis Brand. Curious to know what they were saying, she turned when someone called her name. The brown-haired young man walking over was Miles Gale.

"Hello, Lizzie. It sure is a beautiful day."

"Yes, but it's windy," she muttered, gazing into the blue sky.

Out of the corner of her eye, Lizzie could see the curious looks on the faces of her cousins as they waited for Miles' response.

"Can we talk privately?" he requested.

"Why can't you talk in front of us?" Hannah questioned.

Lizzie felt her cheeks blush in embarrassment. The last thing she wanted was to be alone with Miles, but talking in front of her cousins and Jake could be just as bad. From the surprised look on Miles' face, she could tell he clearly didn't know how to answer Hannah.

"Let's give Lizzie time to talk to her friend," Jake suggested as he reached for Hannah's hand.

Stunned by Jake's words, Lizzie watched them walk to the wagon. As Miles moved closer, she saw Jake looking over his shoulder at her.

"Lizzie? Are you listening?"

Blinking, Lizzie stared at Miles. "I'm sorry. What did you say?"

"I asked if you wanted to go for a buggy ride tomorrow afternoon. We can pack a picnic and eat by the waterfront."

"No, I don't think so."

"What about going with me to next Sunday's Divine Service? I know it's a week away, but you promised to think about it," he urged.

"I need more time."

"Does this have anything to do with the sailor?"

Lizzie hesitated as she debated whether it was JJ holding her back instead of her papa's sudden death. "No, it's me."

Before Miles could continue, Grandfather walked up. Lizzie felt relieved as he shook Miles' hand.

"It's good to see you," he said. Turning to Lizzie he added, "Sorry to intrude on your conversation, dear, but we must be going."

"Sir, since Lizzie's father is out at sea making shipments, I would like to get your approval to court her."

Lizzie's jaw dropped as she struggled with her emotions, knowing her papa wasn't coming back. Grandfather raised his eyebrows.

"This is quite a surprise. Lizzie and I will have to talk about it."

"Thank you, sir. Good-bye, Lizzie."

Miles walked over to where his stepbrother, Thomas, was talking with their neighbor, William Sigley. Lizzie watched, still in disbelief.

"Miles seems to like you," Grandfather mentioned, "but with everything going on, I think you need to keep a low profile. We'll talk about this more later. We have a turkey waiting for us at home."

Following him, Lizzie was so deep in thought she didn't say much as she got into the wagon with Alice and Rebecca. Jake was helping Hannah climb in when John Martin came to speak to Grandfather.

"Mr. Worsley, we've decided to meet after dark at Tunnel Land in memory of the crew. Ye are welcome to join us since ye are Captain's family."

"Thanks for including us, but we shouldn't be secretly meeting."

"I understand. If ye change ye mind, we'll be gathering about an hour after the sun goes down. I also want to extend the offer to ye, Jake. Captain thought a lot of ye, and so did many of the others."

"I'll think about it. I assume no one told Israel," Jake hinted.

"Nay. As far as I'm concerned, he quit being a member of the crew the day he tried to take over the ship."

"Is JJ going?" Jake asked.

"Stephen's going to talk to him since we'll be remembering his father, too," John revealed, pausing to glance at Lizzie. "Miss Lizzie, we would be honored for ye to join us on behalf of ye father. I've got to go. Mother's waiting for me."

Dipping his tricorn hat, John Martin walked away. As they started for home, all Lizzie could think about was the memorial the pirates were planning. Although it was noble to remember their captain and crewmates, Grandfather had a point about it being dangerous. With Captain Brand in Bath, he was literally right across the water from Tunnel Land. Weren't they taking an unnecessary risk, especially since Edward, Stephen, and John had to leave town to attend?

When they pulled into Grandfather's yard, Lizzie still hadn't decided what to do. Pushing thoughts aside, she slid out of the wagon and followed her family inside the two-story house. Hanging her black, hooded cloak on the tall rack by the back door, she went into the kitchen. Aunt Charlotte and Aunt Mary were busy removing iron pots off the hooks suspended over the fireplace by a rod. Every Sunday the sisters cooked dinner prior to going to the Divine Service.

Lizzie helped her aunts scoop the food into bowls while Alice and Rebecca carried them to the table. Aunt Grace set the table with plates, cups, and eating utensils. The only thing that didn't make it to the table was the turkey. On the Saturday before the Day of Thanksgiving, Grandfather went with Uncle Thomas and Uncle John turkey hunting. This time, Trent got to go with them. They even invited Jake on the hunt, which ended with Trent shooting his first turkey.

Once everything was ready, the family gathered around the table. Grandfather sat at the end of the oak table while his oldest son, Thomas, sat at the other end. Everyone else found a place on the long benches lining either side. Sitting between Alice and Trent, Lizzie took their hands as they listened to Grandfather's blessing.

"Father God, thank You for this meal and for this family. We are thankful for all the blessings You have given us. Forgive us for our sins and guide us to do Your will. Bless this food for the nourishment of our bodies. We ask You to lift the burden on our hearts, Lord, for those who aren't with us today. All this we ask in the name of Your Son, our Lord and Savior, Jesus Christ. Amen."

Opening her eyes, Lizzie tried not to cry as she made eye contact with her grandfather. He smiled at her as he got up and went to the other side of the table. Leaning between Aunt Charlotte and Aunt Mary, he reached into his pocket and pulled out a match. Striking it on the table, he lit the candle in the center of the feast. Although they didn't use candles during the daylight, they did light one on the Day of Thanksgiving in remembrance of those who had gone to heaven.

"We light this candle in memory of Mary, Martha, Jared, the Griffin family, and Edward," Grandfather proclaimed.

Lizzie wiped her eyes when she heard her parents' names as well as her grandmother's and uncle's. He even thought to add Jake's family. Grandfather sat at the head of the table as Hannah asked what Mr. Gale meant when he talked about the Lord using a candle to search the insides of their bellies. Her question was serious, but her view of it made the adults chuckle. Grandfather clarified what the Bible verse meant. The book of Proverbs described the spirit of man to be like a candle of the Lord, searching the inward parts of the belly. As Lizzie listened, she thought about another similarity. Like a flame, a person's life was fragile. In a blink of an eye, it could be gone.

"God sees and knows all, Hannah. Now, let's start this wonderful meal. John, will you please bring in the bird?" Grandfather requested.

"Me?" Uncle John blurted out as he looked at his older brother, who usually brought in the turkey on special occasions.

"Yes, you. Go get it, John," Uncle Thomas spoke up.

Glancing at his father, Uncle John went to the kitchen. He returned carrying the golden-brown turkey. Everyone clapped as he placed the silver platter down in front of Grandfather.

"Before I carve this bird, I would like to say how proud I am of Trent and his first turkey. I know your father would be proud, too. You get the first slice. Pass me your plate," Grandfather declared.

Jake handed him Trent's plate as Aunt Grace got up to give her son a hug. Seeing how emotional her aunt was, Lizzie turned away to wipe her eyes. Thankfully, Jake got everyone's mind on something else as he encouraged Trent to tell them about the bear tracks they found while hunting. Soon they were laughing as Trent recounted how he stumbled upon the tom turkey, which wore a long, stringy beard. Eventually, the conversation came back to the bear.

"Is he a big bear?" Hannah wanted to know.

"We didn't actually see the bear," Uncle Thomas told his niece.

"Too bad we didn't," Uncle John commented. "It would be nice to know what we might be dealing with. Maybe we should go back next week. Surely there's some manure piles nearby."

"Judging by its paw prints I'd say the bear is about four hundred pounds. There might be more in the area," Jake informed them.

"Four hundred pounds, huh?" Uncle Thomas responded.

"Can you believe all Jake has to do is look at a paw print? I'm hoping he can teach me how to do it before next week when we take the Plott hounds rabbit hunting," Trent stated excitedly.

Jake explained how he learned about animal tracks while hunting with Red Wolf on Ocracoke. He answered questions about Red Wolf and White Feathers, but Lizzie was no longer listening. If the crew had been in battle with the Royal Navy, then there was a chance Red Wolf and White Feathers heard cannon fire or gunshots. They may have even seen the battle. The more Lizzie thought about it, the more she yearned to talk to White Feathers and Red Wolf. She tried to put her desire to return to Ocracoke Island out of her mind, but it was useless. Until she knew the details of what happened, her spirit would not rest. Still, the dangers of going to Ocracoke were too great. All she could do was wait for the Royal Navy to go back to Virginia. Since Captain Ellis Brand was expecting his comrade, Lieutenant Robert Maynard, to arrive in Bath, it was doubtful they would be leaving anytime soon.

Before long, the men retired to the parlor while the ladies cleared the dishes. Lizzie picked up several plates when Hannah spoke up.

"Can we go outside and play hide-and-seek, Momma?"

Aunt Grace smiled. "Yes, dear, but please be careful not to tear your dresses, and don't forget your cloaks. It's chilly out there."

"Did you hear what Momma said, Trent? Don't tear your dress!" Hannah teased her big brother as Alice and Rebecca giggled.

Trent stuck his tongue out at her. "Ha, ha. Very funny."

Heading for the door, Alice, Rebecca, and Hannah put on their cloaks while Trent slid on his coat. Jake went with them, pausing to get his coat off the rack. Lizzie stayed to help her aunts clear the table. Once the dirty bowls, plates, and cups were in the kitchen, Aunt Mary rolled up her sleeves to start scrubbing them in a wooden washtub of soapy water. With Aunt Grace drying the clean plates and Aunt Charlotte stacking them in the cabinet, there wasn't much for Lizzie to do. Even Aunt Sarah was busy with her two little boys.

"We've got this covered, Lizzie, if you want to rest awhile. I know this has been an emotional day for you," Aunt Grace acknowledged.

"If you don't need me, I think I'll go sit on the porch."

"Okay. I'll join you in a little bit," Aunt Grace promised.

Leaving the kitchen, Lizzie grabbed her black, hooded cloak off the rack and opened the back door. Wrapping the cloak around her, she was surprised to find Jake sitting in a rocking chair whittling.

"You aren't helping your aunts in the kitchen?" Jake inquired.

"They didn't need me," she said as she sat down and watched him shape the small object with his knife. "What are you making?"

"A whistle for John. I've already made Little Thomas and Hannah one. Don't tell them. It's a secret. I hope they'll like them."

"They will, but Aunt Grace and Aunt Sarah might not," she joked.

Jake grinned. "These may get me in trouble."

Rocking back and forth, Lizzie thought about the memorial. She felt she should go, but convincing her family would be hard.

"Are you going to the memorial service?" she asked Jake.

"I feel like I should. After spending so much time with the crew, I sort of owe it to them to pay my respects. How about you?"

"I'm not sure. I want to do something to remember Papa. We can't have a funeral with his body at Ocracoke. I can't even wear the traditional black clothing to show I'm mourning. Grandfather didn't think it was a good idea to go to the memorial."

"Just because they're not going doesn't mean you can't," he reminded her as the back door squeaked open.

Aunt Grace came out of the house, followed by Aunt Mary and Aunt Sarah, who was carrying John in her arms. Lizzie could hear Little Thomas hollering as Aunt Charlotte tried to put his coat on.

Moments later, the two of them came outside, both looking flustered. Jake got up and offered his chair to Aunt Grace, saying he was going to play hide-and-seek with the children. Sliding the whistle in his pocket, he put his knife in its leather sheath and handed it to Lizzie.

"Wait for me! I want to hide!" Little Thomas exclaimed, slipping away from Aunt Charlotte's grasp.

Reacting quickly, Jake scooped up the three-year-old before he could get far. He spun the little boy in the air, making him laugh.

"Look, Momma! I'm flying like a birdie!" he giggled.

"I see," Aunt Sarah responded as Jake brought her son back.

"No!" Little Thomas objected when Jake tried to put him down.

The toddler held on, refusing to let go as he begged his mother to let him play. Although she was reluctant, Aunt Sarah finally gave in after Jake promised to keep an eye on him. Happy to be going with Jake, Little Thomas held his hand as they went to find the others. Seeing his big brother leaving, John started to cry. The twenty-two-month-old calmed down as Aunt Charlotte picked him up. Sitting on the stairs, she bounced the toddler on her lap, pretending he was riding a horse. Lizzie moved to the stairs so that she could play with him, too. Meanwhile, her aunts chatted about Aunt Mary and Thomas' choice to postpone the wedding until spring instead of canceling it.

With all the talk about the new wedding plans, the afternoon went by quickly. Soon the sun was sinking beyond the trees. Aunt Sarah was the first to mention something about heading home as she looked down at her youngest son fast asleep in Lizzie's arms.

"I think I'm going with Jake to the memorial," Lizzie announced.

Aunt Grace exchanged looks of concern with her sisters and sister-in-law. "I don't know if you should go."

"It's Papa's memorial, Aunt Grace. I need to do this."

"We can do a service for him after things settle down. Don't you want to wait for Susannah to get here?" Aunt Grace urged.

"Tonight's different. It's hard to explain how close Papa was to his crew. They were like a family in a way. I feel like it's important for me to be there to represent my father. I'll be okay with Jake."

Aunt Grace didn't object, but she was clearly against it. As they all went inside, Lizzie thought of words to convince Grandfather. Coming into the parlor, she could smell the tobacco smoke drifting from Grandfather's clay pipe. His cheerful greeting gave her hope until Aunt Grace told him about her plans. Rubbing his chin, he glanced at Uncle Thomas and Uncle John, who were sitting nearby. Sensing the tension in the air, Thomas Bustin announced he was leaving. Aunt Mary walked him to the door as Grandfather spoke.

"After meeting Brand, I feel you shouldn't go to this memorial."

"We'll be fine, Grandfather. It will be dark. No one will see us."

"I still don't agree, but you're determined to go. Where's Jake?"

"He's outside with the children," Aunt Grace reported.

"Alright, I'll go talk with him. You can use my carriage."

Following him down the hallway, Lizzie was almost to the dining table when Aunt Grace stopped her to give her a hug. Promising to be careful, Lizzie headed out the door and walked to the shed behind the barn. Grandfather was hitching Whitey to the carriage while Jake untangled the reins. Approaching the white horse, Lizzie rubbed her forehead. Whitey nudged Lizzie's face with her pink muzzle.

"Take Lizzie home as soon as this thing's over, Jake. I don't want her out late tonight," Grandfather instructed.

"Yes, sir," Jake answered as he climbed into the carriage.

"I'll be fine, Grandfather," Lizzie added.

Helping her get in, Grandfather gave her hand a squeeze. He said good-bye to Jake, who promised to bring his carriage back in the morning. Jake flicked the reins to get Whitey started on their journey. With the sun disappearing, the temperature was dropping. The chilly air caused Lizzie to pull her cloak tighter to stay warm. She looked up at the deep purple sky. Even though it wasn't dark enough to make out the first appearing stars, she could see a sliver of the moon above the treetops. It reminded her of the night Cookie and JJ brought them home—the night her papa shot Israel Hands.

Fidgeting with the hem of her cloak, Lizzie considered sharing the burden on her heart. They had crossed Glebe Creek and passed the dock in front of their house when she decided to talk.

"Jake, there's something bothering me. Do you think we should tell Grandfather and Aunt Grace about the French ships? We weren't involved in taking the ships, but we were there."

"Why do you want to tell them now? When we got back to Bath, we agreed to leave some of the details a secret."

"Everything's different with Captain Brand in town. Papa had to come to the hearing Tobias set up for the French ship, remember? He told me there were some men at the hearing who heard Governor Eden order Papa to pay a tax to the government with the sugar. The people of Bath don't know we're connected, but Israel does."

Jake took a deep breath. "Maybe you're right. They should at least know we were mixed up in an act of piracy."

The glow of lanterns shone up ahead, signaling they were nearing the mansion at Tunnel Land. Although it was getting too dark to see, Lizzie could make out several horses tied to the hitching post in front of the house. A group of men had gathered by the base of the stairs. Jake pulled the reins to make Whitey stop. Getting out of the carriage, he helped Lizzie down. In the lantern light, she recognized John Martin, Stephen Daniel, John Giles, and Edward Salter. They stopped talking when Jake and Lizzie walked up.

"Glad ye decided to join us," John Martin greeted them.

"Hope we aren't late," Jake hinted.

"Nay, we're waiting for Stephen Elsey to get his candles. We've all been saving our burned-down candles to use for the memorial."

"Did JJ come?" Lizzie questioned, glancing at Jake.

"He's down by the dock," Stephen Daniel reported.

Knowing she needed to speak to him, Lizzie left Jake with the pirates. Guided by the candlelight from the lanterns, she made her way to the waterfront past a wooden table. She spotted JJ on the dock staring at the water. Inhaling a shaky breath, she stepped onto the boards thinking about waving to her papa from this very spot.

"JJ," she murmured softly, grabbing his attention.

Turning around, JJ stared at her for a moment. Even in the dim light, she could see the hurt look on his face as he stepped closer.

"I'm so sorry for ye loss, Lizzie. I know how empty ye feel."

Lizzie's heart broke as he lost his composure. Burying his face in his hand, JJ attempted to pull himself together, but he couldn't keep the tears at bay. Wiping tears from her cheeks, Lizzie gave him a hug. Someone cleared his throat, causing JJ to pull away from her.

"Jake, I'm glad ye and Lizzie came tonight," JJ commented.

Feeling awkward, Lizzie crossed her arms as she peered up at Jake. His questioning gaze made her even more uncomfortable.

"They're getting ready to start the ceremony," Jake informed them.

Leaving the dock, JJ and Lizzie followed Jake to the table set up by the waterfront as the five pirates joined them. John Martin pulled out items from a bucket and placed them on the table. Lizzie could hardly believe it when she realized they were dried corncobs cut in halves to resemble little boats. He put a nearly burned-down candle in each hole cut in the top of the corncobs. There were eighteen, one for each member of the crew.

"I'm going to call out a name and light one of these candles. Each of ye can take the corncob boats down to the dock. After ye put them in the water, come back for the next one," John Martin instructed as he reached for a long candle and opened one of the lanterns.

Something nagged at Lizzie's soul. She recalled Cookie being upset about the way Vane's crew buried Big Reuben and Shorty at Ocracoke. Finding the courage to speak, she stopped the ceremony.

"Excuse me, can I say something? Cookie told me every man deserved to have a few words spoken before he's put to rest. Can you say a few words before you light the candles?"

JJ spoke up, saying he heard Cookie say something similar. After getting everyone's approval, John agreed to give the crew a proper send-off. Everyone listened as he talked about the crew, comparing them to a brotherhood. He spoke of sweaty workdays filled with chores and nights of drunken merriment. Ending his speech, he added a short prayer. Lizzie wasn't sure who was more surprised, her or the pirates. John lit the candles and called the first six names. John Giles carried the first corncob, followed by Stephen Daniel, Edward Salter, Stephen Elsey, JJ, and finally Jake. Lizzie watched them take the candles to the dock and put them in the water. On the next round, Jake carried Cookie's candle. When the third came, John asked Lizzie to carry the last corncob belonging to Captain Black Beard.

Hearing what John said, Lizzie became nervous. She wanted to represent her papa, but she also didn't think she could go alone. Fighting tears, she looked at Jake, who was waiting beside her, while JJ led the third group to the dock carrying his father's candle.

"I don't think I can do this, Jake. Can you go with me?"

Jake hesitated. "Maybe you should ask JJ."

"Please help me get through this."

By now, the five pirates were back. They stood in a semicircle as John called her up. Glancing at Jake, she was relieved when he nodded, agreeing to go with her. Taking a deep breath, she stepped forward while John lit the candle and placed the corncob in her hands.

The walk to the dock was emotional. Although she barely saw where she was going through her tears, she made it to the dock without falling. Jake stayed close behind, giving her the strength to keep going. Eventually, she came to the end of the dock. Crouching on her knees, she placed the corncob in the water. Overwhelmed with sadness, she cried as her fingers dipped into the creek.

With her eyes on her papa's flickering candle, she whispered into the chilly night air. "I love you, Papa."

Looking at the water, she watched the eighteen candles drifting down the creek. One by one, they started to burn out until her papa's candle was the only one remaining. At last, the flickering candlelight extinguished, sending them into darkness. It was a fitting symbol for the life quenched too soon, the life of Black Beard the pirate.

CHAPTER TWENTY-SEVEN

☠

CIRCLING BUZZARDS

December 6, 1718 ~ Saturday

December arrived without much notice for the residents of Bath Town. Little did they know as they prepared for winter that serious things were happening right under their noses. Unlike many families in the community, the Worsley family had been paying attention. In fact, it was Uncle Thomas who uncovered some valuable information about Governor Charles Eden and Tobias Knight.

Over the last week, Uncle Thomas had gone to Tobias' house twice, hoping to hear news of when Lieutenant Robert Maynard was due to reach Bath. Although he didn't have anything new to report, Tobias did talk about Captain Ellis Brand's inquiries in town. The rumor was that Captain Brand had some very interesting conversations with several people who didn't like either Tobias or Governor Eden.

A man named William Bell also talked to Brand. Tobias guessed that Bell, who lived outside of town, came to tell Brand the same story he told Tobias and Governor Eden in mid-September when he filed an official Hue and Cry. In the warrant, Bell claimed a bearded rogue attacked and robbed him. Lizzie figured this was how her papa came into possession of the chest of goods he supposedly bought, which included the special silver cup. It also explained his broken cutlass.

Uncle Thomas stumbled upon some other disturbing news the day before when he checked in with Tobias again. Due to the strange happenings, Secretary Knight decided to write a letter to Governor Eden. His house guest, Edmund Chamberlayne, delivered the letter to Eden, who added his own questions to the bottom of the document. He sent it by messenger to his friend and trusted adviser Colonel Thomas Pollock, of the Chowan Precinct. They were waiting to hear from the former governor as to what triggered the government of Virginia to intrude into the Carolina territory.

It was unusual for the Virginia government to ignore the Carolina authorities by sending their Royal Navy in a two-pronged attack. From what Lizzie understood, they never should've crossed the Virginia line to hunt down her papa, even if he was a pirate with a high bounty on him. Virginia's lieutenant governor, Alexander Spotswood, seemed to be the one behind it. He promised to pay a bounty of a hundred pounds for Black Beard and various amounts for the other pirates depending on their skills. Making matters worse, Spotswood failed to alert Governor Eden or anyone else, which suggested the group wasn't there just to catch Black Beard. Their other, less obvious goal was to challenge Eden.

While Tobias was bringing Uncle Thomas up to date in his study, his house slave alerted him that he had visitors from town. Telling his slave to let them in, both he and Uncle Thomas were speechless when Captain Ellis Brand walked in with Colonel Maurice Moore, Captain Jeremiah Vail, and several other men. Uncle Thomas departed, acting as if he came to check on Tobias' health. On his way out, he heard Brand questioning him about a load of sugar supposedly left behind by the pirate, Captain Black Beard. Tobias denied knowing anything about it even after Brand mentioned finding sixty casks of sugar in a barn on Governor Eden's property in town.

This concerned Uncle Thomas, who had no idea his brother-in-law had delivered sugar to Tobias' place. Naturally, he asked Lizzie and Jake about the matter. Having already told Uncle Thomas, Grandfather, Uncle John, and Aunt Grace about the stolen French ship earlier in the week, they reluctantly explained the situation further. They also told them about Israel's attempts to take over the ship and the weeklong pirate banyan with Captain Charles Vane's crew.

Knowing how serious things could get, Grandfather suggested that Jake avoid Israel Hands and not go to town unless he had to. Lizzie couldn't go until Captain Brand left Bath. Furthermore, Grandfather recommended they both limit their time with the former pirates. This had been hard since JJ seemed to be spending more time at their house. Luckily, neither Grandfather nor Uncle Thomas considered his presence to be as much of an issue as some of the other pirates.

Lizzie had grown used to having JJ around. He had helped Jake and Trent put wheat straw and dried corn in the barns for the livestock to eat during the winter. Aunt Grace even asked him to stay for supper on Wednesday and baked him an apple pie for his eighteenth birthday. While he was grateful for the birthday meal, he was particularly happy when Lizzie agreed to have a picnic with him on Thursday. Since it was his birthday when he asked her, she felt obligated. The picnic turned out to be better than she thought, and it kept her from being home when Miles Gale came by. JJ wanted to take her on a carriage ride today, but John Martin needed help hauling brand-new barrels he purchased from the cooper back to his mother's house.

With the livestock's food stored away, Jake and Trent went hunting that morning with Grandfather, Uncle John, and Uncle Thomas. They decided to take the Plott hounds back to the spot Trent and Jake saw the bear tracks. Grandfather invited Thomas Bustin to go, but his family was having a gathering at their home. Since he and Aunt Mary were spending the day with his family, it gave the Worsley girls the opportunity to start Aunt Mary's wedding quilt.

For most of the morning, Lizzie, Alice, and Rebecca assisted Aunt Grace, Aunt Charlotte, and Aunt Sarah in setting up the quilting loom. After rearranging the parlor furniture, they finally put the loom together. It was a family heirloom, passed down from Grandmother Worsley's own grandmother. Wedding quilts were special since every girl in the family worked on them. As the bride-to-be, Aunt Mary would receive the quilt on the day of her wedding. Twelve-year-old Alice and ten-year-old Rebecca were thrilled to be helping with their first quilt. Although Lizzie had participated in a quilting, she hadn't experienced making a wedding quilt, which excited her, too.

Thankfully, Hannah kept John and Little Thomas busy so that the toddlers wouldn't bother the women and girls while they worked. Aunt Grace even allowed Hannah to bring Tuffy downstairs so that the little boys could play with her. Occasionally, Lizzie glanced over her shoulder at the boys, who took turns dragging a piece of yarn for Tuffy to attack. The cat purred happily as she tried to capture the yarn.

By dinner, the quilt was off to a good start, though their progress slowed when Aunt Grace stopped to prepare the deer stew. She had just announced it was ready when the men returned from their hunt. To Lizzie's amazement, they not only shot eleven rabbits but also came across the bear. As the family sat at the table eating the stew of potatoes, carrots, mushrooms, onions, and deer meat, Grandfather told them how they tracked and killed the four-hundred-pound beast.

Trent and Uncle John added details while Uncle Thomas tried to get his three-year-old to eat the deer stew. Despite his efforts, Little Thomas refused to eat the deer meat. Aunt Sarah didn't have any trouble getting John to eat. Looking down the table, Lizzie noticed Jake staring at his food. Although he was eating, he played with his spoon between bites. His strange behavior triggered her to remember how odd he had been acting. She caught him and JJ in a heated discussion late yesterday afternoon before JJ left in a huff. Knowing they had just heard the news Uncle Thomas had brought from Tobias' house, she assumed the conversation was about Captain Brand.

Soon they had eaten dinner and were ready to get back to work. Everyone took their empty bowls to the kitchen. They then put on their coats to go see the bear before the men skinned it and butchered the meat. Excited to see a bear up close, Lizzie hurriedly slid her arms into the sleeves of her work jacket as she followed her cousins outside. Stepping out on the back porch, she heard Killer's barking.

Killer went to meet the visitor, barking loudly as she swished her little white tail. The brown and white dog chased the carriage all the way to the yard. Once the carriage was closer, Lizzie was able to see a woman at the reins. It was her papa's younger sister, Susannah Beard Franck. Getting emotional, Lizzie wiped tears from her eyes as she ran to meet her aunt and the three young children with her. Pulling on the reins to get their black and gray horse to stop, Aunt Susannah stepped down from the carriage to give her niece a hug. Holding each other, the two of them wept tears of sadness.

"I'm so sorry, Lizzie. I wish I was here when you got the news of Edward's death," she mumbled, wiping tears from her own cheeks. "Edward loved you very much. I can't believe he's gone."

"He loved you, too, Aunt Susannah."

"Welcome back, Susannah. We're glad to have you, though not under these circumstances," Grandfather spoke up.

Turning around, Lizzie realized her mother's family had gathered to greet them. After receiving hugs from everyone, Aunt Susannah met Jake, whom she remembered from years ago. While they caught up on news, Grandfather and Uncle Thomas helped six-year-old Edward, four-year-old Mary, and two-year-old Elizabeth get down from the carriage. Squeezing Lizzie, they excitedly told her about their traveling adventure. Lizzie knew from experience how difficult the journey was from their Neuse River plantation on Beard's Creek to Bath.

"I'm surprised you came without Martin," Aunt Grace mentioned to Aunt Susannah as they walked to the barn to see the bear.

"I came as soon as I received your letter about Edward's death. Martin had some business in New Bern. He hopes to join us during the week of Christmas," Aunt Susannah explained.

"So, you're staying for three weeks?" Lizzie blurted out.

"Yes," she answered, suddenly looking at Aunt Grace. "We might be able to stay with my stepmother's family at Romney Marsh even if it is a good distance from Bath Town."

"Nonsense," Aunt Grace told her. "You're always welcome to stay here."

"Thank you. I appreciate your hospitality on such short notice."

By now, they were behind the barn where the men left the rabbits and the bear. Buzzards had already picked up the scent of the dead animals and were circling overhead. Unlike other birds, they hardly flapped their wings as they soared gracefully through the air. Lizzie marveled at how they detected animal scents from so far away.

"Wow! He's big!" Hannah exclaimed when she saw the bear.

Everyone admired the beautiful creature on the butchering table. The shiny, black fur coat looked so soft as Grandfather lifted the bear's head. Even though she was still struggling with God over her papa's death, Lizzie had to admit God was an awesome Creator.

Leaving the men to skin the animals and prepare the meat for the smokehouse, the women and children headed back to the house. They were halfway to the porch when a horse and rider came racing into the yard while Killer barked. Hearing the dog, Grandfather came around the barn with Uncle Thomas, Uncle John, Trent, and Jake.

"Where's the attorney Thomas Worsley, ma'am? I was sent to find him," the short, blonde-haired man asked Aunt Grace.

Although she hadn't seen him much, Lizzie recognized the man as their next-door neighbor, Stephen Elsey. The former pirate was in a tizzy, which sparked her interest. His appearance concerned Aunt Grace, who told Alice to take the younger children in the house.

"I'm right here. Who sent you?"

"JJ Brooks. He's in trouble. They all are," Stephen proclaimed.

"What do you mean?" Jake inquired. "Is JJ hurt?"

"Not yet, but who knows what those scavengers will do? I went to town to drink brandy with John Giles. There was a ruckus down by the dock. Most people stayed in their homes, but ones like John Porter, Thomas Harding, Edmund Porter, Giles Shute, and Governor Eden were there. Maurice Moore and Jeremiah Vail went, too. By the time I got through the crowd, that Brand was shaking hands with Lieutenant Maynard. John Giles and Israel Hands were standing near Brand with their hands in chains," Stephen declared.

"Did you say Maynard is here?" Grandfather wanted to know.

"Aye. He brought four men with him. I heard Maynard tell Governor Eden his crew anchored Black Beard's ship at the mouth of Bath Town Creek. He claims to have evidence against Tobias Knight. Brand ordered the officers to arrest Edward Salter and Stephen Daniel. When Brand discovered John Martin and JJ Brooks purchasing barrels at the cooper's shed, he had them arrested, too. John Martin spotted me and asked me to tell his brother what was happening. JJ told me to find Thomas Worsley. I assumed he meant the attorney."

"I don't know what I can do. It's unlikely they'll let me see them. They were probably arrested for piracy," Uncle Thomas responded.

"I thought the same thing, but Brand didn't arrest me. Maybe I'm no longer considered a pirate since I've been in the colony longer than the others. He talked to Israel at some point because

Israel was protesting his arrest, saying Brand cheated him. They're heading for the *Adventure* in chains to join the rest of them. Once they drop them off, Brand and Maynard are planning to visit Tobias with evidence."

"What do you mean by 'the rest of them'?" Jake questioned.

"Apparently, some of the crew are alive. Maynard didn't give any names, but he told Brand nine men had been interrogated."

Lizzie's heart beat faster. "So, there were survivors?"

"Aye, but ten men still lost their lives. Brand asked Maynard if he was sure Black Beard was dead. Maynard said he fought with Captain himself and had just hung the proof on the bowsprit of the *Adventure*."

"What kind of proof could possibly be hanging from the front of the ship?" Uncle John persisted, skeptically.

"Captain's severed head."

Gasping in horror at the thought of her papa's head swinging from his own ship, Lizzie collapsed to the ground. When she finally woke up, she found herself stretched out on her bed. As the details of what happened came flooding back, she started to cry. Sitting up slowly, Lizzie saw Aunt Susannah seated by her feet.

"Are you alright, dear?" Aunt Grace asked as she stood over her.

"You gave us quite a scare," Aunt Susannah remarked.

"I was upset hearing what they did t—to Papa," she stammered.

A knock on the door broke the silence. Aunt Susannah stood and went to open it. Lizzie saw her grandfather in the hallway.

"Is she okay?" he urged.

Aunt Susannah opened the door for him. "She just woke up."

Walking to the bed, Grandfather reached down to kiss the top of Lizzie's head. "I'm so glad you're all right. You scared us. Grace, I was just coming to see Lizzie before we left."

Aunt Grace looked surprised. "Where are you going?"

"Thomas, John, and I are going to Tobias Knight's place."

"Don't you think it's dangerous to be at Tobias' house when Mr. Brand and Mr. Maynard arrive?" Aunt Grace pointed out.

"We're not going to get close. Thomas thinks Maynard has some major evidence on Tobias since Brand was there yesterday. William Martin is going with us. His mother told him Stephen Elsey dropped in with bad news, so he came over here looking for him. He said several men from town are rowing to Tobias' place to see the ship."

"I'm going, too," Lizzie announced. "I have to be sure it's him."

"You don't need to see it," Aunt Grace protested.

Surprisingly, Aunt Susannah spoke up. "I feel the need to go myself. If Lizzie wants to go, I'll take her."

Aunt Grace took a deep breath. "I guess Charlotte and Sarah can look after the children while we're gone."

"You don't have to go, Grace," Grandfather told her.

"If Lizzie's going, I'm going."

Slowly nodding, Grandfather led the way downstairs. As they entered the kitchen, Lizzie put on her cloak while Aunt Grace went to tell Aunt Charlotte and Aunt Sarah where they were going. When she returned, Trent begged to go with them. After much discussion, his mother finally agreed to let him go. Once outside, Lizzie clambered into the back of Aunt Susannah's carriage. Grandfather offered to direct the horse, allowing Aunt Susannah to ride with Lizzie. Aunt Grace climbed in beside her father while Uncle Thomas, Uncle John, Trent, and Jake mounted the horses they rode during their hunt. William Martin and Stephen Elsey joined them as they started down the dirt path to the Knight plantation.

Before long, they crossed the line onto Stephen Elsey's property. Keeping a steady pace, they continued to the Knight plantation, which bordered Tunnel Land. They stopped short of the main yard, choosing to walk the rest of the way. As they walked to the waterfront, Lizzie thought about what would happen to JJ and the others. She also considered if maybe his father or Cookie survived.

Coming to the waterfront, Lizzie saw men standing near the water's edge taking turns looking through a spyglass. Most arrived on periaugers, but some came by horseback. All their attention seemed fixated on the *Adventure* anchored in the center of Bath Town Creek. Staring beyond them, Lizzie spotted boats scattered around the *Adventure*. Above the ship, buzzards circled the bow where an object was swinging in the breeze. It was too far to make out details, but Lizzie didn't need a spyglass to recognize the familiar black beard for which her beloved papa was famous.

Turning from the repulsive scene, Lizzie hugged Aunt Susannah as they cried in each other's arms. Why was her papa displayed like this? Wasn't it enough for them to kill him? Must they hang his head on the ship like a trophy? Anger surged through Lizzie's spirit at the thought of what Maynard and his men did to her papa. Stephen was right; these men were scavengers.

"There's trouble at the Knight home," Stephen pointed out. "Looks like both Brand and Maynard are getting kicked out."

Letting go of Aunt Susannah, Lizzie noticed several men coming out of Secretary Knight's house. Two of the men on the porch wore Royal Navy uniforms. Knowing the blonde-haired officer was Brand, she assumed the other was Lieutenant Maynard. The lieutenant held up a black, leather-bound book as Mrs. Katherine Knight thrust her straw broom at him, angrily forcing the men out of her home.

"How dare you come into my house claiming my husband is a liar while he's sick with marsh fever! I don't care who you are or how you rank in Virginia, but around here Governor Eden is in charge. Just wait until he hears about you calling Tobias a liar," Mrs. Knight yelled, grabbing the attention of several servants and young Scripo.

"We have evidence of your husband's dealings with Captain Edward Teach, otherwise known as Black Beard. Mr. Knight lied to me yesterday. He swore he didn't know about any stolen barrels of sugar and insisted Captain Teach was a reformed pirate who wanted to retire. Governor Eden claims the sugar we found on his property was a tax payment. As tax collector, Mr. Knight should've handled it," Captain Brand persisted.

"There you go again accusing my husband," Mrs. Knight shouted as she jabbed her straw broom at the men.

Captain Brand jumped back to avoid the broom. "Are you going to stand in the way of justice? I can have you arrested for defying the Royal Navy and refusing to allow us to search the premises."

Mrs. Knight's jaw dropped. "Is that a threat?"

"Just let them search the property, Katherine."

A frail man exited the house leaning on his wooden cane. Lizzie could hardly believe it was Tobias Knight. His skin was pale against his white nightclothes, but his face had flushed red in his apparent anger.

"Don't threaten my wife. You can find what you're looking for in my barn. Captain Teach asked to use it as storage until he came back. As far as I knew, Captain Teach was heading to the Caribbean for the winter and had acquired the sugar legitimately. From what little I know about him, he served as a privateer and only in the last two years was a pirate. He took the king's pardon in July. You can confirm it with Governor Eden. He signed the papers," Tobias insisted.

"We know who signed Black Beard's pardon. It was in his desk drawer with his personal pocketbook, which paints a different version of your story. Black Beard wrote a lot about you," Lieutenant Maynard revealed, holding up the leather-bound journal.

Lizzie glanced at Jake, realizing how serious the situation was. There was no telling how many secrets Black Beard had written in his pocketbook diary. Tobias Knight was in it, but were they?

"His pocketbook? Let me see it," Tobias demanded as he reached for the diary.

Maynard yanked it back as he chuckled in amusement. "Let you see it? Over my dead body!"

"Don't offend him, Lieutenant. We have permission to search the grounds. Let's see what we find," Brand stated. "Sorry for the inconvenience, Mrs. Knight."

"I bet you're sorry," Mrs. Knight spat, going back inside.

As the Royal Navy officers made their way to the barn, Grandfather suggested they go home. Following him, they trudged back to the carriage. Jake, Trent, and Uncle John went with them, but Uncle Thomas chose to stay with Stephen and William Martin. Leaving the horrible scene, Lizzie was glad when they reached the carriage. She couldn't get the picture of her papa's severed head out of her mind as they headed home. When they arrived, Lizzie walked into the house behind her aunts. Aunt Grace filled in Aunt Sarah and Aunt Charlotte on the events at the Knight plantation. Exhausted, Lizzie had just taken off her cloak when she noticed Jake standing in the kitchen doorway motioning for her. Wondering what he wanted, she left the parlor.

"You know that sack of gold your papa gave me before he left? Well, it's hidden on a ledge in the outhouse. You can't find it unless you stand on the wooden seat."

"Why are you telling me this?"

"I don't know what's going to happen. Someone needs to know where my money is, just in case. All my money is in the sack. Who knows what's in Black Beard's journal? He gave me the paper I signed, but I don't know if he wrote my name anywhere else. The paper is in the sack, too, by the way."

The back door opened as Trent walked in wearing a strange look. "Uh, ...Jake, the Royal Navy is here wanting to talk to you."

Lizzie felt light-headed. "What are you going to do?"

"I'll have to go out there," Jake said, heading for the back door.

As soon as it closed behind him, Lizzie turned to Trent. "Go tell your momma what's happening. I'm going outside, too."

Trent took off as Lizzie grabbed her work coat and went out on the porch. Lieutenant Maynard and three more men were talking to

Jake and Grandfather by the old, leafless pecan tree. In the distance, she spotted Uncle John as his horse galloped down the dirt road. She figured he was heading to Tobias' house to find Uncle Thomas.

"Are you Jake Griffin?" Maynard wanted to know.

"Yes, sir."

"I'm Lieutenant Robert Maynard of the Royal Navy. It has come to the attention of my commanding officer, Captain Ellis Brand, you were involved with Captain Edward Teach, alias Black Beard."

"Are you insinuating he's a pirate?" Grandfather demanded.

"Not yet, but we have a statement saying Jake Griffin and his sister were hostages on Black Beard's ship from mid-July to the end of October. If this is true, then he was there when Black Beard's crew captured two French ships. I've been ordered to arrest Mr. Griffin and take him to the *Adventure* for questioning," Maynard stated.

"Arrest me?" Jake exclaimed.

"If you refuse, you will be charged with resisting arrest. It's in your best interest to come with us. Captain Brand also wants to speak with your sister. I was told you both lived here," Maynard proclaimed.

Lizzie tried to duck inside as he looked at the house, but it was too late. Maynard had spotted her. Thankfully, Aunt Grace and Aunt Susannah came out as Maynard was walking up to the porch.

"Miss? By any chance are you this lad's sister, Lizzie?"

"Jake's not your brother," Aunt Grace whispered to Lizzie.

"It's a long story. Just go with it," she softly muttered back.

It appeared that Maynard was coming up on the porch but changed his mind when Grandfather gave him a nasty look. He had a wound across his forehead and a bandage on his left hand, obvious injuries from his encounter with her papa.

"The pirates mentioned a girl named Miss Lizzie. Are you her?"

Lizzie recalled Israel talking to Calico Jack about her and Jake. He assumed they were brother and sister, held hostage by Black Beard for a ransom.

"Yes, I'm Lizzie."

"Both of you must come with me. Let's go."

"Why do they have to go with you?" Grandfather inquired.

Maynard appeared irritated. "They have to tell us what they know about the pirates. Brand is waiting for us on the *Adventure*."

"My granddaughter isn't going anywhere," Grandfather objected.

"They *will* have to come or face charges of resisting arrest. She won't be restrained, but I have orders to shackle Mr. Griffin."

"If you insist, then I'm going also," Grandfather informed him.

Although Lieutenant Maynard was clearly upset with Grandfather going with them, he didn't protest as he ordered his men to arrest Jake. Lizzie watched the three battle-scarred men chain Jake's wrists. Giving her aunts a hug, she joined her grandfather as they followed Maynard to the dock. Jake walked behind them with the officers.

Once at the dock, Maynard climbed into the waiting periauger. Sitting down in the front of the periauger, Lizzie made room for Grandfather while the officers helped Jake. The men untied the rope holding the boat to the dock and began to row toward the *Adventure*. Gazing at Jake, who was sitting with his chained hands in his lap, Lizzie tried not to cry. She was thankful to have her grandfather with her, but what could he do besides offer comfort? Even Uncle Thomas had doubts as to what he could legally do to help JJ and John Martin. Would he be able to get her and Jake released?

Soon, they were near enough to the *Adventure* that Lizzie could see the sails and rigging crisscrossing above the deck. Overhead, the growing number of buzzards flew in circles. Lizzie looked at the wooden planks below her feet, not wanting to see her papa again, especially this close. Before long, the periauger arrived at the *Adventure*. Tying the boat to dangling ropes, Lieutenant Maynard instructed Grandfather to go first. Watching him climb up the rope ladder, Lizzie tried to pull herself together. When it was her turn, she gripped the rope ladder as she started to climb. Remembering not to look down, she focused on the ladder, easing her way up until she reached the top. Taking Grandfather's hand, she swung her left foot over the railing.

Memories rushed into Lizzie's mind as she looked at her papa's ship. Having spent three months onboard, she knew every nook and cranny. She could almost see the crew mending sails and rearranging the rigging. On a day like today, she and Cookie would be mopping the deck while her papa stood on top of his cabin with spyglass in hand.

"Take Mr. Griffin into the hold with the others and tell Captain Brand Miss Griffin is here," Maynard ordered. "Afterward, remove Black Beard's head from the bowsprit. We don't want to lose it in the creek with the wind picking up. It's too valuable. Put it in the scented container."

The three men escorted Jake to the stairs leading to the galley. Jake glanced over his shoulder at her. As he disappeared below deck, Lieutenant Maynard led them into the captain's cabin. It was all Lizzie could do to hold back tears as they entered her papa's quarters. Maynard told them to sit in the two straight-backed chairs in front of her papa's desk. He then left to find Captain Brand, stating he should've been there by now. Once he was gone, Lizzie walked over to the side room where she had slept.

"Lizzie! Get back over here," Grandfather hissed.

"Papa made a place for me in here. I worked with Cookie during the day," she explained. Crossing the room, she opened the outhouse, or head as Cookie called it. "When I first arrived, I was attacked by a rat. Cookie chased it out and sent Tuffy after it."

Grandfather looked surprised. Lizzie suddenly recalled her papa's secret place under the floorboards. Curious to see if Maynard found it, she slid back the chair and pried up the loose board.

"What are you doing?" Grandfather asked. "They'll be back."

"I'm checking to see if…yes! It's still here. I can't believe it."

Voices came from the other side of the cabin door. Shoving the board back down, Lizzie moved the chair closer to the desk and rushed to her seat. She barely sat down when Maynard and Brand entered. Relieved, Lizzie prepared to face them. Knowing her papa's treasures were safe, she felt a little glimmer of hope. Now she just had to figure out a way to get them off the ship.

In a way, it was odd for her to be sitting here where her adventure started. This was the exact spot she discovered her papa was a pirate. Although he fought the Royal Navy with pistol and cutlass, she was getting ready to fight them with words. She was not going to let these scavengers win this battle. Just like a buzzard, they had circled their prey and swooped down to capture the pirates, but she was determined they would never uncover her papa's real identity.

CHAPTER TWENTY-EIGHT

☠

HANGMAN'S NOOSE

December 15, 1718 ~ Monday

It had been nine days since Lizzie left the *Adventure* for the final time. After two hours of interrogations, she was tired and frustrated. When Uncle Thomas arrived, he convinced Captain Ellis Brand and Lieutenant Robert Maynard she had nothing to do with the pirates. The men reluctantly agreed to let her go but refused to discuss Jake's fate. Uncle Thomas argued with them, but they weren't budging. Having no choice, Lizzie departed from the *Adventure* with Grandfather and Uncle Thomas, leaving Jake with the pirates and the Royal Navy.

Since then, Uncle Thomas had rowed out to the ship to check on Jake every day. Their meetings were short, but he wanted to be sure Jake was getting decent treatment. Grandfather went with him a few times and so had William Martin, who was worried about his brother, John, and JJ. During Uncle Thomas' first visit on Monday, the eighth, Jake informed him JJ's father wasn't among the survivors. Sadly, Cookie wasn't either. The crew members who lived through the battle were John Carnes and the five Africans: James Blake, Thomas Gates, James White, Richard Stiles, and Richard Greensail. Several other men were also alive, including Tobias Knight's slave, Caesar, and the co-owner of Tunnel Land, James

Robins. A third man named Samuel Odell was on the ship as well, though Lizzie didn't know him.

Jake later learned from James Robins that the man had helped Black Beard's crew get the *Adventure* off Brant Island Shoals, a sandbar near the mouth of the Neuse River. Samuel Odell, captain of a trading sloop, sailed his ship to Ocracoke where the pirates served him and his small crew brandy and fed them for their help. James said the battle started early on Saturday, November 22. He and his comrades, Garret Gibbons and Caesar, arrived at Ocracoke the night before. They gave Black Beard the letter from Tobias Knight and relayed the information about the pardon due in mid-December. With the feast planned for Samuel Odell, they stayed the night to enjoy themselves before returning home. Their plans to leave the next morning changed when Nathaniel Jackson spotted two ships coming into the inlet. Within the hour, the Royal Navy attacked.

The five Africans guarded the *Adventure* while the others boarded Maynard's ship. James and Caesar stayed to help the Africans and to protect Samuel Odell since his crew sailed away on his boat. Unfortunately, Maynard had set a trap for the pirates, killing quite a few of them. Garret was one of the first to lose his life. Seeing they weren't going to win and would hang, Black Beard ordered Caesar to go into the powder room of the *Adventure* and blow up the ship. Even this didn't work out the way they hoped. While James wrestled with Samuel Odell so Caesar could light the fuses, the attackers took over the *Adventure*. Hearing the Royal Navy officers coming down into the hold, they pretended to be Black Beard's hostages.

Ever since her uncle had relayed the account of the battle, Lizzie wondered what took place above deck. James was too preoccupied down in the hold to know what happened at the end of the battle. She recalled hearing Captain Charles Vane say he would blow up his ship to avoid hanging at the gallows. It was also a mystery of what Maynard did with the bodies. There were rumors in town about

Maynard tossing the bodies overboard to the sharks. This seemed a little farfetched, but the most insane story was the notion of Black Beard's headless body swimming around the ship after they tossed him in the sea. He was supposedly looking for his missing head.

On top of being upset about her papa's awful death, Lizzie's new focus was the guilt she felt for getting Jake into this mess. For the first time since her papa died, she called out to God. Alone on her knees, she cried desperate tears. After getting the whys off her chest, she asked God to forgive her and begged Him to save Jake. She prayed for JJ's life as well. It felt good to talk freely with God again, and she realized He would rather her ask why than to back away from Him. Between praying and reading the Bible, she felt much better about the situation, but she still knew Jake could hang.

"Lizzie, can I come in?"

Looking up from her desk, Lizzie snapped out of her daze. Inviting her visitor in, she wasn't surprised to see Aunt Susannah. Her aunt had been staying in her room with four-year-old Mary and two-year-old Elizabeth, who were delighted to share a room with Reba. Lizzie had temporarily taken Jake's single bed while six-year-old Edward slept with Trent in his double bed. Since this arrangement didn't offer much privacy, Lizzie washed and changed clothes in her room.

"Sorry to bother you while you're getting ready. Elizabeth left her rag doll on the bed," Aunt Susannah proclaimed, walking in.

Reba squawked at Aunt Susannah as if protesting her being there. Realizing she had gotten lost in her thoughts, Lizzie silently scolded herself. She came upstairs to change into her dark purple dress so that she could attend the court hearing for Jake at noon. After Uncle Thomas discovered Captain Brand's intentions to take Jake and the pirates to Williamsburg, Virginia, for trial, he pleaded with Governor Eden to call a separate hearing in Bath. Governor Eden didn't want to get involved, forcing Uncle Thomas to go to Tobias Knight for help.

Despite his sickness, Tobias wrote a letter to the governor, pointing out how a court hearing would be for their benefit. By holding a hearing, Brand and Maynard had to give details about the battle and possibly even a reason for their intrusion into Carolina. In the meantime, Governor Eden received a letter from his adviser, Colonel Thomas Pollock, in response to the questions he and Tobias wrote to him about. Pollock had no clue who alerted the Virginia government or how to go forward with the matter. This gave Governor Eden the courage to call for a court hearing, though he made sure only those relevant to the case attended. His announcement infuriated Brand and Maynard, who were planning to leave Bath once they transferred the eighty barrels of sugar onto the *Adventure*.

"I'm ready. I was just putting on my necklace," Lizzie responded to her aunt as she touched the oval-shaped locket her papa gave her. "I can't stop thinking about what they did to Papa."

Doll in hand, Aunt Susannah walked over to the desk. "I know you miss him. We have to hold on to our good memories."

Lizzie nodded as she rubbed her initials on the locket. All the conversations she had with Aunt Susannah lately revolved around old memories. The stories of her papa and aunt's childhood were especially wonderful to hear. Another touching moment occurred when Aunt Susannah shared details of her brother's visit a few weeks before.

Sighing, Lizzie gazed at the open box on her desk. Uncle Thomas and Grandfather managed to sneak her papa's small box of treasures off the ship. For days, she begged them to find a way to get it, knowing the box held family heirlooms belonging to Grandfather Beard. Uncle Thomas finally agreed to try sneaking it off the ship when he went to see Jake the day before, following the Divine Service. Carrying his sealskin attorney's bag with him, he demanded to speak with Jake in private. It took some convincing, but Captain Brand eventually granted Uncle Thomas and Grandfather ten minutes alone with Jake in the captain's cabin. This gave them time to retrieve Black Beard's wooden box hidden under the floorboards and put it in Uncle Thomas' portmanteau. They also got his sea artist's box full of navigational tools once used by Grandfather Beard.

"My necklace reminded me about something I found in Papa's box last night. There are letters and, of course, Grandfather Beard's pistol and Bible, but this one paper is strange. Do you know what it means?" Lizzie questioned, handing the parchment paper to her.

"No, it looks like a bunch of gibberish."

Lizzie took it back as her aunt flipped through the Bible, studying the page with all the family names and dates. Meanwhile, Lizzie examined the jumbled letters, trying to figure out what it meant.

NIFFIRG DAETSEMOH YENMIHC

Her papa had written out the letters and separated them. Clearly, these letters meant something to him, but what?

"I don't mean to rush you, dear, but your grandfather is waiting. We don't want to be late for the hearing," Aunt Susannah commented as she put her father's Bible back in the box.

Placing the note on top, Lizzie started to close the lid but paused as her eyes lingered on the three skull-and-crossbone pendants her papa kept in memory of her mother and his parents. Beneath them was a greenish-blue beaded necklace. Although Lizzie was certain the beads weren't in the box before, she recognized them from Captain Charles Vane's treasure chest. She remembered asking Cookie about them as they transferred the treasure to buckets.

Pushing her curiosity aside, she carried the wooden box to the chest at the end of her rope bed. Placing it with her own box of knickknacks, she spoke to Reba as she followed her aunt downstairs. Coming to the kitchen, she saw Aunt Grace and the girls putting on their cloaks. Reaching for her cloak, Lizzie tied it around her neck while Aunt Susannah helped her children into their coats.

They locked the door and joined Trent, who was waiting in the wagon.

Helping her cousins get in, Lizzie climbed into the back herself. Aunt Susannah rode in the back as well, since Elizabeth and Mary wanted to be close to their mother. Six-year-old Edward sat up front between Trent and Aunt Grace. With a flick of the reins, Trent urged Honeybee to start their journey to Grandfather's. Heading to the small wooden bridge, they crossed the property line at Glebe Creek.

Trent, his sisters, and the three Franck siblings were going to stay at Grandfather's house with Aunt Charlotte and Aunt Mary. Uncle John decided to go to the hearing along with Grandfather, Aunt Grace, Aunt Susannah, and Lizzie. Since they didn't know how long the hearing would be, Uncle Thomas planned to drop off Aunt Sarah and the boys before going with William Martin to the *Adventure*.

William threatened to go to Captain Brand's superior if he didn't bring John and JJ to Bath. In addition, Uncle Thomas requested they testify on Jake's behalf. After listening to their petitions, Governor Eden insisted Brand bring those arrested in Bath to the hearing since they weren't part of the battle. It was uncertain what would happen to the former pirates, but just getting them to Bath was a start.

The trip to Grandfather's house didn't take long. He and Uncle John were waiting for them in their dress clothes and tricorn hats. Aunt Mary, Aunt Charlotte, and Aunt Sarah were also anticipating their arrival while Little Thomas and John played on the back porch. As they pulled into the yard, Grandfather and Uncle John helped the children get down. Uncle John climbed into the back beside Lizzie as Grandfather joined Aunt Grace. Soon they were setting off again.

Traveling the dirt road, Grandfather mentioned Miles Gale approaching him yesterday at the Divine Service. Lizzie stared into the woods as he explained the situation to Aunt Susannah. Thankfully, he told Miles they would discuss it after Christmas. It was a good thing she stayed home with Aunt Susannah and her cousins while the rest of the family went to the last two Divine Services.

The conversation ended by the time they came to the old wooden bridge spanning Bath Town Creek. Honeybee's hooves clip-clopped on the wooden boards as they crossed the greenish-blue water. Feeling a heaviness on her heart, Lizzie peered at the *Adventure* anchored where the creek merged with the Pamtico River. Its sails were hanging limp against the mast in the breezeless morning as if they too had nothing left to hope for. In her heart, Lizzie wanted to believe her uncle could help Jake, but it was possible he would go to Williamsburg, Virginia, with the pirates and maybe even hang. Staring up at the cloudy, gray sky, she tried to gather herself as Grandfather guided Honeybee into the lot beside the Blue Heron Inn.

There weren't many horses tied to the hitching post out front, and the only carriage belonged to Elizabeth Martin. It appeared she just arrived with her fourteen-year-old grandson, Joel, and daughter, Ann. Seeing their neighbors coming, Miss Martin called out to Grandfather.

"Have you heard from our sons, Thomas?"

"No. I'm sure they'll be here soon," Grandfather assured her.

Grandfather stepped down from the wagon and helped Aunt Grace as Miss Martin nodded. Although she knew her oldest son was a pirate, she had been worried ever since his arrest nine days ago. She also seemed concerned about JJ, whom she had welcomed into her family.

Climbing out of the wagon, Lizzie followed her family and the Martins to the porch. Grandfather led them to the door and held it open for Miss Martin and her family. Uncle John brought up the end, pausing to look at the whipping post. Aunt Grace asked if he wanted to stay on the porch, but he said he felt like Jake needed his support.

As before, the tavern was set up for court, with tables and chairs against the walls. Governor Charles Eden stood behind his table at the back of the room talking to Tobias Knight's house guest, Edmund Chamberlayne. Provost Marshal Thomas Harding was sitting where the court's clerk and the registered deputy normally sat. Captain Brand's new friends—Colonel Maurice Moore, Captain Jeremiah Vail, and Colonel Edward Moseley—were also there, along with a fourth man Lizzie didn't know. They sat at a table in front of Governor Eden.

Thomas Harding got up to direct Miss Martin to her seat on the left side of the room. Fourteen-year-old Joel sat between his grandmother and aunt. Aunt Grace and Aunt Susannah filled the last seats against the wall. Mr. Harding told Grandfather and Uncle John to sit at the council's table with Moseley, Moore, Vail, and the stranger, whom he identified as William Bell. He then told Lizzie to sit at the table in front of her aunts since she was on the list to speak if called upon. The chairs beside her were for Uncle Thomas and William Martin.

Sitting down, Lizzie glanced over at William Bell. He was a short man with a stern look on his face. Lizzie wondered if he was going to talk about the night Black Beard attacked him. Behind Mr. Bell, Lizzie noticed Thomas Harding was looking outside.

Moments later, he approached Governor Eden. "Brand is here."

"Good," Governor Eden replied as he adjusted his white, shoulder-length wig and straightened his dark green suit.

The tavern door swung open as Uncle Thomas and William Martin came in. Captain Ellis Brand entered next, dressed in his navy-blue uniform as he escorted Jake in. Five casually dressed officers followed them with JJ Brooks, John Martin, Stephen Daniel, Edward Salter, and John Giles. Israel Hands limped in last on his wooden cane with Lieutenant Robert Maynard, who wore a uniform like Captain Brand's. All seven prisoners had iron shackles on their wrists.

Captain Brand led the way to the right side of the room where he instructed Jake, JJ, and John to sit beside him at the table. Lieutenant Maynard sat behind them with the four pirates and his five officers. As they got situated, Uncle Thomas and William Martin joined Lizzie. Governor Eden banged his mallet on the wooden block.

"Attention! I will be presiding as judge. Our clerk is not here so there will be no written notes during today's proceedings. I asked Provost Marshal Thomas Harding to swear in those testifying."

Thomas made Brand swear to tell the truth on the Bible. He then did the same for Maynard and the pirates. When he got to Israel, the unruly pirate refused to do it; however, he changed his mind after Maynard threatened him. Next, Thomas swore in Uncle Thomas, William Martin, and Lizzie. Placing her hand on the Bible, Lizzie realized to tell the truth would incriminate not only her papa but also herself. On the other hand, the Bible called lying a sin. It was also a criminal offense to lie under oath. Gazing across the room at Jake, she sent up a prayer knowing only God could help.

"Mr. Edmund Chamberlayne will stand in for Secretary Tobias Knight due to his illness. I have temporarily granted him the duty of chief justice of the court. Normally, the chief justice would read out the charges against the accused, but these are unusual circumstances. Since there is some confusion regarding the charges, Captain Ellis Brand needs to enlighten us," Governor Eden declared.

The blonde-haired Brand narrowed his eyes and gritted his teeth as he stood. "As commanding officer of this mission, I was given the authority to arrest anyone associated with Black Beard. We brought these men upon your request, Governor, but I will not release them. They will go to Virginia with the survivors Lieutenant Maynard detained after the battle and hopefully hang for piracy."

"I don't appreciate the Royal Navy coming into Bath arresting people," Governor Eden countered.

"Lieutenant Maynard discovered evidence in Black Beard's personal effects stating these men were pirates. The only issue is Mr. Jake Griffin's involvement. His signature is missing," Brand argued.

"What evidence do you have, Lieutenant?"

The dark-haired lieutenant stood and held up a handful of parchment papers. "These are signed articles for Black Beard's ship, the *Adventure*. There's also a crew roster with many of their names. Black Beard made a new roster for those currently serving. Mr. Griffin's name is on the old crew roster, but his signed article is gone."

"Chief Justice Chamberlayne, get the old roster from Lieutenant Maynard and read out the names," Governor Eden requested.

Edmund took the roster from Maynard. As Lizzie listened to the names, her heart pounded in her chest. She recalled the day she discovered the list in her papa's desk drawer. Jake's name was at the bottom. In her mind, she remembered Jake telling her Black Beard had given him the paper he signed which was now in their outhouse with Jake's gold. When Mr. Chamberlayne finished, he sat down.

"All these men are on the roster and have signed the bylaws. They knowingly signed on as members of the pirate crew and will go to Virginia with the survivors of the battle," Captain Brand said.

"Speaking of the battle, now would be a good time for Lieutenant Maynard to explain his actions," Governor Eden responded.

"He doesn't have to explain anything," Brand objected.

"I am the judge. He will tell us what happened," Eden snapped.

"Fine!" Maynard exploded. "On Saturday, November twenty-second, at about ten o'clock, I commanded the *Jane* into Ocracoke Inlet. Midshipman Edmund Hyde captained the *Ranger*, the other ship in our company. We got stuck on a sandbar, so the *Ranger* went ahead of us. Black Beard spotted us and severed the anchor cables to make a getaway. Once my men freed the *Jane*, we got closer so I could talk to Black Beard through my speaking trumpet. I told him to surrender and his men fired upon the *Ranger*, killing Midshipman

Hyde and many others. My men engaged in battle until there was an opportunity for Black Beard to board the *Jane*. With all the gun smoke, we couldn't see anything, so I ordered my men to go below deck. At the right time, I yelled for my men to come out, and we were able to kill the pirates. I personally fought with Black Beard, but it took both myself and another comrade to kill him. When he was dead, we cut off his head and apprehended the pirates still alive. We found three men in the hull of the ship who claimed to be captives. After the battle, we cared for our wounded and sent the *Ranger* back to Virginia with those severely injured. Ten pirates died, including Black Beard, and nine are captives. Between our two ships, we had twenty casualties."

Listening to the horrible details, Lizzie's eyes blinked rapidly as she tried not to cry. Behind her, she could hear the sniffles of her aunts and the Martin family. Knowing how the crew had prepared for the battle with the French ships, Lizzie could almost see them scrambling across the deck getting ready for battle. She imagined them fighting with the Royal Navy officers, swords clashing in a flurry of hand movements.

"Why did you wait so long to come to Bath? Captain Brand must have been expecting you," Governor Eden pointed out.

"It took two weeks to clean up the bloody mess. We also buried the bodies, interrogated the survivors, and took inventory of the little bit of loot. One pirate, who we assumed was dead, somehow escaped and crawled into the marsh despite his many wounds. The buzzards found him," Maynard answered as William Bell suddenly stood up.

"Where's Black Beard's loot? He stole a variety of items from me as recorded in the official Hue and Cry statement. Secretary Knight took my complaints and promised to have the provost marshal investigate. The most important was a silver cup. Did you find it?"

"We did, but it's going to Virginia as evidence against Black Beard. There was no gold or silver. Just a little gold dust," Maynard reported.

"No gold?" Israel blurted out, his face as red as his shirt. "Where's the plunder and the ransom money Black Beard got for the captives?"

Eden beat his mallet on the block. "Gag him for disruption!" After Thomas Harding had gagged Israel with a neckerchief, the governor continued, "What was he shouting about, Captain Brand?"

"He told me Jake Griffin was on the *Adventure* and served under Captain Edward Teach, alias Black Beard. Mr. Hands claims Black Beard was holding Mr. Griffin and Miss Griffin for ransom, which he apparently received in October. The ransom money was never discovered."

"Who is this Miss Griffin?" Governor Eden inquired.

Surprised, Brand pointed to Lizzie. "She's over there."

All eyes turned to Lizzie. Uncle Thomas leaned over and whispered in her ear for her to tell the truth. Shaking slightly, she stood to her feet and prayed for God to guide her words so that she wouldn't let it slip that she was Black Beard's daughter.

"My name is Lizzie Beard."

"Hold on," Maynard interrupted her. "You told me you were Lizzie Griffin when I came to your house."

"No, sir. You asked if I was the same Miss Lizzie the pirates talked about. It was your own assumption I was Jake's sister."

"If you aren't siblings, then what were you and Mr. Griffin doing on the ship? Were you even captives?" Brand persisted.

Nervous, Lizzie glanced at Jake. "There were rumors about Black Beard capturing ships. I went looking for my papa, who captained my grandfather's merchant ship. He wasn't a captive like I thought. Jake followed me to the ship, but by the time he found me we were stuck onboard. The crew discovered us in the storage room. Black Beard forced Jake to serve on the crew and made me work with the cook."

"You may be seated, Miss Beard," Governor Eden declared. "Mr. Griffin, please stand and give your account."

Hastily sitting down, Lizzie watched Jake scramble to his feet. With his hands shackled in front of him, he addressed the court.

"Lizzie's right. Black Beard forced me to become a member of his crew. I did whatever was necessary to keep both of us alive."

"So, you admit to joining these pirates?" Brand remarked.

Uncle Thomas stopped Jake from speaking. "May I say something?" Governor Eden gave his approval. "I'm Thomas Worsley Jr., Lizzie's uncle. I also represent Jake Griffin as his attorney. On behalf of my client, I'd like to point out he was only on the ship to find my niece. Joseph Brooks Jr. and John Martin will testify this is true."

"Mr. Brooks, tell us what you witnessed," Eden stated.

"Miss Lizzie and Jake came aboard just like they said. Jake is not a pirate, and never tried to be," JJ revealed as John Martin mumbled his agreement and the two of them sat back down.

"Assuming he is charged with acts of piracy like the others, I ask you to dismiss the charges," Uncle Thomas urged.

"Jake Griffin was on the roster," Maynard reminded them.

"Yes, but you said there was no article with Jake's signature. He was forced to serve," Uncle Thomas responded.

"After hearing both sides, I have concluded Jake Griffin had no intentions to get mixed up in piracy. I order all charges against him to be dropped and grant his release," Governor Eden announced.

"What about my brother?" William Martin inquired.

"He's going with us. I have the proof for him!" Maynard exclaimed as he held up the papers.

"We have proof against Secretary Tobias Knight as well. Lieutenant, read them Knight's letter to Black Beard," Brand instructed.

Flipping through Black Beard's pocketbook, Maynard pulled out a piece of paper and read it aloud. "November seventeenth, 1718. My friend, if this finds you yet in harbor, I would have you make the best of your way up as soon as possible your affairs will let you. I have something more to say to you than at present I can write. The bearer will tell you the end of our Indian War and Ganet can tell you in part what I have to say to you so refer you in some measure to him. I really think these three men are heartily sorry at their differences with you and will be very willingly to ask your pardon. If I may advise be friends again, it's better than falling out among yourselves. I expect the governor this night or tomorrow, who I believe would be likewise glad to see you before you go. I have not time to add save my hearty respects to you and am your real friend, and servant T. Knight."

"Governor, what do you think Mr. Knight meant by saying you would be glad to see Black Beard?" Captain Brand wanted to know.

"You will have to ask him," Governor Eden answered. "I'm sorry, Mr. Martin. Lieutenant Maynard has given enough evidence to charge your brother and the others with piracy. From what I understand, the pardons I gave them are no longer valid."

"This isn't over. I plan to be at the hearing in Virginia," William replied. "Can you at least allow my mother a few minutes with John?"

"And JJ, too! He's like a son," Miss Elizabeth Martin piped up.

"I grant you fifteen minutes. Court is adjourned," Governor Eden declared, slamming down his wooden mallet.

Brand went to speak with Moore, Moseley, Vail, and William Bell while Maynard unlocked Jake's shackles. He also unlocked JJ's and John's. Miss Martin threw her arms around her son's neck, crying as she talked about her baby hanging at the gallows. John tried to comfort her and his sister. Wanting to see JJ, Lizzie joined Uncle Thomas as he went to shake Jake's hand. Relieved that Jake escaped a hanging, Lizzie gave him a hug as her uncle spoke with the Martins about the trial in Virginia. Jake let go of her as JJ came over.

"I'm sorry, JJ. I wish I could do something," Jake apologized.

"It's not ye fault," JJ mumbled as Miss Martin came to hug him.

When she let go, she told him they would do everything possible to help them. She then returned to listen to the discussion John was having with William and Uncle Thomas. Now alone with JJ and Jake, Lizzie searched for the words to say as JJ grabbed her hands.

"Cookie told me God listens to ye, Lizzie," he began. "Before I hang, I need to know God will overlook my skeletons. Pa didn't get a chance to make things right. I don't know if he went to hell, but I can't risk it. I know my mother's in heaven."

"You have to believe that God loved the world and gave His only Son, Jesus, to die for our sins. Then you must ask God to forgive you. Anyone who believes in Him will have eternal life."

"How can I be sure. What if it's too late?"

"It's never too late. There were two thieves crucified with Jesus. One talked nasty to Jesus, but the other sought forgiveness and asked Jesus to remember him. Jesus forgave him and promised to take him to paradise. If Jesus took the thief to heaven, then He'll forgive you."

JJ nodded as he closed his eyes in prayer. Closing her own eyes, Lizzie listened as JJ asked Jesus to forgive him. By the time he finished, all three of them were wiping tears. Lizzie tried to be supportive, but all she could imagine was the hangman's noose waiting in Virginia.

Hugging JJ tightly, Lizzie knew this could be the last time she ever saw him. Maynard announced their time was up and started to put the iron shackles back on John's wrists. Letting go of Lizzie, JJ looked over his shoulder at John and then at Jake.

"Don't forget about what we talked about and remember to keep our pact. I'm counting on ye," he whispered.

"I won't forget," Jake replied.

JJ removed his navy-blue neckerchief from his neck and placed it in Lizzie's hand. "I want ye to have this to remind ye of me. I've grown fond of ye, Lizzie, and well, I love ye."

Clutching the neckerchief, Lizzie didn't know what to say. Jake seemed just as startled by JJ's admission of love for her.

"I know ye promised to come up to Virginia, Jake, but under the circumstances, maybe ye should lay low," JJ stated.

"Don't worry. You're my friend, and I'll see you in Virginia."

"I said your time was up," Lieutenant Maynard snapped at JJ.

Lizzie watched Maynard roughly lock him in the shackles. He then led JJ outside as the other officers took hold of John Martin, Stephen Daniel, John Giles, and Edward Salter. Captain Brand brought up the end with the limping Israel Hands. Miss Martin followed her son as close as the Royal Navy would let her. Leaving the Blue Heron Inn, Lizzie was surprised to find Giles Shute standing on the porch. Brand ignored him as he led his prisoners to the docks with the Martin family trailing behind. Uncle Thomas and Grandfather stopped to find out what was going on with Mr. Shute. As Mr. Chamberlayne and the governor stepped out on the porch, Mr. Shute told them he just received news about Stede Bonnet's death five days ago. Apparently, the pirate hung at the gallows down south near Charles Town.

Thinking about Stede Bonnet's hanging made Lizzie feel worse. She knew her papa's crew had done wrong, but it was still hard to watch the pirates leave Bath to face the hangman's noose.

CHAPTER TWENTY-NINE

☠

LONESOME SOUND

December 18, 1718 ~ Thursday

Squally weather kept the *Adventure* stranded in port longer than Captain Ellis Brand or Lieutenant Robert Maynard anticipated. For two days, Bath Town endured a nasty mixture of gusty winds and heavy rain. The chilly December gales caused everyone to stay behind closed doors. By dawn on Thursday morning, the wind and rain stopped. Lizzie figured the break in the weather would hasten the *Adventure*'s departure from Bath, though the eighty casks of sugar weighing down the ship would make travel slow. A handful of Royal Navy crew members waited on the *Jane* for them at Ocracoke.

Her suspicions proved to be right when Uncle John came galloping to the house on his black and white horse. His arrival startled Lizzie and her family, who were cracking pecans on the back porch. With so many pecans to pick out, Aunt Grace had decided to work on them so that she could roast some next week for Christmas. While Hannah, Edward, Mary, and Elizabeth played with Killer and Tuffy in the leaves, Lizzie helped Aunt Grace and Aunt Susannah shell the pecans. Even Alice and Rebecca helped crack the brown, oval-shaped nuts. Trent and Jake were busy chopping wood and piling it on the porch so it would be close to the house during the winter.

Uncle John reported going to Harding's General Store where he learned that Giles Shute and his son, Philip, had spent the last hour stacking barrels of food on the loading dock for Maynard. The lieutenant's men transferred the supplies to the *Adventure*. After a little snooping, Uncle John discovered Brand wasn't going back to Virginia on the ship. Instead, he and his servant planned to leave on horseback as soon as Maynard set sail. His choice to travel by land was odd, even if he came to Bath on horseback in the first place.

In addition to Brand's strange behavior, Uncle Thomas found out through Edmund Chamberlayne that Governor Eden arranged to leave Bath as well. The governor was heading to his mansion in the Chowan Precinct to celebrate the Twelve Days of Christmas with his two grown stepchildren and their families. His wife, Penelope, died in January 1716, leaving him with no children of his own. Both of his stepchildren belonged to Penelope and her first husband, who died when they were young. Although this was a justifiable reason to leave, it was possible Eden wanted to get away from the stench of piracy.

Once he delivered the news, Uncle John hurried back home to fill in his father and brother on the latest developments. Knowing the *Adventure* should be getting ready to set sail, Jake headed down to the dock. Lizzie started to go with him, but Aunt Susannah stopped her.

"Wait, I'm going with you," she announced as she called her six-year-old son over. "Edward, stay on the porch with your sisters."

"But we were playing chase with the puppy and kitty, Momma."

"The children will be all right, Susannah. Alice and Rebecca can watch them. We won't be long," Aunt Grace assured her.

Not wanting to miss seeing the ship, Lizzie made her way to the dock. By the time she got there, Trent and Jake were sitting on the edge of the dock with their legs dangling over the water. Crouching down beside Trent, Lizzie did the same. The *Adventure* hadn't departed yet.

"Do you think JJ will hang?" Trent asked Jake, who was looking through a spyglass he acquired during his days as an apprentice.

"I don't know. Hopefully, your uncle can do something to help."

"Have they left?" Aunt Susannah wanted to know.

"Not yet," Lizzie answered.

Jake lowered his spyglass and passed it to Trent. "Looks like they're preparing to hoist the anchor."

"They're scrambling around the deck," Trent reported as he looked through the spyglass. "What are they doing to the sails?"

"To get the ship headed in the right direction, they have to adjust the sails to the way the wind is blowing," Jake explained.

Trent handed the spyglass to Lizzie. Closing her right eye, she peered at the *Adventure*. The crew of Royal Navy officers were using the iron capstan as a crank to lift the heavy anchor out of the water. As it emerged from the greenish-blue creek, the men tied it off while others made sure the sails were secure. Lizzie spotted Lieutenant Maynard on top of the captain's cabin staring into a spyglass.

Soon the ship began to move as the wind filled the sails. Sighing, Lizzie gave Trent the spyglass. He passed it to Jake, who took another look at the ship as it picked up speed. Before long, the *Adventure* had eased into the Pamtico River as it slipped away from Bath. Lizzie thought about the souls aboard the ship. She imagined JJ and the others huddled together, cold and damp with their hands bound in chains. In the captain's cabin, her papa's severed head would be in its scented container where Maynard could make sure it stayed safe. Overwhelmed, Lizzie closed her eyes to pray.

Please help JJ, God. I know he has sinned but have mercy on him. Save him from the hands of these men. I ask this in the name of Jesus. Amen.

When Lizzie opened her eyes, only the sails were visible as the *Adventure* went around the bend of the river. She kept her eyes on the sails and mast until it disappeared into the horizon.

Aunt Grace was the first to speak. "There's a lot of pecan cracking to do. I want to crack out some walnuts, too. Come on, Trent."

Clambering to his feet, Trent followed his mother. Lizzie stood as well, staying close to Aunt Susannah as they walked to the house. Jake was reluctant to leave the dock, but he eventually trailed behind them. Peering over her shoulder, Lizzie wondered why he had been distant.

As they passed the barnyard, Lizzie heard the shrieks and laughter of the children as they played with Tuffy and Killer. The little brown and white dog tried to catch the ball Hannah and four-year-old Mary were tossing to each other. Alice and Rebecca were playing a game of scotch-hopper while Edward marched around the yard blowing the whistle Jake made him. Elizabeth was chasing Tuffy, though the cat didn't like it when the two-year-old grabbed her black tail.

Getting her tail pulled was probably the reason Tuffy refused to come inside at night. Lizzie had been bringing the one-eyed cat up to her room since Cookie left. When Aunt Susannah and the children arrived, the cat suddenly didn't want to stay in the house. For a few days, Tuffy slept near Killer's small, wooden doghouse on the back porch. Not wanting her to get cold, Lizzie tried to relocate her to Trent's room. This didn't go over well, so Trent made Tuffy a cat house that fit on top of Killer's.

Nearing the house, Aunt Grace said she was going inside to check on the fish stew simmering on the hearth. While she was gone, Aunt Susannah and Lizzie started back shelling pecans. Ten minutes later, Aunt Grace came back to help crack the nuts. Working together, the three of them made progress on the pecans, putting the empty shells in a wooden bucket. Jake and Trent returned to cutting and stacking the wood. After an hour, Aunt Grace announced dinner was ready.

Everyone entered the kitchen, took off their coats, and washed up in one of the four wooden buckets of water Trent brought from the well. Grabbing a bowl from the counter, they formed a line so that Aunt Grace could fill the bowls with fish stew. Meanwhile,

Aunt Susannah brought the milk pitcher to the table and poured some in each cup. Getting her own bowl of fish stew, Lizzie found a place to sit between Hannah and Edward, who was practicing the tune Jake taught him on the whistle. His musical concert ended when his mother threatened to take it from him. Once everyone was around the table, Aunt Grace asked Trent to bless the food before they ate.

The combination of trout, potatoes, onions, and herbal seasonings made the stew delicious. Listening to the conversation, it was obvious the children were getting excited about celebrating the birth of Jesus. With the Twelve Days of Christmas starting next week, everyone was looking forward to making wreaths and decorating the house with festive greenery. Thursday would be December 25, the first day of the celebration, which would end twelve days later on Tuesday, January 6. During the twelve days of festivities, families and neighbors shared feasts and played games. There was also a community gathering held on the last day of the celebration at Governor Eden's home. Since he was heading to the Chowan Precinct, Lizzie didn't know if someone else would host it.

A knock on the door interrupted the conversation. Aunt Grace got up to see who it was. She returned with a dark-haired man. Lizzie recognized him as her uncle, John Martin Franck.

"Martin!" Aunt Susannah exclaimed, quickly standing up.

Edward and his two sisters ran to their father as they excitedly gave him a hug. "Papa! You're here! We missed you."

"I missed you, too," Uncle Martin responded, giving them a hug.

"Look, Papa! Jake made us all a whistle. Want to hear it?" Edward prompted as he started to play the whistle again.

"Edward Franck, I told you not to blow that whistle. Give it to me," Aunt Susannah scolded her son.

"Yes, ma'am," the six-year-old murmured dejectedly, handing the whistle to his mother before sitting beside Lizzie.

"What happened to your plans in New Bern, Martin? You weren't coming here until next week," Aunt Susannah mentioned.

"Several men who were supposed to meet had to cancel. We'll have to reschedule. I decided to come early. Is there any stew left?"

"I'll get you a bowl," Aunt Grace offered, going to the kitchen.

After giving Lizzie a hug, Uncle Martin spoke to the other children. Trent introduced him to Jake, making sure to mention Jake's family being neighbors with them on the Neuse River. As Uncle Martin sat at the end of the table, he told Lizzie how sorry he was about her papa's death and asked his wife if they had learned anything from the Royal Navy. Aunt Susannah poured him a cup of milk as she gave him a short version of what they discovered. When Aunt Grace returned with the fish stew, Uncle Martin was shaking his head.

"Do they know about Edward visiting us?" he wanted to know.

"It didn't come up at Jake's hearing," Aunt Susannah answered.

"What about the other pirates? He wasn't the only one. Do you recall the names of the other two men?" he persisted.

"I think they had the same first name. Wasn't it Joseph?"

"Maybe Joseph Brooks and Joseph Curtice?" Jake interrupted.

"Yes, those were their names," Aunt Susannah confirmed.

"They were Papa's friends," Lizzie piped up. "They died."

"Let's hope the men who survived don't spill their guts about coming up the Neuse River then," Uncle Martin commented.

"Momma, can we go play outside?" six-year-old Edward urged.

"Yes, can we?" Hannah pleaded, looking at her own mother.

"Go ahead, but put your coats back on," Aunt Grace agreed as she took a stack of dirty bowls to the kitchen.

Hannah, Rebecca, and Alice got up while the three Franck siblings waited for their mother's permission. When she gave her approval, Mary and Elizabeth scampered to the kitchen to grab their own coats.

"Can I have my whistle back, Momma?" Edward asked.

Aunt Susannah hesitated for a moment. "I suppose you can."

"Thank you! Thank you!" he shouted happily as he slid off the bench and hurriedly grabbed the whistle from his mother.

"Don't forget to put your coat on," she reminded him.

The older children helped the little ones put on their coats before heading outside. Trent and Jake got up to follow, but Aunt Susannah asked Jake to stay. As Trent left, she began to give Uncle Martin a better account of what happened to her brother. Lizzie remained at the table, listening as she told the gruesome details of Black Beard's last hours. By the time she got to the part about his severed head, Aunt Grace was back. Uncle Martin asked Jake and Lizzie to tell him about their summer with the pirates. Glancing at Jake, Lizzie shared parts of their adventure. Occasionally, Jake added to the story, which led to Uncle Martin thanking him for looking after Lizzie.

Finally, Jake said he was going outside. Getting up herself, Lizzie went to help Aunt Grace wash the dishes. Meanwhile, Uncle Martin got his belongings off the porch where Trent left them before taking his horse to the barn. Bags in hand, he followed his wife upstairs to Lizzie's room. Watching them, Lizzie sighed, knowing the sleeping arrangements would change again. Since Jake was back in Trent's room, Lizzie had moved in with Alice and Rebecca. Hannah slept with her mother. Now Mary and Elizabeth had to sleep on a pallet of quilts.

Before long, the dishes were clean and put away in the cabinet. As Lizzie went to get her coat, there was a knock on the door. Turning around, she spotted Grandfather entering the kitchen.

"Hello, Father," Aunt Grace greeted him.

"Hello, dear. The children said Martin arrived."

"Yes, Susannah took him upstairs to get settled in. What brings you over here? I hope there's no more bad news."

"I'm afraid so. Thomas Bustin came to see Mary. He brought me a copy of the *Boston News-Letter* fresh off the boat. It has an article about Captain Richard Worley's capture in November by Governor James Moore of southern Carolina. I think he's Richard Worsley."

"He came to Ocracoke in October to tell Papa and Captain Vane about Stede Bonnet's arrest. Papa said he's related," Lizzie declared.

"Jake told me about Richard stopping by Ocracoke when I shared the news with him. Richard is my brother's only son. I know his father is devastated to hear this news. He was a good young man growing up, but he wasn't satisfied. All he talked about was traveling and finding gold. Guess it caught up with him. It's a shame."

"Are you going to go see your brother?" Aunt Grace mentioned.

"No. I'll send him a letter and perhaps visit after the holidays. The paper also had an article about William Howard's release. Apparently, the new royal pardon just arrived from England. Maybe Richard, John Martin, and JJ can get the new pardon, too. Thomas is going to talk to Tobias Knight about it," Grandfather proclaimed.

"I hope so. William was Papa's quartermaster prior to July. I was told his family lived east of Bath," Lizzie commented.

"The Howards have a lot of land," he responded.

Aunt Susannah and Uncle Martin returned to the kitchen. Reaching to shake hands, the two men greeted each other. Surprisingly, Uncle Martin said he had something he wanted to talk to Grandfather about and suggested they go into the parlor. Aunt Susannah insisted Lizzie and Aunt Grace join them. Entering the parlor, Lizzie sat down in a straight-backed chair while her aunts seated themselves in the rockers. Grandfather had just pulled up a chair when Uncle Martin began to speak.

"Susannah and I feel it's best if Lizzie lived with us for a while."

"What?" Aunt Grace blurted out as Lizzie felt her jaw drop.

"Grace, we only want what's best for her. She's been through a lot. Maybe it would be helpful to leave Bath. We don't want anyone to connect her to Edward's piracy," Aunt Susannah stated.

"She should stay with us for at least a few months. What do you say, Thomas?" Uncle Martin asked Grandfather.

"Don't I get a choice?" Lizzie objected, jumping to her feet.

"Yes, but we are responsible for you," Aunt Susannah told her.

Upset with her answer, Lizzie crossed her arms. Fighting tears, she waited to see what Aunt Grace and Grandfather would say.

"Perhaps we should talk about this after Christmas. Things have been difficult lately," Grandfather mumbled at last.

"We want her to go home with us. Since I came early, I doubt we'll stay through the new year," Uncle Martin persisted.

Not wanting to hear another word, Lizzie left the parlor. Her aunts came after her, but she pushed them away, stating she needed to be alone. Going upstairs, she opened the door to her bedchambers and went to the wooden chest at the end of her rope bed. In the corner, Reba squawked from her cage. Gazing at the green feathered bird, her eyes drifted to the turtle shell basket White Feathers gave her. As she sifted through the contents of the chest, she found the small wooden box belonging to her papa. She tucked it under her arm and lowered the lid of the wooden chest. Then, she went down the hall to her cousins' bedchambers.

Crawling onto Alice's single bed where she had been sleeping, Lizzie opened the box and flipped through the stack of letters, looking for the one from Pennsylvania. Remembering Margaret's comment about her papa not heeding her warning, Lizzie guessed she wrote the letter. With no address or last name, there was no way to let her know of his death. Regardless, Margaret would find out soon enough. Considering how Stede Bonnet, William Howard, and Richard Worley were all mentioned in the *Boston News-Letter*, she figured her papa's death would make the front page. Since news was two weeks late due to the time it took to receive information, print it, and ship it to the colonies, she felt her papa would be in the next edition.

Lizzie placed the letter in the box as she picked up the greenish-blue beaded necklace. Holding it, she located her papa's note. It frustrated her not to be able to understand the code. She debated what the code meant and whether it had anything to do with her papa's missing treasure. Maybe she needed to show Grandfather.

Creaking floorboards alerted her to someone coming up the stairs. Quickly putting the beads in the small box, she realized the footsteps weren't coming closer. From the partially opened door, she saw Jake enter his room. When Jake didn't come out, Lizzie wondered what he was up to. Deciding to show him the note, she went across the hall and gave a gentle knock before stepping over the threshold. Jake was dragging out items from under his rope bed.

"What are you doing?" she questioned, making him look up.

"I'm trying to get my things together."

"There's no need to move your things. Uncle Martin will stay with Aunt Susannah. Mary and Elizabeth will be fine sleeping on a pallet. Anyway, I wanted to show you something. I found this in Papa's box. It looks like a code. Papa put it in the box with the beads we found in Captain Vane's stolen treasure chest. I think it may have something to do with the missing treasure we helped Cookie hide."

"I'm busy. What makes you think I can decipher the code?"

"Come on, Jake. It'll only take a few minutes."

Getting up from the floor, Jake took the note from her. After studying the jumbled letters, he handed the note back. He picked up the canvas bag on the floor and began stuffing clothes in it.

"I don't know what it means. It could be anything."

"Weren't you listening? You don't have to move your things."

"I heard you. I've been doing a lot of thinking and have decided to leave Bath. It'll take me a week to get to Virginia. The sooner I leave, the better," he announced as he continued to pack.

"What? When were you going to tell us, on your way out? Can't you go with Uncle Thomas after Christmas?"

"I only planned to be here through the summer. It's time to move on, and Virginia is a good place to start. If I get a job, then I can support myself while waiting for JJ's hearing."

Lizzie's heart sank as she grasped what he was saying. "Sounds like you aren't planning to come back."

"Why are you surprised? My plans were to go to Pennsylvania."

"I figured you changed your mind after what happened to you up there. For goodness sakes, you have your own bed now."

"I'm thankful for all your family did, but I should move on."

"First, Aunt Susannah and Uncle Martin insist on me going to New Bern, and now you're leaving Bath. What else will happen?"

Jake turned to look at her. "You're going to New Bern?"

"I don't want to, but apparently it isn't my choice. They're concerned people might find out I'm Black Beard's daughter," she replied. Wiping tears, she added, "I wish things could stay the same."

Turning away, Jake pulled out the bow and arrow Red Wolf gave him and picked up his spyglass from the side table. He placed it in another canvas bag with his sack of gold from the outhouse.

"Maybe you should get away from here," he remarked. "Who says you have to stay for months? If you're old enough to court Miles, then you should be able to decide what you want to do."

Struggling to hold back her emotions, Lizzie felt like a rock was in her throat. "Will you at least write occasionally so we know how you're doing?"

The door creaked as Trent came in. "I got concerned when you didn't return from the outhouse. What are you doing, Jake?"

"I'm packing. Lizzie was trying to talk me out of leaving," Jake explained as he closed the bags and swung them over his shoulder.

"Leaving? What are you talking about?" Trent prompted.

Jake picked up the bow and arrow. "It's like I told Lizzie. I'm grateful for everything your family has done, but it's time to leave."

"Are you going to Virginia?" Trent asked.

"Yes, I promised JJ to be there during his hearing," Jake confirmed, exiting the room with his belongings and tricorn hat.

While Trent argued with him, Lizzie took the coded note to her cousins' room. Placing it in her papa's wooden box, she slid the box under the rope bed and ran to catch up with Trent and Jake. By the time she joined them, they were at the bottom of the stairs. Trent still hadn't changed Jake's mind. As Jake entered the kitchen, Trent went to the parlor to tell his mother. When he returned, Aunt Grace, Grandfather, Aunt Susannah, and Uncle Martin accompanied him.

"What's this about you leaving?" Aunt Grace confronted Jake.

"I'm going to Virginia, Miss Grace. There's nothing anyone can say to change my mind. I'll never forget the kindness you have shown me."

"At least let me pack some food for your journey," she advised, grabbing a sack as she spoke. "Bring me those apples and pears, Trent. I'll put some biscuits in here and several jars of preserves."

"Why don't you wait to go with Thomas?" Grandfather mentioned. "He'll be leaving after the Twelve Days of Christmas."

"I need to get settled in and find a job. Please thank him for all he did for me. I'm sure he can find me when he gets to Virginia."

Sliding on his coat, Jake picked up his belongings and the sack of food before heading out the back door. Trent offered to saddle Buckwheat while Grandfather made suggestions on which way he should travel. As Lizzie stepped out onto the cold porch with her aunts and uncle, she tried to hide her feelings. Even without her coat, the numbness she felt had nothing to do with the chilly December air. Soon, Trent had Buckwheat ready. Seeing their brother guiding the horse across the yard, Alice, Rebecca, and Hannah stopped playing to see what was going on. The Franck siblings followed them.

"Where's Jake going?" Alice inquired.

"Jake's leaving for Virginia, dear," Aunt Grace informed her.

"When are you coming back, Jake?" Hannah piped up.

"I don't know, Hannah. It may not be for a very long time."

The little girl started to cry as she ran to him and threw her arms around his waist. "Please don't leave us, Jake! We love you."

Bending on one knee, Jake gave her a hug. "I love you, too. You'll always be my special friend. Take good care of Reba, okay?"

Hannah nodded as Jake let go of her to hug Rebecca and Alice. Even Edward, Mary, and Elizabeth were upset to find out he was leaving. The six-year-old little boy was particularly disappointed that Jake wouldn't be around to teach him any more songs on his whistle. Jake passed his bags and Red Wolf's bow and arrow to Trent so that he could fasten them to the saddle. He then shook hands with Uncle Martin and Grandfather. Once they said their good-byes, he gave Aunt Susannah and Aunt Grace a hug. Finally, it was Lizzie's turn to say good-bye. Wrapping her arms around his neck, she hugged him tightly. His firm embrace made her wonder if part of him really didn't want to leave. Pulling away, he stared at her as if he wanted to say something. His penetrating gaze caught her off guard, reminding her of the time he helped her up from the sandy beach at Ocracoke.

"I'll try to write," he whispered.

"Please, be careful," she mumbled back. "You're in my prayers."

Putting on his three-cornered hat, Jake walked over to Trent. Giving the fourteen-year-old a hug, he mounted his light brown horse. Buckwheat's cream-colored tail swished as Jake got situated on the saddle. Saying good-bye, he nudged Buckwheat's sides as they trotted away.

Standing with her cousins, Lizzie waved, though she couldn't muster the strength to shout good-byes like the others. Jake's departure was almost too much to bear. When he was nearly out of sight, Edward held up his whistle and played the tune Jake taught him. The lonesome sound drifted through the air, causing a light gray dove in a nearby tree to add its own mournful coo. Tears welled up in Lizzie's eyes as she listened. Closing them, she prayed for Jake's safety and asked God to fill the emptiness Jake's absence would undoubtedly leave in her heart.

CHAPTER THIRTY

CHRISTMAS TREASURE

December 25, 1718 ~ Thursday

Nothing prepared Lizzie for the heartache she experienced in the days following Jake's departure from Bath Town. She knew his absence would be difficult, but she had no idea how close they had become. All she could think about was the special moments they shared, which gave way to memories of Cookie, JJ, and her papa.

Staring at the wooden boards of the ceiling, Lizzie sighed. Today was Christmas morning. In an hour, the children would be getting up excited to begin the festivities. Normally, they went to Grandfather's for a feast, but this year was different. Elizabeth Martin invited them to share Christmas with her family in hopes to lighten their heavy hearts. Grandfather accepted her invitation.

Turning on her side, Lizzie tried not to feel sad. For days, she dealt with regrets of what she should've said to Jake. It hurt to know she let him leave without explaining how much he meant to her, particularly since he probably wouldn't come back to Bath. There was a possibility she could talk Uncle Thomas into letting her go with him to Virginia, but with Aunt Susannah insisting on her going back with them, the chances were slim. Her other reason for wanting to go to Virginia had to do with her papa.

She talked to Grandfather and her uncles about what would happen to her papa's severed head. More than anything, she wanted to give his head a proper burial, which she doubted his body received at Ocracoke. In addition to his head, she wondered what would happen to the *Adventure* and her papa's pocketbook diary. The skeletons in his journal would soon be public. There was no telling what he wrote while he was sick and drinking. Consumed with emotions, she tossed and turned until shrieks startled her.

"Look outside! It snowed during the night!" Hannah reported cheerfully.

Sitting up, Lizzie peered over her shoulder at Hannah. Her loud voice woke Reba, who fluttered around her cage squawking. Lizzie was glad they moved the bird into their newly shared room, knowing her aunt and uncle would have had a fit if the bird was making such a fuss in their room. Rebecca and Alice scrambled out of bed to join their little sister at the window overlooking the waterfront. Following them, Lizzie could see gorgeous white snow covering the yard. Everything glistened from the barn to the outhouse. The morning sun made the snow appear like it was shimmering on the tree branches.

"Wow!" Rebecca exclaimed.

"Isn't it beautiful?" Alice sighed.

Aunt Grace walked into the room still dressed in her white nightgown and mob sleeping cap. "Did you see the snow?"

"Oh, Momma, it's so pretty," Rebecca commented.

"Can we go play in it?" Hannah begged.

"I'm sorry, but we've got to get ready. You can play in the snow when we get to Miss Martin's. Get dressed so we can eat breakfast."

As her mother left the room, Hannah picked out a dress from the wooden wardrobe where she and her sisters kept their clothes. Meanwhile, Lizzie fixed her covers and started to put on the light pink dress she laid out on the chest at the end of the bed. With

Aunt Susannah and Uncle Martin staying in her bedchambers, she had been keeping clothes in her cousins' room.

Reaching for her locket on the side table, Lizzie unhooked the latch and wrapped it around her neck. Her eyes lingered on the navy-blue neckerchief her necklace had been lying on. JJ's words came to her as she stared at his neckerchief. She didn't love him the way he loved her, but she liked him more than Miles Gale, whom she dreaded seeing after the Twelve Days of Christmas. Deciding to wear her hair down, she used her mother's hairpin to pull back strands of her hair. Looking to see if her cousins were ready, she spotted Hannah in the corner with the conch shell Jake brought her from Ocracoke. The little girl was holding the shell up to her ear.

"Do you think it's snowing at Ocracoke?" Hannah inquired.

"Probably," Lizzie answered, watching her put the shell back on the shelf.

"I wish Jake was here. I miss him," Hannah continued sadly.

Lizzie's mind drifted to Ocracoke Island. Part of her wished she could see the snowy beach and the wild ponies running across the snow-covered sand dunes. She thought about Red Wolf and White Feathers staying warm in their hut. Memories came flooding into her mind from the whale to the pirate banyan. As she recalled Captain Vane's buried treasure, she wondered why the Royal Navy couldn't find it. Although she wanted to know what happened to the treasure, Lizzie realized the real treasure wasn't the chest of gold and jewels, but the friends she made and the memories she held in her heart.

Soon, the girls were ready. As they entered the hallway, they met Trent, Edward, and Uncle Martin, who were heading to the kitchen. Aunt Susannah stayed behind to help Mary and Elizabeth dress. The little girls had been sleeping with Edward in Trent's big bed while Trent took Jake's. Trailing behind her cousins, Lizzie tried to put on a happy face, knowing what Christmas truly meant. All of them were bursting with excitement as they descended the stairs decorated with greenery. Going to the kitchen, they discovered the new woolen mittens, scarves, and little gifts Saint Nicholas secretly left for each child.

Delighted with her pair of mittens, Lizzie put them away as she tied on her apron and helped Aunt Grace roll out dough for biscuits. Uncle Martin went outside with Trent to feed the livestock while Aunt Susannah poured the milk. In no time, they were back and the ham biscuits were ready. Gathering around the decorated table, they held hands to pray and started to eat as the children talked about the Christmas festivities. Lizzie ate her salted ham biscuit in silence, staring at the holly wreath centerpiece. When breakfast was over, she helped clear the table and assemble the baskets of food. The vegetables cooked yesterday evening would be reheated at the Martin homestead. They also made a couple of pecan pies and blackberry pies in memory of Lizzie's papa.

Making his favorite pie was emotional for Lizzie. The sadness lifted some when Aunt Susannah shared a childhood memory about one summer when her brother got a bellyache from eating too many blackberries, or as he called them, briarberries. Wanting to share a recent memory, Lizzie showed her family how to make Cookie's false chocolate, explaining how they ate it on Ocracoke Island. Her cousins enjoyed helping her collect and boil down the live oak acorns before mashing them to form the so-called chocolate, which paired well with Aunt Grace's cornbread hoecakes.

While Lizzie helped pack the bowls of food, her cousins slid on their coats and went outside to feed Killer and Tuffy. Trent and Uncle Martin returned to the barn to get the horses hitched to the wagon. Now alone in the kitchen, Aunt Susannah and Aunt Grace discussed when to give the children their sticks of sassafras candy. The two of them had purchased the Christmas treats Tuesday when they went to see Mrs. Charity Shute at the general store. They decided it was best to wait until they returned to Grandfather's house later this afternoon. Aunt Grace went to the oak chest under the staircase to get quilts to wrap up in. Wanting to feed Reba before they left, Lizzie grabbed a leftover biscuit and hurried upstairs. As she entered the room, the redheaded green parrot screeched loudly.

"Lizzie! Lizzie! Reba pretty girl! Reba pretty girl!"

Smiling at how well Reba learned to say her name, Lizzie opened the latch to her cage. "Yes, you're a very pretty girl, Reba."

Breaking up the biscuit, she dropped the crumbs into Reba's food bowl and checked her water. Closing the latch, she was about to leave when she got an idea. For days, she wanted to share her papa's coded note with her grandfather, hoping he had insights to what it meant. Deciding to bring it with her, Lizzie pulled her papa's wooden box out from under the bed. Opening it, she dug through the contents until she found the note. Sliding the box back under the bed, she stuffed the note in her blue cloth handbag.

By the time she got to the kitchen, her family was putting on their mittens and cloaks. Removing her own black, hooded cloak from the peg on the wall, she tied it around her neck, slid on her new woolen mittens, and grabbed a basket of food off the counter. With arms full of goodies and blankets, everyone trooped out onto the back porch. Tuffy had curled up in the old blanket they put in her cat house while Killer whimpered sadly, expecting someone to rub her.

Being careful on the slippery steps, they trudged through the five-inch-deep snow to the wagon. Uncle Martin took the baskets of food, passing them to Trent who was standing in the back. He then picked up his children and put them in the wagon as well.

Taking big steps in the icy snow, Lizzie helped Hannah into the wagon and got in herself. Rebecca, Alice, and Aunt Grace climbed in behind her. As they settled down, Trent spread out the patchwork quilts so that they would stay warm during their journey. Meanwhile, Aunt Susannah joined Uncle Martin up front on the bench seat.

Flicking the reins, Uncle Martin guided his horses to the path leading to Grandfather's property. Since their load was heavy and the traveling was going to be rough in the snow, Uncle Martin hitched both horses to the wagon. Travel was slow as the horses pulled the wagon over the snow-covered wooden bridge crossing the partially frozen Glebe Creek. Lizzie remembered hearing Aunt Grace and Aunt Susannah talking about the storm off the Carolina coast. Mrs. Shute told them the nor'easter was keeping merchant ships from coming into Port Bath and trapped two ships in the Pamtico Sound. After hearing this news, Lizzie thought about JJ and the crew. With the inclement weather, Lieutenant Maynard had most likely hunkered down at Ocracoke until the storm passed and it was safe to travel on to Virginia.

Looking at the winter wonderland, Lizzie soaked in the scenery. Everything appeared renewed under the blinding-white blanket of snow. Warm beneath the quilt, she studied the glistening trees and bushes lining the path. It reminded her of a Bible verse in the book of Psalms where David asked God to wash away his sins so he would be as white as snow. Lizzie couldn't help but wonder if her papa had ever asked God to cleanse his sins before he took his last breath. Had he changed his heart after she asked him to consider giving up piracy and accepting Jesus? The chances of a pirate seeking forgiveness seemed crazy, but hadn't she shared with JJ the account of the thief dying beside Jesus on the cross? In the Bible, God told Samuel He looked at the heart of a person instead of the outward appearance. Only God knew what was in her papa's heart.

Pondering all this, Lizzie caught a glimpse of red in the woods. Searching for it again, she spotted a bright red cardinal perched on a prickly holly bush. The red berries on the holly blended with the pretty red bird. Surprisingly, the cardinal stayed still as the wagon rolled past the holly bush and crossed over onto Miss Elizabeth Martin's land. In no time, Uncle Martin was pulling the reins to make the horses stop beside Grandfather's carriage and Uncle Thomas' wagon.

"Merry Christmas! What do you think about this snow, children?" Grandfather exclaimed, helping Aunt Charlotte out of their carriage.

"We love it!" Hannah replied excitedly.

Shrieks of laughter coming from the backyard caused everyone to turn around. Lizzie spotted a handful of children running around as they threw snowballs at each other.

"Oh, Papa! Please let us play in the snow," Edward begged his father, who was helping him and his sisters get down.

"Well, I don't see why you can't for a little while," Uncle Martin agreed as Aunt Grace gave her approval.

The children joined in on the fun while the adults gave each other hugs. Aunt Grace had just asked where Aunt Mary was when she and Thomas Bustin came up the snow-covered path on his buggy. Knowing this might be her only opportunity to talk to Grandfather about her papa's note, Lizzie walked over to him. She already had the note out of her blue handbag when William Martin came up to greet them. Disappointed, Lizzie stuffed the note back in her handbag as William shook hands with Grandfather and her uncles. By the time he made his rounds, Thomas Bustin and Aunt Mary were walking up. Aunt Mary started giving out hugs while Thomas passed Grandfather a folded newspaper.

"What's this?" Grandfather wanted to know.

"It's a copy of the *Boston News-Letter*. I thought you might want to see it. Edward made the front page," Thomas murmured.

"Thanks," Grandfather responded solemnly as he unfolded it.

Uncle Thomas leaned over to see what the paper printed while William asked Thomas Bustin if the article mentioned anything about his brother. Wanting to see it herself, Lizzie moved closer. Aunt Susannah did the same, passing two-year-old Elizabeth to Uncle Martin.

"I also have a letter for you, Lizzie. Mr. Shute said whoever sent it paid the postage," Thomas Bustin revealed, handing her the letter.

Stunned and excited, Lizzie took the letter wondering if Jake already made it to Virginia. The excitement disappeared as she looked at the fancy handwriting knowing Jake didn't write neatly. Her sadness turned to curiosity as she saw where it came from.

"A letter for Lizzie? Is it from Virginia?" Grandfather questioned.

"No, it's from Philadelphia, Pennsylvania," Thomas stated.

"Pennsylvania?" Aunt Susannah blurted out. "Who would be sending you a letter from there, Lizzie?"

"I met several of Papa's friends when we were in Pennsylvania," Lizzie informed them, knowing it was possibly from Miss Margaret.

Flipping over the letter, she started to pull apart the wax seal, but stopped as Elizabeth Martin called to them from the back porch.

"We're coming!" William yelled back. Looking at Grandfather he added, "Can I help carry something? You brought plenty of food."

Grandfather chuckled. "Yes, I think we have enough food to feed half the town. John and I also brought some of our homemade apple brandy to go along with your famous peach brandy."

"Great! Can't wait to try it," William answered, rubbing his chin.

With baskets in hand, they followed William to the house. Pulling Lizzie aside, Grandfather handed her the *Boston News-Letter*.

"I'm sure you want to read this."

"I'll put it in my handbag with the letter," she told him.

Grandfather put his arm around her as they walked behind the others. Looking around the Martin plantation it was difficult to imagine they were here a month ago for the Harvest Day Celebration. Stepping up on the back porch, Lizzie hugged Miss Martin. As they entered the decorated house, they took off their cloaks and coats. The Martin siblings and their extensive families were there to welcome them. Thankfully, there appeared to be enough food for the crowd of around fifty people. Moving to the kitchen, which smelled like the evergreen decorations, she helped her aunts unload the food and set the pots near the hearth.

Thirty minutes later, Miss Martin announced dinner was ready and stepped outside to get the children. Despite the full house, she insisted everyone eat together. She carefully planned the seating, allowing the adults to eat at the dinner table and the children to gather around tables in the kitchen. Lizzie joined her nine cousins and the twelve Martin children as William said the blessing.

Once he finished, Lizzie scooped food onto the plates of her younger cousins and started to fill her own plate with collards, corn, a slice of goose meat, and leather britches beans. John and Elizabeth sat beside her eating their mashed potatoes, green beans, and ham. Before long, the ladies brought out the desserts. Picking from the selection of sweets was difficult. They had brought a pecan pie, a briarberry pie, a peach cobbler, and a black walnut cake. Miss Martin and her daughters also prepared a carrot cake, a cherry cobbler, and a basket full of apple turnovers. Everyone even seemed to enjoy Lizzie's false chocolate and Aunt Grace's hoecakes.

After sampling a sliver of pecan pie, cherry cobbler, and an apple turnover, Lizzie got some false chocolate and a piece of briarberry pie. With each bite of her papa's favorite dessert, she thought about the adventure with him. Pausing to sip her apple cider, she glanced at the half-eaten goose in the center of the table, recalling her papa's story about swan hunting with Grandfather Beard. Remembering her papa's laughter, she felt blessed to have the opportunity to spend the summer with him and to have collected memories she would treasure forever. As she looked at Edward, Mary, and Elizabeth, she thought about another blessing. Perhaps she should spend time with them in New Bern. What if she only stayed a few weeks?

She had just taken another bite when there was a knock on the door. Miss Martin asked William to get up, stating it was most likely one of the servants who had the day off to celebrate Jesus' birth with their families. William returned with someone behind him.

"Jake!" Hannah shouted as she jumped up.

Shocked, Lizzie stared into the other room still holding the fork in her hand. Jake stood beside William grinning as Hannah threw her arms around him in a hug.

"You're back! I can't believe it!" Hannah gasped, squeezing him.

"Welcome back, Jake," Grandfather said, giving him a hug.

Waiting for everyone to hug Jake, Lizzie got in line behind Alice. Finally, it was her turn to get a hug. She wanted to tell him how much she missed him, but Uncle Thomas didn't give her a chance as he came up to give Jake a hug of his own.

"How did you know to come here?" Uncle Thomas asked him.

"No one was at Mr. Worsley's house. I went to Nathaniel's quarters where they were gathering to eat. He told me about Miss Martin's party. Hope I'm not intruding," Jake commented.

"Nonsense! Come get something to eat," Miss Martin insisted.

Jake sat beside Grandfather while Aunt Grace made him a plate and Aunt Susannah poured him some apple cider. The table grew quiet as he silently prayed. Lizzie prayed too, thanking God for bringing Jake home, though she felt it was only temporary. When he finished praying, Jake started to eat as he answered everyone's questions.

Listening, Lizzie learned he almost ran into Captain Ellis Brand and his servant on his way north to Virginia. Jake saw the two of them leaving the store he stopped at as he waited for the wooden, roped ferryboat to arrive back at Bell's Ferry. He also found out Governor Eden was waiting for the ferryboat at the home of a local couple who rented rooms to travelers. Unfortunately, word arrived that bad weather delayed the ferry, which took passengers with their horses or wagons across the Albemarle Sound. Not wanting to travel with Captain Brand and Governor Eden, Jake decided to rethink his decision to leave. Choosing to return to Bath Town, he began the thirty-mile trip back, which proved to be difficult in the snowstorm. Jake made it clear he was still planning to go up to Virginia to support JJ and the others, but said he wanted to be with them for Christmas.

After Jake took his last bite of briarberry pie, William showed the men to the parlor while the ladies cleared the tables and put away the leftover food. Instead of helping her aunts with the cleanup, Lizzie followed her cousins to the parlor so she could speak to Jake.

"I'm so glad you came back," she proclaimed.

Picking up Little Thomas, Jake replied, "It's good to be back. I didn't think I would miss all of you as much as I did."

"Gather around. I want to say something," Miss Martin declared.

Once the room grew still, Miss Martin went to her desk and returned with a small, brown package. Unwrapping it, she passed out peppermint candy sticks to her grandchildren as well as Lizzie and her cousins. Surprised, they thanked her for thinking of them.

"I know it's unusual for neighbors to give gifts, but I wanted all the children to have something. Keeping the tradition of the Twelve Days of Christmas celebration, I asked Thomas Worsley Sr. to read the account of Jesus' birth from the Bible in Luke chapter two, verses one through twenty. William will then lead us in song. You can start when you're ready, Thomas," she stated, sitting in a cushioned chair.

Grandfather read the account of Joseph and Mary going to Bethlehem. Mary was great with child. She brought forth her firstborn Son, wrapped Him in swaddling clothes, and laid Him in a manger because there was no room for them in the inn. There were shepherds keeping watch over their sheep nearby and the angel of the Lord came to them. The angel told the shepherds a savior was born in the city of David, which was Christ the Lord. After hearing this and seeing the heavenly host praising God, the shepherds went to Bethlehem like the angel told them. They found the babe lying in a manger with Mary and Joseph nearby.

The Scripture was familiar to Lizzie, who had read it numerous times and heard her grandfather read it to the family every Christmas. Next, William Martin started singing the song "While Shepherds Watched Their Flocks," while the entire room sang along. Adding her voice to the crowd, Lizzie sang out the words, which were a paraphrase of the second chapter of Luke's Gospel and written in rhyme a few years before in 1700.

While shepherds watched their flocks by night,
All seated on the ground, the angel of the Lord came down,
And glory shone around, And glory shone around...

Continuing to sing, Lizzie looked at the happy faces. Each one joyfully sang as they celebrated Jesus' birth together. When the song was over, two members of the Martin family brought out a couple of fiddles while others moved the furniture. Once they cleared the floor, they began to play music to dance by. Surprisingly, Grandfather asked Miss Martin to dance. Several other couples stepped forward to dance with them. Uncle Thomas and William dispersed cups of peach or apple brandy to those who wanted it and held up their cups in a toast.

"Come on, let's go play blind man's bluff," Alice suggested as she went into the room where they ate dinner.

Most of the younger children followed her while Trent joined fourteen-year-old Joel Martin and two of his cousins in a game of marbles. Hannah asked Lizzie and Jake if they wanted to play, but Jake informed her he was going to the kitchen for some false chocolate and hoecakes. Deciding she would watch the fun, Lizzie went into the adjacent room with Little Thomas, John, Mary, and Elizabeth. At first, they were too timid to play, but once they discovered two of the Martin children chasing each other, they joined in.

Sitting on the bench at the table, Lizzie watched Trent and Joel set up the marbles. The four older children huddled in a circle flicking their marbles in the corner. Staying out of their way, Alice wrapped a blindfold around ten-year-old Rebecca's eyes. Spinning her, she let go of her sister and instructed the other children to make a circle. They walked around her until Rebecca clapped three times. Rebecca then pointed to one of the children and guessed who it was. Guessing it was Hannah instead of Edward, she had to chase him down which proved difficult and hilarious as she fumbled all over the room trying to find him. Lizzie couldn't help but laugh as Rebecca finally caught Edward. She had just tagged the little boy when Jake returned with his dessert and a cup of apple cider. Placing them on the table, he sat down in the straight-backed chair and slid it closer to the table.

"Did she get him?" Jake asked.

"Yes, now it's Edward's turn," Lizzie responded.

"So, are you going to the Neuse River with your aunt's family?" Jake inquired as he sopped up false chocolate with a hoecake.

"I think I'm going to go for a few weeks. Papa would want me to spend time with his sister. Maybe going to the Neuse River will help jog my memories so I can figure out what his coded note means."

"How did Miss Grace react to your decision?"

"She doesn't know yet. You're the first one I've told."

"I need to look at the note again. A few nights ago, I was thinking about the note and realized part of it seemed familiar to me."

"I brought it with me to show Grandfather, but haven't gotten a chance," she said as she hurried to the door where the cloaks hung.

Locating her blue cloth handbag, she brought it to the table and took out the letter, newspaper, and coded note. Jake raised his eyebrows in surprise as he slid his empty plate and cup away from him, asking what she was doing with so many papers. Explaining how Thomas Bustin brought the letter and a copy of the *Boston News-Letter*, she picked up the paper to read the article. Tears came to her eyes as she read the horrible details of her papa's death apparently seen by a passing ship. Handing it to Jake to read, she opened the letter. Like she guessed, the letter was from her papa's friend, Miss Margaret. Returning the paper, Jake said he was sorry she had to read such terrible things, then asked who sent the letter. Telling him it was from Miss Margaret, she shared what the lady wrote, which included her sympathy for her loss and a strange comment about hoping to see her again.

Wondering what Miss Margaret meant, Lizzie reread the letter as Jake studied the coded note. He gave her a nudge, stating he may have an idea of what it was. Giving him her full attention, she watched as he pointed to the first set of jumbled letters.

"This first part reminds me of my last name. If you take NIFFIRG and spell it backwards it's GRIFFIN," he informed her.

"Do you think the rest of this gibberish are words, too?"

"Possibly. Let's see. The letters DAETSEMOH spelled backwards is HOMESTEAD and YENMIHC is CHIMNEY. Together the message reads: GRIFFIN HOMESTEAD CHIMNEY."

The excitement faded a little as Lizzie realized they had a new puzzle to solve. Why did her papa write the strange note, and what did it have to do with the greenish-blue beads?

"Well, I guess we solved the code, but we still don't understand the message Black Beard left," Jake commented.

"I can't figure out why Papa wrote these words and left it with the beads. It sounds like he's talking about your old house."

"I'm not sure what he's referring to. I doubt there's much left of our homestead except maybe the chimney."

"Do you think he went there?"

As soon as the words left her mouth, the two of them stared at each other apparently thinking the exact same thing.

"It all makes sense now," Jake muttered as he lowered his voice. "Maynard claimed he didn't find any gold and jewels. We know Black Beard had Captain Vane's treasure and the communal plunder. Your aunt said Cookie and JJ's father were with Black Beard when he visited them. What are the chances they buried the treasure there? I'm sure he was concerned about Calico Jack hunting them down after he found the treasure gone."

Staring at the code, Lizzie considered what he was suggesting. Was it possible her papa wrote this note as a reminder of where he buried his treasure? Thinking about this, she felt a sense of urgency come over her. She knew for sure she wanted to go with Aunt Susannah. Looking at Jake, she suddenly realized he wouldn't be going with her.

"What's wrong?" he prompted. "I thought you'd be happy to discover what the note said. You might get to do a little snooping."

Knowing he was joking with her, Lizzie tried to smile but the sadness in her heart refused to let her. "I wish you could go."

"I've got to go to Virginia."

"I know, you made a pact with JJ."

Surprisingly, his demeanor tensed. "My pact with JJ had nothing to do with Virginia. He asked me to keep Miles away from you."

"I can't believe JJ's thinking about him when he's facing death."

"Well, he did. He also told me where his portion of the plunder is. If he's sentenced to hang, I'm supposed to give it to you. The gold is in the hay loft in Miss Martin's barn."

Overwhelmed with emotions, Lizzie didn't know what to think. JJ's choice to give her his gold showed how much he loved her.

"I have a confession to make," Jake admitted awkwardly. "I left because it's hard for me to sort this out. I have—um—feelings for you. Do you know what I mean?"

"I—I think so," she stammered as her heart beat faster.

In her mind, she recalled the conversation she had with her papa the day he left. His approval of JJ courting her had been his focus, but he also discussed his misgivings about Miles and his admiration for Jake. Until now, she had never considered courting him. Although she didn't want to mess up their friendship, she realized she felt something for him that she didn't feel for either Miles or JJ.

"Are you still planning to permanently leave Bath?" she hinted.

"I don't know."

"I've been miserable since you left. The thought of never seeing you again upset me. I know you need to go to Virginia for JJ, but hopefully you'll return. You mean a lot to me, Jake," she whispered.

"I'm not sure I should stay in Bath."

"Why not? You just said you had feelings for me."

Jake shook his head. "Yes, but JJ's in love with you."

Lizzie started to protest but froze as Aunt Grace entered the room. Her appearance caused the children to stop their game.

"I came to check on you," she explained. "Are you having fun?"

"We are, Momma," Alice said, peeping out from the blindfold.

"Sorry I interrupted your game," Aunt Grace declared.

The children went back to playing while Aunt Grace turned to leave. She paused in the doorway to look at Lizzie and Jake.

"Why don't the two of you come in here? Everyone's having a good time dancing," she suggested as she returned to the parlor.

Once she was gone, Jake took his dirty plate and cup to the kitchen. Watching him go, Lizzie let out a sigh. Why did Aunt Grace have to interrupt them when they were finally being honest with each other? Sliding the newspaper into her blue handbag, she picked up Margaret's letter and the coded note. Pulling the strings of the bag, she took it to where her cloak was hanging. When she came back, she approached Jake.

"I know you don't like dancing, but we can watch."

"I don't dislike dancing, I just haven't done it much. If you would like to dance, I'll try."

Grinning, Lizzie walked with Jake to the parlor. As the next song started, he extended his right hand for her to join him on the dance floor. Jake did fine with the lively tune, but when the second song started, he tensed up. It was a slow song, requiring them to be close.

Dancing with Jake made Lizzie incredibly happy. She hoped to have a deeper relationship with him, though it would be difficult with her family wanting her to court Miles. If JJ survived the hangman's noose, she would also have to deal with him. Not wanting to ruin this special moment, she tried to block out her thoughts.

Gazing at the faces of her loved ones, Lizzie thanked God for all her blessings. Thinking about her papa, she self-consciously felt her locket dangling from her neck. For the first time in a long time, she recalled the words her papa told her when he gave her the necklace so many years ago for her birthday.

Lizzie, my darling, no matter where I am in this world, when you wear this necklace my heart will be close to yours.

Despite the fact he was no longer in this world, Lizzie still felt comforted by his words. No matter what, his heart was close to hers. He said so himself a month ago when he told her he loved her. Beneath the fearsome beard and harsh personality of Black Beard the pirate was the soft heart of her father. Even with the skeletons of his past strewn all over the colonies, he had always been her beloved papa. After living with him for months, she had seen him for who he truly was and unlocked many of those buried skeletons as she searched for the man she once knew.

Thinking back over her journey, Lizzie remembered what her papa said when they were alone together on the *Adventure* only hours before he shot Israel Hands. He had been right about her life changing. She wasn't the same person she was when she left Bath in July. Her outlook on life was different now as she reflected on what Jesus meant when He said your treasure will be where your heart is.

Thankful for the time she had with her papa, she realized she already had a treasure far greater than all the gold and jewels in Captain Vane's chest; she had a relationship with Jesus. Between the love of her family and Jake's return to her life, she had so much to be grateful for. One of the best things this Christmas was the treasure of her papa's love. God gave her a second chance with him and put her in the position to impact his life as well. Her papa's love would live on in her heart forever, just like the legends of Black Beard the pirate.

GET THE SCOOP
BLACKBEARD THE PIRATE

- Whether you call him Edward Teach, Edward Thatch, or Edward Beard like this story suggests, the identity of Blackbeard is a mystery. If he changed his name to keep his family's name clean, he did an excellent job. Over three hundred years later, we are still trying to figure it out.
- Not much is known about Blackbeard's origins. His birth date, family, and life prior to piracy are all secrets. There are claims he came from Jamaica, Scotland, England, and everywhere in between, but there has been no proof of exactly who he was and where he came from. After researching colonial records, I chose to place him in the Beard family. There is some evidence he may have married one of Thomas Worsley Sr.'s daughters, but this is not certain. What about his fourteen wives? Who knows?
- Blackbeard was a pirate for roughly two years. Historians believe prior to piracy he was a privateer, legally plundering enemy ships during Queen Anne's War.
- In June 1718, Blackbeard's ship, *Queen Anne's Revenge*, wrecked off the North Carolina coast near present-day Beaufort. Some say it was accidental, but it may have been on purpose to downsize the crew. After abandoning *Queen Anne's Revenge*, Blackbeard transferred supplies, cannons, and men to the *Adventure*. He sailed on this ship until his death.
- Many men served under Blackbeard during his short career. At one point, there were as many as seven hundred men on four ships. When he died, there were only seventeen. The crew members of the *Adventure* listed in this book were based on the real pirates.
- Blackbeard died on Saturday, November 22, 1718. Two Royal Navy ships called the *Jane* and the *Ranger* cornered him at Ocracoke, North Carolina. Lieutenant Robert Maynard led the attack by water while his comrade, Captain Ellis Brand, came to Bath,

North Carolina, in search of the pirates. The remaining captured pirates of the *Adventure* were all taken to Virginia for trial.
- Events and people such as the Tuscarora Indian War, Cary's Rebellion, the Woccon Indians, John Lawson's explorations, government officials, and other pirates were all real.
- Colonial records mention Blackbeard's pocketbook which Lieutenant Maynard discovered after his death. In it was Tobias Knight's letter to Blackbeard. No one seems to know what happened to the pocketbook or Knight's letter, but the contents of the letter are in the Colonial and State Records of North Carolina dated 1719 during the inquiries into Tobias' business with Edward Teach.
- Blackbeard's severed head went to Virginia, though it is unknown where it ended up. His so-called buried treasures were never located even after three centuries of treasure hunters scouring North Carolina, other coastal areas on the East Coast, and every island in the Caribbean.
- When we think of pirate treasure, we picture a chest overflowing with gold, silver, and jewels. Pirate treasure didn't typically consist of such things. Many stolen "treasures" were cargos of sugar, cocoa, cotton, indigo die, and other highly desired merchandise that were scarce in the colonies. Pirates could sell the cargo or trade them for needed supplies.
- Records do indicate pirates took smaller amounts of gold or jewels from stolen ships, but it wasn't the main prize. Pirates also stole navigational tools, maps, spare anchors, extra sails, tar for careening, weapons, barrels of rum and wine, and anything else they could use. Carpenters, coopers, sail makers, and musicians who were on captured ships were either forced into serving or chose to join the pirates. Even doctors were pressed into the ranks.
- Unfortunately, human cargo was a great prize. Pirates kept servants or slaves—Indians, Africans, Mustees, and Mulattos—to do the worst chores, but they sometimes sold them. Many colonists desperately needed them for their crops, especially since families had lost their men to disease, drought, and the Tuscaro-

ra Indian War. Some of the captive servants wanted to be pirates because they typically had rights and received part of the plunder.
- Blackbeard went to Pennsylvania in August 1718. His stay was brief, and we don't know why he went. Some say he was terminally ill and was seeking another doctor's opinion on treatment. This conclusion comes from the fact Blackbeard blockaded Charleston, South Carolina, in May 1718. Although he had the entire port at his mercy, the only thing he requested was a chest of medicine. He reportedly captured a ship prior to the blockade and forced a doctor to come onboard his ship, *Queen Anne's Revenge*. The discovery in recent years of a medical instrument found at the wreckage of *Queen Anne's Revenge* supports this claim.
- Out of all the pirates known to us today, Blackbeard continues to be one of the most legendary. Many pirates did kill people as documented in the records. People expect Blackbeard to be an evil man who tortured and killed his victims. Interestingly, there are no records of his supposed murders. He did threaten captives, so it's possible some of his victims may have later died from their injuries. We know more about Blackbeard because of the eyewitness accounts his victims told.

Hope you enjoyed this adventure in history!

Robin Reams

Made in the USA
Columbia, SC
06 April 2023